Lady's Night

Also by Mark Anthony

Paper Chasers

Dogism

Lady's Night

MARK ANTHONY

 ST. MARTIN'S GRIFFIN 🐝 NEW YORK

THIS BOOK IS DEDICATED TO my son, Mark Jr., and to my daughter, Savannah. Although you both are too young to read these words, you both should know that you are my inspiration and the reason why I tirelessly strive to fulfill all of my dreams. *Lady's Night* was conceived in my mind before you two were born, and the book is tangible proof that dreams do come true. So know that whatever it is that you want out of life can be yours if you just believe! And if either of you ever have any doubts about what you can accomplish, just remember that *your daddy is the American Dream.*

Lady's Night

1

"THAT NIGGA DIDN'T RAPE YOU!" my mother screamed at me with the most disgusted look on her face, like I was annoying her by bringing these accusations to her.

"Yes, he did!" I shouted as tears ran down my face. "Why would I lie about something like that?"

I couldn't believe it. My mother's disgust quickly turned into a devilish smirk as if something was got damn funny.

Slurring her words, she added, "Wha? Wha? What? . . . The nigga probably pulled your pants down and bent you over and gave it to you like a dog in the street, right?"

I stared at her, feeling as if my spirit was slowly being stepped on.

"And I bet you was just parading around this apartment half naked and showing off your ass!"

"Mom, he raped me! What is wrong with you?! I wouldn't lie to you about something like this."

"Did you come out of the shower butt-naked with no towel on or something? Tina, you coming at me telling me that my man raped you and I'm telling you that I know he ain't like that! You just like my so-called friends that wait for me to turn my head so that they can lay up with my man! You're lucky you my daughter!"

"Mom!"

"Bitch, you listen to me! Whatever happened to you, it wasn't rape! He ain't rape you! Junie ain't no rapist! If you had any got damn sense in your head you would have closed your eyes and enjoyed it!"

"What?" I asked in total disbelief.

"You heard what I said, Tina! It wasn't no rape! If you had any sense in your head you would have simply closed your eyes and enjoyed it! I don't believe in a woman getting raped. All these fast little tricks out here can't handle it when somebody gives it to them real good and they immediately wanna scream, 'He raped me, he raped me!' The next time that happens—if you're laying on your back or doing it standing up like a dog—all you gotta do is just relax and close your eyes and enjoy it!"

Next time? I thought to myself. *There ain't gonna be no next time!* My mother's boyfriend had physically violated me, one of the worst things that a woman can go through, but in that moment, listening to my mother, I couldn't tell which experience had been worse, having had someone force themself on me or listening to my mother tell me that I should have *closed my eyes and enjoyed it.*

"Tina, did you cum?"

"Mom, what are you asking me?" I screamed in rage.

"Did you have an orgasm? That's what I'm asking you!" my mother replied in a slurred tone, her screw face making her look as if Satan had entered her. Her lips and eyes were frowned up as if she had eaten something with a real sour taste.

Vivid and violent pictures entered my mind. I pictured myself plunging a knife as deep into my mother's lungs as I possibly could and turning the knife inside of her to gut out anything and everything that was in her body. I envisioned cutting off her boyfriend's penis and putting it in his mouth and watching them both bleed to death.

"You know you had an orgasm and that's why you're ignoring me. None of your little skinny boyfriends ever did it to you like that before, right? . . . Tina, am I right? None of those so-called thugs of yours ever did it to you like that, right?"

I knew that I had to get out of that apartment as quickly as I could.

I also knew that if I stayed around and had to live through the ungodly sight of seeing my mother's boyfriend, Junie, come home that I would have flat-out lost it. Plus at that point I couldn't tell if my mother would have stood by while he raped me a second time, just like she had looked the other way in the past when a few of her other boyfriends had molested me.

"Tina, just answer the damn question and I'll leave you alone! I need to know this!"

I gave my mother a deathly stare but it didn't intimidate her slightly drunk ass.

"Yes or no, Tina! Did he make you cum?"

Other than the sound of me sniffling and trying to suck the snot back into my nose—and to keep the streaming tears from going inside my mouth—there wasn't a sound that could be heard in the room.

"Yes or no, Tina?" My mother's voice was so loud and piercing it was as if the walls and everything in the house were trembling.

"Yes! . . . A'ight? Are you happy now?" I said it in a way that sounded like I was just trying to get my mother to shut up. But unfortunately I was telling the truth.

"See, that's what I knew! I knew it. You little whore! How in the hell is it gonna be rape if you enjoyed it enough to have an orgasm? And I bet that was probably your first real orgasm at that!"

I stormed to my room and violently pulled clothes out of my closet and stuffed them into a backpack. With tears of hurt and anger still flowing out of my eyes, I bolted out of that apartment because I just couldn't take it anymore. I cried uncontrollably once I got in the street. I must have looked like a disoriented street bum or something. My hair wasn't done and my outfit was some lounging-around-the-house type of gear. I had some house slippers on and I had no clue where I was gonna go or who I was gonna turn to. All I knew was that I could not stay in that apartment anymore. Both my mother and Junie would have been dead and their blood would have been on my hands.

I thought about walking into a police station for help but I couldn't bring myself to do that. I couldn't go to the police because of the horrible fact that I had indeed had a real powerful orgasm while I was being raped, and that was something that confused the hell out of me. I wasn't trying to have no cop in my face screaming at me and trying to convince me that I was just some freak or something.

I walked from 205th Street in Hollis, Queens, all the way to the F train on 179th Street in Jamaica, Queens. I got on that F train as a fourteen-year-old child but I knew that I had to quickly grow up and become a woman.

I rode the train all day, just me and my thoughts. The ride did me a whole lot of good because I had resolved in my mind that I would do whatever it took not to be helpless again.

The incident with Junie was sort of the culmination of a long history of enduring all kinds of dangers, obstacles, dysfunctions, and instability. My mother had never held down a decent job for more than a year and she never claimed her own independent living space. For as long I could remember we never had our own house or apartment. She was always dependent on some nigga and so it was like my younger sister and I were constantly moving. I guess as soon as the sex got boring to the nigga or whatever, it was then always time for all of us to get on to the next place to live. Thank god that most of the guys were pretty predictable in that they didn't get bored with the sex until after a year or so; otherwise we would have been moving like every two or three months.

It's hard to put into words what an unstable upbringing like that does to a person. But it also created a fierce survival instinct in me and a burning desire to never be dependent upon anyone for anything. Even at the tender age of fourteen I knew that I had to have the mind of a woman at least twice my age if I was gonna make it in this world—and more importantly if I was gonna go a different route than my mother.

But being raped by my mother's boyfriend and having her tell me I should have enjoyed it . . . well that was simply more than my spirit could bear. It was my point of no return.

I hated to be leaving behind my little sister Mya, because I didn't want her to have to fend for herself. I was afraid that with me out of the house Mya would become the sexual focus of my mother's boyfriend. It really hurt me but there was really nothing else that I could do at that point. Leaving was my only option.

That day in April of 1993 was when I began living on my own.

2

I DIDN'T KNOW WHERE MY next meal was coming from. I spent countless hours riding the New York City subway system with no destination in mind. I had to figure out where to get clothes from, where to take showers at, and where I was gonna sleep each night. I had to figure all this out while still going to school.

A young, sexy, brash girl who was, at that point, literally from the street, and trying to make it, I learned very quickly that I had to form the right affiliations. But like anything in life, most people want to do more than just survive, they want to thrive in whatever circumstances they are faced with and I was no different.

I attended Hillcrest High School in Jamaica, Queens, and I was involved in all kinds of activities at school. Mainly I got involved because it gave me an excuse to stay late after school. Being that I was involved in everything extracurricular I naturally knew everybody in the school and everybody knew me.

But for obvious reasons I really didn't let too many people get close to me, especially females, who, if they knew my circumstances were liable to blow me up. I had associates more so than friends. Most of the girls on the cheerleading squad were from a section of Queens called Long Island City. More specifically they lived in the Queensbridge housing projects. Nobody who was from Queensbridge would dare say that they were from Long Island City. Rather, they had to make it known that they were from "*Queensbridge.*"

The girls from Queensbridge literally dominated the cheerleading squad. So no matter how talented you were, if you weren't from Queensbridge then you were not gonna make the squad. Although I wasn't from Queensbridge, I think that I made the squad simply because of my popularity and looks.

I recognized that they were a good affiliation for me so I went out of my way to hang out with them in Queensbridge on the weekends, after school—whenever I could get the chance.

In fact it was my traveling back and forth on the train to Queensbridge for more than a year that indirectly helped me land a job in a donut shop located near the Queens Plaza train station at the corner of Twenty-eighth Street and Queens Plaza South, just walking distance from Queensbridge projects. And it was at that job that I hooked up with a customer who would forever change the course of my life.

3

I THINK EVERY HOOD IN the country has somebody who is notorious for some type of ghetto-fabulousness. In New York City there is a long list of ghetto-fabulous people, but none more infamous than Kevin "Cream" Johnson from Queens. Kevin "Cream" Johnson gained his ghetto celebrity and mythical status for masterminding and leading one of the most violent and profitable criminal empires in the country that he labeled the Cream Team.

In fact, to this very day it is alleged by many people that Raekwon from the Wu-Tang Clan got the inspiration for his smash rap record *Cream* from members of the Cream Team. Legend has it, and I was able to later verify that the driving force behind Kevin's illegal ambition was an acronym which he derived from the letters that make up the word cream. Cash Reigns Everywhere Around Me.

I was only making like seven dollars an hour as a cashier in the donut shop and to be honest I hated the job. Considering that I was homeless and had tons of idle time on my hands, I still hated the restraints that the job put on my time. I guess it clashed with my independent will. But for the time being I knew that it was a good situation for me. It was a twenty-four-hour-a-day donut shop located in a commercial/industrial high-traffic area right near and underneath the outdoor elevated train tracks. The donut shop had a steady flow of customers. It was located on the Queens side of the Fifty-ninth Street Bridge right near the base of the bridge. The Fifty-ninth Street Bridge is the bridge that connects Queens to Manhattan and is also known as the Queensborough Bridge. Hence, that is how the projects and the community which they encompass came to be known as Queensbridge.

Even though I had to be in school by 8 A.M. every morning, I still managed to work from 9 P.M. until 2 A.M. three days out of the week and sometimes more than that.

Those part-time hours helped me buy clothes, which I would keep stashed in the three lockers that I had in school. They also helped me pay for my train fare, giving me access to the subway, which is where I would usually sleep on the train for a few hours a night. On my breaks I would do homework or study at one of the tables in the shop. I would sometimes use my breaks to try to get fifteen minutes of sleep.

All kinds of people would come into that donut shop, but there was always a group of about three guys who would stop in every other day or so. Besides being cute, they were always very niggerish. And that was kind of attractive to me. By niggerish I mean, in addition to being very brash, loud, and cocky, they would do things like take out a bankroll of money in order to pay for two sixty-cent donuts and a bottle of Snapple.

At the time I had no idea that the three guys were part of the Cream Team. And I definitely had no idea that one of them was Kevin "Cream" Johnson himself. And to be honest, I think that my ignorance was probably the best thing that could have happened to me. I would just sort of vibe with them without feeling like I had to act any differently.

My first verbal interaction that I remember having with them was actually sometime around October of 1994.

"Yo what's up, ma? Lemme get two bowties and two jelly donuts," Cream stated, completely skipping the customers in line. He placed one of his Timberland boots on a footrest and his elbows next to the cash register while he peeled back money from his wad of cash.

"Sweetie, how you gonna just disrespect the line like that?" I asked.

I didn't come off rude, and to be honest I wanted to serve him instead of the other customers, but I wanted to see what his reaction would be to my comment.

Cream adjusted his sleeve to his jacket, deliberately showing off his expensive Presidential Rolex watch.

"Come on, ma, I don't care about these people," Cream said in a tone that was mixed with surprise and cockiness.

"But I'm saying, these are my customers and they waited on line and I can't just treat them like they don't exist," I told him.

One of Cream's boys stepped up and asked, "Yo, what's up man? Is she trying to play you or something?"

I ignored the two of them and took the next order. There was an uncomfortable smile on Cream's face as he stood up straight and took two steps back from the counter so that the other customers could get serviced.

The next customer was a middle-aged man who looked like he was either on his way home from a stressful day at work or on his way to start a stressful day at work. He looked at Cream and said, "Sir, it's okay. You can order ahead of me."

Without saying thank you, Cream nodded his head at the gentleman and stepped a little closer to the counter with his wad of cash fully exposed. I don't remember exactly what designer names he was wearing that day but I know that everything he had on had that brand-new crisp look to it. He was wearing some nice baggy jeans along with some construction-type Timberland boots and a matching jean jacket.

"See now, was that so bad?" I asked him with a smile.

"Come on, ma, you killing me," Cream said, sounding as if his patience was running low. He had a disgusted look on his face.

"Yo, just hurry up and get the order. We ain't got all day!" Cream's boy said.

"Nah, chill, don't flip on shorty. I like her style," Cream said, then asked, "You still remember what I wanted, right?"

I nodded my head and proceeded to fill his order. By the time I was done two other customers who had been on line had been helped by the other cashier. And the remaining customer had left in an apparent attempt to catch his bus which had pulled up in front of the store.

I handed Cream his donuts in a white paper bag but I didn't put the Snapple in a bag, I just handed him a straw.

"How much is that?" he asked.

"Nah, don't worry about it," I responded. "I got you."

"A'ight, cool. I like your style, shorty," Cream said.

See, although I didn't know who Cream was at the time, I figured that I had nothing to lose by trying to find out who this cocky customer was. And he had that look that said he liked being treated as if he was the man or something. So I knew that I again had to say something that would keep him off balance if I wanted to score some points with him. See, just like with the most skilled football player or boxer, if you're able to catch them off balance then that makes them vulnerable and it increases your chances of scoring on them. You control the situation.

"It's just about respect, baby. Next time y'all come in here, y'all gotta just respect the customers and respect the establishment," I told him.

"What?" Cream asked with a smile on his face and took a bite of his donut. "Ma, you must not know who I am!"

He was right, I didn't.

"But see that's the whole thing. It's not just about you," I said, trying my hardest to come across with some street class and wit, all the while trying not to be completely disrespectful.

"Y'all come in here all the time, making all kinds of noise and acting real niggerish. Y'all expect all the respect in the world, but I'm saying y'all gotta give some respect too."

Cream's third associate who had been silent up until that point said rather matter-of-factly, "Yo, we should take her and put her ass out on the track!"

The three of them laughed.

I had no idea what a track was, but said, "See, that's exactly what I'm saying. Just listen to your boy." I deepened my voice, " 'Yo, *we need to put her ass out on the track.*' What the hell? How you gonna just talk to me like that and you don't even know me! Y'all gotta start treating me like a lady. Y'all be in here all the time holding your balls, cursing, and calling everybody 'ma' and 'bitch' and 'shorty' and all of that. And I know that y'all just being y'all but I'm saying can y'all at least start showing a little respect to a sister and start treating me like a lady?"

The three of them burst into laughter so hard they were almost crying.

"Yo, shorty is really bugging out," one of them said.

"Uh-huh . . . See, that's exactly what I mean. I'm not your shorty!" I said.

Cream said, "Okay, okay, ma . . . I mean okay, I feel you, so what's your name?"

"Tina, and yours?"

"Cream."

"No, I mean what did your momma name you? What's your government name?"

"See, come on now. Now you're pushing it. Why you need to know my government name? But you know what, Tina? I'm a start treating you like a lady from now on. We gonna be cool, a'ight?" Cream asked as he extended his hand. I took it. "From now on when we come in here it's gonna be nothing but love."

"Cool," I replied as I purposely held onto his hand. "See, now wasn't that easy?" I asked.

"No doubt, no doubt," Cream replied. Then he brought my hand to his mouth and kissed it.

"See now that's what I'm talking about, got damn it!" I shouted as I playfully laughed and poked Cream in the chest with my index finger.

"You know what? I ain't gonna even call you by your government name. From now on I'm gonna address you as Lady. A'ight?" Cream said.

I smiled. I really liked the ring of that.

"I'm cool with that. That'll work."

"A'ight Lady," Cream said as he gently extended his closed fist to me. "Can I get a pound before I bounce?"

I tapped Cream's fist with mine before he and his crew walked out of the donut shop.

At that point I still had no real idea just who I had been talking to but I knew that inside I felt damn good about myself. I felt good because I was confirming something to myself. I was starting to recognize and develop a talent that I must have been born with. And that was what I call my mojo. Mojo is what most people call charm, or magnetism. My mojo had allowed me, as a tender underage minor who looked five or ten years older than her age, in a matter of minutes, to get a thugged-out-looking cat who was loud and brash and cocky and flashing all kinds of money to kiss my hand and treat me like royalty and to brand me with a ghetto-fabulous street name of Lady.

4

ASK ANYBODY IN NEW YORK who was around at the time and they'll tell you that in 1994 if you had an Acura Legend coupe then you were the man! If it was chromed out with some nice rims and tinted windows and all of that then you were liable to get treated like a rap star.

I was like everybody else who admired the car and it was like my eyes would bleed with lust whenever I saw one. So when I left work at a little after two in the morning my eyes were instantly drawn to the white Acura Legend coupe that was parked about half a block away from my job.

It was only November but it felt like January. The weather had been crazy in New York and lately it had been getting colder with each passing day. Although it was real brick outside I decided to walk on over in order to get a closer look at the whip. It also gave me a good excuse to kill time because I really had no particular destination. I got within ten feet or so of the car which was parked in a bus stop and I just stood and pretended I was a pedestrian waiting for the next bus.

No one but me would really understand why I would just brave bitter cold weather in order to stare at a car that wasn't mine. Most people would think that I was doing it in order to attract attention to myself from the car's owner. But to me, my fascination with the car and the need to look at it was so that my brain could burn that image of the car deep into the subconscious part of my mind. I needed that image burned into my mind while at the same time putting my body through the torture of the cold weather.

As I stared at the car I kind of played it off so that it would not be so obvious what I was doing. My teeth chattered and parts of my body were numb from the cold winds that were acting as if they had a personal vendetta against me. I stared and told myself, "Tina you can have that car. It's just a matter of time. Not only can you have that car but you will have that car and all of the luxuries of life that go along with owning a car like that. You deserve those types of toys in your life."

I repeatedly spoke in a positive way to myself because I knew that whatever my mind could accept and grasp in a tangible way without doubt, would be the things that would manifest themselves in my life. And the negative things that were also real to me, such as feeling the bitter cold and not having a place to go where I could call home—I needed those negative feelings as well because I wanted my mind to repel them so that I could find a way to have the negatives seamlessly replaced with the positive things of life.

My philosophies were just that, my philosophies. I rarely shared them with people, out of fear that they might label me as delusional. I didn't want anyone, nor did I need anyone to embrace what I was thinking and feeling. I knew what I had to do in order to get out of life the material comforts that I was so desperately seeking.

As I stared at the rims on the car, the tinted window began to roll down and I could hear the sound of a DJ Clue mixed tape coming from the car.

"Lady! What's up?" someone in the driver's seat of the car asked, while leaning across the passenger's seat trying to get my attention.

I ducked a little and bent my body slightly forward in order to confirm who was trying to get my attention.

"Cream! What's up, boo?" I shouted as excitedly as I possibly could, considering how frozen my face was.

"Ain't nothing, ma. Yo, why you standing in the cold? What's up? Where you headed?"

I hesitated.

"Yo, get in," he said.

As soon as I stepped into the car and sat down, I felt the heat coming from the vents and it felt better than sex.

"So what's up with you? I ain't seen you in a minute," Cream said.

"You know where I work, all you had to do was stop in and check on me. I mean, I was all wondering about you and wondering if everything was okay."

"Nah, I was cool. I was just back and forth, in and out of town."

"Oh, word?"

"So yo, like I was saying, why you just standing out in the cold? I know you just got off work but where you going?"

I knew I had to give some kind of an answer. "Oh, I was supposed to be getting picked up by somebody but I don't know what's up because they should have been here by now."

Cream, who was puffing on some weed, blew some smoke out his driver's side window which was slightly cracked.

"You invite me into your car and question me and you don't even ask if I smoke?" I asked teasingly.

Cream smiled and said, "My bad. Is the smoke bothering you?"

"Nah, that's not what I'm saying. I mean if roles were reversed and I was smoking that Purple Haze, what I would have done was extended the blunt and asked if you wanted some. You know what I'm saying?"

"You right," Cream said and handed me the blunt.

I took a pull on the weed.

"Lady, you know I'm a tell you something . . . Nah, matter of fact, where are you from?"

"Hollis," I replied quickly, hoping that Cream wouldn't continue to question me about where I rested. I also hoped that he wouldn't ask me why I would travel from Hollis all the way to Queensbridge just to work in a donut shop.

"I could shoot you to Hollis real quick if you want."

"Nah, I'm cool. I told you I was waiting for somebody. And plus it's not like I know you like that to be driving around with you," I said as I took another pull on the blunt.

"That's true. But peep what I'm about to say, and if I'm wrong I won't stress you."

"Talk to me," I said, beginning to feel more relaxed as the weed kicked into my system.

"You weren't really waiting for a ride and right now you're really trying to figure out where you're gonna go tonight."

There was a brief moment of uncomfortable silence.

"Am I right?" Cream questioned.

I was trying to figure out how the hell he was pulling my card like that and I knew that the best thing for me to do was to be honest and up front.

"Yeah, but I'm sayin', how did you know that?"

"When you told me that you were waiting for someone to pick you up I saw how your eyes shifted when you responded. I knew you were lying."

Still not really knowing where Cream was going with all of this fake-ass mental telepathy crap and not really wanting to get all into my business, I knew that I had to keep him on his toes.

"So I was straight up with you, now you be straight up with me. Why were you just sitting here, chillin' in your car this late at night?"

Cream confidently answered, "I'm working."

By now the weed had me totally comfortable and all of my inhibitions were gone.

"Working? You look more like you were trying to get a professional from one of these tricks out here on the corner."

"A professional?"

"Yeah that's my word for blow-job," I said while cracking a smile.

Cream fell out laughing. "Yo! I'm feeling that! I'm a run with that from now on."

I chuckled a bit and nodded my head and continued to claim the blunt as my own.

Cream continued, "Actually I'm just making sure that all of these girls that you see out here are a'ight. You kna'imean?"

It was late as hell and I was enjoying the warmth of the car, but I wanted to get somewhere and try to sleep. So I needed to be more direct in order to speed things up.

"Cream, stop talking to me in codes. First you come at me on some ol' 'I can read your mind' tip. Then you tell me you're out here because you're working. And now you're telling me that you're making sure that all of these chicks are a'ight. Just talk to me plain."

"Lady, this is me," Cream stated while touching his chest. "This is how I get down. But I tell you what. Why don't you let me see you one day this week, like on a day that you're not working or something and I can be more plain with you. . . . A'ight?"

Cream looked good as hell and I didn't know what to make of his words, but I just assumed that that was his way of trying to get with me. His car alone had me open, and besides that, the way he looked, he had this certain street way about him that was just *ghetto-fabulous*. To be honest it was that thug in him that had me open ever since I noticed him in the donut shop.

I was thinking about whether or not I should let him know how old I was, but my instincts were telling me no. I mean since the time that I left my mother's house I'd turned fifteen but I looked twenty-one. Guys had a saying, "Fifteen will get you twenty and sixteen will get you ten." Meaning if they messed with a female who was only fifteen years old they could get twenty years in jail and if she were sixteen then they could get about ten.

So I didn't want that type of noise running through Cream's head. I wasn't trying to derail the train before the engine got started.

"I'm cool with that," I stated. "We could hook up this Sunday or something. I'm usually not doing anything on Sunday."

"Sunday?" Cream thought for a moment.

"Yeah, Sunday. Now stop trying to think about what it is that you gotta do on Sunday 'cause whatever it is you can just dead it."

Cream looked at me with a cold stare.

"So let me get your number," I said while reaching into my large Coach bag for a pen, all the while hoping that I didn't expose what was inside of my bag.

"Lady, I'd bet a grand that your favorite sex position is with you on top."

"What?" I asked.

"You heard what I said!"

Cream's tone of voice caught me off guard. He sounded as if he was about to check my ass or something.

"You seem like you like to control a nigga and the situations. When I first met you, you were trying to control what me and my crew said and how you wanted us to act. Now in my car you just took control of my blunt and now you're coming gangsta with yours, talking about 'so let me get your number.'"

I didn't know what to say or how to respond, I was just hoping that I hadn't disrespected Cream in any way. Thankfully I was feeling high as hell. And hopefully so was Cream.

Cream continued, "Not that I'm saying it's a bad thing. I'm just saying I never met anybody that gets down like you on that control tip. You're good at it. . . . But I'm better!"

"Oh my god! That is so not me," I said, lying through my teeth. There is power in control and I hated to give up any of my power. But Cream was keen at noticing the slightest details in things, things that most people don't realize or think about. And that's why he was able to pick up on all of my moves and traits.

Cream simply gave me a half smile and nodded his head while he wrote his phone number on a piece of paper and handed it to me.

"That's my cell number," he stated. "So we good for Sunday?"

"No doubt," I replied as I prepared to open the door to Cream's car and let myself out.

"So you sure you don't want a ride?"

"Nah, I'm good."

I paused and then I added with a smile, "I'm keeping this." I was referring to his blunt which I held up to make sure that he knew what I was talking about.

"That's cool," Cream nonchalantly replied.

I then extended my hand to Cream in a playful way as if I was a dude and asked, "Can I get a pound before I bounce? I mean I know that you gotta get back to work and all."

Cream smiled and extended his hand to my hand.

With my door slightly cracked open I clasped Cream's hand and made sure that I didn't let it go too quickly. I was feeling nice and free and my words were uninhibited because of the weed. I pulled Cream toward me, closed my eyes, and leaned in and gave him a kiss on his lips. I paused for a moment. And although I didn't say exactly what I wanted to say, I simply stated, "You were wrong about me liking to be on top . . ."

Cream laughed.

I removed my hand from his and then opened the door fully and stepped out. "I like it from the back."

Cream was no longer laughing.

"I'll call you," I said, then firmly closed his car door.

5

WHEN CREAM AND I ARRIVED at Club New York in midtown Manhattan, I had to try really hard to contain myself. I didn't wanna come off as someone who had never been anywhere and didn't know how to act. But there was just so much energy outside the club and I couldn't wait to get inside and release some of it. We pulled up to the front of the club and Cream had the valet park his car.

The line to get inside the club was intimidating, as it ran the entire length of West Forty-first and wrapped around onto Broadway.

Cream held onto my hand and immediately guided me to the front of the line. A big, black, bald-headed bouncer who looked as if he was about six foot five and three-and-fifty pounds removed the rope that was blocking the V.I.P. entrance to the club.

"What's up, Cream?" the bouncer asked as he extended a pound to Cream.

"My man," Cream replied as he clasped the bouncer's hand and pulled him close to his chest, giving him one of those quick ghetto embraces.

"Cream, she's with you?" the bouncer asked, referring to me.

"Yeah, she's with me," Cream replied as he introduced me to the bouncer.

"Nice to meet you," I politely stated as the bouncer waited for me to walk past so he could place the rope back in its position to block off the V.I.P. entrance.

As we made it into the crowded club I could hear the sounds of DJ Ron G blasting Snoop Dogg's hit song "Gin & Juice."

"Lemme get your coat so I can take it to the coat check for you!" Cream shouted over the loud music while speaking directly into my ear.

Earlier that day, Cream had taken me out to eat and he had also taken me shopping, specifically to buy an outfit for the club. Although he had purchased the outfit, he had yet to see me in it. So as soon as I took off my full-length coat, Cream shouted, "Got damn, Lady! Your look is off the meter!"

I must admit that Cream was not overdoing it in his excitement about my look and my outfit. I had on some black high-heel stiletto shoes along with a black leather miniskirt and a tight white wrap shirt with a plunging neckline. My skin was flawless and I made sure that the baby oil had been applied to all of the right places. I also placed a very small and tasteful amount of glitter on my legs and near my neck and face so that the lights from inside the club would bounce off my skin and make my honey complexion look that much more appealing.

I had purposely chosen the heels and the miniskirt because I knew that my butt and my hips were my two best assets. Not to mention that my legs had that strong, firm, and shapely look to them—my thighs and calves were every man's dream. I stood five foot six and weighed about 135 pounds and I liked having attention directed my way. I was sure that my outfit would bring me all sorts of positive male attention. Not that I wanted to play Cream or anything like that, it was more that the looks from other men would help to boost my ego and make me feel better about myself.

Whenever I haven't met a person and if I have only spoken to them over the phone, I always ask them to describe themself by telling me which famous person they look like. And I have learned that it is easy to do the same thing when describing myself. Although Beyoncé and the rapper Trina were not really on music's radar screen at that time, looking back I would have to say that my look was a cross between the two of those stars, especially my complexion. The major difference with them and me is that they both wear extensions and weaves in order to produce that long and wavy hair look. But I was born that way. I had natural brown hair which I added honey blonde streaks to. Many people have also told me that I look a lot like Chilli from the group TLC, only that I'm much thicker than she is.

That old ghetto adage of "you look like you got Indian in your family," definitely holds true for me. My hair is not as straight as an Indian person's hair would be but it is straight enough to mix with my natural African kinky-hair genes to give me the perfect look of long hair that goes down to my shoulder blades.

As far as personality goes, I definitely had that no-holds-barred, in-your-face mentality of a Trina or rap star Foxy Brown.

Cream handed my coat to the coat check girl who had managed to give Cream a kiss on the cheek and whisper something into his ear. Although it caused a smile to plaster Cream's face and I could have taken that as a sign of disrespect, I gave the coat check girl a free pass.

Cream proceeded to lead me through the crowded club. It was like he was a famous celebrity because everybody knew him and was acknowledging his presence.

"Who don't you know?" I yelled into Cream's ear over the music.

"This is my spot. I'm always in here," Cream responded. "Come on, let's go to the V.I.P. area," he instructed.

I followed closely behind Cream, holding his hand, and I was like a kid in a candy store. Or a kid at Disney World where the characters that they see on TV suddenly come to life and are tangible and real to the point where they can touch the characters and take pictures with them.

I had been out partying and had been to clubs before but this felt way different from what I was used to. There was something more next-level about this club. In the short time that I had been in the club I could tell that this was my ghetto Disney Land and I wanted to meet all of the characters and experience all of the joys of the glamorous street and nightlife combined.

The music was thumping and I could feel the vibrations from the speakers running up and down my body. At that point the deejay threw on Rakim's old-school joint "Erik B. For President." The joint that goes, "I came in the door I said it before I never let the mike magnetize me no more . . ."

When that song came on everybody in the club lost their minds, including me. I didn't even need any liquor or weed to open me up and have a good time because the atmosphere and the music had me on a natural high and I was ready to let loose.

I grabbed Cream's hand and turned him in my direction and began dancing in front of him. I had my hands raised into the dimly lit air and was snapping my fingers and just having a good time.

Cream, who looks a lot like the rapper DMX, was trying to play that cool "I don't dance" role. But I was determined to get him to open up.

I kind of blocked him out of my mind and just concentrated on dancing and having a good time and being loose and I knew that my energy combined with the music would eventually rub off on him and I was right. Cream began doing his cool Mac Daddy two-step dance but he eventually got more into it.

Then the deejay switched up the song and threw on another old-school song by Milk D, called "Top Billin'," which went, "Milk is chillin', Giz is Chillin', what more can I say top billin' that's what you get . . ."

Needless to say the whole atmosphere was just sick and everyone in the club went wild.

"You know you feeling it, Cream!" I shouted into his ear.

"This is my record!" he replied as he threw his hands into the air and moved his body a little closer to mine and continued to dance with me.

Club life is what life was all about and what I could see myself doing every day. Everything just felt so right.

"Come on, let's go to the V.I.P. area so I can introduce you to my people," Cream instructed.

I wanted to stay on the dance floor and continue partying but at the same time I wanted to experience the entire atmosphere of the club.

"Okay," I replied.

We snaked our way past the crowded bar area and underneath numerous strobe lights, walked up a flight of stairs, and made it to a large plush-looking room that had what appeared to be a fiberglass enclosure. There were small tables and little chairs all around the V.I.P. area and many people were dancing while some were sitting and drinking liquor.

We walked toward the rear of the V.I.P. area and I could look through the fiberglass partition. I was able to sort of look down on the crowd and see the strobe lights and all of the people partying. The V.I.P. room was somewhat crowded and the music was just as loud as it had been downstairs on the main floor.

"Yo, Cream, what up baby pa?" someone shouted.

"What up kid?"

Cream and I finally made it to an area of the V.I.P. room that had couches and small tables. Some chick was dancing on one of the tables like she had lost her mind but I was feeling her energy.

"You can have a seat if you want," Cream instructed. "You want something to drink?"

"Yeah, get me a Bacardi and Coke," I replied.

"Yo Shamgod, y'all up in here dry, nigga? Why y'all ain't get no drinks going yet?" Cream questioned.

His man Shamgod responded, "We was waiting for Spinach to get his ass in here but we can't wait on that nigga no more, let's get this on and poppin'!"

By the way, Shamgod was given that name at birth by his mother. And believe it or not it is his government name. Yup, it's on his birth certificate. But that's a whole other thing.

Anyway, Cream got the attention of the waitress and she came over to where we were sitting.

"What's up sexy?"

"What can I get for y'all, baby?" the waitress asked.

"Bring me a Bacardi and Coke and get us five bottles of Moët."

I was sitting there thinking to myself, *Got damn! It's like that?! I can't believe this nigga just ordered five bottle of Mo'.* I was wondering if had I ordered the wrong thing.

"Cream, who is this?" Shamgod asked as he looked and gestured in my direction.

"Come on man! That's Lady."

"Get the hell outta here! That's Lady?" Shamgod asked, sort of in astonishment.

"Shamgod, you see me at work like almost every day, so don't try to front like you don't know who I am," I responded.

Spinach, by the way, got his name because he always kept a large wad of green unfolded and wrinkled bills in his pocket. Hence, spinach is green and clumpy and messy and money is green and when not neatly folded looks clumpy and messy. But anyway, Spinach and Shamgod were both right-hand mans of Cream and they accompanied him just about everywhere he went.

"Nah my bad, I'm just sayin' from behind the counter in that donut shop a brotha just didn't know that you had all of that going on," Shamgod replied while motioning to his thigh and hip area.

I had known that I would bring a lot of shock value to both Shamgod and Spinach when I eventually saw them. And in fact that was one of my intended goals. I knew that I would be meeting a lot of Cream's people and I wanted to be on point.

Cream began to escort me around the room and he introduced me to so many people who were all down with him. Earlier in the day he had explained to me in a real brief and general way that he ran with and headed the Queensbridge-based Cream Team and that he would introduce me to a lot of the members and associates at the club.

I met Dame, Prince, Pete, Ci-Lo, Stretch, and so many other people that I simply just could not keep track of the names and faces. But everybody that I met seemed to show me a whole lot of love and a whole lot of respect. Cream also introduced me to some chicks who had all kind of hate just oozing out of them. Just from the vibes that they were giving off it was apparent that they were somewhat jealous of a sista.

But I was like *whateva*. If they were coming at me with the screw faces and ice grills I made sure to come back at them with the same kind of shade. Even though I was young, I had had my fair share of street battles over all kinds of things and all kinds of stupid beefs. But without a doubt the majority of my street wars were with women who were simply jealous of me. And I learned early on that disrespect and all of that was just simply not gonna be tolerated by me. In fact my motto was I didn't care who the chick or the nigga was, they were not above me bringing it to them if I felt the need to do just that.

By the time Cream had finished introducing me, the drinks had arrived and I proceeded to sip from my drink. But I could just sense the hate that was coming from this one chick Nikki in particular. I had seen her talking to her girl who Cream had introduced as Diamond. My intuition was telling me that they were plotting something but I wasn't exactly sure if they would start some nonsense in the club.

I spoke as loudly as I could into Cream's ear over the music but in a tone that was relative to a whisper. "Cream, what's up with that chick, Nikki? Word is bond, I came here to have a good time but I won't have no problem bringing it to that bitch!"

"What happened?" Cream asked.

"It's just them stank looks that she's dishing out. And I know she's plotting something with her girl. Cream, I'm sayin' I know you don't have time for this pettiness and I know that you didn't come here for no beefs and all of that but . . ."

"A'ight . . . A'ight hold up, just chill," Cream responded. "It ain't nothing, that's just how Nikki rolls with hers."

"But she don't know how I roll with mines!" I shot back.

"Lady, just finish your drink. Have some Mo' and just have a good time and just chill. I'll talk to Nikki. She works for me so it ain't nothing."

I took Cream's advice, calmed down, and sat near Shamgod and Spinach, who had finally arrived.

Shamgod had sensed what was going on and he told me, "Lady, don't worry about Nikki. She's just trying to intimidate you so that she can protect her money."

I had no idea what Shamgod meant by that but I was like *whateva*. I had finished my drink and I proceeded to drink some Moët. The whole atmosphere was still crazy as the deejay continued to throw on hit record after hit record.

I was dancing by myself with my drink in my hand and just surveying the crowd when I noticed someone that I had known for some time. She was older than me by like three years but that age gap didn't mean anything because I knew how to carry myself so really almost everybody that I hung out with was always older than me. I got so excited that I had to go locate her. I was just hoping that she wouldn't leave her location before I got a chance to get to her.

"That's my girl! I can't believe my girl is up in here," I shouted as I accidentally spilled some of my champagne in my excitement.

"Shamgod, I'll be back in a minute," I stated. "I see one of my girls from back in the days that I haven't seen in a while. I gotta go talk to her."

"A'ight," Shamgod responded.

I started to make my way out of the V.I.P. area and I bumped into Cream and told him where I was going.

"A'ight but hold up, before you go I wanna introduce you to somebody."

I really didn't want to delay because as crowded as the club was I was certain that my friend would bounce to another part of the packed club and I wouldn't be able to locate her.

"Okay, but I gotta hurry up 'cause I don't wanna miss her."

Cream nodded to show that he had heard my concern. But as we walked and snaked our way to another section of the V.I.P. area this tall guy grabbed Cream by the shoulder and was like, "Yo, what up nigga? How you gonna just brush past me like that?"

I could not believe who had just grabbed Cream. It was LL Cool J! Although I was from New York and seeing celebrities was not really a big deal, this was a little different because I was actually right there in the mix with this star, the same rap star that I loved and worshiped from as early on as I could remember.

"Yo, L, what's up, dog?" Cream stated while giving LL a pound. "L, this is Lady. She's cool peoples and a good friend of mines."

LL, who was looking sexy and diesel and smelling good as hell did his trademark licking of his lips as he said, "Lady? I'm feeling that name. That's different. . . . You having a good time?"

"I always have a good time," I replied. "It's nice to meet you."

"Nice to meet you too," LL responded. "I'll be in here for a minute so I'll see y'all."

"No doubt," Cream replied. "And yo, L, come by the couches and have some champagne when you get a chance."

"I'll make it over there before the night is out," LL replied.

I could not believe that I, a young fifteen-year-old high school kid who was living on her own and making it on her own was literally chillin' and speaking to LL Cool J like it was a normal everyday thing or something. I really felt like I was about to have an orgasm! I was feeling so damn good about myself.

"Lady, that wasn't even who I wanted you to meet. Come on, it's gonna be quick, I just wanna introduce you to this nigga real quick."

Meeting LL had been more than enough for me and my mind was definitely fixated on catching up to my girl.

"Yo Biggie, I wanna introduce you to somebody. This is a good friend of mines and she's real cool. Her name is Lady . . . Lady, this is Biggie Smalls a.k.a. the Notorious B.I.G."

My jaw was literally ready to drop to the ground. Biggie's career at that time was just about to get sick and his single "Juicy" was a smash and constantly being played on the radio. Plus he had that hot single "How to Sex an R&B Chick" or something like that. At that time in his career no one knew how big of a star he would eventually become, but it still was off the hook just meeting him. And not meeting him like some crazy screaming fan, but to meet him on a regular vibe. That was what made it feel so good.

Biggie, who was really big as hell, was in his classic form with his slow-speaking sort of drawl.

"What's up, ma? Anybody that runs with Cream is cool with me. It's good to meet you."

"You too," I replied. "I'm feeling that 'Juicy' record, word is bond."

"Thanks, ma. I'm just trying to do me right now and trying to rep Brooklyn, that's all. . . . Yo, let me introduce you to some of my people. Matter of fact, remember them because they're about to blow this music game out of the water. This is my girl Lil' Kim and this is my man Lil' Cease. They're part of my group called the Junior M.A.F.I.A."

"Nice to meet y'all. Good luck with everything and I hope y'all blow."

I had no idea at that time who Lil' Kim was nor did I know that she and I would later become close friends. And I certainly had no idea how big she would become but her vibe and Lil' Cease's vibe was just so street and at the same time she was just so real.

"Cream, I'm gonna jet downstairs and talk to my girl and I'll be right back."

At that point I had mixed emotions because I wanted to see my girl but I also wanted to drink champagne and mingle with the stars. It was a tough thing to leave all of the glamorous people so soon without having really kicked it with them, but I was hoping to quickly find my girl and bring her back to the V.I.P. area.

Since the club was so crowded it took me forever to make it down to the dance floor. Along the way I got all kinds of catcalls and heard all kinds of comments about how I looked but I had no time for that, I just wanted to find my girl and make it back to the V.I.P. area.

I searched for about ten minutes and then I finally saw Shauna, my friend, dancing it up with some guy. I made sure I wasn't too rude but I had to butt in.

"Shauna! What's up, trick? What the hell are you doing in here?!"

"Tina? I know that is not you, Tina!" Shauna and I both let out yells of excitement as we embraced each other.

It had been at least three years since I had seen Shauna but it felt like just yesterday.

"Tina, look at you! You look grown as hell!"

"I'm sayin', girl! You look good too."

Shauna added, "The last time I seen you you ain't have all that ass and all them hips!"

Shauna and I had lived on the same block for about a year or so. The two of us had become real close during that time but when I moved off the block we lost contact with one another.

We continued to exchange excited small talk. Shauna told me that she was gonna be heading out in a few minutes so that she could get some sleep before going to work the following morning.

Shauna gave me her number and then I was able to convince her to come with me up to the V.I.P. area. I promised her that it wouldn't take long and that she could bounce in five minutes.

As the two of us were allowed into the V.I.P. area, Shauna was impressed that I was able to get the both of us inside the exclusive area of the club without any special passes. The song that was blasting at that time was En Vogue's smash hit, "Hold On."

Shauna proceeded to follow me to the V.I.P. lounge area where Cream and all of his boys were chillin'. As I was walking in, LL Cool J was on his way out and it was like he went out of his way to acknowledge me. "Lady, I'm out. I know I'll see you around. Take care."

Shauna was shocked and grabbed my shoulder. "Tina I know that was not just LL Cool J talking to you like he knew you!"

I had to play things cool like it was no big deal. "Yeah girl, when we talk I'll bring you up to speed on everything. And by the way everybody in here calls me Lady. That's my street name."

Shauna couldn't believe what she was witnessing or what I was telling her. I proceeded to introduce her to everybody in the Cream Team who were present.

Biggie was chillin' right there next to everybody and I waited for him to get off of his cell phone. I walked up to him and said, "Biggie, I want you to meet my friend Shauna. Shauna, this is Biggie. Biggie, this is Shauna."

"Nice to meet you," Shauna stated, sounding all shy and silly.

"You too, ma . . . Lady, do all of your friends look as good as y'all do?"

I smiled and said, "Yeah, you know, we try to do our thing, but we just like having fun. We work hard and we play hard, you kna'imean?"

Shauna's mouth simply would not close. I just wanted her to get off of the starstruck tip and play everything cool. This was not the time to be acting like a groupie.

She stayed for a while and drank some Moët and then she pulled me off to the side where we just chitchatted. Craig Mack's "Flava in Ya Ear" blared in the background of our quick conversation.

"Tina, you better make sure that you call me! You're living on your own and rolling with the Cream Team and talking to stars and all of that. I just wanna know, how can a sista be down?"

We both began laughing as we slapped each other five.

"I still can't get over this. So you're saying that you came here with Cream and you're leaving with him?"

"Yes, Shauna!"

"Trick, listen, you better call me this week!" Shauna said as she hugged me and prepared to leave.

She hated to go but she had to because of that damn nine to five. Shauna had told me that she was making good money, like thirty-five thousand dollars a year working as a legal secretary for some large prestigious corporate law firm.

The night went on and everybody had a good time. Ron G was off the hook with the music. The hip hop, reggae, R&B—it was just all off the meat rack.

I had never had so much fun in my entire life. And that night at the club was sort of like an epiphany for me because I knew that eventually the club scene would be where a major part of my future would lay.

Around four in the morning, Cream and I found ourselves back in his car. We had already made plans for me to spend the night with him at his house in Astoria, Queens. My ears had like a constant ringing to them because of the loud music that I had been exposed to all night. I began feeling tired from all of the liquor that I had consumed in the club, especially since the intoxication of the booze had started to wear off.

We weaved our way through the streets of Manhattan and made our way to and over the Fifty-ninth Street Bridge and were back in Queens. Cream stopped his car at the corner of Twenty-eighth Street and Queens Plaza South, just yards from the base of the bridge and right near my job.

"I just gotta take care of something real quick. I'll be right back," Cream stated as he placed the car in park and stepped out while leaving the engine running and me in the passenger's seat.

I made it my business to be nosy as I spied on Cream's every move. I saw Cream talking to three guys who were on the corner along with the rest of the street-walking prostitutes who were out there.

Cream had been out of the car all of two minutes and when he made it back to the car he just sat there without saying anything.

"Is everything okay?" I asked.

"Yeah, everything is cool. I just gotta wait for one of my girls," Cream explained.

As I sat there things started to hit me like a ton of bricks. *Cream was pimpin' the hoes that were out there on the street corner.*

Suddenly it all made sense why Cream had said Nikki worked for him, and why Shamgod had said that the chick Nikki was trying to protect her money. It also explained why Cream had told me he was working that night when I saw him parked on the exact same corner that we were currently parked on and why he had said he was making sure all of the girls were okay. That and Spinach's comment about putting "my ass out on the track."

I thought real fast. I wanted an affiliation with Cream. After tonight I knew that hooking up with Cream would bring me all that I was desiring in life. But I was no fool. I knew Cream wasn't about to be *marrying* no pussy. I knew that he was about the Benjamins and I also knew that with him, regardless of how things looked on the surface, that underneath it all, everything in his world was designed to serve and please him. That was a'ight though because it was not like I was looking to get tied down in no relationship or anything like that. I was way too young for that. Plus I knew that when it came to guys that I had to come at them the same way they would come at me. I mean I really only needed a nigga who could put it down in the bedroom, and who could help me raise my status on some level. But no matter what, I definitely needed a nigga who would keep me in check.

So as I sat there in his ride, I didn't let myself get all flustered.

Cream is pimping these hoes, I kept telling myself. I knew that he more than likely had plans for me to get out on the track and sell my body for him. In fact, his taking me to the club and treating me all good was probably just his way of recruiting me to be one of his hoes.

"Cream," I said. "Why the hell do they call this a track?"

I knew the question had caught him off guard, which had been my intent.

"I mean, I know these girls are selling pussy out here but why does that make it a track?"

Cream laughed a little bit.

"Yo, that's just an old-school term. Everybody in every hood since way back in the day has been calling it a track."

Then one of his girls came to the window. Cream rolled it down.

"What's up, *papi?*" the sexy young Latina asked him.

"Just chillin'. We just came back from Club New York."

"'We'? What the hell do you mean, 'we'! I know you ain't just come from the club with this bitch!" the girl disrespectfully shouted as she looked in my direction. Her accent was reminiscent of Puerto Rican actress Rosie Perez. "Where is Nikki and Diamond?"

"Trick, who the hell are you calling a bitch?" I stated as I quickly unbuckled my seat belt and prepared for battle.

"Chill! Got damn! What the hell is wrong wit' y'all? Mercedes, this is Lady and Lady, this is Mercedes!" Cream said in a disgusted tone as he attempted to calm things down. His face was twisted. The last thing he wanted to be doing was refereeing a catfight.

"Lady? Whateva . . . Here baby," Mercedes said as she handed Cream a wad of folded cash. And then she asked again, "Why you ain't with Nikki and Diamond?"

"Y'all a'ight out here?" Cream replied, totally ignoring her question.

"Yeah, we good but it's just slow 'cause these damn cops keep circling the block and posting their car on the corner," Mercedes explained.

"A'ight. Just do what y'all gotta do. I'm a bounce to the crib. If you need me call me on my cell. Spinach should be leaving the club soon and he'll swing through and scoop y'all up, a'ight? Nikki is rolling with him."

"A'ight baby. Be safe," Mercedes said as she gave me another ice grill before walking away from the car.

Seeing the amount of cash that had just been placed in Cream's hand confirmed for me that he was definitely just about the money. I mean he might have been attracted to me and liked me in some way, but there was no doubt that his main goal was to get me to sell my ass and put some more money into his pockets.

It was a tough thing to picture and consider but I knew that if Cream asked me to work for him that I would have to accept. He would definitely provide that sense of security that I was looking for, and I knew that he was in a position to take care of me. And in light of the circumstances I was facing—being homeless and all—working for Cream seemed scary but at the same time it seemed like the right move to make.

Plus, I didn't really know who Nikki and Diamond were, but they seemed like they held some kind of rank in Cream's eyes. And if that were so, then I could probably bounce them two chicks up out of Cream's life and get in good with him and rise with him and his crew.

My major dilemma was my sister Mya. She was my heart, and although I hadn't seen her in a while I cared about her like she was my daughter, and there was no way I would have wanted her to see me or hear about me whoring around. But at the same time, by doing it I would be able to provide a way out for Mya.

I looked at Cream and thought the current pimp game wasn't like the old-school game had been. It was more low key. There weren't anymore flamboyant players' balls. Nah, the game had completely changed. You couldn't tell the current pimps from the local hand-to-hand drug dealers.

Even the hoes on the street were not all old-school like they used to be. The current prostitutes were likely to be average-looking girls from the hood. They would be on the corner with tight jeans and Reebok sneakers and unless you knew the game you could have easily been fooled.

"Sorry about all of that," Cream said, referring to Mercedes's behavior.

"You ain't gotta apologize for her. I know the deal, she's looking at me and resenting the fact that I'm riding with you."

Cream replied, "Yeah, but she is good peoples though. Mercedes definitely holds me down."

"Nikki and Diamond hold you down too, right?" I asked.

Cream just looked at me and didn't say a word.

It was now nearing, like, five fifteen in the morning and there was silence in the car as Cream drove through the streets of Queens and headed toward Astoria.

I knew that we were headed back to his crib and that he would wanna sex me. And to be honest I didn't have a problem with that because that's what I wanted too. In fact I had been horny as hell for like the past two weeks so I was definitely down for whateva, not to mention that sexing him would also give me somewhere to sleep for the night. I just didn't want it to be a one-time sex thing where I wouldn't get anything else out of it. But I knew that it more than likely wouldn't be. I mean, I doubted that he would dis me by sexing me and then throwing me out of his house. I knew that he wanted me to work for him.

Cream broke the silence in the car as he glanced over to me and stated, "You know I wanna be your daddy, right?"

I knew that daddy was the slang word for pimp but I didn't say anything to him. I just looked straight ahead and slowly nodded my head to the music playing in the car.

"Lady, what's up? Look at me," Cream instructed.

I looked at him and continued to slowly nod my head to the music.

"You see me nodding my head, right?" I asked instead of just answering Cream directly.

"Lady, I'm dead serious! I'm not playing games. I don't have time for games."

"Cream, ain't nobody ever come at me like that," I replied.

"So you frontin' on me or what?" Cream asked as he slowed the car down and pulled to the side of the curb.

"What? You putting me out of your car?" I asked.

Cream didn't say anything. He just slightly twisted his bottom lip.

"Cream, I nodded my head yes when you asked me. I'm whichu, daddy," I replied.

From out of nowhere Cream snapped. He reached over and snatched me up by my arm and pulled me closer to him. His face was right in my face and I could smell the weed on his breath as he spoke.

"Let me explain something to ya ass. When I ask you a question you open up your got damn mouth and you give me an answer! You think I'm a mind reader?" Cream shouted with a rage that was totally unexpected.

I didn't know what to think. My heart started pounding as I wondered if he was just high or really pissed off.

"Cream, I'm sorry," I stated with a nervous smile on my face.

"Lady, I swear to god, I'm two seconds from slapping that silly-ass smile off your face! You must really think I'm a joke or one of your little friends or something?" Cream asked as he gripped my arm even tighter.

"Cream, I'm sorry! I wasn't trying to disrespect you." I made sure to wipe the smile off my face.

Cream finally relaxed his position and let go of my arm. He waited about thirty seconds, not saying a word to me. Then he resumed driving. Before long we had arrived at Cream's crib.

My head was spinning now as all kinds of thoughts were racing through it. Cream hadn't spoken a word to me since he released his tight grip on my arm and I was wondering to myself what in the world had I just committed myself to. I have to admit that I was nervous as hell.

Cream led me to his bedroom, not saying a word to me the whole time. He didn't ask me if I wanted anything to drink, or if I had to use the bathroom or anything cordial like that. He didn't even show me around his house. But he finally did break the silence as he began unbuckling his pants.

"Daddy gotta make sure that you ready for dem streets," he stated as he stood with his pants down to his ankles and his dick fully exposed.

I realized that my first training session was about to take place. I hoped that I would perform well and I was also fearful of saying the wrong thing or not responding in the right way. So without any instructions I walked over to Cream, got on my knees, and placed him inside my mouth, much to his satisfaction. I knew that I didn't need any training session as far as my sex skills were concerned. I mean after all, ever since I was twelve years old I had learned and understood how to put it on niggas.

I orally put it on Cream that night. I had also managed to get undressed and I was backing it up like a Mack truck all night long and I know that he was open to my forty-four inches of booty. Yeah, Cream didn't expect me to handle him the way I did but I wanted to turn him out the best I could and make him happy. I mean, he handled his business and I got mines off but it wasn't about me that night. It was all about keeping Cream, my daddy, happy and showing him that I could make money for him.

And I did just that.

6

ON MONDAY MORNING, CREAM'S BED felt real good and I didn't want to get up, but I had to. I knew that I wouldn't make it to school until about third or fourth period but I had to be there if I wanted to cheer in the basketball game which was scheduled for later that evening.

Surprisingly, when I woke up at around nine that morning Cream was already up and about the house. I had assumed he'd be the type to just stay in bed and roll around until like one in the afternoon or something. But that wasn't the case.

Being that it was my first time in Cream's house, I didn't just wanna take it for granted that he lived alone and just start parading around the house half naked or anything. But at the same time I needed to get to the bathroom and shower, brush my teeth, and get the hell to school as quickly as I could.

I quietly sat up in the bed, pulled back the covers, and shifted both of my legs until they dangled from the side of the king-size water bed. Wearing just a long T-shirt that Cream had loaned to me, I stood up, quietly made it to my bag, and knelt down in an attempt to retrieve an outfit from the bag.

"Lady, you want something to eat?"

I quickly let out a small yell of astonishment as I had been startled by Cream's presence.

Cream laughed and said, "Chill, it's just me."

"You tryin' to give me a damn heart attack or something?" I jokingly asked with an embarrassed smile on my face.

"I'm making grits with cheese and bacon. You want any?" Cream asked. That thug side of him, the side that caused him to grab me up by my arm—it seemed like it had disappeared and his calmer side had resurfaced.

"Nah, I'm good. Actually I gotta hurry up and bounce."

"Where you gotta be this early?"

I knew that now was as good a time as any to spring the news on Cream and let him know that he had unknowingly committed statutory rape and also that I was on my way to high school. But I decided to just play things cool for the meantime and not be too up front. I didn't wanna say anything that would trigger that thug side in him.

"Oh, I gotta go near Archer and Parsons," I nonchalantly replied.

The intersection of Archer Avenue and Parsons Boulevard was located in the heart of downtown Jamaica, Queens. There are tons of stores in that area along with a major movie theater, a gym, courthouses, etc. There is even a college bustling in the area. But most importantly, there is a major public transportation hub at Archer Avenue and Parsons Boulevard. Since the day that the transportation hub opened, everyone has referred to it simply as Archer and Parsons. A large majority of the Queens residents who take the train to work pass through Archer and Parsons; it's sort of like the first leg of anyone's trip to work or to Manhattan.

"Archer and Parsons? For what?" Cream questioned.

Playing everything cool, I replied, "I gotta go to school."

I was hoping that Cream would just assume that I was referring to York College which was within a two- or three-block walking distance from the Archer and Parsons train station.

"School?" Cream questioned with a puzzled look on his face.

"Yeah, school," I replied, making sure to verbally respond to him and show him the respect that he had commanded.

"Word! You in school? I ain't know that. You're doing your thing like that? That's cool."

"Yeah, I'm just tryin' to do me."

I wanted to change the subject and used time as a diversion.

"You should have woken me up when you got up. I'm a be late," I stated, sounding as if I was anxious.

"Nah, don't sweat that. I'll drive you over there. You go to York College or do you gotta get on the train?"

This was definitely not the direction that I wanted the conversation to take.

"Cream, I'll be a'ight. Thanks for offering to take me but just chill and eat your food. I'll call a cab, it ain't no big thing."

"You sure?"

"Yeah, trust me. I'll be a'ight. Where is your bathroom? I just wanna jump in the shower real quick. . . . And can I use your iron?"

Cream pointed me in the direction of the bathroom and told me where I could find the iron and the ironing board. I quickly made my way to the bathroom. I desperately wanted to take a tour of every room in Cream's crib just to see how he was living. From the looks of things it appeared as if he kept his house immaculate, and that to me was a pleasant surprise. But there was no time for a real tour because I had moves to make.

After I made it out of the shower I brushed my teeth, put on some deodorant, rubbed lotion all over my body, and tied one of Cream's towels around my body in order to cover up my private parts just in case his mom or some other unsuspecting guest was lurking around. I didn't know who he lived with and I didn't want to assume anything.

Cream had a two-story brick house and it appeared as if all of the bedrooms were located on the second floor. Cream was downstairs on the main floor in the kitchen. From the smell of things it sounded as if he knew what the hell he was doing in the kitchen.

Anyway, I decided to be a little daring before going downstairs to iron my clothes. Even though I was running late I had to make time for a quick tour. I casually walked over to a closed door which looked as if it led to a bedroom. It was located down the hall on the opposite end of the house from Cream's bedroom, which was located right next to the bathroom. I made it to the closed door and gently twisted the knob. I was hoping that the hinges were new and would not make any squeaking sounds as I prepared to slowly push the door open.

After quietly opening the door I realized that I could not see who or what was inside the room unless I ventured inside the room a little bit farther. So I proceeded to tiptoe into the room in a brisk and silent manner. Although the sun was shining brightly outside, the room appeared kind of dim because the vertical blinds were closed.

Now that I was in a position to accurately see the inside of the room, I noticed that it was quite large. In fact it was just as large if not larger than Cream's bedroom. It was large enough to accommodate a king-size bed and a love seat. Sprawled across the bed were two half-naked, dark-skinned girls that both had butt for days! One was wearing just some red lace panties and the other was wearing a black thong and what appeared to be a black matching bra.

On the love seat was a light-skinned girl who was dressed in a pair of gray leggings and a tight, short, white tank top that exposed her entire stomach. All three women appeared to be no older than eighteen or nineteen years old. They were definitely highly attractive. And I wasn't sure but two of the girls looked like Nikki and Diamond, the chicks that were scheming on me at the club.

I should go over there right now and snuff they ass, I thought to myself. *Nah, now ain't the time, Lady.*

I turned and quietly left the room and closed the door. Before making my way downstairs I went back into Cream's room and got the clothes that I was gonna wear that day.

As I made my way down the stairs all kinds of things were racing through my mind. I was wondering who and what was inside of the other rooms in the house and if I should risk venturing into those rooms as well. I was hungry as hell but I knew that there was no time to eat because I had to get going.

When I landed in the living room I noticed that Cream was really *livin'* in terms of his living room floors. He didn't have no carpet or nice hardwood floors or anything like that. He had what looked like black marble floors. But I later found out that it was not marble, but granite. It was as if the entire floor was just one big sheet of black shiny ice. It was off the chain and instantly had me open.

I definitely needed a pair of slippers because although the heat was on inside the house, after having come out of the shower my feet were freezing. With cold feet I gingerly walked across the granite floor until I made it into the kitchen.

"Cream, I am feeling your floor!"

"It's hot, right?" Cream cockily answered. "That's thirty thousand dollars that you were walking on."

"It's worth every penny of it," I replied, stroking his ego.

"Oh, excuse me, I'm sorry. I'm all rude, I didn't realize that you had company," I remarked to Cream as I saw yet another attractive black girl sitting at Cream's kitchen table. She was wearing an off-white, short silk robe and slippers and her legs were crossed as she sipped some type of beverage from a mug.

Who in the world is this? I silently thought to myself.

"Nah, nah, nah, it's cool, don't even trip. This is Trish. Trish, this is Lady."

I was bracing and preparing for the shade and the impending drama that I just knew was about to come my way from Trish.

But to my complete shock Trish spoke up in an accent that I could not make out. I didn't know if it was a Southern accent, a West Coast accent, or what.

"Lady, why don't you sit down? Do you want me to get you anything?"

Is she the got damn maid or what? I was asking myself.

"Oh no, I'm good. I can't really hang around. I just came to ask Cream where exactly the iron is."

"You sure? Please, just be yourself around me and relax," Trish replied.

She definitely wasn't from New York because she just came across too damn green and polite sounding.

"No, really, I wouldn't mind staying but I gotta hurry up and iron my clothes and bounce."

Cream added, "Yeah, Trish, Lady's in school."

"School? When the hell do you have time for that?" Trish wanted to know.

I found the question weird because I was like she didn't even know me so how could she know what I had time for and what I didn't?

"Yeah, I gotta stay focused and just do me," I replied.

"More power to you. I just don't know how you have the energy for school. So what are you taking up there?"

The lightbulbs went off in my head. Trish must have thought that I was already out on the street tricking every night and too damn worn out and sore to be waking up every morning to go to some college.

I decided to play along with the whole college thing.

"I haven't really decided on anything yet but I'm really feeling the whole economics thing and the finance thing. I just love money and knowing how everything really operates behind the scenes."

That statement was actually accurate in that I loved my economics class that I was taking at Hillcrest High School. I had learned so much from that class and it had sparked such an interest in me that I started reading and studying anything and everything that I could get my hands on that related to the economy and stocks and corporations and business and all of that.

"Really? That's cool," Trish replied.

By this time it was nearing nine thirty in the morning and I really had to bounce. Cream was finished cooking his grits and the bacon was ready.

"Lady, you sure you don't want none?"

"No, I'm good. Cream, just show me real quick exactly where your iron and ironing board is at."

Cream told me to follow him.

As he led me in the direction of the basement steps I blurted out, "Cream, you know what? You can make me a BLT. Wrap it in aluminum foil and call a cab for me and I'll eat it in the cab."

"Damn, see now you're sounding like the controlling and loud person that I know!" Cream jokingly said.

Then he turned on the light to the basement and led me right to the closet that held the iron and all else that I was looking for.

His basement was also plush and it looked like it was made for a bachelor whose only purpose in life was to have liquor-filled stripper parties and Super Bowl parties. There was a real nice full-size Jacuzzi, a nice bar area, and a sixty-inch-looking projection television.

But there was also a sofa bed with yet another nice-looking young lady sleeping under the covers.

I whispered in a joking fashion to Cream, "Damn Cream, what are you? Hood Hefner or something?" I was playing on words, comparing Cream to the *Playboy* magazine founder and ultimate pimp, Hugh Hefner.

Cream laughed and told me that he just takes real good care of all of his girls.

Just then, a door opened up in the basement and it was that ghetto-Goya-trash Mercedes. She immediately started mouthing off and she was in rare form.

"Cream, I know that this bitch ain't spend the night! Why is she parading around in a towel and all of that?"

I immediately struck back. "Cream, please speak to your girl because I'm telling you, I will cut that ghetto-Goya-trash!"

After I said that, Mercedes flew into a rage and just rushed me. She looked as if she had every intention of literally beating the hell out of me. Actually, I hadn't expected her to come at me like that and my first reaction was a bit slow but it was fast enough for me to drop the clothes that I had in my hands and prepare to beat Mercedes' ass.

I don't know if it was my upbringing or what, but I was never one to fight like the typical woman with an open-hand slapping style. From my earliest fights I only remember fighting with a closed fist, boxer style. I always fought like a dude and this time was no different.

As I dropped the clothes and threw up my hands, Mercedes was lunging at me and her foot landed on the clothes that I had dropped on the floor, which caused her to lose her balance and sort of slide into me. She grabbed onto me to keep her balance and to keep from falling flat on her face. She had gathered enough momentum and when she grabbed onto me she was sort of pushing me backward at the same time and taking me down to the ground.

I felt myself falling backward but I managed to grab hold of Mercedes as tightly as I could with my left hand, and with my right hand I sent three of the hardest and fastest punches to her face and head that I could throw. I knew that I had caught her good and that I had hurt her because I saw her grimace in pain.

Her force of falling into me had caused us both to violently slam into the closet that held the iron, ironing board, and the clothes dryer. The sound of us slamming into that closet must have sounded like a plane crashing into a building. It was extremely loud and at the same time extremely painful for me. An intense pain shot up my back and I felt as if I had had the wind knocked out of me.

But I was high on adrenaline or something and I totally blocked out that pain and the fact that the wind had been knocked out of me. There was no way in hell that I was gonna let Mercedes beat my ass. I guess from the punches that I had thrown and connected upside Mercedes' head, she didn't have the confidence to pick her head up and look me in the face. She still sort of had her head down like some charging bull and she was attempting to throw punches. Her punches weren't really having any effect because she was not looking to see where she was throwing them.

With her not looking at me, I reached over and grabbed the iron and like a person doing karate who lets out a yell before they throw a kick, I let out a yell in order to summon more energy from my body as I bashed Mercedes upside the head with the iron. I had definitely hurt her and caught her off guard. It was what I needed to get out from under her.

I quickly stood up and in the process the towel that had been wrapped around me managed to come off. And there I was, standing barefoot and butt-ass naked and not caring. In my mind I remember thinking, *Yeah, now it is really on!*

"Get up, Goya bitch!" I yelled as I kicked Mercedes with the sole of my bare foot.

As Mercedes was desperately trying to get to her feet I remember seeing the young lady who had been asleep on the couch in the basement waking up and asking what was going on. Cream had tried to grab hold of me in order to calm me down and Trish must have heard the commotion as she came running down the stairs to assess the situation.

When I saw the young lady wake up from her sleep, and Trish coming down the steps, instinctively I thought that I was gonna get jumped. I was waiting for all of the tricks in that house to come to Mercedes' aid. And before I knew what was what, Nikki and Diamond had appeared from upstairs.

I had a bad feeling. Filled with adrenaline, it was nothing for me to jerk my arm free of Cream's grip. Hell, for all I knew he could have had plans of holding me down while his girls beat my ass, and I was not trying to let that happen.

I grabbed the iron and took the cord and wrapped it around Mercedes' neck. I was squeezing as tightly as I could.

"What's up now bitch! What's up now?" I screamed while choking Mercedes.

Mercedes at that point was on all fours. I violently helped her to her feet with the assistance of the iron's electrical cord.

"Get the hell up!" I barked at her.

Now her back was to my chest and I still had the electrical cord around her neck. This was the position that I wanted to be in. From here I could survey the room and see exactly what was going on and be prepared to handle mines just in case anyone tried to rush me.

Trish was yelling for me to calm down and let Mercedes go. The other young lady who had been asleep on the couch was asking what was going on.

"Diamond, go get my knife! I'm a cut this bitch! I know this ain't the same bitch from the club last night that was all up in my face!" Nikki barked out as she came toward me. "Get your hands off my girl!" she added.

"Take one more step closer to me and I'll beat your ass worse than I beat your girl!" I shot back at Nikki.

Cream was trying to get me to let go of Mercedes.

"Lady, a'ight! That's enough! That's enough! Stop choking her!" he screamed.

You have to understand that like in most fights, things just happen real quick and your survival instincts sort of take over, but the amazing thing is the speed at which things transpire.

Like one minute I was talking to Cream and in a matter of seconds

Mercedes and I were fighting and I was standing butt naked, choking her, and trying my best to kill her.

Mercedes was really struggling and I knew that she couldn't breathe. In a minute or so I knew that she would pass out, but I needed some assurances before I let her go. I also wanted her to know that I had just kicked her ass.

"Cream, I'll let her go but tell her to calm down! And tell Nikki to back up off me! I ain't letting her go until she calms down!" I yelled those words as Cream was trying to pry my fingers from the electrical cord.

"Tell her to relax and I'll let her go!"

"Nikki, back up!" Cream commanded as he told Mercedes to just chill and relax. Mercedes knew that she had no choice but to do as I said via Cream's words.

"Don't you ever disrespect me again! And don't ever come at me like that again!" I instructed as I sort of pushed Mercedes forward while releasing the grip of the electrical cord.

My titties were bouncing in the air, but covering up and putting on clothes was the last thing that I was worried about. I was still in combat mode and I knew that at any moment things could flare right back up.

And I was right. Diamond came back to the basement with a knife in her hand.

"Diamond, put the knife down right now!" Cream ordered. Diamond quickly dropped the knife.

Mercedes was coughing and I guess trying to free up her windpipe. But she was visibly the loser of that encounter. And as I suspected, her shame and embarrassment caused her to rise up and try to come at me again.

"Word is bond! Mark my words! I'm gonna kill you!" Mercedes threatened with Cream holding her at bay.

"Whateva, bitch!" I replied.

"Cream, I'm sorry about all of this. Trish, I know it ain't good to meet you on these terms but I just had to look out for myself," I explained while breathing very hard from the excitement.

That was more of a rhetorical statement because I wasn't looking for a response from either Cream or Trish.

At that point Mercedes was still vexed and venting. Nikki and Diamond were trying to calm her down and had walked with Mercedes into her room. I could hear all kinds of rumblings and dresser drawers opening and closing inside the room, along with all kinds of swearing and F this and F thats.

I threw on my wrinkled jeans with no panties and I threw on my shirt with no bra and I also threw on my Timberlands. At that point I could have really cared less about how I looked. I knew that I had three lockers in school that held my clothes and that I could just change into something else once I got there.

Cream summoned everyone back into the center of the basement and ripped into us.

"Y'all broke the got damn hinges off my door!" Cream screamed. "Y'all can't be doing this, man!"

"Cream, come by my job tonight and I'll give you the money for that," I replied.

"It ain't even about the money. It's about respecting a nigga's crib!"

I knew that Cream was upset and rightly so. And I knew that he wasn't all that thrilled at the fact that his money—in the form of Mercedes—now had defects to her face in terms of bruises and scratches.

"As of last night Lady is your new *sister-in-law*. I want y'all to respect her and show her some got damn love!" Cream barked.

All of the girls looked on with twisted lips and blatant contempt for me. They were straight hating.

After I finished throwing on my gear, I ran upstairs to Cream's room and got the rest of my things. I wasn't in the frame of mind to be waiting for no cab nor was I in the frame of mind to eat a BLT sandwich.

When I returned to the living room with my things and was prepared to leave I told Cream, "I'm not gonna call the cab. I'm just gonna bounce."

Cream didn't respond.

I walked over to Cream and I kissed him on the cheek. "I'm sorry about this," I said, not sure what else to say.

"If you can take this for what it means, daddy, I had a real good time last night. Everything was off the hook. The club, the drinks, your crib, and of course the sex with you was crazy! I'm ready to get that money for you."

Unfortunately I didn't get an enthusiastic response from Cream. But I kind of could sense why he was reacting the way he was. I could be a real loose cannon. My will and everything about me was strong like the realest cats in any hood. And I think it was that energy about me that probably made Cream hesitate now. He was wondering if I could really be of any value to him or if I would just be one big headache.

I had to erase all doubts and I had to do it fast.

"Cream, I know that I'm a loose cannon, but before I go I just wanna ask you to please be down for me," I said.

I smiled a little. "Now Cream, after what you just seen, with me tearing up your house and fighting butt naked like I was on the *Jerry Springer* show, I hope you know that I need some serious home training! Otherwise I'm gonna be a mess."

I was relieved to see Cream crack a smile. "Yeah, you right. Your ass definitely needs some home training!"

"Let me hurry up and go," I said as again I prepared to leave. But this time instead of just kissing Cream on the cheek, I walked up to him and placed my tongue in his mouth and held him in a way where he had no choice but to kiss me. His mouth felt warm and silky and smooth. It felt as if I had just bit into a slice of warm apple pie. My nipples instantly became perky and since I didn't have a bra on underneath my shirt I knew that they were probably poking through my shirt like two California raisins.

If I had had more time and wasn't in a rush to make it to school I would have suggested to Cream that we pick up where we had left off in terms of our first sexual encounter—which had taken place only a few short hours ago. Yeah, I was definitely in the mood for a second round but I had to control myself.

"Whew!" I said as I stopped kissing Cream and pulled away from him. "You definitely know how to get a sista open."

Cream smiled.

"I might start calling you Hood Hefner from now on!" I said.

"That's peace, but only you can call me that."

"A'ight," I replied, laughing. "So I'm one of your bunnies now."

"Bunnies?"

"Yeah, you know, Hugh Hefner has his *Playboy* bunnies so if you're Hood Hefner you gotta call your girls bunnies as well," I said. "Oh, I got it! You know Honey Buns are the schiznit in the hood, right?"

"Yeah," Cream replied. "Everybody loves them damn things."

"So if Hugh Hefner has *Playboy* bunnies, that means that you should refer to all of your girls as Honey Bunnies!"

Cream smiled and looked at me.

"Tell me you're not feeling that?" I asked.

"Yeah, I'm feeling that," Cream replied. "No doubt. I like that."

"So daddy, are you gonna hold me down?" I asked.

"Yeah, I'm a hold you down," Cream replied.

I remember thinking to myself, *Yes!*

"And I'm a hold you down too, just like I told you last night in the car, daddy."

7

A FEW DAYS HAD PASSED since the incident at Cream's house with Mercedes and I had not spoken to Cream since then. He had not stopped by my job nor did I see him or any of his girls on the track near my job. The only thing that I could think was that he had gotten locked up or something. The last thing that I wanted to think was that he had gotten stabbed, shot, or killed or anything drastic like that.

To me, working for Cream represented so many things that were missing in my life. For one, it represented a source of physical security. It represented financial security. It also represented a source of shelter. It would mean that I could stop staying with one friend one night and then staying with another friend the next. It would mean that I wouldn't have to go to a YMCA or Bally's health club to take a shower. It would mean no more train rides without a destination. It would mean normalcy and a greater sense of hope. And it would ensure that I would, in fact, be able to help remove my sister Mya from the situation I had fled from.

I decided that I would reach out to Cream by calling him on his cell phone just to see what was up. When I dialed his number from my job I have to admit that I was a bit nervous, I didn't know what to expect from him. I didn't know if he was mad at me or what. I mean, had he been expecting me to show up at his crib for work or what? I hoped not. But I was curious why I hadn't heard from him.

His phone rang four times and then went to his voice mail.

"Yo, this is Cream, leave a message."

Making sure not to sound like a clucking-chicken-head, I spoke into the phone, "Hey, daddy, what's up? This is Lady. I'm just calling to say what's up. I haven't spoken to you in a few days and I wanted to make sure everything was okay. I'm a try you back later, but in case I don't reach you for some reason, I wanted to know if you are going back to Club New York on Sunday? If you are, can I roll with you? A'ight? I gotta bounce, I'll speak to you later."

I hung up the phone and exhaled a little bit.

Cluck cluck cluck, I said to myself. I immediately started to beat myself up. *Damn Lady, what was all of that about the club? You playin' yourself. Don't you know that the nigga already hit it and he ain't tryin' to mess with you like that? All he needs you for now is to make him some money. You should have mentioned that you are ready to get this money for him.*

I really didn't need those kinds of negative thoughts flowing through my head and I had to get myself to switch up my mindset to something more positive. I immediately decided to call my girl Shauna who I had bumped into at the club that night.

Shauna picked up on the first ring.

"What's up, trick?" I said while speaking into the phone.

"Tina, this can only be you. . . . It's about time you called me! I don't see you in I don't know how long and then I see you all Hollywooded-out up in the club looking like Janet Jackson and you take all this time to call me?"

"Shauna, it's only Wednesday."

"Yeah, and Wednesday night at that! What happened to Monday and Tuesday? You can't keep a girl hanging on like that! Over the past couple of days all I've been thinking about is you. So come on, come on, fill me in . . . Waz up waz up waazzzzup?"

"Shauna, you are so crazy! A'ight, sorry that it took me so long to call you but now I got you."

"Yeah, yeah, Tina, enough with the small talk, I wanna know where the hell did you get all of that body from? That's number one and number two, how the hell were you up in V.I.P. at Club New York with LL Cool J and all of them Cream Team niggas?"

"Shauna, it's not Tina anymore, call me Lady from now on."

"Yeah, and what the hell is that all about? Look, just talk, I'll shut up and you fill me in."

Shauna's excitement was making me laugh but I didn't have the time to fill her in on everything because my break was almost over and I had to get back to that damn cash register. But I didn't want to tell Shauna where I was or let her in on where I was working. In no way could I let her know that I had a *regular* job. I mean that would have totally killed the Hollywood image that she had in her mind concerning me. And I wanted her to keep that Hollywood image of me until a later time. So I knew that I had to throw in a diversion until I could speak to her more at length. At the same time, I wanted to prep her for any and all future revelations. I wanted to tell Shauna how I would be working for Cream; in fact, I was hoping that if I sold it right that she would even be down to do it with me.

"Shauna, you know that nickname is hot. Don't front on me."

"Yeah, it is a hot name but how did it come about?"

"Easy, easy, easy, Shauna, I'll get to all of that. But as far as my body is concerned, you know that all you gotta do is let the right niggas hit it from the back and then your butt and hips will naturally fill out," I remarked while chuckling into the phone.

"Tina . . . I mean Lady. I know that you're not having sex?" Shauna stated, sounding all concerned, shocked, and surprised.

In my mind I was like *okay, here we go.* I was hoping that Shauna wouldn't try to come at me like a parent or with some holy-rolling you-should-wait-until-you-are-married-to-have-sex nonsense.

From the time I first met Shauna years prior, I always thought that she was an old spirit and an old soul trapped inside of a young body. She was always more responsible than the next person. She always did the mature thing versus doing the free-spirited thing, like she would have absolutely no problem watching the Discovery Channel on a regular basis versus watching something like *Showtime at the Apollo*. But even though Shauna at times displayed attributes of an old soul, she was still with the times and was crazy, crazy, crazy cool.

"Shauna, come on! Like you ain't out there screwing everything that moves!"

"But Tina—"

"Lady!" I interrupted.

"My bad. But Lady, I'm sayin' you're so young."

I could not believe that my girl was coming at me like that. She knew how everybody in our old 'hood got down. Hell, she knew how everybody in every 'hood got down. So why was she frontin' on me?

"Well, all I know is that's where my body came from."

"Lady, you are so crazy. So okay, now about this Cream Team thing. . . . Fill me in."

My boss was breathing down my neck and I really had to bounce.

"Shauna, I gotta go, but don't kill me. Just hear me out. This is what I wanna do. Are you working tomorrow?"

"Yeah."

"Well, what time do you get off?"

"I get off at five o'clock."

"Okay, you gotta convince your boss or whoever is in charge to let you leave early."

"Why?"

"Because I want you to come to the Hillcrest versus Jamaica basketball game tomorrow. I'm a cheerleader for Hillcrest."

"Oh, you go to Hillcrest?"

"Yeah, but trust me. Leave work early and be at the school a little bit before five P.M. The line to get in is gonna be bananas so trust me, get there early. I'll leave your name with the security guard and let them know that you're my guest and you'll get in with no problem even if the game is sold-out."

"Okay, I'll be there. So the game starts at five?"

"Yes, but be there early."

"Should I tell them I'm a guest of Lady or Tina?"

I laughed and replied, "Tell them Tina. They know me as Tina."

"Okay, trick, I'm a be there but I wanna hang out with you after the game."

"Yeah, that's a definite. That's exactly why I want you to come. We'll chill together and I'll fill you in after the game. But yo, Shauna,

I'm telling you the game is gonna be crazy tomorrow. Everybody is gonna be there so come looking correct. You can't be embarrassing a sista. I got a reputation to maintain!"

"Oh trick, please. You know I'm always on point with mines," Shauna laughingly replied.

"A'ight, so I'll see you tomorrow."

"Later."

I was glad the call was over because my boss was acting like a complete idiot. He was all rushing me, and it wasn't even like there were any customers who needed to be serviced. See, that was the type of crap that I couldn't take. I hated that feeling of being told what the hell to do and when to do it. I wanted so bad to tell my boss that I was gonna be quitting.

It was getting to the point where the job was interfering with my self-image. I mean, like the conversation I had just had with Shauna. How would it look if I were to tell her that I was working in a damn donut shop?

Thoughts like that were causing me to decide that even if Cream fronted on me, I would find another way to get into his world. I knew that was where the treasure trove was.

Anyway, I did what I had to do and I went back to the cash register. I was able to get through that work session because I had something promising to look forward to. Yeah, I had no idea where I would lay my head on that particular night but I felt good. I knew that if I could at least make it to the next day I would hopefully be able to spend the night with Shauna and sleep like a normal human being.

8

THE FOLLOWING DAY, JUST ABOUT every thug from Queensbridge was in the gym rooting for their boy Ron Artest. But Southside Jamaica, Queens which is where Rafer "Skip to My Lou" Alston was from, also had a whole slew of thug representatives in the gym to cheer him on. I was hoping that no violence would break out and thank god everyone had come in peace and things stayed on the up and up throughout the entire night.

During the game I had finally been able to make contact with Shauna. At halftime she ran up to me, got my attention, and let me know that she was in the house.

"Y'all was off the hook, girl!" she screamed as she ran up to me, referring to the way we as cheerleaders had performed.

I gave her a hug, and told her that I was glad that she had made it. I asked her if she was enjoying herself.

"Hell yeah, I'm enjoying myself!" she emphatically stated.

Then she went on to tell me that she wanted me to reintroduce her to Cream and his boys because they didn't remember who she was.

"Yeah, I kinda played myself and I was like, 'Hi Cream,' and he just looked at me like, 'Do I know you?'" Shauna informed me.

"When was this?" I asked in amazement.

"Today, you trick! I was sitting right behind him in the bleachers."

"Today?" I asked in even more astonishment. I became a little bit nervous, wondering if Cream had indeed seen me cheering.

"Yeah today! What's wrong with you?"

"Nah, I just didn't know that he was gonna be here today, that's all."

"Yeah, him and all of his boys were sitting in the first row like right near the middle of the court and I was sitting right behind them. How could you not see them?"

Yeah, that was exactly what I had wanted to know. *How in the world did I not see him and his boys?*

"Were you here from the start of the game?" I asked.

"Yeah."

"And Cream was there from the start as well?"

"Yeah, he was right in front of me the entire time. We saw how y'all came out and killed that cheer to the Shabba Ranks song."

I knew that there was no sense in getting all nervous and scared at that point. The cookies had been out of the bag and Cream had to know how young I was and exactly what he had been dealing with. I just wanted to make sure that I had a chance to speak to him before he left.

"Yeah, Shauna, I'll definitely reintroduce you to him if I get a chance. But I didn't even know that he was gonna be here so I need you to do me a favor. Make sure that you know where he is at all times and when the game is over, I need you to point me in his direction."

"Okay," Shauna replied.

"A'ight, I gotta go to the locker room for a minute. If I don't see you, just meet me underneath the basket that's at the far end of the court from where we'll be cheering when we come back out."

"Okay, no doubt."

For the remainder of the game I could not really concentrate but I had to make up my mind to not even sweat it. I mean, after all, Cream was only about twenty-two or twenty-three years old and it wasn't like I was a nine-year-old kid or anything. I thought about just lying and telling him that I was in my senior year and that I was eighteen years old, but I was like *to hell with that.* See, I figured it was time for me to man up—if women could do such a thing—and just be up front with

Cream and let him know exactly how old I was. There was no sense in lying because that would only lead to telling more lies and having to keep track of lies for no reason at all. Cream had to know that I was live and my age didn't have to be and wasn't gonna be an issue.

When the game was over there was a sea of people trying to navigate their way out of the gym. Thankfully I was able to locate Shauna.

"Tina, I don't know where Cream disappeared to in this crowd of people. When everybody rushed onto the court I didn't see where he went."

"Okay, don't sweat it," I quickly instructed. "I'm gonna run and get dressed real quick. Go outside and wait for me on Parsons Boulevard, right in front of the barbershop. I'll be there in like ten minutes."

I raced to the locker room and quickly changed my clothes. I also grabbed an outfit to wear the next day. I wanted to freshen up because I had been sweating, but there was really no time for that.

When I made it out of the school and met up with Shauna, she told me that Cream and his crew were chillin' in front of the bodega on the corner of Hillside and Parsons, smoking weed and playing Cee-Lo.

"Okay, cool. Shauna, do me a favor. Just walk with me but when I get close to Cream I need you to just fall back a little bit and lay in the cut. I think he's upset with me about something and I kinda gotta talk to him alone."

"A'ight, is everything cool?"

"Yeah it's all good, I just don't wanna run up on him the wrong way."

So as we walked the fifty yards or so to Hillside, I got the attention of Cream. Shauna dropped back just like she had been instructed to do.

"Lady . . . What's up? You did your thing out there, ma," Cream joyfully stated.

Whew, I thought to myself. The weed had put Cream in a good mood.

All of his boys began making comments like, "I didn't know you was flexible like that with the splits and all that," and "You probably be turning niggas out with all kinds of freakiness in the bed!" Others made comments and inquiries about some of the other cheerleaders. But I kinda blocked that out and pulled Cream aside.

"What's up with you? I ain't seen you since Monday."

"I been good."

"So why didn't you get in touch with me? I thought you wanted me to get this money for you."

Cream replied, "Yeah, I do. But on the low, I had to switch up spots for a few days because five-o was stepping up the heat near the bridge. And I didn't even want them to see me in that area and start questioning me."

"Oh," I replied.

"Yeah, I had to lay low for two days and then I shifted things to a track in Brooklyn. We'll be there for a few days until the heat dies down in Queens."

"Cream, I ain't gonna front . . . I gotta keep it real with you and tell you that I didn't know how you would react if you knew how old I was."

"Yeah, I mean I figured you was young but I didn't know you were in *high school*. I came to see my boy Ron Artest. I was surprised to see you out there. But I'm sayin', how old are you anyway?"

"Fifteen."

"Fifteen! Got damn! You really tryin' to get a nigga locked underneath the jail!" Cream replied.

To myself I have to admit that I was like, *You a pimp, nigga! Why all of a sudden you acting like you got morals?*

In actuality Cream was so full of it. He really didn't care how old I was. In fact I would later learn that Cream preferred girls who were like fourteen and fifteen years old. Cream preferred the younger girls because they were more submissive and easily manipulated.

There was a pause before Cream spoke up. He took a pull on his weed, blew out the smoke, and said, "A'ight, we still gonna do this. We definitely gonna do this. . . . So who you staying with?"

"I told you I'm living on my own. It's like every day is up in the air for me. For the most part I'm living out of like three lockers in my school. But as far as where I rest at night, that all depends. Some nights I sleep at different friends' houses and some nights I gotta just rough it and ride the train all night long."

"Word? It's gulley like that?" Cream asked.

"Daddy, it's like that."

"A'ight, so here's the deal. What time are you getting outta school tomorrow?"

"I have cheerleading practice but that should be over by like four thirty."

"Okay, so at a quarter to five tomorrow I'm a meet you right here. I'll be in a burgundy Jeep Cherokee with tinted windows."

"So, it's on tomorrow?"

"It's on. At four forty-five I'm a pick you up and we'll take it from there."

"Cool."

"And yo, Lady, you ain't gotta worry about where you gonna be resting at from now on 'cause daddy got you."

9

THE NEXT DAY, BEFORE I knew it, practice was over and I was leaving the school. I had all kinds of thoughts running through my mind, body, and soul. Being that it was the dog days of colder weather, the atmosphere was still and it had that look of just about being dark at only a quarter to five in the early evening. I stood on the steps of the school with my large bag of clothes and books on my shoulder. I zipped my coat all the way up in order to keep the cold air from reaching my chest.

I peered out onto the street and sure enough there was a burgundy Jeep Cherokee sitting idle with the engine running and steamy smoke coming out of the tailpipe. I didn't hesitate, I immediately said my good-byes to the other cheerleaders who had walked out of the school with me, and walked in a brisk fashion to the Cherokee.

When I reached the car, I just took it upon myself to open the passenger door and let myself in. Thankfully for me it was Cream who was in the driver's seat because I would have been totally playing myself if it were someone else's car.

"What's up, baby?" I asked after closing the passenger door and reaching over to give Cream a kiss on the cheek.

"It is brick out there!" I shouted while rubbing my hands together.

"Word," Cream replied as he put the car in drive and pulled off.

"So, what's up?" he asked.

I sighed and then blew out some air and stated, "I'm ready to do this."

"Chill, we got some time. I mean it's only like five o'clock. Ain't nobody hitting the track until like ten o'clock tonight so we got some time to kill."

"A'ight," I replied while adjusting the radio station to Hot 97 FM.

We listenened to the radio in silence a while and then Cream spoke up. He reached over and turned down the radio so that he wouldn't have to talk over the music.

"Lady, I need you to look at me."

I turned so I was giving Cream my full attention.

"There is one thing that you gotta know about the streets. And it don't matter what your hustle is. I don't care if you're running guns, if you got an illegal numbers spot, or if you're selling crack or selling sex. It's all the same when you boil it down."

Cream reached forward and turned the radio off completely.

"Lady, the one thing that you gotta know about the streets in order to be successful is you gotta know how to keep your mouth shut. You can't have loose lips. Remember this and you'll always be a'ight. Don't help the cops and feds under any circumstances. If it ever comes down to you doing twenty-five years in a box versus ratting somebody out, then the twenty-five years in the pen is your only option. Ya heard?"

I looked at Cream and nodded.

"Nah, Lady, I'm dead ass right now! It's more than just keeping your mouth shut, it's like on the streets you gotta be silent about anything and everything. I mean, you're gonna see a whole lot out here on the streets working for me and you're naturally gonna be taking in a whole lot. But the thing you cannot do is be out here running your mouth."

"In other words, Cream, what you're saying is that on the streets you can't be a rat," I said.

"Well, that is a flat-out given. You can't have any part of the streets if you're a rat or a damn informant. The worst creation in the world is niggas who rat to the police and rat to the feds. Informants are even worse."

I decided to remain silent and just listen as I nodded my head.

"You're nodding your head, but I know that you don't understand what I'm saying. See, what I'm saying is this: of course we can't rat to the cops, but when I talk about remaining silent I mean it's more than being an informant. Lady, you can't be out there just casually talking because that casual talk is what ruins niggas just as much as the flat-out blatant ratting to the cops."

"Okay, I'm feeling you Cream, but help me be a bit more clearer on what you're telling me."

"This is what I'm telling you. Matter of fact, I'll tell you by asking you a question and then explaining from there. How many people in your school know that you spent the night at my crib and how many people in your school know that me and you had sex?"

My heart started racing because I had no idea where Cream was going with what he was saying. I just decided to tell the truth.

"Well, I only told this one person."

"Who?"

"This chick named Shonnie."

"Why?"

"Why what?"

"Why did you tell her? I mean is that your ace, is she real cool with you or what?"

Now I was really getting nervous. I was wondering if Cream knew someone in the school who I didn't know and if they had reported the gossip back to him.

Cream didn't give me any time to answer.

"Lady, you gotta remember this. One spy can do a whole lot more damage than an entire army of soldiers." He pulled up to the curb and shut off the car's engine.

Without saying anything to me in terms of where we were going, I simply got out of the car and followed him into USA Diner which was located on Merrick Boulevard in the Rosedale section of Queens.

We made it into the diner and I followed Cream and a waitress to a rear booth where we sat down to order food.

Cream continued on. "See Lady, the thing is you or no one else is ever *just talking*. There is always a motive behind words whether you know that or not. Like I can guarantee you that when you were speaking to Shonnie you had some kind of agenda that you wanted to get across. . . . Am I right?"

I was humbled and simply had no choice but to agree.

"See you take it as causal talk with Shonnie to get across whatever your agenda might be. But that's not how things will play themselves out later on. See, even if you had no agenda your words shouldn't have been spoken to her because those same words can come back and bite you in the ass. You can never be wrong by just keeping your mouth shut. Remember that!"

We ordered our food and then I spoke up.

"But Cream, the only reason that I said something is because the whole school was gossiping about me and you. They saw me talking to you after the game."

Cream replied, "Lady, there will always be gossip and that we cannot control. But just make got damn sure that it never originates from you and make sure that you don't fuel it in any way. Check this out. Let's say that some bitches in your school get jealous of you because they saw you with me. And then you start talking about all kinds of stuff and your talking just further fuels their jealousy. Behind the scenes you don't even realize what kind of trap you're laying—not just for yourself but for everybody. See, when you go out on the streets suppose that you get knocked by the cops and they start checking into your background and want to find out information on your parents and if you've been going to school and all of that. You follow me?"

"Yes."

"While they're investigating they go to your school and start asking questions. The school counselors don't know any dirt on you so what they start doing is the counselors start talking to the people that know you. And then those people that know you, especially the jealous ones, will start relaying all of the information that you told them and all of the gossip that you helped validate. Then the counselors turn around and call the cops and say, 'I've been checking with other students and the other students are telling me that the young lady that you wanted information on goes by the street name of Lady and she's been spending a lot of time with this guy by the name of Cream.' See

Lady, when that happens or if that were to happen a whole new can of worms would open up and it just gives cops all kinds of trails to go on. But if there were no words behind all of the talk at the school then it eventually would die and even if the cops were to come questioning the school counselor, that counselor would get no information that she can relay back to the cops that would help them. I know this sounds complicated but am I making any sense?"

I felt so bad that I had opened my mouth to Shonnie. I was so frustrated thinking that I had just ruined a prime opportunity. I couldn't help it, I began to softly cry. I said, "Cream, I am so sorry for opening my mouth. Please, just trust me. My mouth will stay shut from now on, you don't even have to worry about that!"

"Lady, look at me. There ain't no need for tears. I trust you and the reason that I am telling you this is because I'm training yo ass."

I wiped away a tear that had rolled down my cheek and continued to listen to Cream.

"This is the main thing that you have to learn. Keep your mouth shut! If something goes down, you don't know me other than you've casually talked to me at times in passing. . . . You understand?"

I nodded my head in agreement.

"Lady, do you hear what I'm saying?" Cream asked with a bit of firmness in his voice.

"Yes," I softly replied.

Cream went on to explain to me that he would get me a fake Ohio driver's license that would show that I was seventeen years old and lived out of state. He said that in the past he had a few girls who were under sixteen work for him and he learned "the hard way" that it was imperative that if the cops were to stop me, in addition to not giving him up, I could not tell the cops my real age or where I was really from. The reason it was imperative that I not tell my real age was because in New York if I were to get busted for prostitution as a sixteen-year-old or older then all I would have to do is pay a fine and then I would be released on my own recognizance. I'd be back out on the street within a few hours. But if I were busted and the cops could prove that I was under fifteen then I would have to go through family court and all of that nonsense and the city would try to get in touch with my parents or put me in some kind of program or some waste-of-time protective services.

"We all have that close nigga who is just down for us, who has always been down for us and will always be down for us. Those are the people that you wanna keep in your *inner circle* and you better think long and hard before you just let anybody into that inner circle. You gotta treat that inner circle like gold, like it's sacred."

"Well, the only person who is part of my inner circle is Shauna," I replied.

"But can you trust her? I mean a person can be as cool as hell and then turn around and cut your throat. Snakes are always cool and calm and before you know it they reach up and strike your ass."

"Nah, Shauna is cool and I can trust her. That's my girl."

"If you say so, but just keep these words with you, trust me I know what I'm talking about. Keep your inner circle small and keep it tight. And don't let nobody in that inner circle until you have tested them and you are satisfied that they have passed the tests."

"Okay," I humbly replied.

"See with me, you might always see me with a lot of niggas but all of them niggas don't make up my inner circle. Niggas be running around talking about they down with the Cream Team and all of that. But to me my inner circle ain't everybody that's in the Cream Team, my inner circle is my nigga Shamgod, and my nigga Spinach. Dame, Pete, Ci-Lo, and all of them other cats are cool with me and they are down with my team but they ain't in my inner circle. See, them two are the only two that I trust, and I know this, if something ever goes down in terms of rats or whatever the case may be, I'm holding one of them two niggas responsible, yup, either Spinach or Shamgod is who I would step to. Because it's like this, I entrust them with things and they better know how the hell to handle it and they also damn sure better know who the hell it is that they should be trusting on their end. If something goes down and if it's because of someone in Spinach's or Shamgod's inner circle, I'm coming for Shamgod or for Spinach. It's about accountability and them two niggas are the only two that I'm holding accountable for anything and everything that goes down in my organization."

"That makes sense," I replied while taking a bite out of my pickle.

"I know it makes sense. But the only hard part about all that I just said is that if that trust that you have in your inner circle is ever broken then you can't hesitate to lay them niggas down. Ain't nobody exempt from dying."

Cream took a bite out of his cheeseburger and then he reached into his coat pocket and told me to look under the table.

"Here, take this and put it in your bag."

My heart skipped a beat as I looked and saw a chrome .22-caliber handgun.

"Just take it and be cool about it," Cream calmly but firmly instructed.

I grabbed hold of the gun and did as Cream had instructed and placed it into my bag.

"Just keep eating," Cream quickly instructed in order to make sure that I didn't suddenly start looking nervous.

"See, I just told you what you needed to know in terms of the codes of the street. Now I'll tell you the rules to this streetwalking game and what you need to know in order to survive."

"Okay," I said. I eagerly wanted to take in every one of Cream's words.

"That deuce-deuce that I just gave you is the perfect size for you. And trust me when I say I don't usually give any of my girls no biscuits because that would do nothing but create all kinds of problems for me. But I'm giving you that biscuit because I really wantchu to be a'ight out there. Later on I'm gonna show you how to cut the lining in your bag and how to put that biscuit in your bag so that no one will know that it's there. Even if five-o were to search your bag they wouldn't find it that easy. Now listen, when you're out there working, somebody from the team is always gonna be out there with y'all to protect y'all and to make sure that y'all are a'ight. But the thing is this, when someone picks you up and you get in their car or y'all go off to a room or wherever, you'll kinda be on your own because my niggas can't be everywhere at the same time. And trust me, at times things will get real thick out there on the street. You got all kinds of nuts and psychos out there, and at times you're gonna be dealing with the scum of the earth and the bottom of the barrel–type niggas."

"So in other words you want me to keep this piece with me at all times in case I have to protect myself?"

"Exactly! You gotta be prepared to protect your neck, and only you'll know when to use it and I can't prep you for every situation. Just always remain in control of situations and use your head. I mean, I know that you're street smart so just keep your eyes open and you'll know when something ain't right or when something is about to go down. The thing is this though, if you think you need to pull your burner on a nigga, then decide that and do it. Because it's that second or two that you'll waste thinking about what to do, and your life will rest in that second or two that you take to make a decision."

As I sat and listened to Cream I remember reality setting in. I was just starting to understand what I was getting myself into and I was thinking to myself, *Okay Tina, not Lady, but Tina, are you sure you wanna do this?*

There was a brief but awkward silence as I sat amongst my thoughts.

"What's the matter?" Cream asked.

I didn't want to tell him what I was really thinking so I just played it off and said, "Oh nothing, I was just wondering about the money and how that would work."

"Eighty-twenty," Cream stated while bringing his glass of Sprite closer to his face and taking a sip. "Those are the percentages for everybody so don't think it's just because you're new. Whatever you make you keep twenty percent and the other eighty percent goes to the team and to track fees."

The team? I thought to myself. *What the hell are got damn track fees?*

"But listen, as far as food goes, I got you! As far as a place to stay goes, I got you! And no matter what, just remember this: I'm gonna make sure that you're a'ight! You gonna be safe with me so don't worry about nothing. And as far as gear goes, I got you with that too! In the car right now I got you these hot Steve Madden stiletto boots and this nice red leather jacket. I picked it up today, the tags are still on them and everything. I mean I'm gonna get you some more gear but I just wanted to hit you off with something real quick." Cream paused and took another sip of his Sprite.

He continued. "And like I was saying, trust me, eighty-twenty is good. You got some cats out here that'll have you working for them and you won't see anything close to twenty percent. Word! You got niggas out here that'll take a hundred percent and just get you some gear, some Chinese food, and a place to stay. . . . You kna'imean? But I do good by my girls and I know in the long run everybody will eat."

Considering all that Cream was gonna be doing for me I guess that the percentages weren't all that bad. The thing that had me thinking was that I just wasn't sure why Cream was treating me so good. I knew that there was no way he could have been this good to all of his girls. *Maybe he's just like this in the beginning,* I thought to myself. *Yeah, and then later on I bet the nigga will be on some ol' guerilla pimping.*

"And that same cut in the lining where you'll keep your heat, keep your cash in there as well. Every so often one of my boys—and by the way, eventually you'll meet all of them—but whoever is out there protecting y'all, he'll be the one to pick up the cake from y'all. It's better that way in case five-o rolls up on y'all. You don't wanna be holding cash and condoms like that. It won't look good, you kna'imean?"

I nodded in agreement. We both were just about finished eating our food.

"You getting scared?" Cream asked. "You look like you bitchin' up on me."

"Nah, I'm good."

"Lady, you ain't never this quiet."

"Nah, for real I'm good. I'm just taking in everything that you were saying."

"You sure?"

I thought for a moment and decided that if there ever was a time to be honest and to speak up, that this was the moment to do so or I would forever hold my piece.

"There is one thing," I stated.

"What? Get at me."

"You said that you have a track in Brooklyn, right?"

"Yeah, we got tracks all over, everywhere except for Staten Island, why?"

"'Cause I'm just sayin', a whole lot of Hillcrest people live in Queensbridge and I wouldn't really feel all that comfortable working on that track near the bridge. And especially with the donut shop being right there and everything, I mean I'm quitting that job, but between old customers and classmates and all of that I don't want people that I know to be seeing me out there like that."

"Oh, I see what you sayin'. Yeah, don't even worry about that. Like I told you, that spot is kinda hot and it'll be hot for a while with five-o, so we won't be working out there for a minute anyway. But I'll put you in Brooklyn. You'll be on this track that's over near Starrett City."

A sense of relief had come over me after hearing Cream's words. I mean, I had been all gung-ho up until the time we sat down to eat. But with reality setting in I was realizing that there were a lot of things that I had not really thought about.

We got up from the table and were making our way back to the Jeep when Cream added, "Tonight, I'm a put you with this girl named Lisa. You'll work with her the whole night and she'll show you how to work, how to walk, how to talk, how much to charge, and what and who to look out for. A'ight?"

I noticeably blew out some air from my mouth as I realized that showtime was quickly setting in.

"A'ight, cool," I replied, making sure not to reveal my nervousness.

10

AROUND EIGHT THIRTY THAT FRIDAY night I found my-self back at Cream's house. Three other girls and I were getting ready to hit the track. Lisa, who Cream had told me he would pair me with was also there. I was kind of thankful that the ghetto-Goya-trash named Mercedes was not around, nor was Nikki or Diamond, because I was in no mood to be fighting. I was trying my hardest to change my frame of mind and muster up the nerve to go through with everything.

Lisa was real cool and she helped to make me feel at ease.

"You from New York?" she asked.

"Yeah, born and raised in Queens," I replied. "And what about you?"

"Oh, I'm from Chicago."

"Word? Chicago? I never been there," I said as I took a drink of my vodka and orange juice. I wasn't really into vodka but I had to drink something in order to help get my buzz on. Liquor always helped to open me up and relax my nerves.

I had just come out of the shower and was in the midst of getting dressed in the room with Lisa.

"Chicago is cool. It kind of reminds me of New York," Lisa added.

I didn't reply as I took another gulp from my glass.

"Girl, you better stop drinking like that, or you'll be pissing like a Russian racehorse all night long. Are you nervous or something?"

"Hell yeah, I feel like a virgin all over again . . . I don't know."

Lisa began to laugh as she assured me that I would be a'ight.

"So how did you end up in New York if you're from Chicago?"

"Well, I met some of Cream's people who were out in Chicago and they kind of *convinced* me to come to New York."

I frowned, not sure what she meant.

"So you haven't been in New York long?"

"I've been here since the beginning of June."

"And if you don't mind me asking, have you been on the track since you came to New York?"

"I started working about a week or two after I got here."

Lisa was definitely raising my level of curiosity. I wanted to know what was so bad in Chicago that she would want to come halfway across the country to walk and work the streets for Cream. I wanted to probe but I remembered Cream's words about loose lips. And the last thing I wanted was for word to get back to Cream that I was probing like a damn detective.

But what I would eventually find out from Lisa was that Cream and his Cream Team associates would often go on trips out of state, to places like Chicago, Detroit, Ohio, and Virginia and they would take those trips in order to recruit young ladies for their prostitution ring. The lure and hook was they would find young ladies in group homes, or foster homes, or shelters, or girls who didn't have much going on and who were at a vulnerable or transitional stage in their lives. If they had the right personality, looks, and body, the Cream Team would sell them on how great New York City was and how they had this legitimate organization that the girls could come and work for. They'd earn all kinds of money modeling and dancing in music videos and working in music studios as backup vocalists.

Surprising as it was to me, numerous girls would buy the Cream Team's game and were seduced into dropping everything and heading to New York in order to work for the team. The monkey wrench was that the girls had no idea that once they reached New York the promises would drastically change. Upon reaching New York the girls' lives would be turned upside down by Cream and his team who used fear, control, and manipulation in order to cut the girls off from their old lives. They would end up basically brainwashing the girls and turning the unsuspecting females into sex slaves.

Like I said, that night I didn't want to probe so I made sure to quickly switch subjects.

"Even though I feel like a virgin again, I do feel sexy. I love dressing in sexy clothes," I stated.

"Yeah, I hear you," Lisa nonchalantly added.

I had put on the black stiletto Steve Madden boots that Cream had bought for me. I also put on some tight jeans. In fact the jeans were beyond tight, they were more like skin tight, and I had no panties on underneath my clothes. For some reason wearing no panties always made me feel extra sexy. Up top I had a red Angora sweater that looked real good with my jeans and small Coach bag. It also worked well with the red leather jacket that Cream had bought for me, which was real sleek and trendy-looking.

"Girl, you look real good in them jeans but can you walk in them?" Lisa asked, laughing.

"Yeah, I'll be okay," I remarked. Then in an attempt to inject some humor I stated, "Plus, I like wearing my jeans tight like this because it keeps the jeans pressed up against my clit and it be sending chills up my body when I walk."

Lisa laughed again and told me that I was crazy. Then she added, "Lady, you gotta remember, *easy access*, baby. You don't want to be struggling with them jeans all night long. Not to mention that with you drinking like a fish you'll be constantly trying to wiggle out of them jeans just to squat and piss somewhere."

I hadn't thought about all of that but I was willing to just roll with the punches. Lisa looked real nice and shapely and she was also very pretty in the face. She began to apply some eyeliner and lipstick as she spoke to me and schooled me on the game.

But before I knew it, it was after nine o'clock and we had all piled into Cream's car looking sexy as hell and smelling like a bed of roses. No one was really speaking in the car but that was okay because

Cream was blasting a DJ Clue mixed tape. Lisa and I sat in the back-seat of the car along with one of the other young ladies. She had reached into her bag and pulled out a blunt which had already been rolled. She sparked it with her lighter and passed it around. Lisa didn't want any but I didn't have to be asked twice. I sucked on that blunt and inhaled it as if my life depended on it.

We continued to smoke weed until we had arrived at our destination on Pennsylvania Avenue. Cream parked the car in a White Castle parking lot and we all piled out into the frigid December weather. Cream stayed behind and the four of us made our way to Stanley Avenue. We weren't too far from this nightclub called the Ark.

When we reached Stanley Avenue we paired off and I walked with Lisa.

"I didn't know it was gonna be this brick out here tonight," I said as my teeth began to chatter and I stuck my hands in my jacket pockets. "I thought the wind would die down and it would be a little warmer."

"Don't worry about it," Lisa told me. "You'll warm up in a minute. Now Lady, you don't wanna really stand too stationary and you don't wanna really walk around too much. You kind of gotta mix it up but the main thing you wanna do is kind of flirt with all of these cars and guys that will be driving by and walking by. Make sure you make eye contact with them and try to get their attention. The bottom line is that you gotta work what you got in order to sell what you got."

"Okay."

"You gotta remember too that this is all straight business! Niggas are gonna wanna talk to you and BS you but if they ain't serious you gotta keep it moving. . . . Remember it's twenty bucks for a blow-job and a hundred for the real deal and if they want a room they gotta shell out for that too. A'ight?"

"Okay," I said, even though Cream had already versed me on what to charge niggas.

"And whatever you do, make sure that you use a condom no matter what!"

"Even for blow-jobs?" I asked.

"Hell yeah! Especially for blow-jobs. Lady, you out here trying to make money, you ain't trying to get killed. The last thing you need is some nigga splashing off in your mouth!"

I began laughing because I had never heard that term used before to describe a male orgasm.

Lisa smiled and said, "Yeah, you laugh now but I'm telling you what's real! And these nasty guys out here, don't let them game you, they gonna be like 'I don't feel nothing with a condom.' And you make sure that you tell them that's just too damn bad! Basically you gotta lay down the rules and be firm with these niggas."

Lisa was a petite girl who looked to be about five feet or so. But she had a mouth on her that wouldn't quit. And in spite of her being nice, she still had a feisty side to her that I liked and respected.

Giving a guy a professional with a condom on was something that I had never done before but I knew that Lisa was right, I wasn't trying to catch nobody's disease.

"And Lady, if you sense that a nigga's been drinking, make sure you ask him. Me personally, I don't mess with these cats that have been out here drinking."

As cars slowly drove by and gave us stares and catcalls, I asked Lisa about the drinking thing because I was real curious.

She explained. "Listen. Time is money and you wanna give these guys like fifteen minutes to splash and really that's it. You ain't making love to nobody and nor do you care about them. And the thing with the guys that have been drinking is that the alcohol numbs their senses or something because it takes them forever to splash off."

"Oh, I got you," I replied as if I had been hit with some type of divine revelation.

"You see what I'm sayin'? We ain't got all night for these cats. If they wanna make love then they need to go home to their wife or to their girl or to their mistress or whatever. Fifteen minutes, that's it! Thirty minutes max if it's for the real thing but even with that you gotta keep it moving. . . . And whatever you do, make sure that you don't kiss any of these guys on the mouth! Word, that is way too intimate and it's too risky in terms of catching something."

I thought Lisa was done but then she added one more jewel of advice when she said, "Oh yeah, Lady, believe it or not, some of these guys out here are gonna wanna pay you to lick your carpet. But don't even try to go there with these niggas. No muff-diving and all of that, 'cause don't nobody know where the hell their tongues have been at, and besides, that's just too intimate and that's not what this hustle is about."

I nodded my head in agreement.

As soon as Lisa finished talking to me a black Mercedes-Benz pulled up alongside of us. It was as if the car had come right on cue. The passenger-side windows to the E-class Mercedes began rolling down. I could see about four guys in the car.

"What's up, ladies?" they asked.

"How y'all doing?" Lisa replied as she kept walking. I followed her lead.

"Ma, where you from? You sound like you got an accent," one of the passengers asked.

Lisa replied in a nice way but she was showing me what she meant about time being money. "Baby, I can't really tell you all of that about where I'm from. I mean it's not where you from, it's where you at, and right now I'm here talking to y'all so why don't y'all tell me what's up?"

"We feeling your friend," they replied, but not in a way that would have made Lisa feel slighted.

I looked in the direction of the car and I smiled. At this point Lisa and I had stopped walking.

"What's up, ma?" one of the passengers asked me.

Suddenly, I didn't feel cold anymore. I kind of felt more like I was in my element. It was an everyday thing for me to have guys trying to kick it to me and that's exactly how I looked at the situation, as just some guys trying to kick it.

I walked closer to the car so that they could get a better look at me. Leaning over and looking into the car I replied, "What's up? What y'all wanna do?"

The same passenger replied, "Yo, it's my man's birthday, so we wanted to take care of him."

I looked in the backseat of the car in the direction of the *supposed* birthday boy and smiled.

I wanted to take the lead and I did so by assuming that they just wanted to get a professional. "If y'all got twenty dollars we can make this happen."

"No doubt!" they responded, sounding like a bunch of sex fiends. But I noticed that the birthday boy was being real quiet.

I wanted to make this quick because time was money. And I knew exactly how to put them on the spot.

"Well, listen, since it's his birthday I know that y'all ain't gonna make him pay. Why don't one of y'all shell out the money and let's do this?"

Almost immediately the driver handed the passenger a twenty dollar bill and he handed it to me. I was reaching to open the back door of the car and get in but Lisa, who had kind of faded to the back, hustled over to the car and spoke up.

"One second y'all," she said while looking into the car.

Then she turned in my direction and quickly whispered, "Lady, you did good but don't ever get in a car with a bunch of guys like that. If it's one guy in the car then that's cool. But if it's more than one guy you gotta make them other cats get out and wait and lock the doors and windows to the car. Make sure the driver gives the keys to whoever is gonna be in the car with you."

I quickly thought about how right Lisa was. A group of horny guys were liable to gang rape me or do whatever with me if they were given the right opportunity and the right conditions.

I turned back to the guys and instructed, "This is what y'all do. Drive around the corner and the three of y'all get out and leave your man in the car. I'll meet y'all around the corner so we can do this. Okay? And make sure that y'all leave the car keys with the birthday boy."

"A'ight, no doubt," they replied as they pulled off and headed in the direction I'd told them to go.

"Thank you," I said to Lisa after the guys were out of sight.

"That's why I'm out here. You did good though. Now go handle your business, and if you don't see me when you're done, don't worry about me just do your thing."

I walked off to meet the guys in the car around the corner. I was a bit excited and somewhat nervous, but I knew that I could go through with it.

When I made it to the car I noticed that the guys had followed my instructions. I got in the backseat of the car and the birthday boy was there and he showed me that he had the keys to the car. It was just him and me inside the car but he looked nervous as I don't know what.

After making sure that all of the car doors were locked and the windows were all rolled up, the birthday boy told me that his name was Kareem.

Kareem looked to be about twenty-six or twenty-seven years old. He was real cute, which was a definite plus in that it made it easier to go through the process with an attractive guy as opposed to some bum.

I reached in my bag and took out a condom but I noticed that Kareem was just sitting there. His boys were acting like voyeurs. They cheered him on as they tried their hardest to look through the slightly tinted windows.

"You ready?" I asked.

"Yeah," Kareem replied. His light-skinned face turned red.

Time is money, I thought to myself.

"You can pull down your pants, I won't bite you," I instructed, reminding myself of a nurse or a doctor or something.

Kareem followed my instructions and in doing so his boys began acting even more immature.

When Kareem pulled down his pants I noticed that he was just average size. But to me that was neither here nor there. I also noticed that he wasn't ready in terms of *it* wasn't *up* yet. That let me know that he was indeed nervous so I decided to just calm him down and get things poppin'. The fact that Kareem was nervous kind of took the edge off because I knew that I was in total control. The guys being nervous was never something I had envisioned about the track, but it was a plus in terms of the control that it gave me.

I began to give Kareem a hand-job and I asked him, "Are you nervous?"

He was honest and replied that he was. He also told me that he was married and that his wife was on his mind.

Oh great! I remember thinking. *The first trick I pull and the nigga is some married cat who seems as if he's going against his own code of morality.* But hell, it wasn't no time for me to start worrying about morality and ethics.

"Don't be nervous. Just relax and tell me who you want me to be."

"Huh?" Kareem asked.

"You want me to be Janet Jackson, Toni Braxton, or somebody like that?"

"Oh," Kareem replied as the smile on his face showed that he was starting to loosen up. "Nah, you Heather Hunter right now."

"The porn star?"

"Yeah, her."

"A'ight, close your eyes and relax and let *Heather* take care of you," I seductively replied.

Kareem followed my instructions and sure enough he soon began to come around. Before I knew it the condom was ready to be applied and I put it on and was doing my thing. It was wild because that was the first time that I'd ever given a blow-job to anyone while literally being cheered on by the friends of the guy who was getting the blow-job. As far as the condom, it proved to actually be a plus because it wasn't like I was dealing with skin-to-skin. It was more like rubber-to-skin which helped make it more impersonal and that was just the way I wanted it.

I was so glad that Kareem had on that condom. Apparently his nervousness had quickly vanished, and even more apparent than that was the fact that he was a less-than-two-minute brother! It was like before I knew what happened, without any type of warning, he had splashed off and groaned in ecstasy.

"You came?" I asked with surprise.

"Yeah," Kareem replied while breathing real heavy.

Time is money, I thought to myself. I was relieved that everything was over before it had started.

I definitely knew that I wasn't gonna be the one to clean him up or anything.

"I hope you enjoyed it. . . . My name is Lady, so if you're ever out here again, make sure that you look for me, and if you don't see me then ask for me, okay?"

Kareem replied "okay" as he sat there with the condom still on and his pants and underwear pulled down to his knees.

I got out of the car and I felt this intoxicating high come over me. I was definitely in my element and I knew that it was time to sell and make money.

"That's it, ma?" his boys questioned.

"That's it," I replied. "It don't take long if you know what you're doing," I said in a suggestive and flirting tone. I looked and noticed that other streetwalkers had arrived and were now working the block.

Things were definitely real but everything felt so surreal. I was actually officially turning tricks and living the life of a streetwalker!

"So, what's up with y'all? I mean, I know it's your boy's birthday but y'all can have some fun too and celebrate with him. I know y'all got some more money on y'all."

The three of them looked at each other in an attempt to confirm with each other whether or not they should go along with the folly.

"A'ight. Yo, I gotta test your skills!" one of them demanded.

Before I knew it and in less than an hour I had $160 in my pocket. Two of Kareem's friends had agreed to get professionals and the driver decided that he wanted a dip in the honey jar so he had paid for a room and we got it on in a motel that was like two blocks away.

I couldn't believe how easily I flowed with everything. In fact that night I had grossed close to $700 in about six hours. I profited for myself about $140. The money had me so wide open that there was no way that I was gonna stop. It was definitely on!

11

MY NEXT TWO NIGHTS OUT on the track went just as smoothly as my first night had gone. I made a lot of dough and had gotten more comfortable in my interactions with customers and potential customers. I had also gotten more comfortable in my interactions with the other girls. Besides the three big haters, Mercedes, Nikki, and Diamond, all of the other girls had begun to embrace me. They would refer to me as their sister and some of them would call me their sister-in-law, all signs and gestures of respect and unity, similar to the way we would sometimes refer to Cream as our daddy.

During those next two nights I was again paired with Lisa, and whenever there were slow periods she and I would kick it.

"Lady, one thing about you that I can already see is that you ain't gonna have no problems with Cream, because you know how to make money," Lisa said.

I looked around and surveyed the block. Once again it was freezing. I had my hands in my coat pockets. Trying my best to keep warm, I said, "You think so?"

"Yeah, girl. With you, you be about your business. It's like you really like this hustle. Maybe because you're new, I don't know. But if you keep making money like that, Cream gonna give you them same privileges that he be giving to Nikki and Diamond."

"*Privileges?*" I asked with a puzzled look on my grille. "What are you talking about?"

"Okay, look, obviously you still don't know everything that goes down. See, Nikki and Diamond, they make money and they bust they ass when Cream needs them to. And it's like he treats them better. He gives them more respect," Lisa informed me.

"But how? What exactly do you mean?"

"Like, I don't know what the deal is with you and Cream, but with the rest of us, we can't just up and do as we please. Like we can't just go to Jamaica Avenue and go shopping. We can't go to the mall or anything like that. And god forbid that we try to kick it with a guy that is really feeling us or something. Cream would beat us within an inch of our life if he found out we was trying to have a boyfriend or something," Lisa explained. "But with Nikki and Diamond, it's different. He'll send them out to buy us clothes, and he'll let them go out to eat and all of that. He definitely trusts them, more than he trusts us. He ain't too worried about them trying to get with another daddy or running to the police or anything like that."

I was still cold as hell, but I took everything in that Lisa was saying to me, without commenting. I just let her speak.

"It's all about the money with Cream. You make that money and he'll love you. You don't and he'll hate you. He'll hate you but he'll keep you around."

"What do you mean?" I asked.

"I mean, take all of these chicks for example. They don't really wanna be out here freezing they ass off, sucking somebody's musty dick. So they don't hustle. Like me, whatever they make they make it and that's it. They ain't really dedicated. But I'll tell you what."

"What's that?" I asked.

"Shamgod and Spinach is the boss when Cream ain't around, but Nikki and Diamond, they be on something . . ."

I looked at her, puzzled. "Whachu mean?"

"Just between me and you, Cream trust them, but they dirty . . ." Lisa said.

I kept my mouth shut because I didn't want to be gossiping and have it later come back to bite me.

At that point a car pulled up. It looked like one of Lisa's regular customers.

"What's up, boo?" she said. "Y'all met my new sister?" she asked.

"Oh word! How you?" he asked me.

"I'm good," I said as I stepped closer to the car and looked inside. "Y'all got room for both of us in there?"

"Oh most definitely!" one of the guys in the backseat replied as the door swung open. "Come on."

As Lisa and I both made our way to the car she whispered in my ear, "See, that's what I'm talking about. You know how to get that money. They were only interested in me."

"I'm saying, girl, let's handle our business," I told Lisa.

We pulled around the corner and in a matter of minutes, I was dishing out a blow-job in the backseat, while Lisa had moved to the front seat and was doing the same.

12

OVER THE NEXT WEEK OR so I interacted a lot with Nikki and Diamond. They had finally come around and started showing me some respect. Mercedes still hated my guts, but Nikki and Diamond finally let up. It was like I had passed their initiation or something.

One morning Nikki called me and asked me to come into Cream's bathroom. When I got there, Diamond was shaving her legs and Nikki was just chilling, posted up against the wall.

Not knowing what to expect I stood at the entrance of the bathroom and said, "What's up?"

"We're going shopping later and I just wanted to get your pants size," Nikki replied.

"It depends on how the jeans are cut."

"She's about my size. Don't worry, I got it," Diamond said to Nikki.

I was never one to hold punches or scratch when something didn't itch, but I said, "Not too long ago y'all was ice-grilling me and couldn't stand my ass. And Nikki, you wanted to cut me and all of that. Now y'all seem like everything is everything. I don't get it."

"Lady, we didn't know who you were. And we had to test you. We had some time to see how you get down, and me and all of the other girls see three things that we like about you. We see that you about your money. We see that you don't be running your mouth talking about everybody. And we also see that you don't let nobody disrespect you," Diamond informed me.

"That's what's up," I said. I was still hesitant to embrace Nikki and Diamond, especially after Lisa had told me that Nikki and Diamond were both dirty. I knew that she didn't mean physically dirty, so she had to mean dirty in the sense that they shouldn't and couldn't be trusted. So as I sat there I was telling myself to just roll with the flow. They had came at me humbly so I was gonna honor that. But at the same time I knew that I had to watch them more closely than I would watch a friend simply because they were not my friends. *Keep your friends close and your enemies even closer.*

"Yeah, we respect your gangsta," Nikki said.

"A'ight," I said as I continued to stand at the entrance to the bathroom.

There was an awkward moment of silence, which I broke by saying, "Okay, so I guess I'll check for y'all later on tonight."

"Okay, and Lady, you our little sister. Everybody wants you to know that it's all love from here on out," Nikki said.

"A'ight. That's what's up," I said as I nodded. "I'm a bounce downstairs and get something to eat real quick. I'll see y'all later."

As I made my way downstairs, I didn't know what to think. Something just didn't seem right about them all of a sudden just showing me love. I mean true, all of the other girls in the house had started to show me love and embrace me. They did respect me for the same three reasons that Diamond had stated. But I wasn't buying Nikki and Diamond's newfound love.

WHEN I MADE IT TO the kitchen, I greeted Cream by giving him a hug and a kiss on the cheek.

"Good morning, daddy."

"What's up, baby girl?" he replied.

I said nothing as I opened the fridge and poured myself some orange juice. At that point it was just me and Cream in the kitchen. So I decided to test some of what Lisa had told me.

"Cream, is it okay if I spend the night with my girl Shauna tomorrow night?"

Cream didn't look at me or even acknowledge what I had said.

"You open up my refrigerator, pour my orange juice, inside my glass, and you don't even pour me none?" Cream asked, sounding real pissed off.

"Oh, I'm sorry," I said as I retrieved a glass and proceeded to pour him some orange juice.

"Lady, Sunday is a money night. You know that," Cream stated.

I took that as a no and made sure not to press the issue. The last thing I wanted was to get smacked.

Cream drank his orange juice and after burping ridiculously loud, he said, "Listen. Don't tell the other girls this, but I was gonna take you to Club New York tomorrow night. Me, you, Nikki, and Diamond. Well, Nikki and Diamond are supposed to meet me there. You been doing good by me. And all of my girls that do good by me, I do right by them."

"Thank you," I said.

"Shauna is cool people?" Cream asked. "I think you told me about her before."

"She's definitely cool," I told him.

"She know what the deal is with you and me?" Cream asked.

I had to lie because I didn't want Cream wary of any of my friends, especially Shauna. "Yeah, she know. But she ain't trippin'."

Cream looked at me and said, "This early in the game, I don't let my girls do whatever it is that they wanna do. But like I said, you been doing right by me, so I'm a do right by you. Chill with your girl tomorrow, and on Monday make sure you take care of me. A'ight?"

"Definitely, daddy. You know I got you."

13

SHAUNA IS A VERY SEXY girl and she reminds me a lot of the singer Toni Braxton. She keeps her hair real short like Toni Braxton and it looks hot as hell on her. She also has that same round face and complexion. But her body is much better than Toni Braxton's body. Shauna is only about five foot four and she doesn't have the typical black girl body. In fact she kind of has the opposite. She's top heavy and kind of light in the butt. She has a shapely butt, it isn't a white girl butt or anything. Her butt wasn't no big ghetto booty like I was lugging around.

"Now Cream, why is that I hear you always trying to play my girl?" I asked Cream as soon as he pulled up in front of Shauna's building.

"What are you talking about?" Cream asked with a twisted look on his face as he stepped out of his car.

"My girl Shauna!" I stated as Shauna looked on. "She spoke to you at the game and you played her! She said she saw you on Farmers Boulevard and spoke to you and you played her and didn't even say hello! Don't you remember I introduced you to her at the club that time?"

"Oh my bad, my bad. But I mean it was dark in the club and I had been drinking so you gotta understand," Cream explained.

"Yeah, yeah, yeah," I jokingly commented.

"So, what's your name? Shauna?"

"Yes," Shauna replied. "Don't pay Lady no mind, I wasn't trippin' like she's making it seem."

Cream had called me while on his way to his house to get dressed before going out to the club. He had told me that he and Spinach were right near Rochdale, which was the name of Shauna's apartment complex. He wanted me to come downstairs so that I could prove that I was really where I had said I would be. Cream took a pull on his blunt and then asked us what we were doing for the night.

I explained that we had no real plans other than just chilling at Shauna's house for the night. So Cream invited me and Shauna to come with him and Spinach to this lounge that was located in the Springfield Gardens section of Queens, on Merrick Boulevard.

We accompanied them and had drinks and bugged out for about thirty minutes. I could tell that Spinach had Shauna wide open. And I was just hoping that she knew how to spit the right game and didn't come across like some clucking chicken because that would have made me look bad.

Fortunately for me, before we all departed ways Shauna had given up the digits and she had gotten Spinach's digits. So everything was everything.

Shauna had driven her cute little Honda Civic so when we left the lounge Cream and Spinach went their separate ways and me and Shauna went ours.

"Shauna, he was feeling you! We should have all just gone back to Cream's crib and chilled there," I said to Shauna as we drove away in her car.

"Tina, I mean Lady . . . I ain't trying to get that close to that nigga that quick!"

"But I'm sayin' you gotta know how to roll with yours. Do you have a man?"

"Yes, and for that reason alone I shouldn't have even given him my number, so that was more than enough."

I could tell that if me and Shauna were gonna be kickin' it, I would have to help her to totally change her perspective on things. I mean, I knew that I had grown accustomed to things on the street in a way in which she probably hadn't, but her thought pattern, I could tell, was just way too slow.

"Trick, you ain't married! You can do whateva the hell you want to! I mean wasn't you feelin' Spinach?"

"Yeah, I mean he looks good and all of that but I'm sayin' . . ."

"You sayin' what? What you should be sayin' is why you didn't follow his lead and go back to Cream's crib with him and give him some."

"Give him some?"

"Yeah!"

"Give him some what? I know you ain't talking about no poohnonnie!"

I could not believe what I was hearing.

"Shauna, I can't believe that you're so tight like that! We definitely have a *whole* lot to talk about tonight," I said as I began to chuckle.

Shauna was older than me and I knew that she was still relatively green and innocent to a lot of things, but in a way I kind of liked that. See, I needed like a female ace that I could always call on and lean on. And I knew that I wanted that female ace to be someone who I had known and also someone whose mind didn't think as fast as mine did.

Yeah, I was thinking ten steps ahead as usual and I knew exactly what role Shauna would play in my life, or I should say what role I wanted her to play. The same way I had her fall back and chill while I spoke to Cream that day after the basketball game, that was exactly what I would need for her to do for me in the future. Sort of just be my right hand and listen and follow my lead. I mean that whole tight-twat Virgin Mary mentality would definitely have to fall by the wayside but I knew that I had time to work on that. And I knew that my influence would eventually be enough to get her to start acting similar to me even if she didn't think it was appropriate. One of my corny sayings was "A rising tide lifts all boats." My work with Shauna would definitely be cut out for me, but at the same time it wasn't gonna be all that much that I would need from her.

So I figured that that night was as good as any to lay everything out on the line and open up to Shauna and tell her all that I had been doing with Cream. I would have no problem sharing things with her but I would need her absolute word that whatever we discussed would stay between the two of us at all costs. I didn't even want her to discuss what we would talk about—even if it was with her nerd-ass clown boyfriend who I had not even met yet. I also didn't want her running her mouth if she happened to bump into any of our mutual friends. But most importantly, I especially didn't want her running her mouth to my younger sister, Mya. Mya was my heart, and for her sake I had to keep what I was doing hidden from her.

14

WHILE AT SHAUNA'S BEAUTIFUL CO-OP apartment in Rochdale Village, I thought about how I would explain, if Shauna asked me, what it was like that first night out on the track. The only thing that I really could compare it to was the time I lost my virginity to an eighteen-year-old dude when I was only in the seventh grade. Yeah, looking back to that time I would say that I had a whole lot of nervous energy flowing through my young twelve-year-old body. I also felt fear as I anticipated the pain of the experience. That's what it had been like for me on my first night out on the track.

"I'm done," Shauna stated as she emerged from the bathroom with a white towel wrapped around her body.

"Okay."

"Don't forget that we gotta talk when you get done," Shauna reminded me. "You've been telling me that you would fill me in on what's been up and you ain't leaving here until you do."

When I was done showering I purposely baby oiled my naked body right in front of Shauna.

"I can't believe that all you ate was some cereal," Shauna remarked as she walked toward her kitchen. "Especially with all of this food that I keep in this place."

Shauna prepared to warm up some leftover Southern food that she had made for herself and her man, whose name I learned was Tavon. I was actually surprised that he had a black-sounding name.

"Oh, and um, Lady, can you please just go grab one of my robes, or put a towel on or something? I mean I ain't tryin' to be stank or not make you feel welcome or anything like that but I just ain't all that comfortable with a naked woman walking around my apartment. . . . You know what I'm sayin', *sister girl?*" Shauna said in a comedic way.

I looked at Shauna and replied, "Girl, why you trippin'? Don't pay me no mind." Then without heeding Shauna's request to cover up, I simply changed the subject.

"Shauna, I saw all of the pictures with you and Tavon. Y'all been everywhere together, Disney World, Niagara Falls. You in love with him or what?"

"Yeah, he treats me good and that's what it's all about. A good man who is gonna respect you and look out for your best interests."

I stuck my finger in my mouth pretending to gag myself.

"What?" Shauna asked.

"You gonna make me throw up with all of that," I said.

"All of what?"

"All of that about you need a man that can treat you good and who respects you."

"Yeah and what's wrong with that?" Shauna asked as she took my plate of food out of the microwave.

"Okay, first of all, Shauna, I don't want you to think that I'm jealous or hating or anything, because it's totally not like that at all. But I think that you are way too young to be tied down. And second of all, you gotta know that when it comes to guys you gotta come at them the same way they come at us. You only need niggas that can put it down in the bedroom, and you need niggas that can help you raise your status on some level, even if it's just buying you a pair of jeans or something. But no matter what, you definitely need a nigga that can keep you in check!"

"Keep me in check? I don't need no nigga telling me what to do."

"Nah, what I'm saying is that you need a man that can let you do your thing but at the same time you need that type of nigga who will have no problem slapping your ass when you start talking too much or being disrespectful."

"Lady, you are really, really trippin' right now."

"No, I'm not! Think about it. Let's say that you're out with your man and some beef breaks out or whateva, things just start getting real thick. You wanna know that no matter what happens, your man will be able to defend himself and protect you. A real live-ass nigga is what you need."

"Yeah, there is nothing wrong with that but I still ain't letting no nigga put his hands on me."

Before putting a bite of baked macaroni and cheese into my mouth I simply and nonchalantly stated, "Okay, you'll learn."

Switching subjects, Shauna said, "Now Lady, what is this about you living on your own?"

I felt good about saying what I was about to say because I knew that it was a reality in my life and I wasn't just homeless and fronting.

I replied, "Well, I'm not really living on my own per se, but I am living on my own in that I live with Cream."

"When did all of this happen?" Shauna asked.

"For a while now, I've been staying at his crib in Astoria," I said, exaggerating the truth just a bit.

"Lady, I don't know . . . I mean the nigga is cute and all and he got money . . . I mean I could see going out with him and all of that but living with him? Nah, he is way too thuggish!"

I simply smiled and ate some more of my food.

"The more thuggish the better," I replied.

"With all of that history with his father and all of that, you better be careful. What happens if the cops run up in his crib and arrest him and they see you're in there?"

I didn't know what Shauna knew about Cream's father and I didn't wanna let on that I didn't know what she was referring to.

"Well, tell me what you know about him and I bet you that it's all just lies that you heard from the street. Cream is gangsta but at the same time he is sweet to me."

Shauna replied, "First of all Lady, there ain't no such thing as a gangsta with a sensitive side. But all I know is that his father ran one of the most violent drug gangs until he got locked up. And you gotta be careful because the apples don't fall too far from the tree."

I knew that Cream and his boys were into the drug game but I didn't know to what extent. Shauna was making me think but at the same time she didn't really know what she was talking about.

"Shauna, it's not like that. The cops ain't running up into his crib like that. Everybody knows that you don't crap in the same place that you eat. Cream ain't stupid."

"Okay, but all I'm saying is just be careful. . . . So, you're like his *girl* or something?"

I knew that now was as good a time as any to just spill the beans and not beat around the bush.

Putting Red Devil hot sauce on my chicken and collard greens I replied, "Nah. I mean he has *hit it* before, but I'm not his girl."

"So, how is it that you're living with him?"

"Well, let's just say that I'm one of his girls."

"Huh? You're losing me," Shauna said.

"I work for him."

"Oh! It's like that?" Shauna stated in a surprised but calm manner.

I was surprised that Shauna was coming across as calm as she was. And in a way that helped me to relax a little.

"Girl, you got a whole lotta heart. But I'm saying what's up with your mom and your sister? What happened?"

I explained to Shauna how I just got tired of the instability and the dysfunctional living that being with my mother brought on. I also told her how many of my mother's boyfriends had molested me and introduced me to pornography and how they would at times beat the crap out of my mother. Breaking down with anger, I told her how my mother's last boyfriend had raped me and how my mother didn't side with me after I'd told her what happened.

"What? I can't believe that!" Shauna remarked.

Through some tears I added, "Yeah, and do you know what that bitch had the nerve to tell me? She told me that I should've just closed my eyes and enjoyed being raped. And she had the balls to ask me did I cum while I was getting raped! I wanted to kill her when she asked me that but at the same time, Shauna, I felt guilty and confused because I did cum. Some people can't have an orgasm when they sexing somebody that they love, and there I was getting raped but yet having an orgasm."

Shauna stood up from her chair and came and caressed my shoulders. She could see the pain and bitterness that was inside of me and how all of it was just flowing out of me in the form of tears.

"And Shauna, to this day I still don't know how I had an orgasm while that nigga was doing that to me. I mean he was actually hurting me and I was screaming for him to get off of me and the next thing I know my body was feeling all good. Oooh! I could just kill that nigga for violating me like that!" I said while slamming my fist on Shauna's glass table.

"Shauna, you really just don't know how I be wanting to kill that nigga Junie. You don't know. Especially now that I'm running with niggas that would have no problem killing him. Yup, all I would have to do is just give the word to Cream and he would have my mother's boyfriend taken out!"

"Lady, you know what? I can feel everything that you are saying, but your mother's boyfriend ain't worth all of that. What you gotta try to do is, if anything, you gotta be there for your younger sister because she's still there, living through what you escaped from."

I had managed to slow down the tears, because Shauna was saying something that I had been trying my hardest to block out for too long. I had managed to not really think about my sister and what she must have been living with. With me not being around as her anchor she was probably dying a slow death. I knew that I would have to somehow start checking on her, and as soon as I possibly could, get her the hell out of that living situation with my mother.

"Lady, listen to this. Imagine if you really loved someone. I mean really loved them to the point where you would die for them, and while you were cooking one day you turned around with a knife and accidentally cut them. If that were to happen would that person bleed?"

"Yeah, if the knife managed to break their skin," I replied.

"See, even if it's accidental the blood would spill out because that's the way God designed us. He designed us in a way where if you get cut you bleed. No matter what the circumstances were that led up to you getting cut."

"Okay?" I said with a questioning tone in my voice.

"Lady, what I am getting at is this. I believe what you said about your mother's boyfriend violating you. That is a horrible thing, but I don't want you beating yourself up just because you had an orgasm in the process. Just like in that example that I just gave you, God designed our sexual organs in a way that once certain places are touched it is that touch or series of touches that can trigger an orgasm. The orgasm came about because that is naturally the way the body functions. Just like blood will spill out of your body if you are cut, simply because that is the way our bodies were designed."

I sat there for a moment and I sort of felt relieved because Shauna had managed to help me understand something that had been eating at me.

"So my having that orgasm had nothing to do with me just being a slut or anything like that?"

"Lady, that is what I'm trying to tell you. Of course not, because you're not a slut, you're a beautiful person."

Now I was thinking, *Okay, I'm gonna test that beautiful person statement.*

"So even though I work for Cream you still would label me a beautiful person?"

"Well, now Lady, all I'm saying is this, I'm not here to judge you or anything like that, but you yourself know the dangers and realities that go with hustling drugs. And I bet when Cream sends you on those drug runs you are alone and by yourself, probably somewhere way out of state, right?"

"Drug runs? No, Shauna, you got it twisted. I don't work for Cream like that. I *work* for him," I said, opening my mouth and simultaneously making the fingers on my right hand form a circle. I moved that same right hand up and down as if I were giving someone a blowjob.

Shauna smiled. "Oh, so he's like your sugar daddy? See, even them so-called gangsta niggas can get juiced as well."

Shauna wasn't getting it. "No, Shauna. I'm not juicing him. He's my pimp. Or as they say on the street, he's my *daddy*. I work on the street for him selling my body."

Shauna spit the food that she had just started to chew out of her mouth.

"You what!" she asked in disbelief.

"Yes, Shauna. And there's no need to be all that dramatic. I mean come on now, it's not that serious."

"Not that serious?"

"Yeah, not that serious, you wouldn't understand if I explained it."

"You're right about that!"

I stood up from the table to present my case as if I were a lawyer talking to a jury.

"Okay, let me ask you this. Have you ever given Tavon a professional?"

"A what?"

"A professional . . . You know, a blow-job, sucked his dick?"

"Oh, of course I did," Shauna emphatically replied.

"Well see, then you're doing the exact same thing that I'm doing only I get paid for it."

"But I know Tavon. It's not like I'm just sucking on any ol' body's sweaty dick!"

"It's all how you look at it, Shauna. I mean yeah, you might know Tavon but really what you're saying is that as long as you know the nigga then it's okay. But when you think about it, it's all relative. I mean if I meet a guy and I know him for a day, a week, or five minutes, it's no different than if I was with him for six months before I decided to give him some."

Shauna looked at me and she was about to say something but she paused and then began laughing.

"What?" I asked as I started laughing also.

"You are so damn scandalous that's what!" Shauna said as she continued to laugh. "Oh my god, I can't believe that you actually be out on the street sucking dick!"

Shauna continued to laugh. "And all this time I'd been calling you a trick. . . ." She laughed harder. I had to admit I did see some of the humor in what she was saying.

"And look at you. You're really comfortable with the whole thing. I guess that's just you. I mean, look at you right now, right this very second. You're just as comfortable as ever, eatin' in front of me with no clothes on. I guess taking your clothes off is nothing to you."

Shauna was right, I was comfortable with who I was and what I was about and what I was doing with my life. And it was bugged because I didn't even realize that I hadn't put on any clothes since I'd come out of the shower.

"Shauna, but you don't understand, I got a real good game plan behind what I'm doing. I'm a get rich off this hustle by flipping it and expanding it into other hustles. I'm gonna have my own little empire. . . . Watch. And until that plan fully materializes I just have to make the most of it. Really it's not hard. I mean come on, be honest, like when you get out of the shower and you look at your body in the mirror, tell me that at times you don't get turned on by your own body? Or if you put on some lingerie don't you feel sexy? I know you do, and all I do is look at myself the same way. When I'm out there I just think about how good I look and how sexy I feel and I get turned on knowing that men are lusting over me. . . . Basically Shauna, with anything the hardest part is getting your mind to accept your actions, and once that happens then actually doing the act is easy."

Shauna looked at me, shook her head and said, "Girl I don't know . . ."

"Shauna, all I'm saying is you just watch how my plan unfolds. Mark my words. You watch. Like a few minutes ago you were saying that I need to think about my sister and all of that. Well, this is the vehicle that is gonna allow me to do just that. You watch. I'm gonna be able to afford my own place and I'll make sure that Mya is up outta my mother's place and living with me."

There was a brief pause.

"And don't worry, you'll be right out there with me one day," I said.

"Who?"

"You!" I replied with laughter. "All you gotta do is throw on your tight jeans and some pumps and get it on!"

"You definitely got jokes now. 'Cause these lips won't be sucking on nobody's dick but Tavon's!"

"Nah, but for real, I could speak to Cream and I know on the strength of me, he would let you work for him. We could just change your name to something like Toni B since everybody thinks you look like Toni Braxton."

"You are really bugging! 'Cause Lady, you know there ain't no way in hell I'm gonna be turning tricks!"

I continued to joke. "Yeah, you could be one of the Honey Bunnies," I said.

"Honey Bunnies?" Shauna asked.

"Yeah that's what we call ourselves."

"Who is we?" Shauna asked.

"All of Cream's girls. Actually it's a name that I came up with."

"Oh my god! Lady, I can not believe you just said 'all of Cream's girls.' I can just see pimps from back in the days with the big Afros and the pink Cadillacs . . . and Honey Bunnies. I'm sorry but ain't nobody dippin' in my honey jar!"

We both laughed.

"And Lady, don't tell me that you're out there letting these guys dip in the honey jar also?" Shauna asked with renewed passion in her voice.

I just smiled and looked at Shauna.

Shauna and I continued to talk. Overall I guess that her reaction to everything was not all that bad. She didn't disown me or anything, and she promised to be there for me, and most of all she was genuinely concerned about me and my safety. I had managed to do a real good job of concealing the truth about what I had also been through, in terms of sleeping on the trains and sleeping at different friends' houses and all that I had to go through just to shower and eat decent meals. And at no time did I let on to her that I had had a regular job at the donut shop until I'd abruptly quit.

In my own twisted way of thinking, it was like I was somewhat embarrassed to admit all of my hardships to Shauna. I knew what my future plans were. I knew how I wanted to hustle and build and control my own little empire. And I also knew that in order to do just that, I would have to have a certain image. My image would be everything. So I didn't bring that bad stuff up at all but instead I glamorized the life of a streetwalker. I glamorized and fictionalized stories of hanging out with stars on a regular basis. I talked up a storm and I could sense that Shauna was buying every word of my game hook, line, and sinker. Not that she would ever do what I was willing to do, but I know that she wanted to keep me around so that she could sort of live through me and indirectly take part in all of life's taboos.

By the time Shauna and I were done talking, she was tired but I wasn't. It was close to eleven thirty at night and she had to go to work in the morning. I was used to being up and my body wasn't tired, nor was I worried about being tired for school the next day. I had finally put on some clothes and I asked Shauna if it was okay if I smoked some weed on her balcony.

"Nah, girl. You can go downstairs and smoke. Go right on the side of the building and you'll see some benches. Sit over there and you should be okay. Security might say something to you though, and if they do, you don't know me . . . okay?"

"So I guess you ain't coming with me then," I stated.

"I'm going to bed. I gotta work in the morning," Shauna said as she handed me her key and told me to take her cell phone and to call her if anything happened.

"Okay, I'll be back in about ten minutes. The blunt is already rolled so it won't take too long. Weed helps me unwind at the end of the day," I told her as I proceeded to leave her apartment and head for the elevator.

I made it outside and found the benches that Shauna had referred to. There was a good amount of people still hanging outside near Shauna's group of four buildings, which was surprising considering how cold it was. I sparked the blunt and proceeded to puff on the weed.

From the bench that I was sitting on, I noticed a nice white Mercedes-Benz sitting idle directly in front of Shauna's building. And who do I see emerging from Shauna's building? Nikki and Diamond.

I stopped smoking the weed and stood up and in my head I was like *what the* . . .

I walked a little closer to make sure that it was really them and that the weed wasn't playing tricks on me. As I got closer I could tell that it was definitely them. In my head I could only think that Cream was so damn controlling that he actually had Nikki and Diamond following my every move.

Got damn! I thought to myself.

But then I saw this Jamaican Rasta get out of the driver's side of the Benz to greet Nikki and Diamond.

Who the hell is that? I asked myself as I saw Nikki all hugged up on the Rasta, who had a green knitted cap with long dreadlocks sticking out of it. His dreads hung all the way down his back.

I was trying my hardest to remember if I had ever seen that Jamaican cat before. And for the life of me I couldn't remember ever having seen him. I didn't know what to think or do and right at that moment I remembered what Lisa had told me about Nikki and Diamond being dirty.

Damn, them chicks gotta be up to something sheisty, I thought as I put out my blunt and retrieved Shauna's cell phone. I called Cream right away on his cell phone but he wouldn't pick up. I called him about ten times in a row and each time it went to voice mail.

I stepped back out of the visible light so that I could see Nikki and Diamond but I didn't want them to be able to see me. I had been told by Lisa that there was a lot of competition between pimps. Pimps were always trying to get girls to leave their current pimp in order to roll with a new one who would gas them and promise them the world. And the thing about it was pimps only went after the best girls that the other pimp had.

I had a strong feeling that this Rasta was a pimp who must have promised Nikki and Diamond the world as well as protection in order to persuade them to dis Cream and let him be their new daddy.

Being that I couldn't get through to Cream I called Spinach on his cell phone and fortunately he picked up. There was all kinds of noise in the background and he couldn't really hear me unless I spoke up. So I had to practically yell into the phone.

"Spinach, what's up? This is Lady," I shouted into the phone.

"Who?" Spinach asked.

"Lady! Let me speak to Cream. It's real important."

Spinach put me on hold and handed the phone to Cream. "Yo!" Cream said as he took the phone.

"Cream, it's Lady. Are y'all having a good time?" I asked.

"Yo, look! Lady, don't be calling checking for me like that. I'm not one of your little-ass friends. Don't worry about what I'm doing! You better be calling me for a good reason!" Cream hollered over the loud music in the background.

I knew exactly how to play it off just in case the cat that Nikki and Diamond were with was a legit dude in Cream's eyes. Had that been the case I would have come across like a snitch and that would not have been good at all.

"I see Nikki and Diamond in front of Shauna's building and I just wanted to know if it was okay if I rolled with them and the *Rasta dude* to the club tonight since Shauna already fell asleep. I mean they are still meeting you there, right?" I asked.

"What did you just say? Yo, hold on, let me step outside," Cream said.

I held on for about five minutes until Cream came back on the phone. "Lady, repeat what you just said."

I repeated myself. And he asked me if I had spoken to Nikki or Diamond.

"No, I just stepped out of Shauna's building to smoke some weed and I see this Benz pull up and the Nikki and Diamond come out of Shauna's building and they all hugging and kissing up on the nigga so I figured he had to be fam and that they were all getting ready to roll to the club together."

"Does the dude have long dreads?"

"Yeah."

"Does he have those white five-star rims on his Benz?"

"Yeah."

"A'ight listen, I'm gonna call Shamgod and tell him to pick you up in front of Shauna's building. Whatever you do, do not let Nikki or Diamond see you and do not let them out of your sight. If they look like they are about to leave, then you let them see you and you stall them until Shamgod gets there. He ain't that far away, he should be there in about ten or fifteen minutes, and I'll be there as soon as I can. I'm leaving the club now," Cream said, sounding rushed and amped.

"Okay," I said. I then called upstairs to Shauna and told her that something seemed like it was about to jump off and that I would be back before she left for work. I assured her that I would bring her car keys and her cell phone back to her before the sun came up. Shauna was alarmed but she didn't press me. She just told me to make sure that I didn't run up her bill.

I froze my ass off waiting for Shamgod because I wasn't dressed real warm. I had simply thrown something on to run outside, smoke real quick, and come back in.

I called Shamgod and he informed me that he was like two minutes away and for me to walk to Bedell Street and wait for him at the bus stop so that Nikki and Diamond wouldn't see him when he pulled up. I did as I was told even though it meant that I would lose sight of Nikki and Diamond and the Rasta.

Before too much longer, Shamgod pulled up and I got into the car.

"Thank god you came when you did. I was freezing my ass off!" I said as I began chattering.

"Yo, where they at?" Shamgod asked.

I pointed to where they were. Shamgod got out of the car and carefully trotted over to see if he could spot Nikki and Diamond and the Jamaican dude. After about a minute he came back to the car.

Breathing kind of heavy, he yelled out, "Them snake-ass bitches!" He immediately called Cream and as soon as Cream got on the phone he asked, "Yo, are you strapped up or do you want me to handle this nigga and these bitches myself?"

There was a pause.

"Hell yeah, the nigga standing there hugged up with them. . . . Nah, I'm parked right on Bedell Street. They can't see me. . . . A'ight cool," Shamgod said as he hung up the phone.

"Listen, Lady, as soon as Cream gets here, I want you to go back into the building and chill with your girl. If Nikki and Diamond see you, just act like everything is everything," Shamgod instructed.

"Okay," I replied, knowing that he and Cream had plotted to set up Nikki, Diamond, and the Rasta.

About fifteen minutes later Cream and Spinach arrived, and Cream was vexed. He also parked on Bedell Street and immediately got inside Shamgod's ride. Spinach and Cream both kissed me on the cheek.

"Thanks, baby girl," Cream said as he gave me another kiss on the cheek. Then he asked me to go back inside.

I kept my mouth shut and did as I was told. But as I began to walk back to the building I noticed that Nikki was walking toward the lobby of the building and it seemed like Diamond and the Rasta were in the Benz about to pull off. I immediately called Cream and relayed the info to him, because from where they were parked they could not see what was going down.

"Okay, Lady, stall that bitch at the elevator or keep her in the lobby until I get there. I'm coming right now," Cream quickly said. Before he hung up I could hear him tell Spinach and Shamgod, "Make sure that y'all light both they asses up!"

"Nikki?" I said just as I was about to enter the building's lobby.

"Lady?" she said as she turned and looked at me. She sounded like she had swallowed a canary and looked like she had seen a ghost.

"What's up girl?" I asked. "What the hell are you doing here?"

Just then, I heard the sound of tires screeching followed by what sounded like a car crashing. Then I heard the sound of multiple gunshots, at least twelve or thirteen shots.

"You heard that?" Nikki asked. She looked shook like I don't know what.

Before I could even answer her, Cream had arrived at the lobby door. He seemed to have sprung up from out of the ground, because even I hadn't seen him coming. And without hesitation he grabbed Nikki up by her hair and rammed her face upside the glass window in the lobby, completely shattering it.

Nikki began screaming her head off as blood ran down her face.

"Shut up, bitch!" Cream screamed as he continued to grasp a fistful of her hair while repeatedly punching her in the face. "Lady, go upstairs to Shauna's right now!" Cream commanded.

I quickly made my way to the elevator and as I pressed the button I could hear security coming and Cream yelling at the security guard, telling him to mind his business.

"Mind your business, toy cop!" Cream yelled. "Mind your business! This ain't got nothing to do with you. . . . Nikki, you tried to play me and you thought I wouldn't find out, right, bitch?" Cream yelled. "Answer me! Where's that punk-ass Rasta at now?"

Those were the last words that I heard Cream speak as the elevator doors closed. I went upstairs to Shauna's apartment. When I arrived at her apartment, I unlocked the door and went inside. Shauna was sound asleep. She had no idea what was taking place twelve stories below her. And I didn't wake her to tell her.

I went to bed, and the next morning went to school like everything was normal. I never told Shauna what had happened downstairs in front of her building. To be honest, I never even asked Cream to fill me in on the details. All I know is that I never heard from or saw Nikki or Diamond again. Cream simply told all of the girls, myself included, that Nikki and Diamond had went *down south*.

Lisa would later explain to me that whenever one of the girls went *down south* they never returned. She told me to read between the lines. I did read between the lines and I never told her what I'd known about Nikki, Diamond, and the Rasta—who I was sure had also been sent *down south*.

I continued to gain the respect of the girls. And I realized that this Cream Team that I was a part of was no joke. They were about their money and about their respect. I know that Cream's respect for me from that point forward skyrocketed because I knew how to make money, I knew how to keep my mouth shut, and most important, I was loyal.

15

ABOUT FIVE MONTHS HAD PASSED since that first time I walked the track on that cold December night. And during those five months I gained so much street knowledge, so much game, and had witnessed so much. My sex was tighter than it had ever been before. I had learned the streetwalking business inside and out. I knew how to exploit it and was ready to do just that.

During that time I had also turned sixteen and managed to stay in school while I worked the streets. It was so damn hard but I put my mind to it and I was determined to do both no matter how draining. Subconsciously I think that I was motivated to excel in school in order to prove my mother wrong. I knew that if I dropped out or failed classes I would be giving weight to my mother's perception of me as being nothing more than a fast, dumb, little hussy.

I knew that I was way above any negative labels that my mother or any of her boyfriends had placed on me. I knew that I was a brilliant girl in terms of book smarts and I wanted desperately to prove that, if for no other reason so I could one day throw it in my mother's face and show her that I had accomplished much more with my life than she ever thought I was capable of.

The major bright spots during those five months were the times that I chilled with and spoke to my little sister, Mya. Mya was growing up quick and she was also living through the same dysfunctional nonsense that I had been through when I was living with my mother. She looked up to me and admired me and I loved that. She would come to some of the basketball games that I cheered at and she wanted nothing more than to be a Hillcrest cheerleader as soon as she was old enough.

I went to extremes to keep Mya in the dark about my trickin'. For example, I wanted her to continue to believe that I was working at the donut shop, so one day after school I arranged to meet Mya in front of my old job so that I could give her some money. Then I waited until she left before breaking out. Mya wouldn't have labeled me if she knew what I was doing on the street, but I didn't want her to ever have a negative impression of me. Plus, I couldn't take the chance that she might slip up and tell my mother what I was doing. I just made sure to hit her off with cash on a regular basis.

"Mya, Ma is not getting a dime of this money, right?" I asked.

"No, I told you that. You don't have to worry about me giving her anything," my sister responded.

I couldn't help but look at her and marvel at the fact that she looked just like me. Except for me being more physically developed than Mya, she and I could have passed for twins.

"I'm just saying, I work too hard for this money and I would give you the shirt off my back if I had to, but I ain't trying to give Ma no money so she can trick the dough on her bum-ass boyfriends."

Mya just looked at me as she folded the money and stashed it away in her pocket.

MY PLAN HAD NOT CHANGED. As soon as I had enough cake and all of the circumstances were right, I was gonna get an apartment of my own, one that Mya and I would share together.

I knew one thing though. I was tired of being small time and I had a plan to move myself from the streets right into management. I would have to sell that plan to Cream and hope that he would bite. Since Nikki and Diamond had been sent *down south*, there was really no girl that stepped in and filled their leadership spots. Mercedes was likely the next in line to fill their shoes but since she had been so tight with Nikki and Diamond that kind of went against her as far as trust was concerned.

I was more than confident that Cream would be open to whatever I pitched to him. In fact, I think had Nikki and Diamond not been in the picture from the jump and had I come at him with the idea of him putting me into management from early on, he would have went with the idea. But I wanted to prove to myself and to him that I was a soldier and worthy of being a boss.

And even though I was netting for myself close to a thousand dollars a week, sometimes it came with too much sacrifice.

Around the beginning of April, I had been working the track on Rockaway Boulevard near the North Conduit Avenue intersection in Jamaica, Queens. I had been on that particular track for about two weeks, and for the most part I liked it. It was slower than Brooklyn and some of the other tracks that I had worked on in the Bronx, so it was more tranquil in a sense. Ghetto tranquility if you will. But I quickly learned that the tranquility was real deceptive.

One April night there was this black Lexus parked right near the track and the Lexus was blasting the Notorious B.I.G.'s hit song "Who Shot Ya?" So while all of the girls on the track were dancing to the car's loud sound system this Spanish guy, who had to weigh close to 350 pounds, pulls up on the track in a big white Bronco.

All of the girls were too busy getting they groove on, but I had my eyes open and I saw the Spanish guy was looking for some action. I quickly made it over to the Bronco and found out what he wanted—a professional.

"You got forty bucks?" I asked.

The Spanish guy had sort of balked at my question. Forty was more than he was used to paying. Charging a premium for my services was something that I had quickly implemented about a week or so into my streetwalking career. I had to get my hustle on in the smartest most lucrative way possible. It was only right. And I quickly found out that niggers would pay extra for my shit.

Besides, Spanish guy was fat and disgusting-looking, and I wasn't putting my mouth on his dick for anything less than forty dollars. I mean, we all had to constantly endure servicing guys that stunk like you wouldn't believe, or who had all kinds of issues below the waist. Dealing with those dirty mofos squashed any glamorous images of being a prostitute. Needless to say I treasured my clients who were cute and had good hygiene. They made it easier for me to get into my job.

Dude agreed to the forty dollars price and gave me the money. I got in his Bronco and we pulled into the parking lot of this motel right across the street from a Burger King. He pulled down his pants and I somehow managed to make it through the hairy rolls of fat and started servicing his joint.

While I was down on him, trying my hardest not to inhale the foul odor that he was giving off or let his sweaty rolls of fat touch my face, I noticed that he was constantly shifting in his seat. He would shift to the left every few seconds or so. It seemed as if he was trying to reach for the driver's-side door handle or something, I wasn't exactly sure because my head was down. I was focused on one thing and that was to hurry the hell up and help him bust a nut.

So all of a sudden the guy kind of leans forward, and my worst nightmare came true. His big, sweaty, hairy-ass, jelly-roll belly was pressed right up against the entire left side of my face. I wanted to puke right there on the spot! I had no idea what the nigga was doing but I had to kind of adjust my face from off of his belly, and when I did I was able to get like a two-second glance of what was going on.

The guy appeared to be reaching for something that was either on the side of his seat or underneath his seat. I didn't know what was going on or exactly what he was reaching for, I just wanted him to sit still and to concentrate so that he could hurry up and splash off and get the dirty ordeal over with.

My mind had flashed back to what Cream had told me on the day that he had given me my small .22-caliber hand gun. *"It's that second or two that you will waste thinking about what to do, and your life will rest in that second or two that you take to make a decision."*

My instincts were telling me something was up and fortunately for me I had my bag on the floor of the Bronco. But unfortunately I had never practiced reaching into the cut in the lining and actually retrieving the gun that was stashed there. All I knew was that if my instincts were telling me that something was up then I had to react quickly. So I took my right hand off of his penis and began to just use my mouth. I didn't wanna just stop completely because I figured that if anything was up then that would have been the wrong move to make. It would have sort of telegraphed my move of defense.

I had my hand in my bag and I was silently rummaging through for the gun. I could feel it but I couldn't really tell exactly how to get it out. My heart began to race because I knew that I had to get out of that Bronco but I wanted my gun for security. My heart raced even more when I realized that the fat dude had stopped being so shifty and I wondered if he had seen me searching for something in my bag.

Hurry up, Lady! I pleaded with myself while I simultaneously sucked on his joint and desperately reached for my gun.

Finally, I felt the chrome handle of the gun. I managed to snake it through the hole in the lining. I made sure that I had it gripped right and once I was confident of that, I didn't hesitate. I immediately pulled my head up and violently jerked my body away from his and in less than a second my back was leaning against the passenger-side door. I knew that I couldn't try to open it just in case it was locked, but that was okay because I wanted to make sure that I was in control of the situation before I even opened the door.

With the guy's pants pulled down I aimed the gun directly at his head. I had both of my hands gripping the small gun so that I wouldn't drop it. I knew that I had totally caught him off guard and that was exactly what I wanted.

"If you move I will blow your got damn head off!"

"*Mami*, what? What?"

"Shut the hell up and open the door!" I screamed.

"*Mami!* Come on!" the Spanish guy pleaded in what sounded more like a Mexican accent.

"You got two seconds to open the door otherwise I'll blow your balls off! Word is bond I'll murder you right now!"

The guy had no choice but to comply with my orders. He reached across his body and opened his door with his right hand. I knew something was in his left hand but I didn't know what.

"Don't even pull up your pants. Just open the got damn door and roll your fat ass out the door!" I wanted the sound of my voice along with the gun to intimidate the guy as much as I could. I was still mad nervous and my heart was pounding but I was also angry like I had never been before. The seconds that the guy was taking to comply with my orders felt more like minutes, and my anger was really testing my trigger finger.

Finally the guy's door was open and he was making his way out the door. I reached for the door handle on my side. I grabbed hold of it, opened the door, and quickly made it around to the other side of the Bronco. It was much warmer than those cold winter days so I had on a pair of white Daisy Duke shorts, white high heels with straps that crisscrossed around my claves, and a white wraparound-type shirt.

The heels made it difficult to move but I still managed to get around to the other side of that car in what seemed like a split second. See, I still wasn't sure what he had had in his left hand and if it was a gun I knew that I would have to be quicker on the draw than he was.

With the gun still aimed at his head, I screamed, "Don't even touch your pants! Leave your pants right where they are and move your fat ass away from the car!"

The guy did just as I had commanded. The driver's door was still open and with the guy standing away from the car I was able to get a closer look as to what he had been reaching for. I noticed that there was a shiny machete wedged just to the left of the driver's seat.

"Turn your fat ass around and walk!" I commanded. "You was trying to kill me or something? Why the hell was you reaching for that machete?!"

"No no no! I was not trying to kill you," he pleaded.

"Shut up and walk!"

With the guy's pants and underwear now dangling around his ankles, I forced him to walk to Rockaway Boulevard with his johnson just dangling for the whole world to see. I knew that the boulevard was a high-traffic area and a cop—or anyone for that matter—could see me walking behind this guy with a gun, but I didn't care. The adrenaline was flowing and that had taken over me.

Shamgod was standing across the street and I was thankful like hell when I saw him.

"Shamgod! Yo, Shamgod!" I yelled into the night's atmosphere until I got his attention.

Shamgod came running across the street with two of his boys.

"Yo, what's the deal, ma?! Lady, what's up?!"

Still holding the gun on the guy, I said, "I caught this fat-ass nigga reaching for a machete like he was plotting to kill me or something, so I pulled out my burner and I'm ready to murder this cat right now! That's what's up!"

One of Shamgod's boys immediately suggested that we get off the busy street so that, as he put it, "We can handle this nigga."

We walked the fat Spaniard back to his Bronco and Shamgod and his boys made him get in the backseat. Shamgod took control of the steering wheel and I got in and sat in the passenger's front seat.

"See, there's the machete right there!" I yelled, pointing at the machete's thick red handle peeking out from the side of the seat.

"Lady, don't worry, we got this!" Shamgod said.

The guy began to beg and plead for mercy. But his pleas fell on deaf ears.

After we'd all piled into the Bronco I kept the gun aimed at the dude. Shamgod proceeded to drive us all a few blocks away to a park that was located on 150th Street. Being that it was so late at night there wasn't anyone in the park.

We made it to the park and got out of the Bronco. The fat guy was violently kicked out of the car and he spilled out onto the ground. He still had his pants and his underwear pulled down and they were dragging around his ankles, making it very difficult for him to maneuver. He tripped over his own feet a couple of times while trying to stand up.

"Get up and walk into the park!" Shamgod said.

At that point the guy was literally in tears and sweating bullets for his life as he tried to scramble to his feet. Shamgod ordered his man, Black, to get the machete.

After we'd walked about thirty yards or so we were standing near a park bench. It was a pretty well-lit area, considering the late hour. The light was from the streetlights that were on and hovering over the basketball courts.

"You were trying to kill my girl?!" Black asked.

"No. I keep that machete in the car for protection. That's all I use it for. Please believe me. . . ." he pleaded.

"Shut the hell up!" Shamgod ordered as he took the machete from his boy.

By this time I had relaxed the gun in the sense that it was just resting at my side and was no longer aimed and cocked at the Spanish guy's head.

In a flash Shamgod had swung the machete across his body in a sweeping motion. He swung the machete with all he had. And in an instant the Spanish guy let out the loudest scream of pain that I had ever heard. Both of his upper thighs had been sliced wide open. But that was the least of his concerns. I think that the brunt of his scream was due to the fact that with that same sweeping slicing motion Shamgod had also violently chopped the guy's dick completely off! He'd severed it right near the base of the shaft.

I definitely understood the dude's pain.

"Pick it up!" Shamgod screamed as the guy rolled around on the ground writhing in pain and in a pool of blood.

"Pick up your dick or I will kill you right now!"

The guy had to know that Shamgod was serious because he had just chopped his dick off, I mean what other proof did he need to know that Shamgod meant what he said?

The guy was in excruciating pain but he made sure to follow Shamgod's orders.

"Now put it in your mouth and suck on it!"

The guy quickly did as he was told. Shamgod's two boys fell out laughing. But Shamgod wasn't. He had the look of Satan on his face. I also wasn't laughing. I had just was witnessed one of the most gruesome sights that I had ever seen. I mean, I had seen cats get killed before, but this was way different.

Black managed to stop laughing and suggested that we leave the guy there with his bloody, limp dick in his mouth and in a pool of blood. We also left him with his Bronco, but more importantly for him, we'd left him with his life.

As we scurried back to the track I remember feeling a little remorseful but I had to remind myself that the guy either had plans of raping me or plans of killing me, so he didn't deserve any pity. Under the circumstances he was damn lucky that he didn't die. For all I knew he could have been some sick, sadistic serial killer or something.

When we reached the track Shamgod gave orders to get everyone off and away from the track right away. And in a flash, like midnight marauders, we were gone from the scene of the crime. The track was emptied and we soon found ourselves resting and plotting in a closed-door meeting with Cream at his crib.

That closed-door meeting was one that I will never forget because I felt honored to even be sitting in on such a meeting.

"So tell me exactly how the whole thing went down," Cream demanded.

I quickly spoke up and explained from the time the Spanish dude picked me up until he got his dick chopped off.

Shamgod, Black, his other boy, and I couldn't help but laugh as we painted a picture of the guy with his severed penis in his mouth. Cream, however, did not find it as amusing.

"Wait a minute, hol' up," Cream stated. His head was down, looking toward the ground, and not looking any one of us in the face. "You're telling me that this cat was seconds from taking Lady's life and all y'all did was chop the nigga's dick off!?"

From the tone in Cream's voice it was obvious that he was ticked off and none of us dared to respond.

Cream stood up from his chair and he looked Shamgod dead in the eyes. "Shamgod, come on man! You know you suppose to murder that dude! Y'all niggas got a job to do when y'all out there and y'all trying to act all Hollywood! Man, this ain't no *Scarface* movie, this is my life!"

Shamgod tried to interrupt. "Cream but I'm sayin' . . ."

"You sayin' what!?" Cream shot back. "You ain't sayin' nothing! Man, all you did was help to shut down my track for a couple of weeks!"

Shamgod gave Cream a look as if he didn't understand what Cream meant.

"Now I can't have nobody out on that track for a while! A nigga gets his dick cut off and not only do y'all leave the dude with his life but y'all leave the dude with his car. You know he went to the hospital and if they patched him up or not, if he has any kind of self-respect he's gonna be coming back to retaliate and that puts my girls at risk. All 'cause you ain't handle the situation the way you should have!"

The room was eerily quiet for a few moments as no one dared challenge Cream's authority.

"We gotta let that track cool down for a while. We gonna shift everything out of Queens altogether and just spread everybody out in Brooklyn and the Bronx. And Shamgod, get on top of your game, nigga! That can't be happening on your watch!"

The meeting was quickly adjourned, but not before Cream had given a few more orders. Shamgod gave Cream his word that he would hold everything down from that point on.

After the meeting had dispersed, I retreated to take a shower. I reflected on all that had gone down that night. My life had really been on the line tonight. The bugged thing was I felt like it wasn't really thick for Cream like it was for me. Because no matter how much pressure he put on Shamgod to keep us safe, the truth of the matter was that anything and everything was capable of going down while I was out there.

And like I said, even though I was netting for myself close to a thousand dollars a week, it came with way too much sacrifice, and I wanted to change things. So that night when I came in, Cream was in his room, talking on his cell phone. I sat down on his bed and waited for him to get off and when he was done I didn't waste time.

"Cream, I saw you on your phone and no disrespect, I mean you didn't have to get off for me or anything but . . ."

"Nah, it's nothing. I was getting off anyway," Cream said. "So what's up? Speak to me."

"Well it's like this. I know that since I've been out there that I've been bringing in my money on a consistent basis and I think I've been doing my thing!"

Cream just looked at me, waiting to see where I was going with this.

"Ever since I been out there I've been seeing a lot of things that I would do differently. For example, we always tell niggas to pay forty bucks for a three-hour room that we use only once for twenty minutes. But we could and should shell out the forty bucks and use the same room four times or more within those three hours and not charge the guys anything for the room. If we did that I know we would make more money because a lot of the guys would be saving forty bucks. But guess what? That same forty that they saved, I guarantee you that they will be back at the track later on in the week spending that same forty on us as opposed to just giving it to the owner of the motels."

Cream looked at me and slowly nodded. "And you know what else? I never could see the business sense in just charging cats twenty bucks for a blow-job and a hundred for sex. So what I did was I've been looking at myself as more like a hustler or a saleswoman. What I mean is this, when I'm out there and if I see that I got a nigga open and he's asking for a blow-job, then I'm a get forty, sixty, or a hundred or the most that I can get from him. And if he is asking for sex then I'm trying to get a hundred fifty to two-fifty or whatever I can get from the nigga. I really don't see the sense in losing out on money like that. So I'm saying all of this to tell you that there have been nights where I've not even worked that hard and made so much money because I know how to hustle. Like these so-called ballers that be coming at me, I know that the niggas is really herbs because if they was really ballin' then they wouldn't be paying for no pussy. But those are the niggas that I been getting to come up outta their pockets and pay me and I know what I'm doing 'cause I've been doing it consistently. It's not like I look much better than all of the other broads, it's just that I know how to spit game and hustle."

Cream just looked at me and didn't respond. I wondered what was going on in his head.

"Cream, what I'm asking is this, why don't you let me take Nikki's spot? Well, what I mean is, why don't you let me train all of the girls so that they can hustle the way I've been hustling? In the long run it's gonna mean more money for the whole team."

Cream finally spoke up. "So in other words you're saying you wanna come off the streets?"

I knew enough not to answer that question with a yes. That would have been the wrong card to play.

"Nah, that's not what I'm sayin'. What I'm sayin' is—"

Cream cut me off. "And how the hell do I know that yo ass ain't gonna try to up and bounce on a nigga the way Nikki and Diamond was trying to do?"

"Cream! Come on . . . You know I ain't got a problem grindin' on the street for you. You know that. It could be minus-twenty degrees outside or one hundred and twenty hot-ass degrees. It don't matter 'cause I would still be getting you that dough. You know I would 'cause I've done it," I said.

Cream just looked at me.

"Cream, I see so many opportunities out there that I know I could blow up and I just want you to trust me and give me the opportunity to blow up those opportunities. I want you to back me on what I do and in the end it's gonna make so much more sense for you."

Cream still continued to remain silent.

"Let me train all of your girls, teach them how to really get money when they're out there."

"Lady, this ain't corporate America," Cream sarcastically responded. "This is the streets."

"Cream, I know that but what I mean is this. Niggas be coming up to me asking me to do a threesome with me and any another girl that be out there and to me I'm like let's do it! Let's get that money and charge niggas like five hundred. Every guy's fantasy's to be with two girls at the same time or else they wanna have anal sex! Cream, I'm telling you, every night I get asked about that. So why not get the money? And besides, the bottom line is we need to be getting this money from these cats regardless! Cream, I can teach your whole crew how I get down. I'm telling you. Just give me a shot!"

"You know what?"

"What?" I responded.

"Did you bring this up because of what happened tonight?"

"Cream, no. I swear to god tonight had nothing to do with me saying any of this. But when you think about it, now is the perfect time to implement something like this because look at what's going on. It's starting to get warm and here you were tonight talking about moving things out of Queens for a while. Cream, this is the wrong time to be cutting back on things but in a way it's necessary. But you can cut back from Queens for like two weeks and let me do my thing with the girls and I guarantee you that even without Queens the team will be making more money than ever before."

"I believe you," Cream said.

"About the money we can make?" I asked.

"Yeah that, but I also believe you when you said that you were not just motivated to bring this up because of the incident tonight."

I nodded my head and looked at Cream.

"Lady, to me the main thing is loyalty and being able to trust niggas. Matter of fact, everything is about loyalty. I'm a let you roll with your idea . . . I'm only hesitant because I haven't had a long enough time with you to *really* see how you get down. I'm a let you roll, but I'm also gonna be watching my money like a got damn hawk and see if you frontin' or if you really real."

I beamed inside 'cause I knew that Cream had bought my pitch and that he would likely buy other pitches from me in the future.

Then there was a pause as neither one of us spoke. Cream broke the silence by saying, "Lady, word is bond. I swear to god, if you ever cross me I'll shove a hot curling iron up your pussy before I slit your throat!"

"Got damn, daddy!" I shouted out. "Ouch! A hot curling iron?" I laughed in an effort to bring some humor to the situation. Even though I knew that Cream was dead-ass serious. He didn't have to worry though, because I would never have crossed him.

He continued on. "On the strength though, I knew from early on that you were overcharging niggas because I had sent my own cats to buy from you, cats that you didn't even know were sent by me to test your skills out and to see what was up. Some nights the only customers you had was my boyz that I sent to you."

I smiled but at the same time I was kinda confused.

Cream added, "I did that because I saw that you was making a lot of dough and I wanted to know what your secret was but you probably don't even remember what I told you about testing niggas."

Cream was wrong because I knew exactly what he was talking about in terms of his advice on testing niggas.

"So you sent your own cats to me in order to test me?"

"Yeah, I tested you more than a few times because I wanted to see if you would ever hold back from me any of the dough you were getting by charging them premium rates. I didn't have to test you because my cuts were higher but I'm just sayin' that's my style. I mean, there was nights where I would send five or six cats to you and you were getting money from them just like you told me. And I did that a couple of times and each time you could have jerked me and handed in the going rate for your services but you was true and you never tried to get over on me. Not even once!"

Inside I was so elated because I had never had any idea that Cream had been setting me up like that but I did know that he was absolutely right in that I had never shorted him one penny. And there were numerous opportunities where I had overcharged customers and I could have benefited my pockets but I didn't.

I had to reinforce Cream's words and capitalize on the moment.

"Cream, it's not about me. It's about us seizing what's out there. I wanna think and know that I'm more than just some pretty, tight-bodied, sexy, dick-sucking streetwalker! I can't speak for all of the other girls, but as for me, I wanna know that I run with the Cream Team and that I'm an integral part of that team. You know what I'm sayin'? It's deeper than just me. Trust me!"

Cream did in fact trust me and I know that with him it was more about his trust in the almighty dollar but hey, I was willing to work with whatever I had at my disposal.

Throughout the night I laid out some of my plans to him but I made sure not to show him all of my cards. He wanted me to get started right away but he and I both agreed that I would have to stay out on the streets for a while so that I wouldn't cause resentment to set in amongst the other girls. I had absolutely no problem with that, because while there were elements of the profession that I hated, I knew that I had the ability to endure those elements. With me, I could endure those elements, knowing that my future was headed toward more than just a dead end. I didn't mind the hustle or hustling, but if I was gonna hustle I wanted to be hustling with a purpose and not just hustling for the sake of hustling.

16

BY THE TIME JUNE 1995 rolled around, things were on and popping and the Cream Team was making money hand over fist like they never had before. I was a big reason for that rise in sales. Or I should say my management skills were the reason for the rise in sales.

Unfortunately for me, school had been taking more and more of a backseat in terms of my priorities. Thankfully for me there were only two weeks left in the school year so I didn't really sweat it that much. I just made sure that I showed up for tests and all of that, but plainly put, I just didn't have the time for school.

By that June, with my persistent saving and good personal money management skills, I had managed to purchase a C-class Mercedes-Benz. It wasn't all of that but it was a start and a damn good one as far as I was concerned. I was making more money than most four-year college graduates were earning at high paying jobs. I knew that I could afford my own apartment and I was making plans to move into the same apartment complex that my girl Shauna was living in. That would be cool because I would be physically closer to Shauna and able to spend more time with her. Spending more time with her was something that I had been neglecting to do but not purposely. However, for the time being I was more than happy to be still living in Cream's house in Astoria. It kept me at the epicenter of what was going on in the Cream Team organization.

It had been close to a month since I'd trained the girls on every aspect of the streetwalking business. I wanted everything running as strict and uniform as a McDonald's franchise system. So it didn't matter if it was Harlem, Queens, Brooklyn, the Bronx, or Long Island, all of the girls had been coached and trained for what they needed to do and say in order to increase sales.

In addition to the increase in sales, I was able to report back to Cream and let him know that most of the girls were receptive to the idea. They ultimately knew that for them it meant the possibility of doing less tricks and earning more money than they'd ever earned before. And as expected, there were some chicks who were purely hating on me and were more than jealous of my position of authority. I tried my best to not lord anything over them because I knew exactly what position they were in and I felt that I had to have some compassion for them. For some reason all of Cream's Spanish chicks seemed to always dislike me. I guess it all stemmed from Mercedes not liking me. But there was a young Spanish girl named Anna who had lately been getting on my last nerve and was always trying to test my authority.

The thing was, many of them didn't object to spitting game and trying to get more money out of customers, but many of them had problems with doing anal sex and threesomes. And as far as that was concerned, I knew that I had to be diplomatic, not soft, but diplomatic and stern and yet not act like a dictator.

I still remember approaching all of the girls one night in Cream's basement about anal sex and different kinky propositions.

"Look y'all, at the end of the day it's about getting this money!" I said to them.

"Yeah, but what I'm saying and what some of us are also saying is that we have a serious problem with the whole anal sex thing. I mean it's hard enough to be out there sucking dick and trying not to get arrested and all of that. But with these low-life niggas that be picking us up, if we let them have anal sex you know they ain't trying to be gentle with it. They'll be up in us trying to rip us apart and then we won't be able to work until we heal up. And Lady, the bottom line is that anal sex hurts and I ain't with it! Cream can beat my ass if he wants to but I'm still not doing it," Anna stated.

"Number one, if anybody is gonna beat your ass it ain't gonna be Cream, it's gonna be me! That's the first thing. Now listen, obviously I know where you are coming from. I'm a soldier, I know what it's like. But if some low-life is gonna pay five hundred bucks to hit y'all in the butt, then let him do it! Take the damn money and ya'll are done for the night. It's better than hustling twenty customers for the same money," I said.

"Lady, you just don't really understand though. That's degrading," Anna replied.

"First of all, Anna, don't tell me I don't understand! Because I do! So let's just get that straight. It ain't like every nigga out there is coming for anal sex. I really think y'all are overreacting. But this is how we gonna handle it. Whoever don't mind doing anal sex and threesomes and all of the kinky stuff, raise your hand right now," I ordered.

As hands went up I told everyone to look around at the faces of the girls who had their hands raised. I also instructed one of the girls to write down the names of the girls whose hands were raised.

"Now this is the deal. Anna and everybody else, make sure y'all get this. If somebody wants a threesome or anal sex or something like that, don't y'all let that money go by. If y'all don't wanna do it then point the customers to the girls that wanna do it. And that's how it's going down. We gotta get this money and that's the bottom line!"

I knew that things still had to be taken a step further if it were to really run like a tight ship. I made Cream go into his pockets and spend thousands on sexy clothes, wigs, and weaves so that every girl on the track would appear to be more than worth the premiums that they were charging. With summertime just around the corner, I knew that we had to capitalize on the warm weather.

I had become sort of obsessed with the success of the operation and I knew that the bar had to constantly be raised. So I told Cream that all of the girls had to start working out at least three times a week. The girls really hated me for that but that was one thing that I was not gonna budge on. As far as I was concerned I was not gonna have the girls just sitting around all day watching *Jerry Springer* and sitting on their asses getting fat.

Why should I settle for that when they could be using that time to run on a treadmill and do some stomach crunches and squats? I wasn't gonna settle for that because I knew that the results would eventually pay off big, and I was more than right.

The money began coming in in droves and Cream and I had worked out a deal where he was paying me like two grand a week in order to oversee the operation from a logistics standpoint. I was more than happy with that arrangement. In a matter of seven months I had managed to parlay myself away from the daily grind of turning tricks to that of a street sex madam where I was, in my mind, really getting paid for absolutely nothing.

The week after Cream and I had worked out my two-thousand-a-week pay arrangement school had come to an end. I was so glad. But what was strange was that as quickly as the money began to increase we soon noticed that the money had slowed down by almost 25 percent and we couldn't figure out why. Then another week went by and the sales had dropped by yet another 25 percent and we were all bugging out.

So in a matter of two weeks our business sort of fell off a cliff, and needless to say it didn't look good that this all happened right after my weekly pay arrangements had kicked in.

But the number of customers who visited the track had dramatically declined. And that was the thing that we could not figure out. No one on the team could understand the disappearing act that our customers were going through. The decrease in customers meant a decline in revenue and it was not a good thing.

Cream questioned everybody including myself yet nobody had any answers. In his heart I know that he knew that I had nothing but integrity and he knew that whatever was going on, I wasn't the one who was behind the sudden drop-off in business. He knew I would not do something like steer customers to get serviced at another location which he knew nothing about. What was bugged was that in my mind—even though nothing had ever been said to make me feel this way—it seemed as if Cream trusted me more than he trusted Shamgod and Spinach. Nothing had been made official or even been spoken of in terms of making me a lieutenant or something like that but it was almost as if I was considered part of Cream's inner circle simply because of the things he would ask me and share with me.

Cream is as calculating as a snake in the grass. You might think he doesn't see what's going on but meanwhile he is plotting and testing you, just like he had tested me back in the days by sending his boyz to me on the track. And something was telling me that he had been secretly testing both Shamgod and Spinach. I didn't know for sure, and I couldn't specifically put my finger on it, but lately I could sense that he thought something was up. It seemed to me that his trust in me was growing but decreasing for Shamgod and Spinach. Maybe I was wrong and it was just biased thinking on my part, but I could feel it in my bones.

As we drove in my new Mercedes, Cream began to pick my brain.

"Lady, you think that Shamgod or Spinach is setting up tracks in other parts of the city?"

I didn't want to tell Cream that I had already thought about and dismissed that idea, but in truth I had given it considerable thought. I knew that in the street you never ever show your hand until you know exactly what cards every player is holding.

"I doubt that."

"Why do you doubt it?"

" 'Cause I mean, to me, I just couldn't see them snaking you like that."

"Lady, that's how niggas do."

"You know what? Just go with your gut. Honestly, ask yourself if you really believe that, number one, your boys have the balls to do that. And number two, ask yourself, do you really think they would do that? And number three, you gotta remember that if there was another track that sprang up, don't you think you would have heard about it? Cream, you know what that little voice in your head is really telling you. And that's your answer to this whole thing. Just listen to that little voice in your head."

Cream sat quietly for a second. He must have been pondering my words.

"Lady, you right . . . I'm buggin'! But I just can't figure this out and it's eating at me!" he told me. But I wasn't sure if he really meant that. I had a feeling that he had already had some type of secret investigation of his own going on and he was just throwing things out there.

As we continued to drive I had a pressing thought in my head but I didn't let it out. I kept quiet because of something that Cream had taught me in the past. He had taught me that there really is no such thing as *casual talk*. And he was right about that. So I didn't want to just casually bring up a pressing thought in my head until I had thought about all of the ramifications.

See, even if Shamgod and Spinach—or someone else for that matter—had been steering customers to other tracks in order to circumvent Cream's organization, Cream would have eventually heard about those tracks and been able to simply drive by those tracks and verify what was going down. I knew that if someone close to him was gonna snake him that they would have to be smart about it and that they wouldn't set up a track, they would more than likely set up a whorehouse.

With a whorehouse it would have been easy to run and at the same time keep Cream in the dark because it would have been able to operate undetected for a while. And if it looked like it might be detected, the whorehouse could simply pack up and move to another location.

I didn't wanna tell Cream about the whorehouse idea because I didn't wanna be just *casually* talking and also because I saw a big opportunity in that whole whorehouse concept that I needed to keep to myself for the time being. I didn't want to keep bringing my ideas to Cream and playing my whole hand. I didn't want to appear to be overly ambitious, which is something that could have backfired and blown up in my face if Cream ever took my overambition as a threat. For the life of me I couldn't understand why Cream wasn't using the whorehouse concept. To me it just made a whole lot of sense. But I kept my mouth closed and continued to drive until we reached Cream's crib.

"Cream, all we gotta do is just chill and not even sweat it and things will pick back up. Watch, it's probably nothing, in a week I bet you we'll be back to grossing what we were grossing before the dropoff."

I followed Cream to his room after he'd checked on the girls who were in the basement to make sure that everything was a'ight. Cream pressed play on his answering machine and there was only one message from someone who sounded like a white guy. But he didn't leave a name with his message, he had simply and calmly said, "Cream, it's me. Call me back as soon as you get this message."

After hearing the message Cream immediately dialed a phone number and then put his phone on speakerphone mode so that he could get undressed and talk on the phone at the same time.

The phone rang about eight times until finally someone picked up.

"Detective Lombardi, how can I help you?"

Cream called from across the room, "Lombardi, it's Cream. I just got your message. What's up?"

"Cream, what the hell are you doing to me, man?" the guy yelled into the phone. He sounded like a white guy. His stern and obviously angry tone was in sharp contrast to the mood that Cream was in.

I had no idea what was going on or who the white guy was. I simply proceeded to get undressed in preparation for getting some dick from Cream, which had been the real reason for our retreat to his house and up to his bedroom.

"What's wrong? What happened?" Cream asked.

"Listen, Cream, I've been sticking my neck out for you and putting my ass out on the line, as well as my job and my reputation. The least you could do is give me the respect and the courtesy to call and tip me off before you do something!"

Cream stopped undressing. He walked over to the phone and picked up the receiver so I could no longer hear what was being said. Cream listened attentively.

"What!" Cream screamed into the phone.

"Yo, just listen to me! I got you! Lombardi, you know that my word is my bond. Listen to me when I tell you that I didn't sanction this and I had no idea that this was going down!"

There was a pause in Cream's words and I wondered what was going on. My heart rate kind of sensed that it had to increase. I could see how vexed Cream was simply by looking into his eyes.

"Lombardi, just feel me on this. I'm sitting here trying to figure out why the hell my money is dropping off by fifty percent in two weeks and now I see why. I would never cut my own throat like that, man, come on!"

There was another pause in Cream's words. I could almost see Cream's blood boiling.

Finally Cream spoke again. "Lombardi, word is bond. I'm gonna handle this. This will be handled by tonight, trust me! I'll get back to you by tomorrow afternoon. Just hold me down until then."

There was another pause and then Cream simply replied, "a'ight" and he hung up.

I could sense that sex was no longer an option so I simply asked, "Is everything okay?"

Cream didn't respond but he looked at me with the most evil look. I kept quiet.

Then all of a sudden Cream let out a yell of frustration as he threw the phone. It hit his bedroom wall with such force that it shattered into pieces.

"Cream, what's wrong?"

Cream didn't acknowledge me and he kept at his rampage. He ripped the base of the phone from his nightstand and also threw that into the wall, shattering it in the process.

"Cream, talk to me!" I shouted.

"Niggas is dying tonight! Word is bond! Lady, mark my words, niggas is getting laid down tonight!"

I had never seen Cream that angry. He was so angry that he couldn't even properly hold the saliva in his mouth.

"Put your clothes on. We gotta get outta here!"

I quickly complied with Cream's orders.

"Lady, grab my cell phone. Call that nigga Shamgod and that nigga Spinach and tell them that I said to round everybody up and meet me at the apartment in Queensbridge tonight at nine o'clock!"

Swiftly obeying Cream's orders I still didn't understand what the anger was for or why he was adamantly saying that niggas were gonna die. I also wanted to desperately know who Detective Lombardi was.

"Come on!" Cream instructed as he led us out of the house.

We jumped into his Acura Legend and before I knew it we were on the Grand Central Parkway doing about one hundred miles per hour heading toward the Van Wyck Expressway.

"Cream, I got Spinach on the phone and he wants to speak to you."

Cream yelled, "Yo, tell that nigga to just be at the apartment at nine!"

"Spinach, did you hear him?" I asked.

"Yeah," Spinach replied. The fact was, Cream had yelled so loud that everyone in Queens probably heard him.

Normally, Astoria is about fifteen to twenty minutes away from the Rosedale section of Queens, but on that particular day we managed to make it to Rosedale in like five minutes.

Specifically we made it to 147th Avenue and parked in front of a nice brick house. Cream put the car in park and then he just sat there and listened to the radio for a minute.

"Cream, please just tell me what is up."

Finally Cream spoke. I guess some of his adrenaline was starting to subside.

"A'ight Lady, listen. These words do not leave your ears! You understand me?"

"Of course I understand," I replied, sounding eager to know what it was that Cream knew.

"Lady, if you utter anything about this cat Lombardi then I gotta take you out!"

"Cream, don't worry about me, I don't talk!"

Cream gave me a crossed kind of look and then he looked out of his driver's side window. With his right hand gripping the steering wheel he slouched down in a way that gave him this stereotypical gangster lean. Then he spoke.

"A'ight, see this cat Lombardi he works down at One Police Plaza. I met him through this kid named Mark who I grew up with who became a cop. The kid has always been a real street nigga and when he became a cop he kept that street side about him and he put his connects together for me and that's how that went down. . . . So like I was saying, Lombardi works in what's called the command and control center so everything that goes on in this city, if it's police related he either knows about it or can get information on it. And he feeds me all of the info about any investigations that are related to my team."

I sat there surprised at what I was hearing but the words sounded so good that it made me want to have an orgasm right there in my seat. It sounded like something out of the movies, but besides all of that I couldn't understand why on earth Cream was sharing this type of information with me. It was like he was violating all of his rules about loose lips sinking ships. I didn't say anything in response. I simply sat and listened but I also repositioned my body in a way where I brought my entire left leg and foot completely onto the seat cushion as I turned and faced in Cream's direction.

Cream continued on. He banged the steering wheel with the palm of his hand as he said, "Lady, now check this out. Dude told me that niggas was making complaints to the police that female undercover cops were arresting them for soliciting prostitutes. Then, after arresting them, they would tell the niggas that if they paid them they would let them walk and no charges would be filed. . . . Can you believe that?!"

I usually catch on quick but I just was not making the connection.

"Cream, I'm not following you."

Cream sat up in his seat and he explained himself further. "Don't you see what's going down? Those female undercover cops that were making the arrests for soliciting of prostitution, they were not real cops, they were my girls posing as cops and just shaking niggas down for their money!"

I finally got it and my mouth fell wide open. I was speechless.

"Exactly!" Cream replied in reference to my shocked and silent expression.

"So let me make sure I understand what you're saying. You telling me that they would pick up a customer and instead of turning the trick they would front like they was the police and try to arrest niggas?"

"Yes!" Cream adamantly responded. "And Lombardi told me that they had fake badges, handcuffs, and all of that so I know that they had no problem making these niggas think that they were really five-o and I know that they had no problem getting them niggas to cough up big money! And they probably pocketed a whole lot of that dough!"

I couldn't believe what I was hearing but I shouldn't have been too surprised because if you leave it up to niggas, they will always figure out a way to make getting illegal money even more illegal than the illegal money that they were getting!

I still wanted to make sure that I kept a rein on my tongue but at the same time I didn't want my silence to raise Cream's suspicions about me. Because the absolute truth of the matter was that I had known absolutely nothing about that particular scheme.

"Cream, I just wanna say this. I had absolutely no idea whatsoever that the girls were running this scam. No idea!"

"Lady, I know that you're good money. You don't gotta explain nothing to me. But the thing is this. There is no way that both Shamgod and Spinach couldn't have known that this was going down! One of them had to know! None of the girls would have tried that on their own. It's way too damn risky. The only way they would have done that is if they were told to do it and also told to keep their mouths shut about it."

I couldn't help but think that Cream was right but I had no concrete proof to offer up so I made sure to keep my mouth shut. I still wanted to know more about Lombardi so I geared the conversation back in that direction.

"Dude sounded bent," I stated.

"Who? Lombardi?"

"Yeah."

"Hell yeah the nigga was bent! See the thing is this, I'm paying that nigga. He ain't offering up this information for free and something like this cuts into everybody's money, including his."

"But Cream, if he told you about it all you gotta do is handle it and keep it moving."

"Lady, it's not that simple. See, when these police-corruption complaints come in, the cops gotta pass that off to their cops."

I gave Cream a twisted look of confusion.

"IAB," Cream replied to my look.

I still wasn't getting it.

"Internal Affairs Bureau, now them niggas is involved. See the IAB are the cops that go after the bad cops and in this situation even if they know that the girls were really prostitutes posing as cops they still are gonna investigate it fully. What makes me so vexed is that we had a situation where if we were out of sight then we were out of mind. Lombardi was feeding me with the information so I always knew how and when to move the operation but now even he's in the dark because nobody in IAB talks and he don't have access to that information."

"You think they may trace something back to him?" I asked.

"Nah, they won't. But the same way that thought came into your head, I know it is swimming in Lombardi's head and that's why I gotta handle this right away."

I nodded my head in agreement and then stated, "So niggas was scared to purchase from the track because they probably heard that cats had been getting arrested."

"You see what was going down?" Cream rhetorically questioned. "Wait right here, I'll be right back."

Cream got out of the car and headed inside the house that we had been parked in front of. As I sat, I remember thinking how living on the street was really a constant hustle. I had no real idea that things like this would always be popping up and interrupting the operation. I was learning fast how the game worked and how I had to adapt to it. At the same time my mind was always working and always scheming so I was simply trying to piece together all that I had been through and all that I had been learning so I'd know the best moves to make for the future.

Later on I would learn that the house that Cream had gone into was one of about six properties that he either owned or controlled, in addition to his own personal residence. He would house prostitutes, guns, and marijuana in all of his properties. But on this occasion he had gone to the house in Rosedale in order to retrieve two nine-millimeter handguns in preparation for later that evening.

17

CREAM HAD A STABLE OF about seventy girls who sold their bodies for his financial gain. And of course he had his two lieutenants, Shamgod and Spinach. Shamgod and Spinach each had about four people who reported directly to them. For the most part you could say that Cream, Shamgod, Spinach, and the eight underlings made up the management side of the Cream Team. There were a vast number of loosely fitted Cream Team associates who ran the streets of New York but they didn't make up the management team.

Cream's initial plans had called for all of the management personnel and all seventy girls to assemble inside one Queensbridge apartment where he had planned to personally interrogate everybody until he was able to determine the culprit responsible for the undercover cop scheme.

I had spent the entire day with Cream. We had some hours to spare leading up to the nine o'clock meeting time and we spoke about different things. I understood Cream's need to quickly resolve the situation but I also felt that he was reacting way too emotionally about the whole thing and I made sure to tell him why I thought so.

"Cream, I know that you know the game and the streets better than I do, and I don't mean no disrespect but I think you should handle this situation in a different way."

Part of me could tell that Cream was probably growing closer to me and developing feelings for me. The chemistry between the two of us had seemed like it had gelled and intensified over the past month or so. That was why I think Cream was open to my statement.

"Why do you say that?"

"Because I think you're bringing too much emotion into this whole thing. I mean, you don't really need all of them niggas and seventy girls all in one spot just to find out what went down. If you do that it will show that you are not in control and it will send the wrong message. You're the one who told me a while back that when things go down all you had to do is go to Shamgod or Spinach and resolve it. So you still need to do that."

"Yeah, I know, but Lady, this is a different set of circumstances. I gotta resolve this not now, but right now!"

"Cream, if you handle it the way you're saying, the only thing that's gonna happen is you're gonna get an apartment full of people denying everything. If you want the answer all you gotta do is question Shamgod and Spinach." I knew that Cream could sense and see the reasoning behind my logic. Actually it wasn't my logic at all. Everything that I was saying had stemmed from what he had taught me and schooled me on in the past. Cream was the leader and he was in charge and I wasn't trying to overstep that in any way or disrespect his decision-making skills. He was the teacher and I was the student, and there was nothing wrong with the student reminding the teacher about a past lesson that I had learned from him.

We both paused and were quiet. Creamed placed his face in the palms of both hands and slowly dragged his palms down his face. He sat and thought for a moment.

"A'ight, yo, check it, this is how it's gonna go down. I'm gonna order Shamgod and Spinach to murder their four underlings. I'm a tell them straight up to murder their whole crew. And Lady, I can tell you what's gonna happen. Whoever is the most protective and pleads their case as to why they don't wanna murder their crew, then that's how I'll know which one I can trust and I'll know that he ain't have nothing to do with what went down. But if one of them is calm about going through with the process and acting all cool and collected about mercking his crew then I'll know that this whole scheme stemmed from that line in the organization."

"So you think that if you order these hits and if one of them is acting too calm and cool about executing the hit then they had something to do with this scheme?" I asked for reassurance.

"Hell yeah! The one who doesn't wanna go through with it, he'll say that if he murders his boys and they're innocent then that would be like a mother killing her child. No real mother would easily agree to kill her child, especially if the child was innocent. But the one who is trying to protect himself, he would rather take out his boys in order to protect himself. He would be like the fake mother who would agree to kill her kids. See, it doesn't mean that they necessarily devised the scheme themselves, which they may have, but they had to know what was going on. By them allowing it to go on they were snaking me!"

I nodded in agreement and inside my head I was getting excited in a sick kind of way. And that was because I knew that it was more than likely gonna be the end for either Shamgod or Spinach. Not that I would wish death on anybody, but my ambitions didn't mind if Cream took out a whole leg in his organization so that I could slide right into the void that would be left. I'd fill it, and increase my power and rank.

Cream immediately called Shamgod and Spinach and told them to come to the meeting by themselves later on that night. And they proceeded to go along with his wishes.

When nine o'clock rolled around, me and Cream sat in his car. We were on Twelfth Street, right in front of the entrance to the project buildings. There were a number of thugs standing in front of the building and they were making a whole lot of noise. I looked and saw Spinach and Shamgod both walking toward the building at the same time. I quickly rolled down my window and yelled until I got their attention.

They both came over to the car and I think they were both a bit surprised to see me.

"What's up, Lady?" Shamgod stated as he peered into the car.

Cream stayed silent in order to keep a sense of mystery surrounding what was on his mind and what was about to be discussed.

"What up, Cream?"

Cream didn't acknowledge Shamgod or Spinach.

"Get in," I instructed. "We just gonna drive to another location."

Spinach and Shamgod both got in. Spinach was uncharacteristically quiet and Shamgod was uncharacteristically talkative as they sat in the backseat. I mean I had seen Shamgod talk before and he was always loud in a niggerish kind of way but as we drove he just wouldn't quit talking a mile a minute. And from that point on I could sense that he was nervous about something.

Finally Cream shut him up.

"Shamgod, would you shut the hell up, nigga?! Damn!"

Shamgod had no choice but to quiet down as we pulled to the curb on Vernon Boulevard. We were sitting on a fairly desolate, industrial-looking block and we were parked next to an electrical plant. And being that summer was just upon us it was not completely dark even though it was a little after nine at night. As I looked out the window I could see New York City's famous skyline on the other side of the East River.

Cream knew exactly how to play his cards as he reached under his seat and pulled out the two nine-millimeter handguns. He turned to the backseat and handed each man a gun.

"You got new burners?" Spinach asked.

"Nah, these ain't new," Cream replied.

"So what's up?" Spinach asked.

I had turned my body around because I wanted to see each man's facial expression and body language as they spoke.

"Y'all gotta use these in order to take out everybody in your crew," Cream stated in a cold and calm manner.

"Are you serious?" Spinach replied with a half smirk. Shamgod was quiet.

"I'm dead ass! Everybody has gotta go tonight!"

Shamgod was still quiet as hell and his eyes were way too shifty.

"Cream, what's going on, kid?" Spinach asked.

Cream proceeded to explain and he broke down the whole undercover cop scheme that had been brought to his attention. But he played things smart and held back from telling Spinach and Shamgod exactly how he had come to uncover the scheme.

"Now I'm a ask y'all niggas straight up. . . . And I'm asking y'all niggas one time . . . Did y'all know anything about this scheme?"

Shamgod finally spoke up. "Cream, word is bond. I ain't know none of this dirt was going down! If I had known, then you know you would have known and this would have been handled already."

"So that's why all the traffic slowed down on the tracks," Spinach stated as if he had just been hit with enlightened knowledge from God.

Cream raised his voice and stated, "Yo, word to my seed, I was so heated when I found out what was going down, I was ready to just merck the whole team! And this is the thing I'm still trying to understand." Cream's voice dropped another five octaves. "If y'all niggas is out there every night watching what's going on how did this go down for like two weeks and y'all didn't know nothing? Y'all ain't seen nothing and now y'all playing like y'all don't know nothing! Somebody better tell me something, give the god some answers!"

I knew at that point it was time to relax my position and I turned and faced the front of the car. I didn't have to look at body language or any of that anymore. My mind was convinced that Shamgod would have to go. The nigga had to have crossed Cream. The bitch in him was just oozing outta his pores. He had gotten quiet and he just wasn't relaxed. He was sitting forward in his seat and he kept looking out of the window and running his hand over his mouth sort of like he was wiping dried-up spit from the corners of his mouth. It was almost as if he was desperately trying to think of the right thing to say.

"Cream, I just wanna say something, and this is coming from straight love and no disrespect. You right that I should have known what was going down, especially if it was going down on my watch and that is my bad." Spinach handed Cream the gun and he continued on. "But if you need to take somebody out, then take me out right here 'cause I know what I know and what I know is my crew didn't draw up that plan. And I got honor for those niggas. Word is bond, Cream, I would let you take me out before I could snuff out my crew when I know they ain't snakes. And that's real right there! You can put that nine right between my eyes right now and pull the trigger. Word!"

Got damn! I thought to myself. I had to give it up to Spinach 'cause the nigga must've had balls the size of an elephant. He was the essence of what true street niggas were about.

Cream directed his attention toward Shamgod. And the nigga was talking shifty as hell.

He turned from looking out of the window, wiped the corners of his mouth again, and said, "All I'm saying, Cream, is this. I doubt my crew had anything to do with this. I really think it was one of the Detroit hoes that started working for us like two months back. They been causing all kinds of problems since they got here," Shamgod reasoned.

"Shamgod, your crew is getting laid down tonight! Dame, Pete, Ci-Lo and Stretch! You telling me you 'doubt' they had anything to do with this? I can't roll with niggas that have their boss doubting them 'cause that means that I gotta doubt you. And I can't have nobody around me that I can't trust. You are their boss, right? So then you don't need to have doubts, you need to *know* one way or the other!"

Shamgod remained quiet. And I had to just sit and think that Shamgod was one stupid, greedy-ass dude. 'Cause from what I knew and saw, everything had been all love between Shamgod and Cream so the only way that I could understand him turning on Cream was by simply thinking that he just had to be one greedy nigga. And what was so foul was that he was making good money with Cream so there was no need at all for him to have turned on him, but that's what greed will do to a nigga.

"My girls, they gonna catch heat behind this, but somebody gave them handcuffs and badges and all of that. My girls are my money and I ain't taking them out that quick! I wanted to get all of them down here tonight and beat the hell out of all of them but I realized that I had to get at the root of the problem. And your bitch-ass crew, them dispensable niggas are the root of the problem. . . . Shamgod, it's either them niggas or it's you. Tell me what's up?"

Shamgod sighed from the backseat before speaking up.

"Start up the car. Let's go do this," he instructed.

There was no hesitation in Cream's actions. He turned his body and started up the car. He spoke as he pulled from the curb. "Get your crew on the phone and tell them to come to the apartment in Queensbridge. Don't let on like anything is up, just tell them to be here as soon as possible."

We weren't too far from the apartment, in fact we were like right down the block. In no time we had parked the car and were walking in the courtyard of the projects. There was this eerie quietness amongst everyone.

"Yo, Cream, what up, baby pa?" someone riding on a mountain bike shouted out. Cream barely acknowledged him as we made it into the lobby of the building and onto the elevator. After exiting the elevator we walked to an apartment that was located right in front of the incinerator. This had been my first time going to this particular apartment. There was a strong smell of piss that permeated the air and garbage that had missed the incinerator was strewn about on the floor.

Cream made his way into the apartment and we all followed.

"Y'all gotta hurry up and bounce and I need y'all to take a cab tonight," Cream instructed all of the girls who were in the midst of getting dressed and ready to hit the track. He went to every room and stated the same thing to make sure that he emptied the apartment of any potential witnesses.

"Five minutes, ladies! We gotta get this money!" Cream yelled in order to have his voice heard over the stereo that was blasting in the apartment.

That eerie quietness still lingered among Cream, Shamgod, Spinach, and myself. But before long all of the girls were piling out of the house looking sexier than ever. I could already see the benefits of their workouts.

"Y'all looking good, ladies," Cream complimented them as they kissed him on the cheek and made it out of the apartment.

Cream was taking a chance having anyone out on the tracks, considering the police would possibly be stepping things up but he had to clear the apartment.

With the apartment cleared, Cream turned down the music and went into each bedroom and took black pillowcases from four pillows.

He handed two pillowcases to Shamgod and two pillowcases to Spinach.

"When those niggas come into the crib I'll check to see if they got any heat on them. When I'm done, I'll tell them what's up and then I want y'all to put a pillowcase over each one of their heads, and we gonna tighten their asses up! A'ight?"

Spinach replied with spoken words and Shamgod just nodded.

Cream retreated to one of the bedrooms again and this time he came back with a bat and handed it to Shamgod.

"When the pillowcase is over their heads, Shamgod, I want you to take that bat and crush all four of their skulls!"

Ouch! I remember thinking to myself. I was nervous like I had never been before but I didn't want to show it. I began speaking to myself using my real name. *Tina, are sure you wanted to sign up for this lifestyle?*

"Spinach, if any of them try to run or if they flinch or if anything don't look right then I want you to blast them. No questions asked and don't hesitate!"

Spinach nodded.

"Niggas gotta learn this ain't a game!" Cream shouted as he poured himself a drink. Then he calmly asked from the kitchen, "Y'all want some Bacardi?"

I was the only one who wanted any. I couldn't take that eerie silence and I needed the drink in order to ease my nerves.

After Cream had finished giving his orders the music was turned back up and it blared throughout the apartment. That made it hard to hear the loud banging at the door.

"Cream, somebody is at the door!" I yelled over the music.

Cream took a sip from his glass and then rested the drink on the kitchen table.

"Yo, turn the music down," he instructed Spinach.

He then proceeded to make his way to the door. After looking through the peephole Cream unlocked the door and let in the four cats from Shamgod's crew. They were in classic thugged-out attire. Dame, Pete, Ci-Lo, and Stretch had all arrived together.

"What up, kid?" Cream stated to each one of Shamgod's crew members.

From different encounters and from being out on the track I knew all four crew members. I had spent many different occasions talking to each one of them at separate times on nights when the track was slow.

"What's up, baby?" I said as I gave each one of them a kiss on the cheek.

"Lady, I heard you're pushing a Benz? You doing your thing!" one of them gleefully stated.

Little did they know that I had just given them a sort of kiss of death when I'd kissed them on their cheeks.

With both of my hands squeezed into the back pockets of the tight shorts that I had on, I stated with a huge smile, "It's just a C-class Benz but I'm a step it up soon."

"Nah, the C-class is perfect for a woman. That's peace right there, word!" Pete stated.

Cream had had enough of the small talk and I could sense that he wanted to get to the matter at hand. But Spinach sort of spoiled that when he added some more small talk.

"Yo, y'all want some Bacardi?"

They all agreed that they wanted some.

"Wait, Spinach hold up," Cream instructed. "Let's just get this meeting over with first. Let Lady get the drinks and everybody else, let's go to the living room."

I quickly made my way to the kitchen and played fake bartender while I listened real closely to what was going on.

"Yo, do any of y'all got heat on y'all?" Cream asked.

Both Shamgod and Spinach played everything off and said yeah. But only one of Shamgod's crew members, Stretch, had heat and I think he started to sense something was up.

"Yeah, I got heat on me too. Why, what's up?" Stretch asked.

From the kitchen I could see into part of the living room and I saw Cream walk over to Stretch—who by the way stood about six foot six—and he said, "Let me see your burner."

Stretch was a little apprehensive and as he reached for it Cream wanted to relax him and relax the situation. "It's nothing, just let me see the gun. We got a situation that came up and tonight we all gonna go handle it."

Stretch looked a bit relieved as he stood up and took the gun from his waistband. He handed it to Cream and then sat back down.

"This will definitely work," Cream said underneath his breath but loud enough for everyone in the room to hear. He looked over the gun and appeared to be taking off the safety.

"So what's up? We gotta handle some beef or what?" Stretch asked.

Cream was still holding Stretch's gun at his side. Shamgod and Spinach both stood up and made their way next to Cream.

"Yo, go get the pillowcases," Cream instructed.

I was in the kitchen just standing near the refrigerator. I knew what was up and the drinks were ready but I didn't want to walk into the living room with the drinks at that point. First of all I was nervous as hell and didn't want to show that nervousness. And second of all I really thought that drinks were the last thing that Cream wanted to see at that time.

Shamgod and Spinach retrieved the pillowcases and threw a pillowcase to each one of the dudes.

"Fellas, we run a real tight ship. And when I say we, I'm talking about the Cream Team. I don't know what y'all may have ever heard from Shamgod or from Spinach but I'll tell y'all straight from my own mouth. The Cream Team ain't no democracy-type organization! It's a straight-up dictatorship and I'm the dictator! So if niggas don't do things my way then they gotta go! 'Cause when niggas don't listen and when niggas get greedy and all of that, then what happens is the ship starts sinking."

"But I'm sayin' I still don't understand what's up," Dame stated as he moved to the edge of the couch.

Cream raised his own gun. He held the gun on the four members of Shamgod's crew as he stated, "What I want y'all to do is put the pillowcase over your heads."

"For what?" Stretch asked with a whole lot of concern.

Cream had that same boiling-blood look in his eyes that I had seen earlier. My heart was pounding like crazy.

"'For what?!' Nigga, don't question me! Put the pillowcase over your head!" Cream demanded as he cocked the gun.

Stretch definitely knew what was up at that point and he lunged his six-foot-six-inch frame from his seat in an attempt to get at Cream's gun.

Cream quickly fired two shots and dropped the dude dead in his tracks. Stretch fell to the ground. He was moving a little bit but he was groaning in pain. It looked as if he'd been shot in the head and I was very surprised that he was moving at all.

"We got two ways we can do this!" Cream yelled. "Y'all can put the pillowcases over your heads or I can use this gun to smash your brains up against that wall!"

The other three dudes were looking shook like crazy but they were willing to roll the dice and go with the pillowcases over their heads.

"So you wanna be that hard street nigga, right?! You wanna be that nigga with all the heart and all the balls, right?!" Cream questioned Stretch as he still groaned from the gunshot wounds that he had received.

"Cream, why did you shoot me?" Stretch struggled to ask with blood rolling out of his mouth.

Cream did not answer. He simply aimed the gun at the Stretch's earlobe and pulled the trigger.

I sort of jumped from the gun's powerful boom. There was definitely no doubt that Stretch's life had just ended.

Cream motioned to Shamgod. He pointed toward the bedroom and then he swung both of his arms and imitated swinging a baseball bat.

The room was eerily silent. The only thing that you could hear was the sounds of heartbeats thumping in the room.

Cream finally broke the silence after Shamgod had retrieved the baseball bat. "Fellas, I'm gonna make this quick. I cannot and I will not tolerate punk-ass niggas stealing from me!" Cream yelled with a certain cadence that stressed and emphasized each individual word he spoke.

At that point one of the dudes looked as if he was gonna attempt to take the pillowcase off of his head—I think it was Dame but I forget for sure who it was. Cream quickly motioned to Shamgod, and Shamgod swung the bat at the dude's head as if he was swinging at a fastball in Yankee Stadium.

The dude instantly fell to the ground and the black pillowcase immediately began to turn a blackberry color as it filled with blood.

By that time I had made it into full view of the living room. I was just in time to see Shamgod swing the baseball bat a second time. This time there was more of a thud sound but the same conditions followed the thud. The dude fell facedown to the ground and a huge dark wet spot of blood stained the pillowcase.

Cream took the Louisville Slugger and handed it to Spinach. Spinach knew exactly what to do with the bat, as he almost decapitated the last dude with a pillowcase over his head. I just stood there. I really didn't know what to say or what to do. My nervousness had kind of died down but I just didn't know how to react after seeing four people that I knew get murdered right before my eyes.

"Punk ass!" Cream yelled as he whacked each guy in the head one more time with the bat. "Yo, remember the dude whose dick got chopped off? We need to cut these niggas' balls off! Word! We need to put their balls in a jar and show it to all them *so-called niggas with heart* so that they know ain't no niggas as ruthless as my team!" Cream stated as he and Spinach began to laugh.

Shamgod wasn't laughing and I knew for certain that he had been down with the undercover cop scheme.

I had always heard how deadly and brazen the Cream Team could be, but other than what I had partially witnessed when Nikki, Diamond, and the Rasta had gotten *got*, this was my first time seeing murder, firsthand, up close, and personal. Although I knew that there had been other killings, I never asked any questions to try and confirm them 'cause you just don't talk about that unless you snitching or something.

Cream instructed me to go to his car and look in the trunk for some big heavy-duty black plastic garbage bags and to bring the bags back to the apartment. I did as he had instructed and was back in the apartment in less than five minutes.

Each dead and former Cream Team member was stuffed into black garbage bags and they were dragged out of the apartment one by one. If someone had seen the bags they would have assumed they were filled with garbage. Except for Stretch—he was so tall that it was hard to get him to fully fit inside of the industrial-size garbage bag—but with everyone's help, including mine, we were able to get Stretch's body inside the bag. Cream made sure to take each dude's money and car keys before they were placed into the garbage bags. He pocketed the money and I know that later on he had their cars sent to a desolate location and burned beyond recognition.

As for their dead bodies, well Cream had two bodies in his car and Shamgod and Spinach had two bodies in Spinach's car. I have no idea where they took the bodies that night or exactly how they disposed of the bodies. And I made sure that I never asked the question. My job that night, after I had helped stuff Stretch into the garbage bag and after Cream, Shamgod, and Spinach had left to get rid of the bodies, was to clean every speck of blood from the apartment. I had to have it done by the time Cream, Shamgod, and Spinach returned to pick me up.

All kinds of thoughts ran through my mind as I scrubbed fresh warm blood from the floor and the furniture and the living-room wall. I had just witnessed firsthand exactly how and why the Cream Team had gained such a violent, feared, and notorious reputation throughout New York City. More than that, I was in a big way an accomplice to the murders that I had just witnessed. There was no doubt that things were getting real thick for me as I lived the street life. My wish of wanting to roll with and run with the Cream Team had come full circle. I had turned numerous tricks on the street, I had my Mercedes-Benz, I was learning the secrets of the organization, and how the organization ran. I had seen niggas get taken out and I had even seen a cat get his dick chopped off. Now it was time to see how my affiliation with the Cream Team would continue to play itself out.

What move was I gonna make? Was I gonna fold and lay my cards down? Or was I gonna don my poker face, stack more of my chips on the table, and continue on in the game?

18

THE SATURDAY AFTER THE EXECUTIONS had taken place marked the last Saturday in June. In New York, the last Saturday in June always meant that the Jones Beach Greekfest was gonna be taking place. Shauna and I had made plans to go to the Greekfest and I couldn't wait. I had spent Friday night at her apartment so that we could wake up early, head to the beach together, and not miss anything.

"Lady, I know you're gonna wear some kind of wrap with that bikini, right?" Shauna asked as she watched me parade around her apartment in my white bikini top and thong bikini bottom. I also wore white beach sandals in order to show off my pretty pedicure.

With my butt bouncing all over the place I was real quick to respond.

"I work way too hard to maintain this body, and I do it specifically for days like these," I said while I put suntan lotion all over my body. "Plus I got my Benz so I gotta represent for all of the fellas . . . I can't be all covered up!"

"For the fellas?" Shauna asked.

"Girl, you know the only reason we go to these wild events is for some male attention," I responded.

Shauna knew that I was right. She looked at me and smiled. She had finally started to come around and live like she was a good-looking, single, young, black female and not some thirty-something, married-with-children housewife. I couldn't help but thank god that she had broken up with her chump boyfriend. Their breakup, even though I know she would never admit it, was definitely due in large part to me. Her boyfriend literally hated my guts as well as the fact that I had more influence over his girl than he did. Not to mention that my influence wasn't all that positive.

But their breakup was neither here nor there. I could have cared less about that, all I wanted to do was get to the beach, smoke some weed, and get my flirt on with some cuties.

"Shauna, will you hurry up? I wanna run to the car wash before we go and I know the traffic is gonna be crazy on the Meadowbrook Parkway."

Shauna looked cute in her two-piece leopard-print bikini. She wasn't as daring as I was and wouldn't be caught dead in the street with a thong. Even though she wasn't wearing a thong, she still had this matching leopard-print wrap that she wore tied around her to cover up her butt. She also wore some matching leopard-print flip-flops.

"Come on, I'm ready," Shauna stated as she grabbed her bag and her sunglasses.

I grabbed my bag which contained a spare bikini, beach towels, suntan lotion—and of course I had to have my weed, that was a pre-requisite for any event. As we made our way to the elevator and eventually out of the building lobby I could sense all kinds of looks of disgust and hate from the few girls who were standing outside. But at the same time I got crazy love and catcalls from the guys who were chilling in front of the building.

"You driving," I said to Shauna as I handed her my car keys. Shauna had no problem with being behind the wheel, especially since she was gonna be pushing such a nice whip. But in general Shauna had been slowly and unofficially becoming like my personal driver. She practically chauffeured me around to wherever I went.

"You think we should stop off at the liquor store before we get on the parkway?" she asked.

Now that type of talk from Shauna was definitely attributable to my negative influence.

"Nah, we should be cool, I mean we got our weed. . . . And you know that there will be people out there with coolers full of liquor so we should be okay," I stated before directing Shauna into the car wash which was located on Merrick Boulevard in Laurelton, Queens.

The car wash was the automated type where you had to get out and let the car go through the washing process while you watched from an enclosed area.

"I need full service," I stated to the short Mexican worker who had come to our car. "And sweetie, make sure you vacuum the inside real good for me. I also want hot wax and I need Armor All on all of the tires, okay?"

"Yes, yes, yes. I'll take good care of your car for you," the Mexican stated as he handed me my ticket.

As Shauna and I made our way into the enclosed area of the car wash I could sense as well as see that every guy there was staring at us. But I also knew that I was the real center of attention. After all, it wasn't every day that a dude could go to the car wash and see two sexy sistas in bikinis walking around, especially one in a thong with her ass jiggling all over the place.

In fact the entrepreneur in me thought, *Maybe if there was a car wash with sexy sistas in bikinis walking around it would make all kinds of money. . . .*

My thoughts were quickly interrupted. Before I knew what was what I had recognized someone that I knew. Ironically his name was also Kevin Johnson, but he was in no way related to the Kevin "Cream" Johnson that I was living with.

"Say, word! Tina, I know that is not you!" Kevin stated as his mouth flung open and practically dropped to the ground.

I couldn't help but blush. I had known Kevin from back in the days. He and I had lived on the same block when I was about eleven years old. Although I had only lived on his block for a short time, it was the type of block where everybody knew everybody. And Kevin was about seven years older than me, so back then when I was eleven years old he had to have been about eighteen. And to an eleven-year-old, an eighteen-year-old is basically considered a grown old-ass adult. That was just how all of the girls my age viewed Kevin, but at the same time we all had a big crush on him. He had that light skin, wavy hair, pretty-boy look about him. In fact he looked a lot like the old-school singer Christopher Williams.

"I can't believe that is you! How old are you now?"

"I'm sixteen," I softly stated.

"Sixteen!" Kevin screamed. Then he grabbed me by the hand and lifted my hand in the air and slowly twirled me around like he was slow dancing with me and I was his ballerina. I knew that he was just trying to get a good look at my body and I was more than willing to accommodate him.

"Yo, can't nobody tell me that they ain't injecting cows and chickens with steroids! That is the only way in hell you get sixteen-year-old female looking this damn good!"

Me and Shauna both fell out laughing at Kevin's remark, and after we had regained our composure I introduced Shauna to Kevin.

"So let me guess, y'all are heading out to the Greekfest?" Kevin confidently asked.

"Yup," Shauna answered as we paid the cashier and made our way outside to wait for our car.

Weather-wise, that day was a perfect beach day because it was still morning, like ten o'clock or so, and the temperature was already close to ninety degrees.

Kevin commented on how hot it was, and he continued to make small talk before asking me for my number. There was no way that I was gonna give him Cream's home number. Cream definitely would have punk'd him had he ever called the house asking for me. But besides that I didn't really want him having my numbers and having access to me and annoying me so I took his number and told him that I would catch up with him. After years of not having seen him, he was still fine as hell and I figured that if I was ever bored or horny he would make a good booty call, so having his number was more than enough. He didn't need my number.

"That's your Benz?" Kevin asked.

"Yeah," I proudly stated with a huge smile on my grille.

Kevin nodded his head to indicate that he was impressed. Then he got into his car and prepared to drive off. "Tina, you better call me or I'll come find you."

"Okay," I stated.

Shauna looked at me and said, "Girl, you better be careful. I mean he looks good and all but he's got that stalker-won't-leave-a-girl-alone kind of look about him."

We both started laughing. And no sooner had Shauna finished her joke, maybe like ten seconds after, there was another guy in my face trying to kick it to me. Even one of the pipsqueak Mexican guys who were drying my car was trying to flirt with me.

"Now do you see why you should have covered up your ass or put on a pair of shorts over your bikini?" Shauna asked. "You're gonna be getting it all day long."

Shauna's prediction was right on point. However I was glad to see that at the beach she was also getting a whole lot of attention thrown her way. Only with Shauna, she didn't revel and bask in the attention like I did. I mean, I knew that I was a walking fantasy for the majority of the men who were out at the beach enjoying themselves. To me it was a turn-on just knowing that I would undoubtedly be the subject of many masturbation episodes for many of the men on the beach once they made it home and lusted over me in their minds and in the solace and privacy of their own bathrooms or bedrooms.

Life should be about having fun and just living it up, and that is what I'd set out to do that day. So while walking on the beach I had no problem letting guys film me and take pictures with me or palm my booty. The Greekfest was probably my best excuse for dressing like a half-naked rap-video dancer so I had to make the most of my opportunity and that is exactly what I did.

I guess I must have been born with some kind of entrepreneur gene in my body or something because there was only one thing at the beach that distracted me from having an undistracted helluva time. And that one thing was the great idea that had popped into my head. It simply would not leave.

See, I knew that I had flesh just hanging loose from every which way, and that was definitely why I had been getting so much attention.

But Shauna didn't have as much flesh exposed and she too was being shown much love. I thought about that, and I also thought about the fact that most of the guys who had been showing us love were also in some type of expensive car. *Just combine those two elements and you will get paid!* I thought to myself. My eyes were bleeding green dollar signs at the beach all afternoon.

Later on in the evening, after the events at the beach had ended, Shauna and I had to decide which Greekfest after-party we would attend. But when those plans were finalized I simply couldn't hold back my idea from her any longer. I had to spill the beans, it was an idea that I had been walking around with all day long at the beach.

In a little over six months, Shauna had witnessed firsthand my rise from being a streetwalking, blow-job-giving hoochie into a Mercedes Benz–driving madam-type who was making in the neighborhood of a hundred thousand dollars a year. So I knew that even if she wasn't feeling my plan that I was about to lay down to her, she would definitely not doubt the fact that if I put my mind to anything it would more than likely end up being successful.

"Shauna, you know how they say *sex sells?*"

Shauna looked at me with this real ironic look as if to say, "Ya think?" Considering that I was Exhibit A when it came to the reality of sex sells, I immediately saw the humor in Shauna's look and we both began laughing.

"No, but for real, everybody knows that sex sells, but today I realized something. I realized that lust and sex are in the same category. It's the same thing. If you're promoting lust it would be like selling the promise of sex."

Shauna looked at me as if she didn't understand where I was going.

"Lust sells just like sex sells! Think about it," I instructed.

"What do you mean?"

"What I mean is this. You saw all of the attention that I was getting at the car wash today and at the beach. And hell, you got just as much attention and phone numbers as I did. But the thing is this, we got all of that attention based on the way we look and the way we were dressed. For a lot of those guys out there, just looking at us and being next to us or any sexy girl in a bikini, that alone was more than enough for them."

"Okay?" Shauna asked as if to urge me on for more information.

"The trick is to makey money on that lust. And let me ask you this . . . What did just about every guy out there today at the beach and at the car wash have?"

"You're losing me. . . . Lady, would you just get to the point?"

I was trying to get Shauna to think like me—my mind always worked like a hustler—but I guess that is something you just can't teach.

"Okay, see, this is what I was trying to piece together. Every guy at the car wash and a whole bunch of guys at the beach all had nice, expensive cars. Most people hate going to car washes because they are afraid their cars will get scratched up by those automated brushes. What most people are doing now is getting their cars washed at hand car washes."

"I'm following you so far."

I continued on. "Well, see, all I gotta do is get some spots of vacant land and open up hand car washes. And I'd call all of the car washes Honey Bunnies Hand Car Wash. Instead of just having some short and dirty-looking, wetback, illegal-immigrant Mexicans washing the cars, I would get some thick, sexy, good-looking chicks and have them wear thong bikinis. I'll have some of them in short T-shirts with no bra underneath and some tight Daisy Duke shorts on, and I'll let them wash the cars."

While I was talking, Shauna stopped all that she was doing so that she could give me her undivided attention.

I walked in Shauna's direction with my hand out asking for a pound as I said, "Shauna, tell me that you're feeling that idea."

Shauna clasped my hand five, and nodded her head up and down. "Lady, I think you got something with that."

"I know I do! Ain't nobody in New York doing that! Yeah, there are hand car washes around but come on, do you know how sick my car washes will be with the fellas once the word starts to spread?! Whaaat?! . . ."

"Lady, that is a genius idea. How the hell do you be thinking up crap like that?"

"I'm a hustler and that's what you gotta do. All day long I just think of ways to get that paper. It's a perfect fit with everything that I'm doing right now. I mean I got access to girls who will definitely do it. And if I need more girls then all I gotta do is hit the strip clubs and I know that I could recruit some more girls if I needed to."

"Nah, like I said, you definitely got something with that idea. Put me down with that idea, word! It's time for me to step up my game."

I had to admit that Shauna's statement had shocked the hell out of me.

"Really? You would actually be down, Shauna?"

"Well, I'm sayin' you would need somebody to count your dough for you, right?"

We both fell out laughing because Shauna and I both knew that she definitely was not volunteering to wash cars while wearing a thong. But I knew to be real slow before just dishing out jobs right away, especially to Shauna. She was not cut from the same fabric that I was and she needed that take-no-prisoners attitude to roll with me business-wise. I mean she was my girl and all, but for the time being I had to just keep her around as my driver. It was a position that really didn't require a street mentality in order to succeed.

"Oh my God! Oh my God!" I screamed in excitement as I threw my hands up in the air out of pure joy and excitement. I looked as if I was praising the lord or something.

"What? What?" Shauna asked.

"Check this out. I had been wanting to bring this other idea to Cream for a while now. And now would be the perfect time to pitch it to him. See, when I open up the hand car washes, there will be a steady stream of horny guys flowing in to get their cars washed by half-naked girls. So what I could do is keep everything on the low, and have these guys prepay for sex or blow-jobs when they pay for their car wash. And then later on in the day or even right after the car wash they could take their receipt to one of Cream's apartments or houses and get their sex or their blow-job right there! It will be so sick,

Shauna! The car washes could be profitable fronts and funnels for whorehouses!"

"Okay, now that's where you lost me . . ." Shauna stated. She smiled, proceeded to take off her clothes, and headed toward the shower.

"Lady, you would make a killing just going with the sexy hand car wash idea. Don't throw acid on it by mixing in the whorehouse and prostitution."

Shauna finished making her way to the bathroom and she jumped in the shower. I knew that I had to hurry up and figure out what I was gonna wear to the club that night, but my mind was starting to really obsess on my new idea. I wanted to bring my idea to Cream, but I also wanted the idea to be just that, *my idea*. Cream had made enough money off of me as it was. I wouldn't mind hitting him off with like 20 percent of the profits, but at the same time it was gonna be my hustle and I wanted to reap the financial rewards. Yeah, I definitely needed the Cream Team's muscle and reputation behind me but not at no ridiculous price.

My plan was to do everything right. Monday morning I was gonna scout out possible locations for my hand car washes and then head straight to a real estate agent. They could contact the owners of the land and devise some kind of rental agreement with me. I also wanted to speak to a lawyer and discuss the legal aspects of my plan so that no one, not even the cops, could try and shut me down. After all of that was done, I would bring the idea to Cream. I was sure that he was gonna bite.

19

TWO WEEKS HAD PASSED SINCE the Greekfest and during that time I had been working like a madwoman. I had made contact with a lawyer I'd found simply flipping through the yellow pages. Fate must have been on my side because the lawyer was willing to bend over backward to help me with what I wanted to do. I was completely honest with him in terms of telling him everything that I wanted to do. I explained to him how I wanted to open the hand car washes and have girls in bikinis washing the cars. The only detail I had left out was the fact that while the car washes would be legitimate and making a lot of money, they were also gonna serve as a front to help further the Cream Team's prostitution efforts.

Deep down inside I knew that the white middle-aged lawyer had been very accommodating because he probably liked the idea of a young, sexy black girl as his client, and I'm sure that he didn't represent many people who looked like me. I would have bet anything that he took me on as a client in hopes of one day getting in my pants. And who knew what the future held, if faced with the right circumstances I might have been willing to give the old Jewish fart the thrill of his limp-dick life. Whatever his reasons for helping me, he did a great job as my lawyer and he was worth every penny that I paid him.

He explained to me the benefits of starting a corporation and opening the hand car washes under the corporation's name. This way if someone tried to sue me or anything like that then under most circumstances they would not be able to touch me personally. Mr. Kellman, my lawyer, rushed my paperwork to the state so that my corporation was set up within twenty-four hours. Golden Lady Inc. was the name that I had chosen for my corporation. I just loved the sound of it. I wanted that name and I wanted everything that I touched to turn to gold.

My lawyer also filed all of the necessary permits that I would need in order to comply with the local laws of New York City. In addition, he helped me to open up a corporate bank account, which was the first bank account I ever had in my life.

Mr. Kellman did a very good job of explaining everything to me in regular terms. Since I was bright and usually caught on quickly to things, I found the whole process much easier than I'd thought it would be. But the best thing that Mr. Kellman did was contacting a real estate broker on my behalf who managed to get me three nice high-traffic vacant lot locations in Queens, Brooklyn, and the Bronx. That process also had been much easier than I'd imagined. But I learned that vacant land was pretty much a money-losing situation for most landowners simply because the land by itself did not bring them any monthly rent or revenue. So when they were approached with my proposition, all of the landowners jumped at the idea. To them it was a no-brain situation in that their land would stay intact and they would start to earn five hundred dollars in rent on property that wasn't currently making anything.

I knew that I had put the cart before the horse in that I had not cleared anything with Cream. Not that I truly had to clear it with him but just on GP I knew that it would have been best. I had not even brought the subject up but I had good reason. I kept my mouth shut due to a new hiccup that had arisen. See, like I had learned, just about any and every street hustle always has with it one hiccup after another. Either the cops were breathing down your back for something, or someone was stealing from you, or someone would be beefing with you and trying to get at you in some way, shape, or form. Bottom line is that something negative was always popping up.

As soon as the whole fake undercover cop thing had died down and business started to pick back up, a major negative emerged. And like I just mentioned, it was that new hiccup that caused me to hold back from telling Cream about my new venture.

Actually the hiccup was more of a burp.

What had happened was this. The girl Mercedes, who I used to refer to as ghetto-Goya-trash, and whose ass I'd kicked in Cream's basement, well she disappeared from the track one night. She had been working the track in Brooklyn on Pennsylvania Avenue, which also happens to be the same track that I worked on my first night ever walking the streets.

Mercedes had not been working alone, she had been working alongside many of the other girls. But the thing was, when everybody was done working for the night and started to leave the block, Mercedes's best friend, who also walks the streets, noticed that Mercedes was missing and she reported it to Shamgod. Shamgod had called Mercedes's cell phone numerous times. He kept getting voice mail and no one knew what to think.

Needless to say, Cream was not too happy when he found out that Mercedes had suddenly disappeared. But see, everyone knew that Mercedes was very crafty and her craftiness spilled over and gave her all kinds of street smarts. So with her street smarts, Cream was not really too concerned about her safety, he was more concerned with keeping tabs on her whereabouts, as he was with all of his girls.

Aside from the numerous beatings and tongue lashings that many of the girls received from Cream and the other male team members, I will never understand just how Cream was able to yield so much cult leader–type control over the ladies that he had recruited. I don't know what it was. I guess he was a master at knowing when to be an abusive tyrant and when to be a caring and concerned father figure. It was really hard to label Cream a gorilla pimp because in all actuality he wasn't a gorilla pimp. Like when the whole fake undercover cop scheme went down, he had verbally voiced his displeasure to the girls but he showed a bunch of restraint in the process. Yet at times when the girls didn't hustle enough and bring in the right amount of money they would get the crap beat out of them. It was a real interesting and unique dynamic to witness and be a part of. Fortunately for me, I had a gift of always knowing the right buttons to push with Cream and I found myself always being in his favor.

But anyway, back to Mercedes. See, Cream needed that control over Mercedes and all of his other girls because the last thing he wanted was one of them disappearing and then reaching out to the police or family members for help. That would have basically crippled Cream's prostitution ring. It also could have possibly brought on the attention of the feds since what Cream and his team were really doing was kidnapping women and bringing them across state lines—a serious federal offense.

Cream didn't show it, but I could sense that ever since Mercedes went missing he was on edge and a bit worried.

"Yo, what's up, Lady, it's me," Cream stated through the phone.

I chuckled a bit as I said, "I know your voice. This is only like the third time in two hours that you're calling me."

Cream didn't even respond to my comment as he asked, "Yo, any word on Mercedes?"

"Nah, I still ain't heard from her," I replied.

"Got damn! I don't know, Lady. It don't sound good."

"What's up with Shamgod? He hear anything?"

"Hell no and that nigga keep talking like she probably just went shopping or something. And I'm asking the nigga how the hell does he know that and he got his got damn finger up his ass talking about *I'm sayin' where else is she gonna be, Cream?*' Lady, I swear to god I ain't even calling that stupid nigga no more, 'cause I might have to kill his ass. But yo, I gotta go. Listen, call Shamgod and the rest of them in about an hour and see if they heard anything and then call me back. A'ight?"

"Okay," I replied as I hung up.

But his worries only lasted a day because during the twenty-four hours that Mercedes was missing, a female resident in the Brooklyn co-op housing community known as Starrett City made a gruesome discovery on her way to work. She found the body of Mercedes, half naked, bruised, and with a slit throat.

When word spread about Mercedes's murder it sort of sent shock waves and panic throughout all of the girls.

Cream had called a meeting at his crib and gathered everybody together. There was so much weed being passed around and smoked that even if you weren't smoking a blunt you would have gotten high from secondhand smoke. As everybody sat around sad faced and reminiscing on the funny things that Mercedes had done and the good times they had shared with her, Cream spoke up and took control.

"Yo, anybody else got one last story about Mercedes?" he asked.

This black girl name Octavia spoke up, "Yeah, Mercedes was just so damn cool and we always spoke about what we wanted out of life. But I noticed that she had gotten real negative on life lately. It was like she had given up on herself or something. I know that she had given up on seeing her family again. And maybe that's what got her down, I don't know. But I do know that she got tired of this hustle, Cream. And you know what? She stayed in it and this hustle took her life. And I'm not trying to have this hustle take my life. I'm tired of walking these damn streets for you, Cream!"

At that point the room got deathly silent. Cream didn't look at Octavia. He simply pulled real hard on the blunt that he was smoking, and paused for about five seconds before blowing smoke back out of his lungs. Then he got up walked over to Octavia and literally slapped the taste out of her mouth.

Octavia let out a yell as she went flying to the floor.

"Don't you be spreading no lies!" Cream yelled as he kicked Octavia in the mouth. He then picked her up by the throat and held her up in midair for everybody to see. "Y'all se this hoe? Y'all see this ungrateful, sloppy-ass hoe?"

Octavia was gasping for air as everybody looked on horrified, not knowing whether or not Octavia would soon suffer the same fate as Mercedes. It was something about choking the girls that seemed to get Cream high. He would literally choke girls who got out of line until their eyes bulged out of their heads.

"I feed your ass! I clothe your ass! I let you stay in my house! What are you tired of? Your ass couldn't even give that pussy away if you wanted to!" he said as he finally dropped her to the ground. He spit on her as she rolled up like dirty laundry and gasped for air.

"Anybody else tired of walking the streets? Anybody else tired of me taking care of them?" Cream asked in sadistic tone.

"Speak now if you are!" Cream commanded as no one dared to say a word.

Then he continued on, "Shamgod, get Octavia's ugly ass up outta my face before I kill that hoe!"

Shamgod quickly scooped Octavia up off the floor and took her upstairs.

"I can't believe that here we are trying to have a memorial for Mercedes and Octavia is trying to steal the girl's shine! That gotta be the most selfish thing I ever seen in my life! I'm sorry y'all had to see how selfish she is," Cream said. He knew that he had just enacted his own form of damage control through fear and punishment. Cream was either real sick or real brilliant or a damn psychopath because he followed up that fit of rage with a calm tone. It was almost like he was a skilled actor.

He quickly changed his demeanor and addressed the girls. Not once did he mention making sure that Mercedes's family would have a funeral for her.

"Look everybody, what happened to Mercedes shouldn't have happened and I can guarantee y'all that it won't ever happen again. I mean, to be real, any of us could get killed in a car accident tomorrow, we just never know. Matter of fact that is more likely to happen to y'all than what happened to Mercedes. We about to end this little gathering, and I want y'all to be happy and be cool and know that everything is gonna be a'ight. I got y'all and I got this," Cream stated. No one looked at him and no one dared to say a word.

"Would y'all stop looking so down? If Mercedes was here y'all know that she would want y'all to ride for her. She would want y'all to ride for her and representing like y'all do every night. And that is exactly what we gonna do," Cream added as he stood near the bar. One by one he began pouring rum and Coke for each of the girls.

To me, on the inside, mentally and emotionally I was somewhat shaken up. After all, Mercedes's dead body could have very well been my dead body. Mercedes and I had never seen eye to eye and we were constantly at each other's throats. But at the same time I felt like the two of us had bonded simply because we both were hustling in the sex trade. Unless someone actually lives that life they will never know what it feels like emotionally to be a streetwalker. I know that Mercedes had felt many of the same emotions that I often felt. Even if she and I never talked about those emotions, they were the same feelings that I always keep bottled up inside of me. I know in my heart that she and I shared that emotional bond.

Yeah, she and I had been enemies, but all of that petty nonsense went out the window when I found out that she had been murdered. However, the thing that ate me up the most was that Cream commanded that no one dare step forward and go to the authorities to identify Mercedes's dead body. Cream was so bent on protecting his illegal empire and protecting himself that he allowed Mercedes's body to be turned over to the city and classified as a Jane Doe.

She had literally sold her body for Cream and the team, and I was sure that she had died a terrifying death and now her death was destined to be a lonely one. Not even her relatives knew her condition or her whereabouts. That ate at me. Man, did that eat at me! I knew that Mercedes's unidentified body would more than likely be buried in Potter's Field. Potter's Field is a burial ground for the poor, the homeless, and the unidentified. It's not the type of place where you would want your remains to rest when you say good-bye to the world. To me it was like Cream was spitting on her grave and saying, "She was nothing but a Puerto Rican whore!" It was a tough thing but unfortunately I knew that it just came with the territory.

"Two times! That's two times that Shamgod screwed up!" I remember Cream telling me after the makeshift memorial service for Mercedes was over and everyone had dispersed.

"Lady, he almost let you get killed and now on his watch Mercedes ends up dead! I can't deal with that nigga! Word is bond! See, this is exactly what I was talking about when I said that the cat who tried to get at you that time should have been killed. Shamgod must be thinking this is a got damn game or something! And now look! I bet you the Spanish dude whose dick got chopped off, he's the one who killed Mercedes. I can guarantee you that the nigga's dick was probably sewn back on and he just healed up and got at her for revenge. I guarantee you he was the cat who did this!"

"Cream, we don't know that for sure. For all we know it could have been some random thing and Mercedes just happened to get caught out there," I reasoned.

"Nah, it wasn't no random thing. All I know is that Shamgod's crew was behind that whole fake undercover cop scheme, and I know Shamgod knew about it. Shamgod didn't handle the situation right with you and the guy that tried to get at you . . . Now Mercedes gets killed on his watch? Lady, it's time for his ass to get up outta here! I can't trust having that nigga around me."

I remained silent.

"The next thing that'll happen is that his ass will start singing to the cops about something. That nigga is a liability and he gotta go!"

In a way I kind of understood where Cream was coming from. But I was getting to the point where everything had just started becoming overbearing for me. I was questioning and asking myself if it was really all worth it.

So while all that had been going on it was easy to see why I had never actually brought up the whole Honey Bunnies Hand Car Wash idea. But I knew that I had to bring it up and I had to implement it very quickly. Every time I turned around I was getting tossed in a different direction and I just couldn't take it. And it seemed like all of those new directions had something to do with murder and death.

During the days immediately following Mercedes's death, Cream had approached me with something that would forever change my life. As I lay next to him in his bed, after he and I had finished sexing, he talked to me about a whole lot of things. The lights were off and the room was dark and Cream sat up in the bed.

"Lady, reach over and turn on the light for me?" Cream asked.

I did as he had asked.

"You know I trust you, right?"

I looked at him and nodded my head.

"Lady, I wanna tell you something. I'm getting to the point where I can't really trust nobody that's close to me."

"Why do you say that?"

"It's just how I feel. But yo, I've been thinking a lot about something. Remember how I told you that it's time for Shamgod to go?"

Wondering where this conversation was going, I simply nodded my head.

"Well, it's like I can't lean on Spinach and ask him to do that for me. I mean they're too close. I can't take the risk that Spinach would tip Shamgod off to what's going on."

"So what exactly are you saying?" I asked.

"What I'm saying is this. I need you to help me set this nigga up."

"Who, Shamgod?"

"Yeah."

In my mind I didn't really know where Cream was going but I just went with the flow.

"So, tell me exactly what you wanna do. . . ."

Cream paused for a moment.

"We gonna set the nigga up, but I need you to kill the nigga for me."

What?! I remember thinking to myself. I knew that Cream would never speak words like that unless he meant it, but I couldn't understand why he wanted *me* to actually kill Shamgod.

"Cream, I ain't gonna front. I don't know if something like that is over my head or not."

Cream remained quiet. I know that he purposely remained quiet so that I could feel uncomfortable with my thoughts. But I played the same game that he played and I didn't open my mouth.

After a few uncomfortable moments of silence Cream finally broke and said, "Lady, trust me. It's not over your head. What we gonna do is, I'll pick you up in my Jeep and the two of us will be riding in the front seat. We'll ride and get Spinach and let him get in the backseat. When all of us are in the car Spinach won't even know what's gonna go down. Then we'll go get Shamgod, we could make it like we're all going out to a club or something. But when we pull up to get Shamgod, what I want you to do is get out and tell Shamgod that he can sit in the front seat and then you go in the backseat. Just make up some flimsy excuse like you need more room in the backseat to adjust your clothes or something."

While I was sitting there listening to Cream, I came to the realization that Cream's murderous plot was not really up for negotiation. Cream had already thought the whole thing through and as far as he was concerned I was gonna be his hit woman. I also knew that the only choice I had was to go through with it. If I were to front and not go through with it then Cream would never trust me again.

As I sat and thought to myself, I looked at it this way: Cream knew that he had told me way too many details about his and the team's inner secrets. He had told me about Detective Lombardi. I knew that the girls were basically being kidnapped from other states, and even though they were not forcibly kidnapped, in essence they were still being kidnapped. I was starting to learn a very small amount about his marijuana hustle but not that much. I knew where he stashed his guns, and I also had witnessed him, Shamgod, and Spinach murder four of their peoples in cold blood.

Yeah, with all that I had been exposed to since I started rolling with Cream, I was capable of taking Cream down if the cops or the feds were ever to press me. Cream knew that, and it was one of the reasons that he wanted me to be the one to take Shamgod out. He wanted to have something on me that he could use to balance the scales.

Cream continued on. "So when you get in the backseat and Shamgod gets in the front seat, what I'll do is drive off and start talking and playing things cool and normal. Then what I'll do is start playing a mixed tape and when I turn the music up really loud that will be your cue. Just go in your bag, take out the gun that I'll give you, and don't even hesitate. Just bust the nigga in the back of his head! . . . Boom! Blow that nigga's brains out!"

I just sat there and nodded my head. I thought to myself, *This dude is really one sick psycho dude!* And like most psychopaths, Cream had never shown that side of himself to me before. It's like it was laying dormant inside of him or something.

Cream looked at me for some type of confirmation. So as I thought about what a psychopath Cream was, I simply smiled as I nodded my head up and down. I didn't wanna give him any indication that I was not up to doing the cold-blooded murder. Unfortunately, the truth of the matter was that I was in way too deep. If I didn't go along with it I knew that it would be just a matter of days before Cream would be having the exact same conversation with someone else about killing me.

I sighed and exhaled very deeply. I then reached over and kissed Cream on the lips as I cradled the back of his head.

"I can do it, baby," I softly said.

I know that Cream was ecstatic inside but he didn't show it. He simply replied, "I know that you got it in you, it'll be a'ight."

"But Cream, the only thing is I'll be sitting right next to Spinach. You don't think he'll flip?"

"I thought about that, but on the real, it'll happen so quick that he won't know what the hell is going on. And by the time he does figure out what's going on, we'll be able to calm him down. It won't be until that point that we'll tell him what was up."

"Okay," I replied.

I wanted to come across in the realest way possible but at the same time I didn't want to appear scared. I just had to get out those thoughts that I knew would be in my head. I simply thought out loud so that Cream could hear me, and at the same time I wanted to be lending credibility to my ability to pull off the crime.

"Cream, that time that I saw the Spanish cat reaching for his machete, and I thought I was in danger, I would have had no problem killing that dude because it would have been more like self-defense or a reflex kind of action. But the thing with Shamgod is that this will be the first time in just straight-up cold blood I'll be taking a nigga out. I just gotta keep constantly talking that through in my head," I told him.

"Yeah, I know what you mean. But you know what? What you gotta do is see yourself pulling the trigger. Keep replaying that over and over in your head. Because whatever your mind accepts as real, your body will have no problem in actually carrying out. But if your mind doesn't even accept it is as real, then you won't ever be able to do it."

When Cream said those words, I looked at him and for a brief moment I almost gasped with fear. Almost word for word, Cream had stated one of the philosophies that I use to guide me. It gets me through many tough things that I need to overcome in order to accomplish a goal that I'm after.

"Yeah, Cream, you right about that. That's similar to something that I always tell myself. 'As long as my subconscious mind is convinced of something and can accept something as being real, then it naturally and much easier will come to fruition.'"

Before going to sleep that night, Cream and I ended up sexing one more time. I know I wasn't wifey or anything like that in Cream's life, nor did I want to be locked down in a committed relationship like that at my age. But what was weird is that I was laying down next to a cold-blooded, psychopathic killer, a pimp, drug dealer, hustler, and manipulator, yet despite all of those negative attributes Cream and I were able to connect in a huge way. The bottom line was I could not and I was not gonna knock Cream's hustle. And how could I? After all, he helped me feel complete and he helped me feel good about myself and that was the one quality that I adored about him. Not to mention the fact that he looked good and he knew how to lay it down in the bed.

I was responsible for my own choices and my own actions and I was my own person. At the same time I felt this sense of loyalty and devotion to Cream that I just couldn't explain. Now it had come to the point where I was willing to kill for him. If there was such a thing as the devil, Cream was it, yet I knew that I was willing to sell my soul to him and be one of his demons.

Yeah, after turning out the lights for good that night, I laid there in the dark next to Cream and started the process of mentally accepting and seeing myself pulling the trigger and murdering Shamgod. I didn't get much sleep that night as I wondered if my life would get any crazier. I also wondered how I had gotten so deep in the mud. There was no retreating at that point. I had to go on even if my good side was telling me to bail the hell out for my life's sake.

20

ON A SUNDAY NIGHT IN July of 1995, Cream and I got dressed in his house in Astoria and then we jumped in his Jeep and headed to pick up Spinach. I was dressed like a diva in order to disguise the hit that we had planned. We had simply told both Spinach and Shamgod that we would all be going to a club in Manhattan to party.

As Cream drove, I sat in the passenger seat. I also had a .45-caliber handgun in my Louis Vuitton handbag.

"You ready to do this?" Cream asked.

I didn't even look at him. I just nodded my head up and down a few times.

"Remember, when Spinach gets in the car just play everything cool."

I didn't respond because I already knew all of what Cream was telling me.

We reached Spinach's block, and let the Jeep sit idle in front of his crib while Cream called him on the cell phone and told him that we were ready.

Spinach reached the car and hopped in the backseat. "What's up, Lady?" he asked while reaching forward and giving me a kiss on the cheek. "Cream, what up, fam?" he stated as he reached forward and gave him a pound.

Cream adjusted the radio station and just at that moment, DJ Funkmaster Flex's voice came on. He was promoting a party where he would be deejaying on that particular night at a club in Manhattan.

"Yo, that's where we're going," I turned and told Spinach.

Spinach just quietly nodded his head to the music that had followed Funkmaster Flex's promotional message.

It was quiet for a moment and then Spinach asked, "Cream, you got a burner?"

I was wondering why he had asked that question but I didn't sweat it too much.

"Yeah, it's inside the door paneling. . . . Why?"

"I ain't bring no heat, so just in case something jumps off at the club I wanna know what's what."

It was good to know that Spinach was not strapped 'cause it eliminated the chances of him reacting the wrong way to the hit that was about to go down.

Spinach didn't live too far from Shamgod so before I knew it we were rolling up to his crib.

"Yo, Shamgod, we outside," Cream spoke into his cell phone.

After about five minutes Shamgod appeared. My heart had been racing and thumping from the moment Spinach had gotten into the car and when I saw Shamgod my heart rate really began to increase. I calmly blew out a little bit of air from my lungs. I knew that I couldn't front on the hit that I had to do. For some reason when I had gone over the plot again and again in my head I had never been able to predict and prepare for how nervous I would be.

Shamgod was just about at the car when I opened my door and got out.

"Hey, baby," I stated as I reached for Shamgod's hand. After making contact with his hand I stood on my tippy toes in order to give him a kiss on the cheek.

"Got damn, Lady! Why are your hands so cold and clammy?" Shamgod asked.

I immediately got even more nervous. I wanted to crawl underneath the car because I knew that Shamgod had to know what was about to go down.

Thinking quick on my feet, I replied, "Oh, it's just from the air-conditioning, that's all."

Shamgod laughed and said, "You looking like a diva and all that, you can't be walking around with no clammy hands."

Cream quickly grew impatient. He blew the horn and yelled at the same time for us to both get in the car.

"Shamgod, you can sit in the front so that your legs won't be all cramped up."

"Nah, I'll be a'ight," Shamgod said as he reached toward the rear passenger door.

My heart dropped to my feet and I knew that I had to act quickly.

"Shamgod, just let me sit in the back and you sit in the front. I got this thong on and it's cutting the crack of my ass. I need to take this bad boy off right now!"

Shamgod and I both laughed. His laugh was a genuine one while my laugh was a nervous one. But thankfully he complied with my wishes and he sat in the front passenger seat.

Whew! I was thinking in my head as I got in the backseat. I was definitely not built to be a hit woman. *Maybe Shamgod wanted to sit in the back so that he could kill me. . . . Was Cream tricking me and was this whole plot really designed to take me out?* I was starting to bug out and I wanted to jump out of the car and just bounce.

Shamgod said what's up to everybody and we drove off. There was this eerie feeling in the car as we drove and no one spoke. I was feeling light-headed and then I felt a huge head rush. It was sort of like if you ever stood upside-down on your head and then when you stand up straight you sort of get a flush-like head rush. That was exactly what I was feeling.

Finally Shamgod broke the silence and he started talking about some wild street brawl that had broken out in Green Acres Shopping Mall the other day. Shamgod was known for always overdramatizing things when he spoke. It got to the point where it was a bit annoying.

You would always want to scream at the nigga, "Enough already! Got damn!"

So as he spoke Cream just rudely interrupted him and changed the subject, "Yo, y'all gotta hear this ill freestyle by this kid from Southside on this DJ Clue mixed tape. It's some cat named 50 Cent. Yo this nigga is real. Word is bond!" At that point in time, 50 Cent was an unsigned nobody who rhymed in Jam Master Jay's makeshift basement recording studio but you could tell that he had the skills to compete and that he was gonna eventually blow.

I just could not understand how cold-blooded Cream could be. The nigga was talking about music just as normal as anything, all the while knowing that a hit was about to go down.

As Cream turned up the music I almost forgot that that was my cue. *Now or never,* I said to myself. I slipped my hand into my bag and my sweaty palms gripped the handgun. I remember looking out of the car window and looking at all of the streetlights and traffic lights. There were cars all around us as we drove and navigated through the dark streets.

As Shamgod listened to 50 Cent spit his rhymes he became his usual overanimated self and began excitedly proclaiming, "Yo, this nigga can spit! Word!"

Shamgod was about to say something else, and I knew that I had to just do it. *Come on, Lady!* I urged myself. I waited no more and quickly pulled the gun and placed it just to the side of Shamgod's headrest and fired. Even with the loud music, the sound was deafening! My ears were ringing from the powerful blast and I was sure that Cream and Spinach both had ringing in their ears . . . I had just caught my first body.

Shamgod's nonstop yapping had been immediately silenced by the powerful blast from the .45 and his brains were literally all over the dashboard and the windshield. His body sat quiet and slumped over.

Spinach immediately took notice as he sat up and yelled, "Yo! Lady, what . . ."

Cream immediately turned the radio down and yelled to Spinach, "Spinach just be cool, we got this! It's okay!"

I didn't wait for Cream to finish speaking. I couldn't take a chance that Shamgod was still alive and breathing, even though I doubted it. So I kept firing. My adrenaline had kicked in and I fired about three more shots, all of which either entered the back of Shamgod's head or entered his back. I was certain that I had caused either myself, Cream, or Spinach to go deaf from the powerful and loud gun blasts.

"Lady! That's enough! That's enough! The nigga is dead!" Cream hollered.

My heart was still racing and my breathing was beyond visible as my chest rose up and down in order to inhale and exhale.

"Somebody gotta tell me what the hell just went down!" Spinach screamed. "My man just got blasted and I'm sitting here with no heat. . . . Tell me something!" Spinach looked as if he was ready to open his door and just bail out despite the fact that the car was travel-ing at about fifty miles per hour. I can't say that I would have blamed him if he had. He must have thought he was next.

I put the gun back into my bag in order to give Spinach a little peace of mind. I reached over and grabbed his arm and told him to just relax and that we would explain everything to him.

"Cream, you knew about this?!" Spinach asked, still in shock.

"Spinach, just calm down, nigga! I'll let you know what's going on but just chill and be cool!"

Spinach turned and gave me a look of disgust and mistrust mixed with fear and uncertainty. In a way I respected Spinach a lot more than I respected Cream. Spinach was a real loyal-ass street nigga and if he rolled with you he wasn't gonna snake you. I had quickly learned that with Cream, he was only about the dollars and he would take anyone and everyone out if it meant protecting his own interests. The streets needed more cats like Spinach, who would go to jail and do twenty-five years in the pen before he would snake or rat out his man.

"Spinach, we had to take that nigga out, he was getting way too sloppy!"

Spinach had the most perfect, honest comeback for Cream. "But Cream, what I'm saying is this. I'm supposed to be your nigga, right? . . . Matter of fact, let me ask you, and tell me straight up, am I getting sloppy? Am I still your right-hand man or what?!"

I could tell Cream was uncomfortable with the way Spinach was talking but he surprisingly came across very diplomatically.

"Spinach, you know you my man for life. I would die for you. Word! I mean, you my son's godfather and all of that."

I was thinking to myself, *Cream, you know good and well that you wouldn't hesitate to take Spinach out if it came down to it.*

"Where the hell is the trust at, Cream?! You ain't tell me this was gonna go down! What, did you think I was gonna cross you and let Shamgod know what was gonna go down?"

"Spinach, it's over! The nigga is dead and me and you are cool! Let's leave it at that. We gotta get rid of this body."

Spinach kept pushing the issue and I can't say that I blamed him.

"Cream, you ain't being straight up with me! Just tell me why the hell didn't you let me know what was gonna go down! Lady, no disrespect, but you chose her to be the shooter? You let her in on this and you ain't even run it by me? Do I need a pussy between my legs or what?"

Spinach was now definitely pushing it and getting real close to overstepping his bounds. For people like Cream—or any domineering bully—the worst thing when someone flips the script and then kind of bullies them by not backing down. That's the way you get respect from cats like Cream. It may cost you your life, but it will grant you respect.

"A'ight listen . . . Spinach, I didn't tell you because I thought you would try to talk me out of it and I didn't need that."

Good answer, Cream, I thought to myself. *It was a lie, but it was a good answer.*

"Dog, just know this. Whatever you say, I'm a respect it and be down with it and I've proved myself with you for long enough. Just trust a nigga, word!"

Cream finally relented, "Spinach, you right. You're absolutely right. With all of the things that were going down, I just wasn't thinking straight. My head was spinning and I was buggin'. But let's just get rid of this body and go back to the crib where we can talk. I got a whole strategy mapped out and that's what we need to focus on."

Spinach didn't respond. I think he was a tiny bit pleased that Cream had admitted he was wrong. But once trust is broken it's real hard to get it back. I knew that from that point on Spinach would forever be second-guessing Cream's actions. He'd be looking over his shoulder and fearing for his life. No trust is a true recipe for disaster in any relationship. Only time would tell how things would play out with Cream and Spinach.

While all the talk was going on in the Jeep, Cream had managed to maneuver the car near the Pennsylvania Avenue exit on the Belt Parkway. He didn't exit the parkway however. He pulled to the shoulder of the road and then turned off the lights. Then he proceeded to drive into a bushy area full of weeds that resembled stalks of hay. Those hay-looking weeds stood about six feet tall and they grew in a somewhat swampy area.

As Cream drove into the tall weeds the whole car eventually became enveloped in brush and we couldn't see anything around us. It was dark outside, but even if it were daytime I seriously doubt that we would have been able to see what was around us. There were just way too many weeds. We definitely were no longer visible to the cars that were zipping by on the parkway.

"A'ight, come on y'all, let's get out," Cream ordered. "Lady, you get in the driver's seat and me and Spinach will drag the body a little bit further into the weeds. If you sense that anyone is coming I want you to blow the horn and wait for us to get back to the car. Be ready to floor this Jeep and get the hell out of Dodge!"

"Okay," I replied as we all opened our respective doors and exited the car on the warm, humid, and sticky night.

Oh my god, this is so disgusting! I said to myself as I stepped into the wet and swampy soil. I had just killed a nigga in cold blood but at that moment my mind was focused on my feet. I had on some open-toed high-heeled shoes and the wet dirt was oozing all up on my feet and in between the cracks of my toes. Each time I took a step into the wet swampy land my feet would sink a little bit as if they were in quicksand. All I could feel was the disgusting, wet, swampy, muddy dirt all on my feet. There were also mosquitoes flying around everywhere.

Needless to say I hurried up and made my way to the driver's door and got in. Cream was the one who pulled Shamgod's lifeless body out of the car and dumped it onto the ground. I could tell that Shamgod must have died instantly because other than the blood and brains that were on the windshield and dashboard, relatively speaking there were not huge amounts of blood inside the Jeep. Shamgod was a pretty big guy so Cream and Spinach each grabbed one of his arms and dragged him about fifty yards or so further into the weeds. Then the two of them quickly came back. They instructed me to keep the lights turned off, face the car in the other direction, and head back onto the parkway.

I did as I was told and we eventually maneuvered our way back to Cream's house in Astoria. The three of us went to work cleaning up the pieces of flesh, blood, and brains from the leather interior of Cream's Jeep. After we cleaned the car we took our clothes, placed them in a plastic bag, and put it out with the garbage.

Cream spoke privately to Spinach as I took a shower. I kept replaying in my mind the moment I had pulled the trigger. I could still see the huge spark from the gun as well as Shamgod's head literally being blown wide open. I tried to block those thoughts out but it was hard. Thinking about the disgusting mosquitoes that had bitten me and the disgusting, swampy, dirty water that had surrounded my feet was a way to keep my mind off of the successful hit that I had just pulled off.

How far are you willing to go and what else are you willing to do? I asked myself. And for a moment I had to ask just what exactly it was that I was chasing after and pursuing. I was wondering if it was time for me to bounce from the Cream Team and use my entrepreneurial gifts all on my own. I wanted to and I contemplated it, but I was too damn loyal for that. Still, I knew that somehow I had to map out a plan for myself.

As I dried off my body, I realized that I had come a long way. I had lived enough for ten lifetimes in the days since I'd worked at the donut shop. Never in my wildest dreams did I think I would murder a nigga, help dump the body, clean up the evidence, take a shower, and then literally head to a club the same night and party as if everything was all good.

But that was exactly what happened. Cream, Spinach, and myself found ourselves at a Manhattan club in the V.I.P. section, drinking champagne, dancing, living it up, and mapping out plans to get that future paper.

21

I FINALLY HAD THE PERFECT opportunity to kick my hand car wash idea to Cream. He immediately felt the idea and gave me his blessing to go ahead and do it. I was shocked that he had gone along with the percentages that I had proposed. I would keep 80 percent of the gross monies from the car washes and he would get 20 percent. Really, the thing that allowed him to so easily accept the percentages was he knew the car washes would bring in a whole new slew of customers for the prostitution business. He would keep the brunt of those proceeds.

We talked about the whorehouse idea and Cream loved it. I hated using the term whorehouse. I liked the term sex-house a whole lot better, since I didn't feel that the girls who were selling sex were in fact whores. But that is neither here nor there. Anyway, Cream loved that potentially hundreds of customers would be coming to get sex. On top of that, they would have already pre-paid for the sex.

So with no money needing to exchange hands at the actual whorehouse it would make everything nice and clean. Really, what could the cops say if they were to ever get hip to the scheme? They couldn't say anything, because in essence people coming over to the whorehouses to have sex would have been just like a group of friends going to one friend's house to take part in an orgy or to just have sex. There was no law against that, providing that everyone involved was of the consenting age.

Cream told me that he had often considered opening whorehouse locations throughout the city. In fact, he had actually tried it one time. But he closed it down and didn't go forward with it because it had brought too much heat from the police.

"Where were y'all running the sex-house from?" I asked.

"We were running it from this house that I had rented in Cambria Heights."

"Cambria Heights?" I replied with a puzzled look.

"Yeah."

"That would never work. . . . But that's something that I wanted to talk to you about," I stated.

"Whatchu mean?"

See, right off the bat I could tell that the Cambria Heights location would have never worked because Cambria Heights is too damn residential and quiet! It's one of the nicest predominantly black neighborhoods in Queens. And in a neighborhood like that if neighbors start seeing unfamiliar traffic they won't hesitate to call the police or organize some kind of community-watch patrol.

"Cambria Heights is too much in the open. You can only pull this off in the dark. You gotta do it from the projects and from commercial locations," I said, scheming.

Cream nodded in agreement. I knew that he loved my entrepreneurial genius, which really wasn't as much genius as it was more just plain old common sense. Cream had just as much common sense as I did but he was more of the bold in-your-face type. He did things emotionally and then justified them logically. Like he had a mentality of "I'm doing whatever it is that I want to do because I want to do it." So he would set up anywhere, in any neighborhood and in a sense challenge the residents to fight him if it came down to it.

"I was thinking that we would start off using your apartment in Queensbridge. We would have to find other apartments that are similar to that and rent them out. We also need to find some cheap commercial space. Something like a store with rooms in the back or offices that are above a store. Whatever we do we gotta stay away from the prissy residential areas."

Cream understood exactly where I was coming from. He assured me that he would get Spinach and his crew working on the task of finding spots right away.

"Yo, Lady, on the real, the timing for this couldn't be more perfect because we need to lay low from the tracks for a while and just let everything cool down and smooth themselves out. Especially with the girls scared as hell that they're gonna end up like Mercedes. You kna'imean?"

"No doubt! I know exactly whatchu mean. All we gotta do is just execute on the idea," I said as I confidently steered my Benz while Cream reclined in the passenger seat and sipped on a Heineken.

So the Honey Bunnies Hand Car Washes had been approved by Cream. And they would soon be up and running. It wouldn't take long because I already had all of the hurdles and start-up stuff taken care of by Mr. Kellman weeks ago and I had been working on it without Cream's knowledge.

BY THE THIRD WEEK IN July of 1995, Honey Bunnies Hand Car Wash was up and running in nine different locations throughout New York City. There were three in Queens, three in Brooklyn, and three in the Bronx. I had thought about just opening one in Queens and giving that one time to operate and if it did good then I would open the others. But I didn't like doing things small, and I also wanted to shut the potential competition down before they got a chance to even think about copying my idea.

Physically and emotionally the car washes had come to pass at a huge price. I had worked harder than I ever had before in my life. The hard work helped me to block out the fact that I had murdered, in cold blood, someone who at one point had been close to me and even protected me. Yeah, the thought of Shamgod's murder was something that was constantly on my mind. And anyone who thinks that they are a killer and that they can go out and kill someone without their conscience being affected, well I can say firsthand that that only happens in the movies and in books, not in real life.

I had Cream Team members who I could trust at each of the locations to oversee what was going on. I also had tickets printed up with sequential numbers so that I could keep track of how many cars were actually being washed in a given day. When a customer came to get their car washed, one of the workers would check off what the customer wanted. Then they'd rip off the bottom portion of the paper and give it to the customer. That would serve as the customer's receipt.

To combat theft by my workers, I had a huge sign prominently displayed where all of the customers could see it. It read ANY CUSTOMER NOT GIVEN A TICKET IS ENTITLED TO GET THE CAR WASH FREE.

To me, that plan was a slick way of indirectly keeping the customers on top of my workers. Being as street smart as I was, I knew that my workers would be looking for ways to steal from me. And I figured that they were more than likely capable of having counterfeit tickets printed up at some local printer and thereby granting themselves the opportunity to rob me. So when I had my tickets printed up I made sure to go to a printer who was way out on Long Island. I had him design the tickets in a way where they had a special mark on them that could not be reproduced very easily. See, I knew that if people had their minds set on robbing me then they would do it no matter what, but I figured I might as well make it as hard as possible for them to achieve that objective.

With the administrative stuff out of the way it was time to do business. And all I can say is not in my wildest dreams did I expect the car washes to take off the way they did. I had spent my entire day at one of the Queens car washes. It was located at the corner of Springfield Boulevard and North Conduit Avenue which was across the street from Springfield Gardens High School and also right across the street from a gas station. Not to mention that the Belt Parkway ran adjacent to North Conduit Avenue, so needles to say the traffic that flowed by my newly opened hand car wash was off the chain!

Our first day of business was on a Saturday. We had opened by 9 A.M. Saturday morning and it was some sight to see. We had ten gorgeous, thick, tight-bodied, half-naked females walking around holding signs above their heads that said HONEY BUNNIES HAND CAR WASH. They looked like the half-naked sexy girls who walk around the boxing ring at the end of a round holding up signs to indicate which round was coming up in the fight.

The girls almost caused a number of accidents as guys were breaking their necks to turn and get a glimpse of the flesh that was seductively walking around the new hand car wash. Before I knew it we had a line of about ten cars waiting to get washed. We had recruited illegal immigrants to do the brunt of the work in terms of actually thoroughly cleaning the cars. But the scantily clad girls would purposely make feeble attempts to work alongside the Mexicans. I had instructed the girls that their main jobs were to attract attention, direct traffic into the car wash, flirt with the male customers, and keep them happy. When they did wash cars they mostly did it in a joking way: putting soap suds on one another, spraying water on each other, and other things of that nature in order to produce that wet T-shirt look.

By the time noon had rolled around things were off the hook and out of control and I was quickly finding out why things had mushroomed like they had.

I overheard a guy on his cell phone vibrantly talking to his boy.

"Yo, son! Word is bond, son, there are girls walking around everywhere with thongs on! Son, you better get down here and see this!"

The only thing I could envision was that hundreds of those types of phone calls were being made throughout the city. One thing was for sure, at least at the spot I was at. Word had spread like wildfire about the girls in thongs and wet T-shirts who were washing cars. The proof in the pudding was the fact that the line had quickly blossomed to about fifty cars that were on line and waiting to get a car wash.

I knew that the wait would be kind of long and I didn't want the customers to get tired of waiting and then leave. So I had the girls split up and walk to all of the cars and write up tickets for the customers. They collected the money and gave them the tear-off stubs. That way at least I would have their money before they got bored.

A few of the girls were new and I didn't really know them. But I knew most of them, and they had either been streetwalkers or they had worked in strip clubs, so they were not shy at all when it came to flirting and exposing their body parts. They did an excellent job of keeping the customers entertained and happy while they waited for car washes.

As the day went on and as the sun got hotter, the line never died down and the cash just kept rolling in. By two o'clock there was straight gridlock on the streets. And what I had feared came true. The cops had been alerted to what was going on and they arrived on the scene. Just at the time that the cops pulled up, Cream called me on my cell phone.

"Hello," I said as I answered my phone.

"Lady, you hit the jackpot with these car washes! It is straight bananas out here in BK! And I just talked to Spinach and he said it's a zoo over in the Bronx."

I was trying to talk over the loud music was coming from the sound system of one of the cars that was getting washed.

"Word?!" I yelled with extreme excitement. "It's crazy over here too in Queens! I'm getting ready to call Shauna to see how she's making out at the other Queens spot. But yo, the got damn police just showed up . . . yeah they standing right here in my face right now!" I said as I gave the police officers a disgusted look.

"You got all your paperwork so you straight," Cream stated.

"Yeah I know, but let me go so I can see what they want. . . . I'll call you back."

I looked at the cops and waited for them to talk. They gave me this look like I was supposed to just immediately kiss their ass or something. And then finally after they realized that we would just be standing there all day, they spoke first.

"What's going on here?" they asked.

"What kind of question is that?" I shot back in a sassy manner. "What does it look like is going on?"

"Are you running this car wash?"

"Yes I am, is there a problem?" I said while rolling my eyes and shifting my neck like a turkey.

"Well, look in the street at all of the cars and the traffic that's backing up. It's all related to this car wash."

"And your point is?" I asked in a sarcastic manner.

"My point is that we're gonna have to shut this place down," the officer shot back trying to flex his muscles.

"You do what you gotta do, all I know is that if you shut this place down I'll be on the phone with my lawyer in two minutes."

There was a pause in the conversation. I knew that I wasn't doing anything illegal and I had all of my paperwork in order. I had crossed all of my I's and dotted all of my T's with my lawyer for this very reason. The cops had just been bluffing and they probably wanted to see my reaction.

Calling their bluff I broke the silence. "So are y'all ordering me to shut down or what? If not, can I please go?"

"Listen, we understand that you're running a business, but not for nothing, you got indecent women walking around and you're disrupting traffic. What if an emergency vehicle was trying to get by right now? You gotta take some action to alleviate this problem."

In my defiant and disrespectful manner I shot back, "Okay, first of all there is nothing indecent about my girls, they're wearing bathing suits for crying out loud! And last I checked that was legal in New York. Second of all, if business is doing good I'm not gonna turn these people away, and most of them have already paid. I'm running a car wash. It's your job to restore order to the traffic, not mine! If it's such a problem then I suggest you get some police barricades and section off a lane so that the people coming to my car wash will not be confused with the regular traffic, and then that might help to alleviate *your* problem!"

The cops looked at each other as if to say, "this black bitch!" But they knew that I had done nothing wrong and I was well within my rights to be running my business. In actuality though, I knew that I probably should have planned better and anticipated this disruption that my car washes would cause.

"Listen, we're not trying to give you a hard time. In fact we like what we see, if you know what I mean," the two cops said as they both began laughing. They knew good and well that they would have given a week's salary to lay up with one of my girls. At least they were starting to come off a little more realistic about things.

The cop continued, "See, this is the thing, just try to see what you can do to help us out, because what happens is you get neighbors complaining and then our bosses start breaking our balls. You know what I mean?"

I could respect that, and that was all that I wanted. I wanted them to show me some respect which they finally did, so I was willing to work with them. Plus, it hadn't dawned on me that the Mexicans didn't have any papers to be in this country so they definitely had no business working. And the last thing I wanted was for the cops to pull that immigration angle.

"A'ight, what I can do is have the girls stay on the property of the car wash and I won't have them canvassing the block taking orders. That should help."

"It definitely should. . . . Thank you, and like I said, we're not trying to give you a hard time, we're just doing our job and following orders."

"I appreciate that and I respect that," I said as I motioned to one of Cream's boys and told him to round up the girls and have them stay close by the car wash lot. "Here," I said to the cops as I gave then two complimentary passes so that they could get free car washes. "Use that whenever y'all want."

They took them without hesitation. They knew the passes would give them the chance to come back and get up close and personal with some black and some Spanish booty.

The day continued on at its feverish pace and the money just would not stop. We had been charging twenty dollars for the car washes and I knew we had to have had about three hundred cars, if not more, that we serviced on that one day at that one location. At around seven o'clock that night Shauna picked me up and drove me to all of the locations so I could pick up my money.

I can't describe how good it felt to collect bundles and bundles of cash. It was a crazy feeling and it felt good because it was all legal money. But it was scary because I wondered, as a young female, if I would be able to handle everything. I also wondered if Cream would go back on his word and try to pimp me for my car wash earnings. I knew that he never imagined that the car washes would have raked in so much dough.

As Shauna and I drove, Cream called me on my cell again.

"Lady, I love you! Word! I love you, baby!"

In my head I was like, *Here we go.*

But I replied, "This is crazy, right?!"

"Hell yeah! Yo, I got your dough for you. I can't believe I'm holding more than five grand for you right now."

Yes! I thought to myself. That number sounded right. And even if Cream had taken more than his 20 percent I wasn't gonna nitpick about it. Unless it was a significant amount over the 20 percent.

"Yo, me and Shauna are just leaving the Bronx right now and we'll be in Brooklyn in like twenty minutes."

"I'll be here," Cream stated.

I hung up the phone and just started screaming like I had won the lottery.

"Shauna, I can't believe this! I think I grossed like over forty thousand in just one day! This is so sick!"

Shauna immediately reached over and gave me a pound. I greatly respected Shauna because she wasn't a jealous-ass hater. I could tell that she was genuinely happy for me. And I know that there were stretches that I would up and disappear on her and not get in touch with her for days and weeks at a time. In fact, when she and her man had been going through their little breakup thing that was a time when she needed me to be there for her but I was to busy being Lady and wasn't there. But she was a true friend and never once did she trip about that or trip about much of anything. She was truly always in my corner.

"Lady, I gotta give it up to you! Word is bond."

"Shauna, I don't know where all of this is gonna lead or end up but I just want you to know that no matter what happens you are always gonna be my girl and I got you no matter what! You my ace!"

Shauna knew that but I just wanted to reassure her that I was grateful to have her in my life. She didn't know about the murder that I had committed and she didn't know about a lot of other dirt that I knew about, but she would never try to snake me or hurt me in any way and I knew that I could trust her. Most of all, she accepted me unconditionally.

As we drove on the FDR Drive headed toward the Brooklyn Bridge, I welled up with both tears of joy and tears of sadness. I had all kinds of emotions but I think overall I was just happy as hell.

"What's the matter?" Shauna asked as she turned down the music.

"Nothing," I said. I was finally starting to show signs that I was in fact still just a kid at heart. "I'm just happy that's all."

"You sure that's it?" Shauna asked.

"Yeah, I'm sure. . . . And Shauna, like I said, no matter what, I just want you to know that I got you," I said as I continued to cry. "See, you were there for me when I told you what I wanted to do. You never abandoned me when I told you what I was doing in terms of walking the streets and all of that. You don't know, but word, that just means so much to me!"

Shauna reached over and rubbed my leg and then she said, "Well, I know I've told you this before, or at least I think I have, but even if I don't approve of something that you did or something that you are doing or whatever, I will not judge you. Nor will I look at anything that you do and let that define who you are."

"See, that's what I mean," I said as I continued to cry. "You are my girl! Thank you. . . . Shauna, on the real, there are some things that I just can't talk to you about right now, but when I can I will. But just know that it feels good having people around me that are real. I mean you ain't trying to hide nothing and you don't have no hidden agendas and that is so rare, especially with the niggas that I'm running with."

Shauna didn't comment. And her silence kind of reminded me to snap back into reality and to stop talking so that I wouldn't let something slip out that I would later regret.

We eventually made our rounds to each location, and my forecast had been right on the money. I had grossed a little over forty-two thousand dollars in one day! Even with Cream's 20 percent and the money that I had to pay to my workers, I had made more than twenty-five thousand dollars for myself! Twenty-five thousand dollars in one day! I had to keep pinching myself in order to make sure I wasn't dreaming.

I felt good that day. That day opened my eyes big time and it was a life-changing day. I think the thing that made me feel the best was that I had made so much money in one day and it was all legal money. And on top of that I had not spread my legs for no one in order to earn the money. All I did was simply expand and use my God-given brain.

22

THREE WEEKS HAD PASSED SINCE the opening of the Honey Bunnies Hand Car Washes and business was still booming. I couldn't believe the large sums of money I had been seeing. I wasted no time making sure that I splurged on myself. I took myself on like a seven-thousand-dollar shopping spree. I bought Prada, Gucci, Burberry, Manolo, and everything else that was expensive and looked hot. And you have to remember that it was 1995 and back then people weren't really into all of the big names like Burberry and Prada like they are now.

When I look back I often think about the influence the Cream Team and I had over people. Influence that we didn't even realize we were having. In my opinion, Cream was the first one in New York to start rocking the diamond-encrusted Rolex watches. Cream was the one who started drinking the Moët bottles of champagne as if they were bottles of water. Now people drink Cristal champagne, but they don't realize that Cream started the trend. In fact, all the flossing you see and hear many of the rappers bragging about is a result of the money-flashing, extravagant lifestyle that the Cream Team projected.

I was no rapper but my close ties to the Cream Team definitely influenced my spending habits. I wasn't really one who wanted to show off just so that I could make the next person feel bad or feel less about their circumstances. However, I did want to see my mother so that she could see that I was making it without her. I wanted her to know that I was a strong woman who was succeeding on my own.

Surprisingly, my mother was still living in Hollis, Queens, with her boyfriend Junie and my little sister Mya. And thank god I was finally just where I needed to be in order to move Mya out from under my mother. I wanted the two of us to live together in *normalcy*. It was a surprise that my mother was still living in Hollis with Junie. Usually by now she would have either left Junie, been kicked out, dumped, or been beat up and forced to move on to another location.

As I drove toward their block in Hollis I was hoping that both my mother and Junie would be home. I was also hoping one of them would open the door when I rang the bell. I was gonna say that I had only come by to see my sister, but the real deal was I wanted my mother and her sick-ass boyfriend to see my Mercedes-Benz. I also wanted them to see the diamond bracelet and diamond earrings that I was wearing. I wanted them to know that at the tender young age of sixteen I was living much larger than they could have ever dreamed for themselves.

Why did I want them to see all of this now? I wanted them to see it because I was ballin' and I was beyond bitter at how disrespectfully I had been treated by both my mother and her boyfriend. And to me the best way to get back at somebody who dissed you is to have more success than them and then to flaunt it in their face and make sure that they know about it.

My fingernails were airbrushed and manicured and my toes had received their weekly airbrush and pedicure. I was smelling like a bed of roses and I was looking like a million dollars. I always dressed sexy as hell and that day I made it a point to look incredibly so. I had on my white leather Poom-Poom Daisy Duke shorts, some open-toed high-heeled shoes, and a Prada blouse.

I pulled up to the front of my mother's house. Although there was a fire hydrant in front, I was willing to risk getting a parking ticket—I parked the car right next to it. I wanted my mother and Junie to see my car, which was clean, waxed, and shining with Armor All on all of the tires. Its chrome rims glistened in the sun.

I was kind of anxious about ringing the doorbell. I didn't know what my mother's reaction to seeing me would be. I mean, during the past two years or so I had only spoken to her on brief occasions, mostly when she answered the phone when I called to speak to my sister.

I tried to expel all of the anxiousness inside of me. I confidently rang the doorbell like I was a bitch with power.

"Who is it?" a voice on the other side of the door asked, in what I would say was a rather rude tone.

"It's me," I replied.

"Who?"

By that time I had figured out that the voice belonged to my mother.

"Ma, it's me, Tina. Open the door."

I heard the locks to the door quickly being turned.

"Tina? Baby, what you doing here?" my mother asked.

My mother looked good in terms of her physical shape and her face. I have to admit that my natural instincts were drawing me to hug my mother and embrace her. But I held back because I also had a lot of resentment built up in me.

"I came to see Mya. Is she here?" I asked, making sure to sound as cold as a virgin.

My mother was looking at me. I could tell that she knew I looked like new money. She paused and scanned me up and down.

"Baby, yeah, she's here. But baby, oh my god, look at you!"

In my head I was like, *Would you please kill all of that?*

"Tina, I can't believe how good you look! You look like a grown woman."

"Ma, I am grown," I replied in a smart-ass kind of way.

"Tina, come in and give me a hug, baby . . . Do you know how much I missed you? . . . The only thing that gave me any kind of peace is that your sister would tell me that you were doing okay," my mother said, sounding like a distant relative at a family reunion.

"Ma, can you tell Mya that I'm here to see her?" I said rather bluntly, making sure not to acknowledge any of my mother's words.

"Oh, okay."

My mother obviously got the message that I didn't wanna talk no fake small talk. She was trying to act like she was concerned but that was all phony behavior that I had seen so much of in the past. If she really missed me so much, she knew where I went to school so it would not have been that hard to locate me.

As we sat in awkward silence and waited for my sister to appear before us, I made it a point to pull out my cell phone and act like I was checking my voice mail messages. Mya was in the shower so I knew it would be a little while before she'd be ready.

"So, Tina, are you okay? Where are you staying at?"

That was all I could take! After all that time had passed—not just a couple of weeks or a couple of months, but rather a couple of years—she had the balls to ask me if I was okay and where I was staying! If she really wanted to know, why did it take her this long—and my coming by—for her to try and get answers to those questions?

"Ma, how can you just calmly ask me if I am okay and where I'm staying? I mean, do you really give a damn?"

"Tina, I'm your mother, of course I care about you. I brought you into this world."

I rolled my eyes.

"Look outside . . . You see that car out there? That's my car! You see these clothes? I paid for them. You see this phone? I pay the bill! You see the diamonds in this bracelet? I bought that . . . So yes, I am okay!"

"All of that is nice, baby."

"Nice? . . ." I said with a twisted look. "It's more than you ever had and more than you'll ever have! Don't just try to step on what I got by calling it nice!" All my bitterness was starting to pour out.

"Tina, I'm not trying to downplay anything that you have. Believe me, I'm not. And baby, I'm not upset with you or anything like that, I—"

I cut my mother off. "What do you mean you're not upset with me? You have absolutely no right whatsoever to be upset with me about anything! You should be hoping that I would tell you that *I'm* not upset with *you!*"

My mother did look a little surprised at my anger and my tone of voice.

"Well, are you upset with me?"

I could not believe my mother would ask me that question. She really had no clue.

"How could you ask me that? After what you put me and Mya through, you damn right I'm upset with you! And that's putting it lightly!"

My mother was visibly uncomfortable with what I had just said and she became kind of shifty.

"Tina, come sit in the kitchen with me for a minute."

"Ma, really, I just wanna speak to Mya and then I gotta go."

My mother walked to the kitchen and came back with something for me to drink. I took the drink and just placed it down near the TV without saying thank you or anything. I had no intention of drinking it.

"You want me to cook you something?" my mother asked.

"No, I'm good," I replied.

My mother knew that she wasn't getting anywhere with me so she tried another approach.

"Okay, Tina, listen to me. You want the honest truth? The honest truth is that every day I constantly pray to God for you. Every day I think about you. Every day I wonder if you're okay. Every day I hope that a cop won't come to my door and tell me that something has happened to you. But baby, I can't offer you anything . . . I don't have anything. You know that, Tina. So while my soul cries out and I wanna chase after you and bring you under my wings, I don't because I realize that I don't have anything to give you."

"Ma, you know what? That sounds all nice and good and all of that but it goes in one ear and right out the other. You know why? Because for sixteen years now, you have been in the same circumstance, constantly dependent upon some nigga to take care of you and your two kids! And you care for the no-good niggas in your life more than you care for your own flesh and got damn blood!"

I could hear and feel my mother's spirit being crushed by my words. That was exactly what I wanted to happen.

"Tina, you don't know what you're saying."

"Ma, don't tell me I don't know what I'm saying! Listen to me. For once you don't seem like you're high or drunk, so just listen to me! You're telling me that you can just sit back and watch your teenage daughter try to make it on her own in a city like New York. That the thought of it eats at you and yet you never reached out to me or chased me because you had nothing to offer me. But in essence what you're really saying is that you knew that the street could offer me more than you could? . . . And you know what? I can't accept that, because the streets can't love me like my mother can love me!"

"Tina, but, see—"

I cut my mother off again. "No, let me finish. You always talk fast and talk over people and manipulate and control conversations so that you won't have to deal with the truth. But you know what? I can't make you deal with the truth, but I'm gonna make you hear the truth!"

I began to cry as I said, "Ma, I don't care what you can give me or what you can give to Mya. And I never did care about what you could give us materially or financially. The only thing I wanted from you was to know that you care! I wanted to know that you love me! Ma, that is free! That don't cost nothing! On the real, I wouldn't have cared if me, you, and Mya were forced to live in a cardboard box on a street corner somewhere, just as long as we knew that together and with a whole lot of love, we would be there for each other and we would make it. . . . So you should have chased after me! And you were the answer to your own so-called prayers to God for me. If you loved me you would have checked on me, and if you wanted answers from God, you should have done your part by showing that you loved me!"

"Tina, baby, you know that I love you," my mother said as her eyes began to well up.

"I know that you love getting high, and I know that you love all of these niggas that you lay up with! That's what I know."

There was a pause and then I shot back and stated, "Ma, how could you let your dirty-ass, cheap-ass, stank-ass, no-good-ass man rape me and then tell me that I should have just closed my eyes and enjoyed it?! How? How can you say that to your daughter? I'm your own flesh and blood! And you expect me to believe that you love me?"

My mom began to shed tears.

"What the hell are you crying for?" I asked. By this time my sister had come out of the shower and made her way to where I was standing.

"Tina, I'm crying because I know that I hurt you."

"Hurt me? Ma, you have no idea what you did to me. No idea!"

"Baby, listen to me, please. I don't love getting high, and I don't love any man more than I love you and your sister. I realize that I fall short in many areas, and I've been trying to change. I've started going to this church in Brooklyn and I'm not no holy roller or anything like that but the church has helped me out a lot. They've pointed many of my weaknesses out to me, they've sent me to places where I can get help, and I'm learning a lot. It's been only very recent that I've started to seek help but what I realize is that I drank, got high, and was with men because that was what I used to mask the pain in my own life."

"Whateva, Ma. I mean people are always pulling out the Jesus card when they get down and out. That's why it's hard for me to buy into all of that. And I know you, Ma. Tonight I can come back by here and it will be a whole different story. Instead of you saying you can't believe how grown I look, you'll say something stupid like, '*Tina, look at you! You think you a woman? But you know it was my man that turned you into a woman! You dressing all sexy why? You trying to take my man from me?*'" I said it in a tone that mocked my mother and mimicked her voice, but she knew that I was right.

With her head hung low, my mother took a seat on the couch. She slumped in her seat. "Tina, what can I say? I understand where your words are coming from. And there is nothing that I can say or do that will prove to you that I love you, and I know that. But there is something that I have to say, and I hope that you accept it. And that is this, Tina, I am so sorry if Junie or anyone else put their hands on you or touched you in a way that they shouldn't have—"

I cut my mother off again. "Ma, please, I know you mean well but please just stop right there because your words can't fix anything at this point and it will only make it worse. . . . I'm glad I came by, I'm glad I had a chance to see you, and as far as the future goes, I don't know. All I know is that I hope you start realizing actions speak *a whole lot* louder than words."

My mother humbly nodded her head and wiped her eyes.

"Mya, I'm sorry that you had to hear the tail end of all of that, but I really came by to check on you and to give you some money."

I reached into my bag and I pulled out a bankroll of hundreds, fifties, and twenties. I peeled off two one-hundred-dollar bills and five twenty-dollar bills and handed them to my sister.

My mother saw the amount of money that I had. I was wishing that she would ask me for some money so that I could tell her no. But I have to admit that I was a bit surprised by her humbleness.

"Tina, if you don't mind me asking, where are you working now?"

I sucked my teeth, and then underneath my breath I stated, "I don't work! I own hand car washes."

"Oh, so you have your own business?"

"Yeah," I said. I was on guard for my mother's manipulation. "I own like nine different locations." How could she not have any idea about at least some of what I had been doing, I asked myself. Maybe she did have some idea. Maybe she knew about some of the things that I was doing and she was just fronting 'cause she had another motive. I didn't know, but her complete ignorance seemed somewhat phony and unreal to me.

"Baby, that's so good. I'm proud of you."

When my mother said that, there was something in me that sort of melted. I had literally never heard my mother say anything remotely close to that she was proud of me. And it actually sounded like she truly meant it.

I nodded my head up and down. As I was preparing to go, my mom added, "Tina, you know what? You probably got your father's genes when it comes to business."

My mother almost floored me when she stated that. I mean, she knew that Mya and I had never met our biological father. She had never spoken with any kind of depth about him. She always spoke in derogatory terms about him.

"Really?" I asked. My voice sounded like a normal teenager. I must have sounded like an eager kid who had just been told what he or she was gonna be given for Christmas and wanted to know more details.

My mother continued to remain humble in her posture and in her tone of voice as she softly and calmly replied, "Yeah, your father had a brain for business that was unbelievable. He always knew how to take one dollar and turn it into five dollars. He owned a bunch of different business and he was also real big into real estate."

"I never knew that," I replied.

My mother sighed and said, "Yeah I know, and that too is my fault. Because of my own issues I took you and your sister out of your father's life. And I regret that. . . . But I won't get into all of that, I know you don't wanna hear it."

Actually, I did wanna hear it but I just didn't trust my mother. She had definitely piqued my interest about my dad. All I could picture was this strong, well-respected businessman. Unfortunately all I could rely on was my imagination when it came to images of my father.

I gave my mother a hug and a kiss on the cheek, and I did the same to my sister. As I left I told them both that I would try to come around more often.

"Please do that, baby," my mother stated.

Just then, Junie came into the room. He was looking as if he had been sleeping all day, and mind you, it was like two in the afternoon. The nigga had probably spent Friday night getting drunk and was waking up with a Saturday-afternoon hangover.

"Yeah, I'll definitely be going now," I sarcastically stated.

"Tina? . . . Is that Tina?" Junie asked as he yawned and stretched. He was in his boxer shorts and wife-beater and he stood there scratching his joint. He just looked so pathetic with his broke ass that it was even funny.

I proceeded to walk outside and my mother followed me.

"Tina you looking good, girl," Junie said to me as I walked out. I paid him no mind but I wanted to get a gun and pump sixteen bullets into him. I had already killed a man and I knew that I could easily kill Junie. I also knew that Cream would have taken Junie out for me in a heartbeat. But Junie wasn't worth it and I quickly dismissed the idea.

As I sat in my car and started up the engine, my mother came to the driver's side window. I rolled down the window.

"Tina, I really am happy that you came by . . . Can we start over?"

"Ma, we'll see what's what."

"Tina, eventually I want you to come check out this church with me."

"Okay, but what kind of church is it that is okay with you living in sin?"

"What?" my mom asked.

I was referring to her unwed, fornicating relationship with Junie.

"Never mind, Ma. Never mind. I gotta go."

"Okay," my mom stated as she gave me a kiss on the cheek.

"Tina, can I hold something?"

"Can you hold something?" I asked, not sure what my mother meant.

"Yeah, fifty dollars."

I wanted to scream, "HELL NO!" and speed off, but I just couldn't do that. I reached into my bag and I pulled out a hundred-dollar bill and handed it to my mother.

"Ma, do not give one red cent to Junie! And do not spend a penny on no liquor and no drugs. A'ight?"

My mother gave me her word that she would not. I pulled off and tooted the horn two times. I was off to my world of sex, money, and murder. But I would have given anything to have a world of family, love, and stability.

23

IN MY HEART I KEPT waiting for the moment of sabotage where everything I worked for would come to a sudden and abrupt end. Since I started living the street life, I noticed a pattern that seemed to exist. No good thing lasted for too long without a hiccup. Hiccups were a dreaded reality in the streets.

I was trying to avoid hiccups at all cost, so what I did was I kept in touch with my lawyer and let him know everything that was going on at the car washes. He in turn helped me out a great deal. He put me in touch with this accountant who showed me how to handle my money so that I could start really building a legitimate enterprise. The thing I liked about the accountant was that although he was white and college-educated, he had this real ghetto side about him. For example, since the car wash was a straight cash business, he taught me how to pay the least amount of taxes and yet still be able to live large and floss at the government's expense.

As for my lawyer, he was, in my opinion, a flat-out genius. He could see stuff, potential hiccups, happening way before they actually happened and in doing so he kept me way ahead of any curve balls. One day my lawyer actually took a drive by a couple of my car wash locations and he saw firsthand just exactly how and why I was raking in so much money.

"Tina, I really like your hook," my lawyer stated as we spoke in front of his BMW as it got washed.

I smiled and nodded my head as the sun beamed down.

"But you know, I gotta tell you something," he added.

"What?"

"You told me from the beginning about the bikini thing. But with the way your girls are dressed and with the traffic congestion that your establishment is causing, I see why the cops are constantly dropping by. Tina, what is more than likely gonna happen, if it hasn't happened already, is you're gonna get local residents who will go beyond complaining just to the police. They'll go to the local community board of politicians and start to make a stink with them. They will put pressure on the police to do more than just pass by and pay you visits. They'll put enough pressure on the right people until the police will have no choice but to shut you down."

"But all my papers are in order," I stated. "How could they just come in and put me out of business like that?"

My lawyer laughed and said, "I know that your papers are in place, I'm the one who put everything in place for you. But Tina, the way things work in this world is with money. Money makes the world go round. Listen to me, and this is just between me and you. . . . If you wanna keep your car washes open what you're gonna have to do is make some cash gifts to your local politicians." My lawyer winked his eye as he completed his last sentence.

I was just flat-out blunt and direct as I replied, "So in other words you're saying that if someone doesn't get paid off then I'll get shut down."

"Tina, I don't make the rules and neither do you. All I'm telling you is how to play the game."

Ain't this a bitch? I thought to myself.

I really appreciated what my lawyer had told me. And I realized that the *real world* was just like the street life that I knew. It was just as corrupt. But I was willing to do what I had to do in order to survive, so

I had no problem anteing up a couple of grand and sending it to a few politicians—via my lawyer—in order to keep the heat off of me.

I put Cream onto what my lawyer had told me. When we combined Cream's police contact, Detective Lombardi, with my newfound knowledge of influencing local politicians with cash, we were on the secure road to riches.

At that point Cream and I, more than ever, felt real comfortable stepping up the marketing of the team's prostitution business. We instructed the girls to be real flirtatious with the customers and to hint at the fact that their body parts were for sale. If any of the customers were hip enough to take the hint and tried to get a personal phone number, the girls had been instructed to give out the exact same phone number to all of the guys that tried to kick it to them. And if any of the guys called the number, they would get a real seductive-speaking girl on the other end of the phone who had enough game not to say anything that would get us busted but still let the customers know what was really up and where they had to come to get *serviced*.

Things were a little awkward in the beginning because we simply didn't want to be overt and in the open with everything that we were doing. After all, selling sex was and still is illegal in New York. But after about a week or so, the streets got hip to what was going on at the Honey Bunnies Hand Car Washes. And before long what we did was we printed things on our order tickets that read, FULL SERVICE, or EXTERIOR ONLY. Each description had its own hidden and double meaning. For example, "Full Service" meant that—in addition to the full-service car wash—the customer also wanted to have sex with one of the girls. "Exterior Only" meant that the customer wanted to get a blow-job in addition to the exterior of their car being washed.

We stopped printing prices on our tickets. The customers in the know would pay for their sexual favors at the same time they paid for their car wash. Only with the sex-seeking customers, in addition to receiving their ticket stub, they also received a color-coded hospital-like wristband. The wristband indicted what type of sexual favor they had paid for, and then later on that night or the following day they could show up at one of our sex-houses and get their orders filled.

The plan is hard to explain on paper, but it worked like a charm. Since Cream's money was now at stake I didn't have to worry about anyone stealing from me—or from Cream, for that matter. Everyone knew Cream's reputation and no one was willing to risk getting their hand caught in the cookie jar.

At the sex-houses, we really had nothing to worry about because no money at all was changing hands on the premises. And while that alone wasn't enough to legitimize our business, it definitely helped us ward off any possible detectives who might have shown up undercover with cash seeking a sexual favor. Plus, all of the girls at the car wash knew that they had to be silent as far as what the color-coded wristbands meant and were for. They could not be faulted for possibly selling a wristband to an undercover cop, as long as they never spoke about the meaning of the wristbands. So we knew that we would be okay.

Cream looked at what we were doing as no different from what swingers across this country do all of the time in the privacy of their own homes. And in many ways I would have to say that Cream was right on point with his analysis, because at the actual sex locations it really looked as if people were coming over to just chill at a friend's house or something.

The layout in all of our sex locations was basically the same. We had big-screen televisions which always had a game on, a boxing match, *Def Comedy Jam*, or some kind of movie. There were large couches everywhere for people to sit on, along with folding chairs. We also had sexy-looking hostesses who were responsible for serving sodas and finger foods. The atmosphere was real slick and smooth and no one got in unless they had a color-coded wristband that was still intact and attached to their wrist.

And of course, at all of our locations, aside from the hostesses were numerous scantily clad women who walked around and mingled or sat with the customers who really looked like houseguests. The girls wore things such as body stockings, spandex pants, Daisy Duke shorts, high heels, and just about anything else that was sexy and enticing. The girls knew that whenever a customer would ask them to *"go to the back"* with them, that they simply had to look at the customer's wrist for a wristband. Then they would comply with the customer's orders and go to the back and service them.

In the back were rooms that had futon-style sofas, condoms, baby oil, K-Y jelly, and paper towels—all of the tools needed to perform quick and safe sex acts. We also had cock diesel body-guard-looking thugs who walked around strapped and ready to bring it to any niggas who were drunk and acting stupid, or any niggas who tried to disrespect the girls and got out of control. And of course, each location had a madam who basically oversaw all of the action. She could immediately be in touch with either Cream, Spinach, or myself if something went down. The madams were also responsible for keeping track of how many customers each girl serviced on a given day. This way, all of the girls would get the correct amount of money they were due.

I remember speaking to Cream about how well everything was going.

"Yo, how long you think we can keep this up before we get some heat?" I asked.

"Don't think in those terms. Just by talking about it, you'll end up bringing the exact type of heat that you are trying to avoid," Cream replied.

I knew that he was right, but my instincts were telling me that I needed to just hurry up and go legit with one hustle and not get greedy. I mean my car washes were bringing me all kinds of money, but the thing with car washes was that if it rained, I wouldn't make any money. Also, on weekdays I didn't make nearly as much money as I would make on the weekends. I also realized that when the summer and its warm weather was behind us, the winter weather would not allow us to make as much money either. My business was seasonal. Although the car washes were feeding me lovely, and they were legit, I was still holding on to the illegal money from the prostitution activities. I just loved the street and I loved street niggas, and the prostitution business personified those elements. I also loved the money and the street money was sort of like insurance against my legitimate business.

I just hated going against my instincts. That little voice inside of me was usually right. The voice was screaming for me to be careful and to start to slide out of Cream's business so I wouldn't get caught out there—either by the cops or by Cream and his cutthroat actions.

Before I knew what was what, a few more days had passed by. Money was continuing to pour in. I was in the final stages of getting my own living quarters and I was also making plans to buy either the Yukon SUV or the Toyota Land Cruiser—or anything for that matter, as long as it was hot. But just as expected, the hiccup that I was dreading started to rear its ugly head.

Cream called me on my cell phone and he sounded more nervous than upset, but I could tell that he wasn't his normal self.

"L, meet me at the Rosedale spot in like twenty minutes. I can't really talk right now but just be there. . . . A'ight?"

"In twenty minutes?" I asked in order to confirm.

"Yeah, in twenty minutes."

Immediately my radar went up. Cream had never referred to me as L. And why did it seem he was talking in code? I wracked my brain trying to think if I had slipped up and gotten sloppy during the past couple of weeks. But I knew that everything with me had been on the up and up and I also knew that I hadn't been running my mouth about anything. So I knew that Cream didn't want to meet with me because of some wrong act of mine.

I quickly left Shauna's apartment and made it over to Cream's Rosedale house in about ten minutes. I waited in my car for him to arrive. My wait wasn't long, he showed up no more than five minutes after I had arrived and parked right behind me.

We both got out of our cars and I greeted Cream as I normally did with a kiss on his cheek.

"Is everything okay? You seemed like you was talking to me in code when you called," I stated to Cream.

Cream raised his right hand to his forehead. He rubbed it while simultaneously shaking his head.

"Yo, I spoke to that cat Lombardi about an hour or so ago and the dude is telling me that he can't work with me no more."

"What?" I asked as I began to make my way toward the yard of Cream's house.

"Yo, matter of fact, Lady, let's just talk outside. Walk with me and we'll talk as we walk."

"Cream, what's up? What the hell is this all about?"

"I was talking to you in codes, and I ain't trying to talk in any of my spots because something is going down or it's about to go down."

My heart began to race just a bit.

"Cream, just be straight up with me. What did Lombardi say?"

"He was kicking this garbage about how he has to totally lay low for a while because he's getting a lot of heat on his end inside the police department."

"What kind of heat?"

"Well, he thinks that Internal Affairs is investigating the possibility that someone has been leaking confidential information to me concerning all of NYPD's investigations and surveillance of the Cream Team."

"And?" I asked, trying to make a connection.

"And he's getting nervous, thinking that somehow if the cops get to me I would rat him out in order to save my own ass."

Starting to finally see where Cream was coming from, I spoke up a bit more confidently.

"Nah," I said as I shook my head. "That just don't sound right to me. Tell me this, how did this whole Internal Affairs thing come up in the first place? . . . And don't tell me he's saying that Internal Affairs has been poking their nose around trying to find a dirty trail ever since that whole fake undercover cop thing with the girls."

"Lady, that's exactly what he's saying! He told me that ever since Internal Affairs came in to investigate that whole fake undercover cop thing, they must have inadvertently struck gold. Somehow they got warm to the idea that someone inside the police force was feeding me information which was helping me to run my empire and evade investigation."

"So, what's with you speaking in codes and all of that? You think somebody is tapping your phones? It can't be that serious yet."

"Lady, on the real I don't know what to think. . . . Word! I just can't think straight."

As we continued to talk, I tried to make sense of everything that Cream was telling me. I had to remind myself not to assume anything. I had to just go on what Cream was telling me and take that as truth and work with that.

"Cream, if Lombardi is coming at you saying that he has to lay low for a while then we gotta make a move, and we gotta make it quick. See, listen to me. Imagine if Lombardi was a street cat, and then analyze it the same way you would if some nigga on the street was talking to you and saying the same things that Lombardi is saying. If you do that you'll realize the only reason Detective Lombardi is coming at you like that is because he knows more than he is letting on. He basically tipped his hand to you. Niggas on the street do it all the time, they rat on themselves and they don't even know it."

"Exactly! And that's why I've been bugging out, thinking about what my next move should be. But I don't know what that move should be because I don't know what Lombardi knows."

"Well, you could even look at it like this. Even if Lombardi isn't ratting himself out, let's just say that there is a real Internal Affairs investigation going on and he's legitimately worried about getting caught up in everything. You and I both know that he would sell your ass out in a second if it meant saving his ass."

"Lady, you think I don't know that?" Cream rhetorically asked.

"I know you know that, but Cream, here's the deal. Chances are that somebody is investigating us as we speak. But I look at it like this. We're already one step ahead of the game because I doubt that they can connect you to me in any way. They could try to say that your dirty money is comingled with my legitimate business side. But even if they say that, they need a paper trail to prove it and it's not like you was writing me checks or anything. So how could they prove it? To me that is a dead issue right there. I ain't got no record and as far as the law is concerned if I don't have no priors, then I really don't exist. So, I doubt that they know anything about our sex locations, especially since we're funneling all of the traffic from my car washes. . . . Just lay low from the streets for a while and that should solve half the battle. We won't have any girls walking the streets on the tracks for a while so whatever heat is out there should die down."

"Hold up. Back up. Why you say half the battle?" Cream asked with uncertainty in his voice.

"I say that because Lombardi is too much of a wild card at this point. *He knows* the Cream Team and what he knows is way too much. So he himself is the other half of the battle. And the bottom line is this. He played with fire by being on the good side, the police side, and he tried to mix into the bad side, the Cream Team side. And you know what happens when you play with fire? . . . You get burned."

"So, what are you saying?" Cream asked.

"I'm saying that unless you take out Lombardi, you might as well play Russian roulette because your whole existence and the Cream Team's whole existence will be laying in the hands of that one detective, Detective Lombardi."

"You saying I need to murder him?" Cream asked in a loud whisper so that the neighborhood residents didn't over hear him.

"That's exactly what I'm saying."

"Lady, you are straight bugging! If I kill some thug on the street, it's like his life is worthless, but if I kill a cop, that is like killing God or something. You just don't do that. I think I gotta roll the dice and take my chances," Cream stated in a manner that was totally opposite to his thugged-out nature.

"Cream, trust me. Right now it's me and you talking. That's it. We know where the nigga works, so we could easily set him up and catch him off guard. We could follow him home to his crib or something and catch him out there like that. If and when we get him it will only be me and you who'll know about it and we can take that to our graves."

Cream was quiet for a minute as he thought about my suggestion.

"Nah, Lady, we can't pull that off and get away with it. You only fight battles and wars that you know you can win."

"A'ight, but I'm telling you he is gonna end up hurting you. You watch."

Cream blew out some smoke from the Newport cigarette he had been smoking.

Still holding the cigarette between the thumb and index finger of his right hand, Cream replied, "I ain't doing that, Lady, because if this whole thing eventually goes away, I'll need Lombardi for more information. I can't kill off a resource like that. In the meantime we gotta get everybody to keep their mouths shut about anything and everything concerning our hustles. What I'm a do is just lay off the streets for a while. I ain't gonna speak about nothing on my house phone and I'm gonna switch up my cell phone like once a month. I'm gonna just disappear to my house. If they are investigating me I ain't gonna make it easy for them to find me or any dirt on me. I'll pop up at a couple of the car washes here and there and that's about it. If they do get me for something it'll be for distributing weed and that aint really nothing but a thing."

Cream referred to marijuana because he had been feuding with some Jamaican drug dealers. They wanted to take over his marijuana hustle, and he feared that they would rat him out to the cops. With him off the streets it be easier for them to move in on his turf. Cream's marijuana hustle was the only hustle of his that I did not intricately know the workings of. It had never been my business to know so I never asked. Yeah, me and Cream were close enough where if I had asked him about it he would have filled me in. But I think my not bringing it up made Cream trust me even more. See, the quickest way to get suspected of being a rat is by asking too many questions that don't directly concern your ass. People get suspicious and it doesn't look good. You'd only ask if you were a rat or too ambitious—which could potentially make you a threat. It was all good though, because in a way I really didn't wanna know about his weed hustle. God only knew what type of drama and murder and mayhem went down with that game.

I kind of understood Cream's rationale and his way of thinking, but to me he was the Cream Team. He was responsible for so much dirt. If he was the target of an investigation then he was being investigated for murder, kidnapping, and a whole slew of other crimes. Adding cop killer to that list really wouldn't have changed things all that much. I went along with Cream's plan which called for him to lay low for a while and for us to enforce total silence in every member and associate of the team.

I learned that I was really vulnerable. If something ever happened to Cream—in terms of him getting locked up or killed—then I would lose a lot of my identity. By playing his coattails so close I was taking all kinds of risks. So over the next day and a half I thought about ways to change that. I needed to make the change quickly.

I realized that Cream had really been the brains behind the Cream Team. He had been the master manipulator of many people. He also was able to get over based heavily on the strength of his father's legendary gangster status in the 'hood from back in the days. Cream never really talked about his father because he was trying to establish and cement his own street identity. But from the little that I had heard through the grapevine, I was able to learn that since Cream was the son of this infamous gangster, he sort of walked around like he was a prince or like an heir to the throne. It commanded respect and authority.

As I continued to look at and examine things I also realized that I had way more brains than Cream. I too was capable of being a manipulator. I just needed to elevate my status and my street credibility amongst those in the New York City underworld. If I could do that, then with or without Cream, I would be more than able to handle myself and survive for decades. Eventually I would be the one with the legendary street status.

I had to start getting everyone to know who I was and who I ran with, which was something that was already starting to happen. I had to take it to the next level and let people in the streets know that this young, fine-ass, sexy bitch was an integral part of the Cream Team and not just some trick hanging around to feed off of the crumbs. Hell, I was the one who was helping to make a whole lot of cake for the Cream Team. In fact, many people were starting to eat off the cake I was helping to create.

There was no better time than the present for me to make my move, considering Cream was gonna be laying low for a while. I always loved the club scene, and I had become permanently addicted to it ever since Cream had taken me to Club New York for the first time and afforded me the opportunity to mingle with all of the stars. So, where better than the club scene to promote my image and who I was? I had always wanted to add the title of "club promoter" to my list of hustles, and now was the best time to do that. Not to mention, it would help me create another revenue stream.

Without Cream's knowledge or approval I immediately went to work. I started checking out clubs and trying to find out where I could rent a club in order to throw my own party. Labor Day was right around the corner so most of the clubs in Manhattan had already been booked. But fortunately for me, the Q-Club in Jamaica, Queens, had not been reserved for the Labor Day weekend. I didn't hesitate in paying the owner of the club five thousand dollars to reserve the club for the Saturday of that Labor Day weekend.

I only had about two weeks to promote. I knew that was not a lot of time but it was something. So I began to lean on everybody and started asking people to get me in touch with some of the best deejays in town. I knew that DJ Clue and some of the other top disc jockeys would already be booked but everyone kept telling me about this deejay named Boo-Da-Man. I got in contact with Boo-Da-Man and let him know who I was and what I was doing. And it was funny because as soon as I mentioned that I was with the Cream Team he immediately agreed to do the event.

We agreed on a price of one thousand dollars. I met him at one of my car washes and paid him half of the money. I told him I would give him the other half on the night of the event.

Boo-Da-Man turned out to be a great contact. He knew the club promotion game, a game about which I knew nothing. But I knew enough to use my charm and wit—my mojo as I liked to call it—to get Boo-Da-Man to work with me and make sure my first club event would be successful. Boo said it was vital for me to get one of the local popular radio personalities to come to the club to host the party. It was like one hand washing the other. If I could get a radio personality to do the event then I would get free promotion as well as discounted radio ads.

That was a no-brainer. It was something I was willing to pay for but I was sure almost everyone would be booked. Luckily Boo came through for me big time. Boo was good friends with a famous Queens native named Mr. Cheeks from the Lost Boyz. Mr. Cheeks was cool with Wendy Williams, who worked on a popular New York radio station at the time. So Mr. Cheeks did Boo a favor and reached out to Wendy Williams and she agreed to host the party as long as I was willing to pay her two thousand dollars for the night. Needless to say I had no problem paying the dough. We also worked out a deal where I paid her half of her money up front and the other half when she arrived at the club.

In a matter of days things had started to take form. Everything was moving really fast and looking real nice at the same time. And then I got the luckiest break I could have ever imagined. Boo-Da-Man had been raving about how I looked and about the sexy girls in thongs who I had working for me at the car wash. Mr. Cheeks decided to pay a visit to one of my car washes in Queens, and he didn't come alone. He was accompanied by the man who, in my opinion, started all of the booty-shaking videos, Luke.

Shauna called me on my cell phone in a panic one day.

"Lady! Lady! Oh my god. You will never guess who is standing in the car wash right now flirting with some of the girls."

"Who?" I asked. Shauna's excitement had gotten me excited.

"Okay, let me calm down before they hear me. I definitely don't wanna be looking like no groupie. . . . Mr. Cheeks and Luke just pulled up in a BMW!"

"Shauna, you are lying!"

"Lady, I swear to god! Where are you at? You need to hurry up and get your ass over here!"

I was in Brooklyn getting my hair done. There was no way in the world I would be able to make it to Queens for another two hours. Everybody in Queens knew Mr. Cheeks or at least they knew of him, so my excitement had more to do with the fact that Luke was actually at one of my car washes.

"Shauna, you gotta get Luke on the phone for me."

I was hoping that for once Shauna would muster up a bit of credible game, enough to get Luke to come to the phone. And fortunately for me she was able to do just that.

"Yo!" Luke said into the cell phone.

Assuming it was Luke, I just began to talk.

"Luke, my girl was telling me that you had stopped. I just wanted to say hello and make sure that you are being taken good care of."

"Are you Lady?" Luke asked.

"Yeah, that's me," I said as I smiled the biggest Kool-Aid smile.

"Lady, my man is getting his car taken care of, I'm not the one driving. But let me tell you that you are a straight-up genius!"

I began to laugh into the phone.

"You don't mind if I take your idea back to Miami and use it down there, do you?"

"Luke, of course not! I mean if anything, my idea was kind of inspired from your dancers. You know you the one that started the whole booty-shaking thing in the first place. I'm not in the record industry so I had to pick up your game where I could . . . I had to get in where I could fit in, you kna'imean?"

Luke began to laugh. "I like that."

"Listen, Luke. I know I don't know you from Adam, but you might know this dude named Cream. Well, I—"

Luke cut me off in the middle of my sentence, "Yeah I know who Cream is. . . . I mean I heard of him."

"Well, I'm the Cream Team's First Lady and I'm throwing this Labor Day event at the Q-Club in Queens. I would love for you to perform."

I didn't know where I had pulled that "Cream Team's First Lady" thing from but it sounded smooth as hell.

Luke went on to explain that he was already booked somewhere else in New York for Labor Day but that he would try to shoot by my event and just show his face.

Trying not to sound desperate I quickly said, "Luke, if you could just come by and do like one song, just do that "Doo Doo Brown" song and that's it, and I'll hit you off with like two thousand dollars. Just kill it for five minutes, that's it."

I was hoping that two G's wasn't an insult for someone of Luke's caliber but I mean come on, two G's for five minutes? That had to be a lot of cake no matter who you were.

Luke thought about it and then he said that Mr. Cheeks had already told him about the party that I was promoting.

"A'ight cool, but I gotta get on by eleven P.M. and I gotta be out right away. I know eleven is early but that's the best I can do."

I wanted to drop my cell phone and run out into the street with my hair half done. I was so charged!

"Luke, are you kidding me? I don't care what time you get on, just as long as you can come by."

"You got my word, I'll be there," Luke assured me.

I didn't know then, but that was another day in my life that proved to be significant. I knew that from that moment on I was really something special. I really had something going on for me that others just didn't have. I didn't know what it was but I was glad that I had it.

After I got off the phone with Luke, my first call was to the printer who I had already given an order to print up like twenty thousand promotional postcard flyers for me. I told him that I would there in about three hours and that I had to up the order to forty thousand pieces and that I had to redo the layout of the entire piece.

I changed everything. My radio ads and all of my print promotional material relayed something to this effect:

> Come party with the Cream Team's First Lady this Labor Day weekend at the Q-Club. The party will be hosted by New York's own Wendy Williams, music by DJ Boo-Da-Man and a special performance by Luke. The first hundred ladies are free. $30 at the door and $20 in advance. Doors open at 10 PM. Dress to impress. Virgin-tight security.

I knew that my first experience as a club promoter was definitely gonna be a smash simply because of the big names that I had representing me. But I was never one to rest on my laurels and sit back and wait for things to happen. I knew that I still had to make sure that things would jump off the way I wanted.

So of course I had to leverage the fact that I had hundreds of people coming to my car washes. I made sure that all of my workers told every customer about the Labor Day event at the Q-Club. I also paid the Mexican workers some extra money to go to all of the malls and put promotional materials on the windshields of all of the parked cars. I also had them handing out flyers at all of the major shopping hubs like downtown Brooklyn and on Fordham Road in the Bronx. As Boo-Da-Man had explained to me, the name of the game when it came to club promotion was overexposure of the event. Boo-Da-Man further explained to me that if I wanted two thousand people to show up I would have to expose it to the masses. That would be the only way to guarantee a return on my investment.

I had done a real good job getting all of my close friends and associates hyped on the idea that I was gonna be New York's next big-time club promoter. However, there was one person who was not all that enthused about my newfound way of making money. That person was Cream. Cream had been in the dark about what I had been planning and what I had put into motion, and he took that as a huge slight.

Since I had been planning to move out on my own, I had been spending more of my nights at Shauna's apartment and a lot less time at Cream's house in Astoria. But on the day that he found out about the Labor Day event he got ahold of me on the phone and basically told me that he wanted me to spend the night at his crib. He wasn't real with me about what his true intentions were for wanting me to come over to his crib, and he never let on that he was upset with me. However, as soon as I was face-to-face with him in his kitchen it was a whole different story.

I had let myself into the house and I made it to the kitchen where I saw Cream cooking something. Although it was way past breakfast time it smelled a lot like he was cooking fish and grits.

"Hey baby," I said as I took a seat at the table.

Cream didn't acknowledge me with a hello or any of that politeness. He immediately reached onto the countertop and picked up one of my glossy promotional flyers.

"Lady, what the hell is this?!" Cream asked in a real pissed-off tone.

"That's for a party that I'm promoting at the Q-Club on Labor Day weekend," I replied.

"I know what it is, but what is all of this about 'Come party with the Cream Team's First Lady'?! Who is this First Lady?!"

"Cream, come on, you know that's me—"

Cream cut me off. He looked as if he had snapped into one of those sadistic rages, and I didn't know what to expect.

"Yeah, I figured it was referring to you, but I just wanted to confirm it!" Cream stated angrily as he walked over to me and stood in my face.

He continued on, "Yo, let me explain something to you. This is my team! It's my crew! I'm running it! Who are you to throw some party and then try to play me by not telling me about it?! And tell me, who made you Cream Team's First Lady?!"

As I sat there I felt like I was getting scolded by my mother or somebody. And I ain't gonna front, I respected Cream and I feared his authority, but I knew that I could only let that fear and respect guide me so far. I was far from being disrespected by anyone, even if it meant risking my life.

I rose up from my chair and at the same time I raised my voice. "Cream, hold up a minute. Number one, I was gonna tell you about it!"

"When?!" Cream screamed.

"I was gonna tell you about it tonight!"

"Lady, word is bond. I'm not one of your little-ass friends out on the street! I've killed niggas who showed me more respect than what you're showing me right now!"

"So what are you saying?!" I asked. I was prepared to fight Cream as if I was a dude, even if I was gonna get my ass kicked. I quickly switched up into full fight mode.

"What, bitch?!" Cream hollered as he slapped me and then pushed me. He punched me in the face and then he grabbed me by the throat and lifted me off the floor with one hand.

The pressure from his grip felt like he was gonna squeeze all of the life out of me and I also felt like he was crushing all of the bones in my throat. But that didn't stop me from fighting back. I began throwing punches at his head and face. I was connecting with every punch that I threw but I wasn't sure if they were having any effect. Finally Cream threw me to the ground.

"I should kill your ass right now, bitch!" Cream threatened.

"Well then kill me!" I shouted back while coughing and gasping for air.

Cream looked at me.

"Kill me then! You the one acting like some punk bitch! I can't believe you're choking me because of some party!"

"You see that hot-ass fish grease that's over there on that fire? I should throw it on your ass right now!" Cream threatened. "We need to let everybody see the 'First Lady' with third-degree burns all over her face!" Cream added sarcastically as he tried to mimic and mock me.

I was mad as hell and I was glad that I didn't have a knife or a gun or anything like that on me because I definitely would have attempted to use it on Cream.

"I'm outta here!" I said as I made my way out of the kitchen and attempted to leave the house.

"Bitch, you ain't leaving this house!" Cream screamed as he yanked me by my hair and proceeded to beat my ass.

I was never one to get provoked and not fight back but I knew that if I fought back it would only prolong the beating that I was receiving. I just wanted the whole thing to end as quickly as possible. Cream unleashed a fury of blows to my face and my body and then he pulled me to the ground by my hair and kicked me numerous times in the ribs. He kicked me so hard that I definitely thought he had broken a few of my ribs.

As I laid on Cream's thirty-thousand-dollar living room floor gasping for air, he stood over me with one of his brand new Timberland boots pressed up against my throat. He was applying as much pressure as he could.

"Lady, you ain't nothing but a good-hair hoe! You understand that?! I'm the one that made you what you are! I took your ass off the street and this is how you repay me? By trying to snake me?! You forgetting where you came from or do I need to remind you?!"

Finally, as I felt like I was just about to pass out, Cream removed his foot from my throat.

"Get your ass up!" Cream yelled at me. "Hurry up!"

As I tried to get up and made it to my knees, Cream unzipped his pants and he put his joint in my face.

"This is all you were and all you ever would have been without me! You would have been some trick on your knees sucking dick for two dollars!"

Thank god Cream didn't humiliate me more by making me pleasure him right there on the spot. He pulled up his pants and commanded me to go into the bathroom and clean myself up. And that is exactly what I did as he nonchalantly walked back into the kitchen and finished frying his fish like the true psychopath that he was.

When I made it to his bathroom I could barely stand up because of the sharp pain that ran up and down the side of my abdomen. Immediately I looked in the mirror and I was so thankful that I didn't have any black eyes or any major bruises on my face. My face was basically still intact. I didn't know what to think. But I do remember having a flashback to when I was about ten years old and witnessing my mother being beaten in a similar fashion by her boyfriend. How ironic it was that I was following in her footsteps. Yeah, now I was the one who was sort of dependent on a man and being beaten by that same man.

It's a'ight, Lady, I told myself as I tried to justify the ass-whipping I had just received. Although I had seen Cream beat numerous girls before, I never thought that I would end up on the receiving end of his fists.

You did kind of disrespect him. I was having all kinds of thoughts. And while I knew that no woman deserved to get beat by a man, I still knew that in the world in which I was living in, I should have expected it to happen to me sooner or later. In fact I was surprised that it hadn't happened to me sooner.

Just dust yourself off and apologize and keep it moving like everything is a'ight, I told myself. I applied some water and soap to my face and then I tried to fix up my hair. After doing that, I closed the toilet bowl seat and just sat there and buried my face in my hands. Although I wanted to cry, at that point I would not let myself shed any tears over the situation.

Holding my ribs, I gingerly made it down to the kitchen where Cream was still frying his fish. The look on his face told me that he was still visibly angry and upset.

I walked over close to him and said, "Baby, I'm so sorry . . . I am."

Cream ignored me and continued to cook his fish.

"Cream, please just look at me and hear me out."

Cream still had anger in him and he let some of it vent through his voice. "You waited until you thought I was at a weak point and then you decided to pull this! I know you figured that since I was laying off the streets and laying low for a minute that you would try to use that as your opportunity to steal my shine . . . Right?!"

I couldn't help it anymore and finally tears formed in my eyes. I talked through my tears and said, "Cream, honestly that is not it. Everything just happened so quickly and I figured that you would be okay with it. Really, I was thinking that we had to figure out another way to make money while laying low and still promote the Cream Team so that niggas on the street would know we were still out there."

"Lady, let me call the shots! That's the way I run my ship. You can't be out there just making moves when you feel like it. That's how things get sloppy and that's how everybody goes down! Shamgod got sloppy and I'm still feeling the effects of that!"

I continued to endure a night-long lecture from Cream. Before falling asleep in his bed, I had no idea if I would wake up the next morning or not. I knew that I had put myself at risk of getting killed by Cream or someone else if Cream were to give the order. That was the life and the world that I had willingly chosen to live in and to stay in. Truthfully, at that point the reality was there really was no leaving that life. Even if I wanted to leave it, I was in too deep and subject to Cream's will. I knew that I had to really play by the rules from now on if I wanted to make it and thrive in that life and not just *survive* in that life.

Cream was probably right, I probably would have been some two-dollar street whore if it wasn't for him. I hated the fact that he was probably right, but what I hated the most was that the only reason I had been beaten was because Cream was jealous of me. He knew that I was smarter than he was and that I had a better mind for making money. I think he felt intimidated by that. He wanted to control me. With Cream everything was about him being in control. Either control by manipulation or control by force or the threat of force. Unfortunately, I was under his control, and I had to respect that. After all, I had brought it on myself.

24

IN EVERY TYPE OF CRIME syndicate such as the Cream Team, the Italian mafia, or any other type of gang or crew there is always someone with the brains and someone that provides the muscle for the organization. As I recovered from the beating that Cream had given me, and nursed my sore ribs, I realized that I indeed did have the brains to establish my own street identity apart from that of the Cream Team's. But the one thing that I lacked—and it played a big part in why I had gotten my ass kicked by Cream—was that I didn't have any muscle. By that I mean I didn't have anyone who I could call on who could be at my disposal in a split second and ready to kill for me.

See, Cream had Spinach and a whole host of other characters, including myself who he could call on to *handle* any situations that may have sprung up requiring guns to be drawn or throats to be slit. Aside from my affiliations with the team, I didn't have any muscle that I could call on. I knew that that had to change. I wasn't in a rush to start recruiting hit men or anything like that but I was definitely gonna keep my eyes open for potential hit-man candidates that I could start surrounding myself with.

One thing I had to burn into my head was that my life was more valuable than anyone else's life. And it was damn sure more valuable than Cream's life. If it had been anyone else who had stomped me out the way he did, there is no question in my mind that the person would have been killed. All I would have had to have done was call on Cream or Spinach to handle it for me. But the thing was, I told myself, in the future, even if it was Cream who was the one disrespecting me, I needed to know that I could go to someone and have them take Cream out on my command. Cream put on his pants the same way I did, so he was no superman who was above being taken out.

In the back of my mind, I knew that Cream didn't like many of the Jamaican crews that populated the borough of Brooklyn. He had long ongoing beefs with them over the marijuana trade that he controlled. So I knew that members of some of the Jamaican crews would be ideal candidates to serve as hit men for me. And like I said, I was in no rush to befriend any of the Jamaicans. But I knew that I would eventually have to do that. I would have to keep that top secret from Cream.

The bottom line was I had to watch out for myself and I had to think about my future. Cream was liable to get killed or locked up and then where would that leave me? I wasn't about to leave nothing up to chance and in the background I continued to formalize my plan to be my own independent and self sufficient street queen. I had the brains and all I needed now was the muscle.

In the meantime, I continued to play good soldier. I had to put the beating behind me and I made sure not to tell anyone about what had happened. Verbally, Cream didn't say anything more to me about staying in check. And really he didn't have to say anything per se, he just walked around with this certain persona about him that sort of said, "Yeah, I taught that bitch a lesson!"

The way he walked around, all cocky as hell, made me sick to my stomach, but I sucked it up, blocked it out, and endured it while I continued to get money. I continued to make money, but I also remembered very vividly how Cream had set up Shamgod and had me shoot him in the back of his head. So needless to say, I was constantly looking over my shoulder and wishing that I had eyes in the back of my head. It's an ill feeling to be literally walking around on edge and not sure if someone is plotting to blow your brains out at any second. But that was my reality after having disrespected Cream.

However, with me constantly looking over my shoulder time passed quickly and before I knew it the Labor Day weekend had rolled up on us. I had shelled out close to fifteen thousand dollars for my debut as a club promoter. I wanted to make sure that things would jump off the way I wanted them to. So when that Saturday came I was nervous and desperately hoping that I would recoupe all of my expenses and still make a decent profit. I was also hoping that everyone like Luke and Wendy Williams would actually show up as promised.

Shauna and I had gone shopping the day before the club event. I treated her to whatever she wanted on the condition that she pick out something sexy and revealing. Surprisingly, Shauna said that she was game to wear whatever I thought would look nice on her.

"Girl, you know you shouldn't have told me that!" I jokingly told her.

"Lady, I'm a take a chance and trust you and wear whatever you think I would look good in."

Shauna didn't have to say any more. I wanted to let her wear something that would fit her somewhat conservative style but at the same time satisfy my wild side. After a few hours of shopping, I had finally spotted for Shauna what I thought was a dynamite outfit. It was an all-white velour cat suit. There were slits that ran down the entire side of each of the legs. The slits were so high that they did not stop until they reached Shauna's hip bone. Her back was fully exposed and the suit had this real loose-fitting hood that she could either let hang down around her shoulder blades or she could wear the hood and give herself this real bad-ass mysterious look. The front of the cat suit conformed to Shauna's body and exposed her cleavage, but at the same time it was baggy so that it went with the loose-fitted look of the hood. All I know is that it was off the chain!

Shauna came out of the dressing room and she was beaming from ear to ear.

"Lady, I can't believe that you have me in this," Shauna said, laughing.

"It looks good on you! Turn around . . . Yeah, now all we gotta do is get you the right heels to go with it and you'll be straight. . . . Let me see you walk in it."

Shauna and I both giggled as she modeled the cat suit like some high-powered fashion model.

"Naomi Campbell ain't got nothing on you, Shauna!" I said as I cheered her on.

Shauna stopped in front of a mirror and remarked, "Lady, do you see how high these slits are? My ass will be busting out the sides of this cat suit!"

I smiled and remarked, "I know. That's why I picked it out. You know you can't wear any underwear with that, right?"

"See, now you are trippin'. All I gotta do is put on a white thong," Shauna replied.

"Shauna, look at that slit! I'm telling you, even with a thong it will still look tacky because the thong will be showing."

"Oh my god! Okay, I cannot believe I volunteered to let you pick out my outfit but I'm a go with whatever you say."

I finished off Shauna's outfit by selecting some five-inch heels for her that were smoking! They had a clear-crystal look to the bottom and to the heels.

"Lady, I won't even be able to walk in them things! Picture me trying to dance in that!" Shauna stated.

"You'll be fine. Just practice walking and dancing in them tonight."

So with Shauna's outfit out of the way, it was time to move on to what I was gonna wear. I wanted to wear this bikini set and chaps— basically a pair of jeans where the butt had been cut out and the crotch had also been cut out. The crotch of the bikini and the butt of the bikini would have been fully exposed. But I figured that was too much over the top simply because I would have to be taking care of a lot of business as well as mixing and mingling with the people. Instead I decided to go with this aqua stretch lace mini-dress, and I do mean mini.

"Lady, that dress is so you!" Shauna emphatically stated as she watched me walk in it.

"You feeling it, right?!" I replied.

"Whaaat?!!"

When it came to shopping for myself I was sort of like a guy. It didn't take me too long to figure out what I wanted. I knew that I wanted to rock some high heels with my dress but I had a bit of a hard time finding heels that matched the outfit. Fortunately I finally did find the right pair of heels. They were also hot—five-inch heels that had straps that crisscrossed up and down my calves and then tied behind my calf.

The next day, Saturday, Shauna and I had to arrive at the club much earlier than everyone else just to make sure that everything was in order. Being that it was so early we went to the club in our regular clothes and finalized all of our business matters. But we had brought our outfits with us and had planned on waiting until around ten o'clock to change.

The doors to the club opened at exactly 9 P.M. Shauna and I had been inside the club so we had no idea what exactly was going on outside the club. While we sat in a private office of the club and chatted, the owner of the club knocked on the door and then came inside where we were sitting down.

"Ladies, I'm just letting you know that we opened the doors. Turn on that monitor when you get a chance. . . . I think it will be a good night," the owner stated. He smiled before leaving the room and closing the door behind him.

Shauna proceeded to turn on the little thirteen-inch black-and-white monitor that was located on a table right in front of us. When she turned it on we realized that closed-circuit security cameras were linked to the monitor which would display different areas of the club, both inside and out.

"Lady, I know that is not the line that's outside . . ." Shauna stated as she looked at the monitor.

I immediately stood up and turned the monitor so that it faced me. I leaned in to get a closer look.

"Shauna, look outside!" I said as I raised my voice in excitement. "I can tell that's One hundred fiftieth Street . . . See, look, there's the parking lot that's across the street and there goes the Long Island Railroad overpass."

"The line is sick!" Shauna stated.

"Yeah, I know," I replied. I wanted to get happy and yell and scream for joy, but first I wanted to confirm that all of the people on line were in fact waiting to get inside the Q-Club.

I quickly went upstairs to the main entrance and spoke to one of the bouncers.

"I just looked at the monitor downstairs and I can't believe the line. I came up to make sure this is real and not an old videotape was playing in the monitor."

The bouncer replied, "Nah, that's real. The line is wrapping all the way around the entire building and it's like three people deep per row."

"That is sick! It's only like nine o'clock!" I stated.

"Lady, that's a good problem to have."

"Yeah, I know, I know. I just didn't think that people would start getting here until around midnight. Yo, I'm gonna run down and get dressed. When Wendy gets here make sure you come and find me or send somebody to find me."

I retreated back downstairs to the office.

"Shauna, we gotta hurry up and get dressed. The line is wrapping around the entire block. It's gonna be off the hook in here tonight," I said as I poured myself a glass of Hennessy. I wanted to hurry up and get my buzz on.

Shauna and I quickly got dressed. Not that I would try to big up my own head or anything, but I had to admit that Shauna and I both looked good as hell. Still, I wanted confirmation from Shauna.

When I was done getting dressed I asked Shauna, "So, how do I look?"

"Girl, you know you look good! You ain't gotta ask me that! You're gonna be killing them in that dress."

I felt like I was in my element. I was getting my drink on. The club was gonna be packed. I was gonna make all kinds of money that night and I felt so sexy in my outfit. I literally had nothing on underneath my dress and if you looked close enough, through the lace you could see my entire body—nipples, pubic hair, and all. To me the sexiness of my outfit was what completed me. It was what helped me get in and stay in my element.

Boo-Da-Man was on point with the music right from the jump.

The thing that I didn't want was a whole bunch of people standing around and just looking at each other. I knew that thugs had this thing where they were too cool to dance, but I was determined to make sure that my first club event was gonna be a smash. I instructed Boo to play a whole lot of party songs and to hype the crowd and encourage everybody to get out on the dance floor and have a good time. I wanted to go to each individual person and make sure that they were having a good time but I simply couldn't. I had to remember that I wasn't at a house party and that I had work to do as the promoter of the club.

I had to constantly check with security to make sure that things were tight and on point. Of course I also had to keep checking on my money to make sure that I wasn't getting robbed. I had to do all of this while guys tried to kick it to me, while I bought drinks for people at the bar, and while I tried to party and have a good time myself.

Wendy Williams arrived around 10:30 P.M. I had instructed Shauna to square away all of the money with Wendy's handlers who were with her that night. I took Wendy to the private office that Shauna and I had been in earlier and she and I hit it off right away. I just loved everything about Wendy's vibe. It was like I could connect with her on a real level. We exchanged compliments and had our five minutes or so of small talk. She told me that she would do her best to make sure that everyone who came out that night had a good time.

As the small talk was about to end I made sure that I instructed Wendy to bring me on stage and to introduce me to the entire crowd. I wanted everybody to see me and to know who I was. I also told her how much I loved listening to her radio show. She told me that her show was her hustle and that she was hoping to use that to help springboard her into other endeavors.

"I hear you, I'm the same way when it comes to getting my hustle on," I said. I briefly explained to her how I had leveraged my Cream Team affiliation and how it helped me to make so much money. I told her about my car washes and about my newfound club promoter hustle.

From my slogan of being "Cream Team's First Lady" Wendy assumed that I was Cream's girl and she asked me about that. Right at that moment a lightbulb went off in my head. I realized that I was talking to the gossip queen of all media as far as black people were concerned. Wendy had the ear of millions of people every day. Who better, I thought, than Wendy to help me get that image out to the streets about who I was. But I knew that I had to tread real lightly because Cream was probably already plotting to kill me because of the whole first lady thing.

"Wendy, on the real, me and you should hang out together. Not for business reasons or anything like that. We need to hang out so you can see how I roll. I don't wanna really speak about Cream but just between me and you, I'm the one that masterminds a whole lot of that chedda the Cream Team is making that you hear niggas on the street talking about."

I wanted to give Wendy just enough to whet her appetite but I didn't wanna give away everything. I had to be real careful either way I rolled. See, if Wendy were to ever find out that I used to turn tricks on the street for Cream, I probably would have lost all credibility with her. And the last thing I wanted was to have her blow up my spot about that on the radio. But on the other hand, if I was able to get close to her and sell her on my gangstress way of living, I was hoping that she would be able to relay that to the public. Hopefully that would catapult my street credibility in the city.

I was determined to be "the woman" in New York City. I knew that in order to do that, I would have to take chances. And that is exactly what I was doing.

I guess Wendy was used to people trying to get close to her for their own benefit. She was good at not really brushing me off but at the same time she wasn't really trying to get all buddy-buddy with me and hang out with me. I mean, she had not even known me for more than ten minutes. She probably was looking at me as some cheap, loose, half-naked promoter, hoochie-momma chick who wanted to get close to her just to advance my own agenda.

"Let me hurry up and get out there to the crowd," Wendy said. "But we'll talk. Maybe I'll bring you on the show one day."

I knew that Wendy was just sidestepping me, but that was cool. As far as I was concerned I was glad that I had had a chance to personally meet Wendy and plant some seeds in her head.

Wendy began to hype the crowd. They loved her. They loved the way she looked, the way she was dressed, and most of all, they loved her energy. Just then, Cream and his boys arrived. They were rolling like twenty niggas deep. It was kind of rare for Cream to roll with so many niggas. But I guess he wanted to make an entrance. I was about to make it over to speak to him, but I could hear Wendy on the mic calling out my name.

Needless to say, I quickly made it to the stage where I gloated in the spotlight. Wendy did the perfect job of biggin' me up as she commented on how good "the Cream Team's First Lady's" outfit looked. She also told the crowd how I was on the come-up in the club scene and that everyone need not forget who I was. It was the perfect promo job and that alone was worth the two thousand dollars I had paid Wendy for the night.

After my two minutes of fame, I made it over to the bar area to where Cream was. I got hugs and kisses from all of his boys.

"What the hell do you got on?" Cream yelled into my ear as he grabbed my arm kind of tight.

"Cream, come on! Please don't start trippin' up in here!" I could not believe that he was still jealous over my promoting a party. I think the size of the crowd and the fact that Wendy had bigged me up as the Cream Team's First Lady added more fuel to his jealous fire. I mean, he was now coming across like some jealous boyfriend. He had never tripped about what I wore. So there was no reason whatsoever for him to be acting so stupid! And not for nothing, I'm sure that if I was standing on the street corner making money for his ass he would have had no problem with what I had on.

"Yeah, a'ight! But I'm saying you ain't gotta have your got damn nipples hanging out!"

"Cream, just have a drink, relax, and party. Look at all this chedda that we're making," I said. I was hoping that that would cheer him up and take him out of his jealous funk. I had never discussed giving him a dime of the money that I was gonna make. But just to be loyal to him and to the team, I had no problem with hitting him off with 20 percent of my take. I looked at it more like an advertising fee. After all, I had promoted the party by using the Cream Team name.

"So, what you think you looking at?" Cream asked. I knew that he was referring to money. It was funny how his tone and demeanor quickly shifted when talk of money came up.

Just at that point one of the bouncers came and told me that Luke had just arrived.

"Cream, I'll be back, I gotta handle something," I said as I just ran off without answering his money question.

I was so thankful that Shauna had my back all night long. She was so much my ace. She had already taken care of handling the money with Luke's manager and by the time I made it to Luke's private room it was like I was just being introduced to him as a regular fan who wanted to meet him.

"Lady, what's up, Miss?" Luke asked as he gave me a hug and told me that it was nice to meet me. I could not believe that Luke was telling me that it was nice to meet me! The whole scene was sort of surreal and it reminded me of the night I had met LL Cool J at Club New York.

I was surprised by how tall Luke was, and in my opinion there was just something sexy about him. He proceeded to introduce me to some of the people in his entourage as he flirted with me. His flirtatious way was something that I did not mind at all. In fact, he didn't know it but I was down for whatever. And yes, I do mean *whatever*.

Luke rolled with a huge entourage and of course he had his sexy thick dancers with him. While most women would have looked at his dancers as some stank, half-naked sluts and would have been repulsed, I was the total opposite. I instantly connected with his dancers and had no problem warming up to the girls who were with him.

"So, Luke, I know that y'all are gonna be in and out but just make sure that y'all rip it for me."

"Lady, don't even worry about it," Luke replied. "We even got a surprise for everybody."

I had a drink in my hand the entire night and was finally starting to feel the effects as I made my way back onto the jammed-packed dance floor. The club was literally packed wall-to-wall with people. The Q-Club only held about twelve hundred people comfortably and everything was all on one level. But I had been told that they had to start turning people away after they got to fifteen hundred people.

When Luke took the stage I was kind of terrified that a stampede or something was gonna break out. It was just too jammed inside the hot club. Ironically, I was glad that he had only agreed to do one song. If he had done a full show the security wouldn't have been able to handle the amount of people who might have rushed the stage or caused some kind of stampede.

Luke started off by shouting the end of his hit song. "Don't stop get it get it. Get it get it!"

The crowd went crazy and just sang along with Luke as his dancers took their positions and started to put on their show. Luke began to recite the full lyrics to the song. The song had so much energy that it was just straight bananas inside the club. It was a zoo! I remember grabbing Shauna and telling her that I couldn't believe that I had orchestrated the entire night.

As she watched Luke perform she shouted back, "You best believe it!"

Before long Luke had finished performing the one song. He shouted me out and then told the crowd that he had only come to do one song but that he did have a surprise for all of the fellas. He stated how he knew that all of the guys liked his girls and he asked for a male volunteer to come up on stage. There were hundreds of eager volunteers but Luke picked one guy at random from the crowd and the guy came up on stage. Luke asked the guy which girl he thought looked the best. The guy proceeded to point out the girl that he liked. Then one thing led to another and before I knew what was going on, the guy was getting a blow-job right on stage by Luke's dancer! Luke had the music turned back on and the entire crowd was screaming in unison, "Don't stop! Get it get it! Don't stop! Get it get it . . . Get it get it!"

I was shocked by what I was seeing. I was even more scared that something was gonna break out in terms of a riot or something. I was praying that there were no undercover cops up in the spot. But thank god the guy was a *minute-man* and the sexual act was over in a matter of minutes. Luke said some parting words to the crowd and then he and his entourage disappeared from the stage. DJ Boo-Da-Man followed up everything by continuing to play the exact same Doo-Doo Brown song that Luke had performed. That was a smart move because he kept the whole crowd in a nonstop frenzy.

By that time it was a little after midnight. Luke's performance had electrified the crowd to the point that literally everybody in the club was up and rocking. There were no wallflowers and no thugs just standing around holding their balls trying to act hard. The atmosphere was so charged that even the thugs were dancing. Cream too had loosened up and he was dancing, and that shocked the hell out of me. I began dancing with him and I seized the opportunity to stroke his ego.

I yelled in his ear, "Tell me that this ain't the most fun that you've ever had while making five thousand dollars!"

Cream was all business as he asked, "How much did *you* make?"

I screamed over the loud music, "Well, there are at least fifteen hundred people in here so I know that I had to have grossed at least forty thousand. But I laid out fifteen grand so I know I'm leaving here with at least twenty-five grand tonight. Matter of fact, it will be more because I got half of the bar!"

Cream finally smiled.

"You see! . . . You bitch-ass!" I jokingly said as I punched Cream on his arm.

Then I added, "You know that all of these people are only in here because I promoted it as a Cream Team event, right?"

Cream nodded his head.

"Baby, just trust me! I'm not trying to steal your shine," I added.

The energy of the crowd remained frenzied until about three in the morning. People didn't start leaving until then but the party went on until about five in the morning.

When everything was all said and done, I had further confirmed what had to be my calling in life. I had been in my element all night long and I actually got paid for it! I chilled and talked with stars, I danced, I got my drink on, I got my flirt on, I looked sexy as hell, the whole crowd got to know who I was, and I was the woman of the night! Flat-out, straight up and down, I had been the woman all night long! Or should I say I had been the *Lady* all night long!

Cream was happy with the five grand that I gave him that night. He actually should have gotten more but he was cool with the nice round number. The take for myself, with ticket sales and half the money from the bar minus Cream's five thousand, was right around twenty-seven thousand dollars! And of course I had to break my girl Shauna off with a couple of Gs.

Shauna and I didn't make it back to her apartment until about six thirty in the morning. She was convinced that I was the smartest business person she had ever seen. I agreed with her. I knew that it was just a matter of time before I would be controlling New York City and maybe even running and controlling the Cream Team.

25

Seven months after the Q-Club event.

BY THE TIME THE SPRING of 1996 came upon us, I had reached the age of seventeen. Yes, after all that I had experienced and been through, I was still only the tender age of seventeen. I never went back to Hillcrest High School in the fall semester. Instead I had decided to just take the G.E.D. test, which I passed with flying colors. I liked school and I knew that I was smart enough to graduate with honors, but to me, school was getting in the way of all that I was doing, which mainly was making money.

By the age of seventeen, I was chilling and living larger than most people who were twice and three times my age. I continued to try to make all smart moves and being that I was young I leaned on my lawyer for a lot of expensive help and advice. Looking back, I know that the lawyer's fees that I paid were more than worth it.

My lawyer had helped me to rent a house with an option to buy, which was located in one of the more expensive sections of Queens known as Jamaica Estates. On my own there was no way in hell the white people of Jamaica Estates would have let me move in there, even if I could afford the price of the houses. But by hiding behind my lawyer—having him do all of the paperwork and make all of the contacts for me, I was able to live in an $1,800 a month four-bedroom house. Eighteen hundred dollars a month may not sound like much money, but back in the early part of 1996 it was indeed a lot of money to be shelling out on a monthly basis for living quarters. My house was equipped with a two-car garage, which was perfect for me considering I had my Mercedes-Benz and I also had purchased a Toyota Land Cruiser. Money was starting to become no object for me, and I was planning on purchasing the Lexus GS300.

In all, I would say that the best part about having money was that I was finally able to live independently. I had moved out of Cream's house and I was on my own. Every day I still had still look over my shoulder and watch out for Cream or one of his boys to execute a plot to take me out. Although I was real cool with everyone in the crew, I knew that being paranoid was the best way to function when it came to rolling with those guys. Despite my hidden paranoia I decided to let my sister move in with me.

Mya looked up to me so much and I was glad to finally be able to take her out of the dysfunctional conditions she had been subjected to. Since I had been making so much legitimate money I was able to shield Mya from the money that I made helping Cream manage his prostitution business.

As I said, I was always kind of paranoid that Cream's jealousy and psychopathic ways would one day well up to the point where he would take me out. I could live with that fact, but I was afraid for Mya. I didn't want her to ever come home and find me dead or witness me being murdered. But again, with the street lifestyle that I had chosen, that was just one of the possibilities that I had to coexist with.

Shauna and I were still real cool and I knew that there was no way that our relationship would ever change. She had desperately wanted me to move into her apartment complex, and I had planned on doing so, but I wanted the spaciousness of a big, private house. Shauna had started to spend so much time in my new home, it was like she practically lived with me anyway. So I guess everything worked itself out.

She and I had the best set-up in the world in terms of two young, sexy sisters who were just living it up. Shauna had finally quit her job as a legal secretary and she was working with me full time, helping me to be a successful club promoter. I am damn sure that she liked the tradeoff. She no longer had to work no hectic and demanding forty-hour work week in which she would receive peanuts. Working with me, she was able to sleep late in the process she received a couple grand a week for her efforts.

Shauna had stepped up her car game. She still had her Honda Civic but she rarely drove it. Instead she would always be seen in her dark blue convertible 325 BMW and it was perfect for her. In addition to her being able to floss around town with her top down, the BMW helped her get around town paying deejays and doing all kinds of promotional work. My weekly club promotion was a smash each and every week.

After the success of the Labor Day weekend event at the Q-Club, I had decided to step things up and moved to a bigger venue in Manhattan. In New York the club scene was really on and popping. Every individual borough had their certain *spots*, but Manhattan was really where everything went down as far as clubs were concerned.

There was this popular nightclub at the time called the Palladium. The Palladium was huge and it had all of the amenities necessary for a successful club. It had more than one level, it had more than one bar, it was modern, and could hold a lot of people. Shauna and I were able to work out a deal with the owner where every Saturday night was *our* night at the Palladium, which meant that no other promoter could have Saturday night at that particular club.

What I did was I dubbed Saturday night at the Palladium "Lady's Night." It was a play on words but it worked really well and I loved the way it just flowed. Despite Cream's initial objections, I continued to roll with the tag of "Cream Team's First Lady." Only I changed up all of my promotional material and flyers so that it stated something to the effect of "Cream Team's First Lady presents Lady's Night" at the Palladium each and every Saturday night. In no time I had a cult-like following in New York City and I was netting more than thirty thousand dollars a week just from promoting a club! It was truly bananas but I loved every minute of it and I loved every cent that I was making. The thirty thousand did not even include other monies from all of my other activities.

By the summer of 1996—while I was making so much money each

week—the police had really stepped up their investigation of Cream and as they put it, his *criminal enterprise*. He knew that his days on the street were numbered and that his arrest and indictment was near. Cream did in fact get bagged by the authorities in the summer of 1996. The whole Cream Team knew what was coming in terms of Cream eventually having to be held accountable for his years of criminal activity. So what we did was we had prepared in advance and stashed away money for Cream's defense team and for his bail.

However the authorities pulled a real fast one on Cream. We had known that the New York City police had been investigating Cream, and we also suspected that the feds were investigating him. We were almost certain that he was gonna be indicted on a host of state charges and possibly on a federal charge. We had come to our own conclusions as to what those charges would be. However, when the charges were handed down we found ourselves shocked, surprised, and wrong.

The authorities wanted Cream off the street. In order to successfully prosecute him, they knew that they would have to have a lot of witnesses and evidence to make their charges stick. I'm sure they figured many witnesses would be unwilling to truthfully testify against Cream. We doubted that they had infiltrated the team in a way where they were able to obtain video or audiotape evidence to incriminate Cream. So, with those two factors against them the die was rolled and Cream was arrested and indicted for tax evasion.

At first, the whole team was relieved, but that relief quickly turned to dread. We soon learned from Cream's attorney that indicting on tax evasion charges was a tactic the feds used to put away criminals despite poor evidence. It was a sort of silver-bullet approach.

Cream had lived real high on the hog for quite some time. And never in his life had he had a regular job. He had accumulated so much and not once did he ever pay a single penny in local, state, or federal income taxes. He had to account for the homes that he had, the cars, and the large amounts of cash. Plus the jewelry, the diamonds, the thirty-thousand-dollar living room floor, the different commercial spaces that he used to front illegal businesses—everything that he had accumulated over the years had to be accounted for.

Cream's criminal-defense lawyer recommended that we hire a tax attorney. So we brought in a Jewish New Jersey–based tax lawyer who was considered the best in his field and he pored over everything. He looked for any and every possible loophole that he could find in order to spring Cream from the tax evasion charges. But Cream needed a valid and traceable source of income if he expected to receive some kind of leniency. But even if Cream had been able to come up with a traceable source of income, he still owed his taxes. Add to that figure the interest and penalties, and we were dealing with an astronomical figure.

Cream's attorney suggested he not even go to trial but just plead guilty to the charges and pay the huge fine in exchange for a reduced sentence of five years in prison. Cream was a fighter and he hated to be taken down without a fight but he knew that smart people only fight battles that they know they can win. And in his case there was just no hope of beating the charges.

So by early 1997, Cream had been shipped off to federal prison. All of his assets had been frozen since the time of the indictment. Now that he had been hauled off to prison, everything he had owned had been scheduled to be auctioned off in order to pay his fine.

Just like that, all of the material things Cream had spent time and energy acquiring were stripped from him. In a flash he literally had nothing. The only thing he still had was his name. It still held some weight on the street. But with him locked down and out of sight and with word that his organization had been stripped of its cash, numerous wannabes were ready to move in like hungry buzzards and devour Cream's remains and start building where he'd left off.

When I drove by what used to be Cream's residence in Queens—the same residence with the expensive thirty-thousand dollar floor—the windows and doors were boarded up and padlocked shut. But the writing on the plywood that covered the front bay window literally spelled out what his being hauled off to jail meant to some of his enemies.

Spray-painted in bright red on the plywood was the following:

LADIES, THE CREAM PUFF IS IN JAIL. IF Y'ALL WANT A REAL DADDY COME HOLLER AT THE RUDE BOYZ FROM THE BROOKLYN MASSIVE.

Brooklyn Massive was the name of the Jamaican gang from Crown

Heights, who hated Cream with a passion and had wanted to take over his marijuana hustle. The marijuana hustle was sure to be theirs with Cream locked away. Obviously, they would also be coming after Cream's girls and trying to take over Cream's prostitution hustle.

26

MY FIRST VISIT TO CREAM in federal prison was in April of 1997. I went alone to see him and I also went with an agenda. I gave Cream the biggest and warmest embrace when I saw him, along with a nice juicy kiss.

"How you making out?" I asked with genuine concern and passion in my voice.

As Cream and I sat down he remarked that he was doing well. He could tell that the time he had to do would not be that harsh.

Cream continued to talk and he said to me, "Lady, you know, I've been in here, I've been thinking a whole lot. They may have locked me up but on the real I think I got a real good deal. Word, I mean look at all the dirt I did. A whole host of niggas would trade what I had if they knew that they were only risking five years in the joint."

I could read between Cream's attempt to come across humbly and his attempt to still come across like he was the man. So, I just played along and stroked his imprisoned ego.

"I know what you're saying. But you know what? Most niggas in your position would be facing twenty-five to life. It just shows that all along you had been playing the right cards."

Cream nodded his head in agreement.

"So what's up? Where do we go from here?" I asked.

"You know what? The bottom line is that I just gotta try to maintain, and there ain't really much that I can do from in here. I mean, niggas on the street ain't loyal so there ain't no sense in me trying to call the shots from in here. You kna'imean? And these unloyal hoes already laying up with them Jamaican niggas!"

"Cream, that's not true. From the jump I've been telling you that if you were willing to be down for me then I would be willing to be down for you. I can speak for myself and tell you that I will be loyal to you while you do your bid."

"That's peace right there," Cream stated.

"Nah, it's more than peace. That's love!"

"Whatchu mean?" Cream asked.

"Well, this is what I mean. I've been killing this whole club scene. I'm the hottest club promoter in New York and I think I got a plan that can hold everything down until you get out."

Cream seemed to come to life just a bit after I spoke those words.

"Spit . . . Tell me what's up," Cream instructed.

"I'm netting a little more than thirty grand a week from my one night at the Palladium. The thing is I could be making more but I get zero dollars from the bar. The owner is keeping all of that money. I was thinking hard about how to really do it up with this club thing so I had my lawyer look into properties in Manhattan that I can buy. I need to leave the Palladium and just open my own joint. I can own my own club. There's nothing to it."

"So if you do that how would that hold everything down?"

"First of all it's not a matter of if. It's a matter of when. I got enough dough stashed that I can buy my own club or at least rent one with the option to buy it outright at a later date. Now, if I were to do that, I could rent out six nights a week to different promoters for like ten grand a night. That right there would bring me sixty grand a week and then on top of that I could continue to have Lady's Night, only it will be at my own club."

Cream replied, "Yeah, I'm feeling the idea but how is that gonna hold everything down until I get out? Are you talking in terms of just cash?"

"Well, yeah, I mean I'll still give you your twenty percent. I'll stash your cake for you and when you hit the bricks you'll have at least a quarter of a million waiting for you, if not a whole lot more. But what I'm getting at is this, I could make the club serve as our headquarters and our base of operations. While all of these clown-ass niggas like Brooklyn Massive are out on the street fighting each other over territory and all of that, we could have one central spot that we own and control. We could do whatever the hell we wanna do at that one spot, because it will be ours."

Cream began to get noticeably intrigued by what I was saying.

"We could sell weed, ecstasy, coke, or whatever, right at the club to all of the people that come into the club. Plus we can still have girls on the premises selling sex and blow-jobs. We would just have to do it slick enough so that the cops won't know what's up. I'm telling you, we'll make more dough than we was making when you was out on the bricks."

"Lady, I definitely see your vision and I'm definitely feeling it!"

"See, now this is the thing. I know Spinach is your boy and I know that you probably trust him more than you trust me."

Cream interrupted me and said, "Nah, Lady, you know that I trust you one hundred percent so it's not even like that."

"I'm just sayin'," I added.

"Well, just continue with what you were getting at," Cream urged.

"Well, what I want you to do is just make me acting boss of the Cream Team. You're still the man and still in charge but in order to run things the way they need to be run, I need to be able to make decisions without second-guessing myself and wondering if you would approve of the decisions that I'll need to make."

"Decisions like what?" Cream asked.

"That's the thing. I don't know. Anything could come up and I just need the autonomy to act with my gut instincts. If I need to check with you for everything then eventually that is gonna screw something up somewhere along the line."

Cream remained silent for a few seconds.

"You think you could handle something like that?" Cream asked as he broke his silence.

"I know I could!" I confidently replied. "And plus, it will be my club, so to me it's only right that I have full control all around if that's gonna be the base of the Cream Team's operations."

Cream continued to think.

"Cream, when you come out, I ain't gonna have no problem putting everything back in your hands. And you be honest and ask yourself if you could say that about anybody else. Do you honestly believe that if you put someone other than myself in charge that they would easily hand everything back over to you once you get out?"

"You right," Cream replied under his breath. "A'ight, I'm a cosign on it. But just do me a favor and don't say anything to anyone until I first talk to Spinach and let him know what's up."

"Definitely," I replied. I continued on, "And Cream, I know that back in the days, in '95, you hated me using the whole tag of Cream Team's First Lady, but—"

Cream cut me off and added, "Nah. That's nothing. I was immature back then and I overreacted to all of that."

"Yeah, you sure as hell did," I said sarcastically as we both began to laugh.

I continued on, "But the thing is this. I'm cool with a lot of the radio personalities and I need them to help me get this new image out there of myself. I want people to know that in addition to being this sexy-ass club promoter who runs with the Cream Team, I am also ill and capable of murdering niggas if I have to. Also, that I now officially run the Cream Team while you're locked down."

"What?!" Cream asked.

"Trust me, Cream . . ."

"But why would you wanna put that out there? All it's gonna do is attract unnecessary attention from the police."

"Nah, it won't. What it will do is give me all kinds of street credibility and there will be this added mystique about me and niggas will respect me more."

"Yo, you can do what you want. . . . But to me, that's risky as hell and it's gonna cause you to end up right where I'm at. . . . Plus, how would you just put something out there like that?"

"All I gotta do is sort of hint to the right people that I'm the one who pulled off that hit on Shamgod."

"Lady, now you are straight buggin'! Don't you know that there ain't no statute of limitations on murder? You start putting that out there and your lips are gonna sink you."

"But Cream, just trust me. Even if that's the case, let me take the risk. I would never implicate you or anyone else in anything that I say, so really there's no problem."

Cream humbly replied, "A minute ago I told you that I'm cosigning on you being the acting boss, so really, I don't agree with that part of your plan. But I'll go along with it because you're in charge, Ms. Lady."

I gleamed on the inside as everything that I had ever envisioned, both consciously and subconsciously, was starting to come to fruition.

I left the prison that day feeling so empowered. I finally felt like a dark cloud had been lifted from over me. That cloud of not knowing whether or not I was gonna get killed by Cream or one of his boys. It was time to start really making moves and time for me to really become the queen of New York.

By the summer of 1997, at the age of only eighteen I was fully in charge of the Cream Team criminal empire. Spinach had no problem letting me reign on top. He basically felt that the cops would be watching to see who Cream would hand the crown to and that person would become the new target of their investigation. In a nutshell, he thought that the position came with all kinds of unwanted and unnecessary headaches. So, I was in control of the team, and I was also the proud new owner and controller of my very own nightclub on the west side of Manhattan. My lawyer handled all of the paperwork for the huge real estate transaction and everything went over very successfully. The club was located on Forty-third Street and Twelfth Avenue. My lawyer had structured everything in the purchase so that the building was owned by my corporation, Golden Lady Inc. He had also greased the palms of people in high places so that my club was approved for a liquor license.

When it came time to name the club I decided to name it the Golden Lady. I just loved the ring of that name. Plus, I wanted to give the club a name that had some mystery to it. The Golden Lady was perfect because it alluded to the fact that it was a nightclub, but with the word "lady" in it, it sounded like it might be a strip club too. I had always been a proponent of using sex in order to sell something, and I definitely was gonna use sex to sell people on coming to my nightclub. Therefore, the Golden Lady was, in my opinion, the perfect name.

In the summer of '97 I was determined to continue to make the Cream Team pop off. I was also determined to make my club jump off. But most importantly I was determined, poised, cocked, and ready to make Lady take off and reign as the queen of New York.

27

THERE IS A SAYING THAT goes something like: "Before the truth can even put on its shoes, a rumor and gossip will have laced up its sneakers and made it around the world and back again." This basically means that people don't talk about the truth but when it comes to gossip and rumors, people love to talk. That is why it quickly spreads. Well, that is exactly what happened with my image during the summer of '97. Overnight I was catapulted to the status of a female street legend. In no time I had successfully engineered gangstress publicity about myself using the likes of Wendy Williams and other big radio personalities to spread gossip and rumors that I had created about myself.

When my club was officially opened, it opened to much fanfare. People are fascinated by members of underground societies who are flamboyant and break the law. Just like Al Capone and John Gotti who have this godlike image and persona that surrounds them, I had also garnered that same persona. People came out to my club just so they could say that they partied at "Lady's nightclub."

I still had to work at promoting my club, but things became a hell of a lot easier for me and Shauna. It got to the point where at the drop of a hat I could call up any of the cool New York City radio stations like Hot 97 FM and tell them that I was coming up and wanted to promote one of my events at the club. No matter who the deejay was, they would have no problem giving me free airtime to spit and spew and promote whatever the hell I wanted to promote. You would have thought that I was a rapper or some kind of R&B superstar.

The truth was I was far from being a rapper or an R&B superstar, but I had become "ghetto fabulous" in the full sense of the word. Like I said, it had happened almost overnight, but suddenly as far as New York was concerned I was like a star to the stars. Rap stars, record producers, record company owners, supermodels, basketball players, football players, and boxers all began coming out to the Golden Lady on a regular basis and they all wanted to get close to me. The Golden Lady was the place to be.

Just like no one would ask John Gotti to recant any of his past wrongdoings, no one ever dared to ask me to recant any of my wrongdoings. Everyone knew that I was this sexy, high-profile, money-making street entrepreneur who had killed dudes in cold blood and also did the dirty work of cleaning up murders that Cream and his lieutenants had carried out in the past. It is a twisted kind of thing, but instead of being condemned for such things and such crimes, people began to idolize me for my past sins.

The thing that shocked me the most was that when people learned I had once been nothing more than some street-walking prostitute getting pimped by Cream, there was no fall-off to my image. I chose to reveal my history to the world so I could be the first one to put it out there, sort of like a form of damage control. Never in my wildest dreams did I think that people would become riveted and fascinated by that aspect of my past as well. But that is exactly what happened. People looked at me as being someone who was willing to do whatever I had to do in order to get to the top. The fact that I had been a streetwalker at the tender age of fifteen and now I was running the Cream Team at the age of eighteen gave me mad street credibility in the eyes of many. In fact, I had more street credibility than someone like Cream who had gained a lot of his respect simply because of who his father was.

It felt good as hell to know that at my beck and call I could get

Spinach and a whole host of other Cream Team members to literally kill for me. I just loved having that kind of power and at the same time I knew that I had to respect that power if I wanted to keep it. I was relieved that I had never formed any close affiliations with the numerous Jamaican gangs or any other criminal organizations. With me rising to the top of the Cream Team, that would have caused a great deal of conflict and tension—it could have led to my downfall.

Without a doubt if you ask people in New York to tell you which two clubs were hitting in the late nineties, there are two names that you are gonna hear. People will say that on Sunday nights in New York City, the Tunnel nightclub was the spot. However, in the same breath you will hear people say that Lady's Night, which was every Saturday night at the Golden Lady, was hands-down the place to be.

It got to the point where every hip-hop and R&B artist would have a record-release party at either my club or at the Tunnel. In fact, I think one of my most memorable nights at the Golden Lady was on an October night in '97 when the former rapper MA$E held his album-release party at my club.

Never in my life had I seen so many people and so many stars in one spot at the same time. The V.I.P. area of the club was just flat-out crazy and everything was off the hook. The performances were off the hook, the way people were dressed was off the hook, and everything was on point. Everything from the way my waitresses were dressed, to the music that Funkmaster Flex played—it was just ridiculous! If I had to pick one high point in all of my doings over the years, I would definitely say that it was the MA$E record-release party in '97.

Although the party was thrown in honor of MA$E, it might as well have been thrown in my honor because I was the center of attention all night long. That night I met Sean "Puff Daddy" Combs for the first time. I also chatted with and mingled with Lil' Kim that night, which was especially memorable. Kim had come up to me with her arms outstretched and was like, "Hey Lady, what's up, girl?"

It kind of took me by surprise but I returned her warm embrace.

"Kim, your outfit is off the chain!" I said with excited passion.

"Girl, your club is off the chain!" Kim replied with a drink in her hand.

As we talked over the loud music I had goose bumps running up and down my body because I felt so good. Just then, some excited chick to the right of us began dancing on top of one of the tables. We moved away as we continued to talk. Kim shocked me with what came out of her mouth next.

"Lady, do you remember that time I met you at Club New York when Biggie was still alive?"

In my head I was like, *do I?* I was thinking, *I should be asking her that, and she's asking me if I remember her meeting me?* I just played right along with the flow.

"Yeah girl, of course I remember that. I knew from back then that you were gonna blow!" I yelled into her ear over the loud music.

Kim said that she knew when she'd met me that I was gonna amount to big things. Then she asked me how was Cream doing and I told her that he was keeping his head up doing an easy bid in a federal prison.

The night was real hectic. So Kim and I couldn't talk for too long, but we did exchange numbers. She and I went on to become real close friends—genuine friends at that. I think that she appreciated that I had my own money and my own name and I wasn't looking to ride her coattails for anything.

That same night MA$E and I also connected. It had been my first time meeting him. He was the cutest, most down-to-earth star I think I've ever met. We also exchanged numbers. I knew back then that he would have jumped at the first chance to get in my pants, but he and I never went that route. We remained real cool. Later on, although I had no idea on that particular night, MA$E would end up having a huge impact on my life.

A year and a half had gone by since the Golden Lady had opened. It was late 1998. Up until that point the whole club scene never really got old for me. I lived for it and I loved it! I loved the dark atmosphere and strobe lights. I loved being near the bars and in the V.I.P. section or in the disc jockey booth watching the deejays move a crowd. I loved dancing and I loved socializing with all kinds of people from all walks of life. But the thing I probably loved the most was the money that I was making. I handled all of the *legal* club stuff, and Spinach and his crew oversaw all of the *illegal* activities which included a couple of sex rooms just past the V.I.P. section. They also oversaw the sale of marijuana, cocaine, and ecstasy pills that went on inside the club. I can confidently say without a shadow of doubt that on each Lady's Night alone, we were pulling in more than a hundred grand! That included everything from ticket sales, bar sales, drug sales, and sex sales. That was all from just one night!

Needless to say, the Cream Team and I were truly living. There had never been a drop off even with Cream going to jail. If anything we had stepped things up a notch big time.

By early 1999 at the age of twenty I had purchased a condominium inside Trump Tower on Fifth Avenue in Manhattan. My condo's view of Manhattan was crazy, the condo was crazy, and the price tag was crazy! But to me, the price was nothing because I was pulling in so much cake. By that time I had long since purchased the house I had been renting in Jamaica Estates. I had a fleet of cars, but the two cars that I loved the most were my white 600 Mercedes Benz and my all-white Lincoln Navigator.

I was truly living, and life only seemed to get better and better with each year that passed. My sister Mya began to get more involved in helping me run my club, and I loved that. Even my mother and I began to talk on a more regular basis. She had really taken to the whole church thing and the born-again Christian thing. She always invited me to come to church with her but I always passed on the invitation. One time I told her that I was afraid that if I ever walked into a church building the entire church would burn down as soon as I stepped foot inside of it. However, I did begin to take my mother seriously about her faith in the Lord because she had finally left Junie. In fact, for the first time in her life she was living on her own and making it on her own. So I guess there had to be something about that Jesus thing that she kept talking to me about.

28

AN INTERESTING THING HAPPENED IN the spring of 1999. My mother and I began to talk more often. Her birthday was coming up in a couple of weeks and she had asked me to come with her to church for her birthday.

"Tina, I don't want you to spend no money on me, getting me no gift or anything like that. All I want is for you to accompany me to church," my mother said to me one day as we spoke on the phone. I finally gave in and reluctantly agreed to go with her to this church that she kept ranting and raving about.

"Tina, you're gonna like it. There are a lot of young people there that I'm sure you will be able to relate to."

I immediately had to check what my mother was saying.

"Mom, listen. I said that I would go with you for your birthday, but trust me, I'm not gonna be going to anybody's church on a regular basis, so you don't have to even go there with all of that 'young people' talk."

When my mother's birthday arrived it happened to fall on a Sunday, and I had completely forgotten about the promise I had made to her. I had been at my club for the entire night before my mother's birthday. In fact, by the time I made it home from the club it was a little after six in the morning. The only thing I was thinking about doing was going to sleep and not waking up until my body naturally woke itself up—even if that meant sleeping until late afternoon or evening.

As soon as I laid my head down, my cell phone rang.

"Hello," I said as I answered the phone.

"Good morning, Tina," my mother replied on the other end. She sounded all excited.

I immediately knew what was up.

"Oh, Ma! Happy birthday! I completely forgot about your birthday today." I sat up in the bed, hoping to be let off the hook.

"Were you sleeping?" my mother asked.

"Nah, I just came home and I just got into bed. I haven't actually fallen asleep yet."

"Well, get up and get dressed and get over here and pick me up."

"Ma!" I said, sounding like a little whining baby.

"Tina, it's for my birthday and you promised me . . ."

My mother was right. I had promised her that I would go, but that had to be the worst possible day for me to be going to some church. I was tired as hell and a little hungover and I had no idea what to wear. I had a whole bunch of clothes to choose from, but I had literally never been inside of a church before so I didn't really know what to wear.

"A'ight Ma, but what should I wear?"

"Tina, it really doesn't matter, just come as you are."

I had enough sense to not wear a hoochie-momma outfit. I put on a regular skirt, a regular blouse, and some heels and I was off to pick up my mother.

I made it to Queens and scooped her up and for the first time in my life, at the age of twenty, I was off to church. When we arrived I noticed that there were a whole bunch of people both young and old. The church itself was very big and it had a main level as well as a second level with balcony-style stadium seating.

The closest I had ever been to a church was seeing Creflo Dollar and T.D. Jakes on TV. So as the preacher spoke, I didn't understand what the hell he was talking about, but I tried my hardest to pay attention. Everything just reminded me so much of what I had seen on

TV. As my mother and I were sitting, I picked up her bible and thumbed through it. I had never read the bible and everything in it—all of the words—might as well have been in a foreign language. The only thing I really liked about the service was the music. The church sang what seemed like up-tempo modern gospel songs that were similar to what Kirk Franklin sings. I liked Kirk Franklin's style, so I was able to connect with that part of the service.

Toward the end of the service, the preacher calmed down his tone a whole lot. He began asking for people who wanted to "give their life to the Lord" to come forward to the altar and do so. I didn't know what kind of freakiness to expect. I was expecting them to start exorcizing demons out of people or something, so at that point I was more than skeptical and ready to go home. Then slowly, one by one, people began going to the front of the church and standing there in front of the preacher. The preacher kept pleading for and urging others to come forward and give their lives to Jesus Christ.

All of a sudden, someone in a hooded sweatshirt began to walk toward the front of the church, and people in the congregation began to cheer like they were at a baseball game. The people had not reacted like that for any of the other people who had come forward. Yet they were going crazy because of some thugged-out-looking cat who was walking to the altar with a hood over his head. Then word started to get around that it was the rapper MA$E who had walked to the front of the church! That definitely got my attention. I was like, *yeah right!* The church was so big that it was hard for me to actually see and confirm who the person in the hooded sweatshirt was. So I stood up like everyone else to see what was going on, and when the guy took off his hood, I saw with my own eyes that it was indeed MA$E!

That was something that I couldn't believe.

"Do you know who that is?" my mother asked.

"Yeah I know who that is, and I *know him–know him,*" I said.

"Who is he?" my mother asked.

"He's a famous rapper on Puff Daddy's record label."

"Oh," my mother replied in a surprised manner.

The preacher was finally able to quiet down the excited crowd, and he was talking to MA$E but no one could hear what he was saying. The preacher then began to speak into the microphone, explaining to the people who had come forward just exactly what was taking place. Then he spoke about Jesus and how the bible says that if you believe in Him you will be saved. After that, he had the people who had come to the front repeat a simple prayer which confirmed to everyone that they had accepted Jesus Christ as their Lord and savior. When the prayer was over, the preacher gave all of the new converts some more instructions and some words of encouragement, after which the entire congregation began clapping and praising God and shouting "hallelujah" like they had lost their minds. I remember looking at MA$E and he appeared to have been wiping tears from his eyes.

Truthfully, I had no idea what in the world had just happened inside the church, but I kept quiet and just kept observing all that was going on. As I drove my mother home she tried to explain to me all that had happened at church, but I just could not grasp it. The whole church thing was just so foreign to me and from what I knew and experienced on an everyday basis.

"So, you're saying that because MA$E confessed Jesus Christ as his Lord and savior, that all of the wrong stuff that he may have done prior to today, God doesn't hold it against him anymore?" I asked.

"Yup, that's exactly right," my mother explained to me. "And even if he does things wrong in the future, God will overlook that as well," she explained.

I still didn't get that whole Jesus thing, but it did kind of intrigue me. I remember calling people and telling them about what had happened with MA$E. Nobody would believe that I had gone to church, let alone believe that MA$E had given his life to Jesus. Then, a couple of weeks later, word got out to the media that MA$E was retiring from rap and that he had in fact given his life to the Lord. All of my words were validated.

I kept asking myself how MA$E could have just walked away from all that he had. Yeah, that day at church with my mother was a real memorable day and it was a day that I would never forget. Unfortunately, it hadn't moved me to the point where I was willing to change and "give my life to Jesus." Nah, there was gonna be none of that for me. I was living far too well, making too much money, and enjoying life way too much to do something stupid like that.

My club was called the Golden Lady and as time went on it seemed that whatever I touched turned to gold. The next two years in my life were sweet. During that time I added to my golden touch by opening a string of successful hair salons, which were called Golden Lady Hair Designs. I continued to stack all kinds of money and my popularity and fame continued to grow. I visited and talked to Cream on a regular basis and kept him fully in the loop as far as where the team was headed and what the team was going through. There were killings, of course, and hiccups and all kinds of drama along the way, as is always gonna be the case whenever something or someone is closely tied to the streets. But none of the hiccups were enough to stop me from reigning as the queen of New York. For all of 1999, 2000, and right into 2001 I definitely had the golden touch. Unfortunately though, there was one thing I touched that proved to me that everything that glitters is not always gold.

29

ON NEW YEAR'S EVE 2001, I decided to use my club to throw one of the biggest and best New Year's Eve bashes of all time. Shauna and I had put a lot of energy into making sure that the event would be a huge success. Our club held close to three thousand people and we wanted to make sure that the club was packed. So right after Thanksgiving we began to promote for our New Year's Eve event. By that time in my club-promoting career, I was more than confident that all of my events and parties were guaranteed to be a success. But on a night like New Year's Eve, I knew that there would be a host of house parties and other club events going on throughout the city which would serve as increased competition for my club.

Thankfully, when the New Year's Eve event finally did come around I was happy to see that even with the increased competition we still had to turn away about five hundred party seekers. My club was just way too packed and as always we were afraid that the fire marshal was gonna shut us down. In fact, it was so jammed inside the club that I was worried people would not enjoy themselves. So I decided that for two hours I would have an open bar so everyone could get free drinks to take their minds off the fact that the club was overcrowded. I knew that once people get drunk they don't complain about much.

Nonetheless, people had paid $125 a head just to get in, so I felt that it was only right that I give them free drinks for at least two hours.

As usual the club was packed with celebrities and even the V.I.P. area was full. I couldn't help but notice this one particular guy in the V.I.P. area who kept staring at me the entire night. I hadn't paid attention to him for all that long but I could swear that at times even when I left the V.I.P. area he followed me. So, as I chilled in the V.I.P. area and mingled with the people, I decided to confirm if in fact the guy was definitely staring at me or if it was just my imagination. I made my way to three separate locations in the V.I.P. area and each time I moved, the guy's eyes would stay glued to me. He was far from being a bad-looking guy, in fact he looked good as hell. His looks were the only thing that had allowed me to tolerate his constant stares. Usually I only liked the rough and rugged, thugged-out look when it came to guys. And as far as complexion, I was more inclined and attracted to dark-skinned guys with bald heads or cornrows or a look similar to that. However, this particular guy did not fit that profile at all. He was the complete opposite of what would normally attract me. He was a light-skinned, good-hair pretty boy who looked like the singer Al B. Sure from back in the days.

I whispered very loudly into Shauna's ear and asked her, "What do think about Al B. Sure over there?"

Shauna took my words literally.

"Al B. Sure is here?"

I began laughing kind of hard at Shauna's response. I had definitely had a little too much to drink.

"No, I'm just joking, Shauna," I said, trying not to slur my words. "But look at that guy over there standing next to the waitress . . . Doesn't he look like Al B. Sure?"

Shauna was obvious as hell as she looked in the guy's direction and pointed. She then burst out into laughter and said, "Oh my god! He looks just like Al B. Sure!" Shauna paused and then said, "I guess it is true that light-skinned guys are making a comeback."

We both began laughing. When I regained my composure I told Shauna how he had been staring at me for the entire night.

"Well, find out who he is," Shauna instructed.

"Nah, are you buggin'? I ain't trying to approach no pretty boy!"

"If he don't say nothing to you soon you better make sure that you speak to him. You gotta find out if the guy is some kind of stalker or something."

I smiled at Shauna and then she walked off and went to another area of the club.

She hadn't been gone for more than two minutes when I saw the guy staring at me again. Only this time he smiled at me and I smiled back. I guess that gave him enough confidence to come over and say something to me. As he approached, I noticed that he seemed to be about six foot four and I could tell that he had ripples of muscles underneath his shirt.

"I guess I got busted staring at you, right?" he asked.

I smiled and replied, "Yeah, you were kind of obvious."

He continued on, "I gotta be honest, I've seen you in here a couple of times and I've been dying to talk to you and ask you your name but every time I see you, you have someone around you."

"It's not like I bite or anything, you could have spoken to me. With all of that staring that you were doing you would make a sista think that you were the crazy stalker type."

We both began to laugh, and I could just feel this certain kind of chemistry forming between the two of us.

"Yeah, I know you don't bite but I mean, come on, look at how good you look. It's hard enough for guys to get the courage to talk to someone who looks as good as you do, so if you got a crowd around you then that makes it incredibly difficult . . . It's one thing to get dissed in a one-on-one situation, but I wouldn't feel too good about getting dissed in front of a bunch of cock blockers."

"*Excuse me?*" I asked in response to the cock blockers comment.

"Well, you know what I'm saying . . ."

I turned my lips in a playful but sarcastic manner and nodded my head in agreement.

"So can I buy you a drink?" he asked.

I thought to myself, *I wonder if he knows that I own the club?*

"Well, it is an open bar so you won't really be *buying* me a drink, but yes you can *get* me a drink," I replied as we made our way to the bar area.

As we walked toward the bar a number of people said hello to me and wished me a happy new year.

"You see what I'm saying?" the guy asked. "If I wasn't here someone else would have your attention right now . . ."

"That's true," I calmly replied.

"So, I take it that your name is Lady?" he asked. "That's a unique kind of name . . ."

"Well that's what everyone has called me for years. But my real name is Tina," I explained as we ordered drinks.

"Well, can I call you Lady?"

"Of course, in fact it sounds weird to me whenever anyone other than my mother or my sister calls me Tina."

"So Lady, if you don't mind me asking, what do you do for a living? I mean how is it that everyone in here seems like they know you?"

I took ahold of my drink which had just arrived. Then I replied, "Okay, first you're staring at me for hours, and now you're asking all of these personal questions and you didn't even tell me your name."

"Oh my bad, that is kind of rude. Well, my name is Sha-Boogie."

"Sha-Boogie?" I asked with a half a smirk on my face.

"Yeah . . ."

I couldn't help it and I almost spit out my drink as I began to laugh.

"What's so funny?" Sha-Boogie asked as he too began to laugh.

"Nah, I'm sorry but you just look way too pretty to have a name like Sha-Boogie!" I couldn't hold it in and I began to laugh some more.

"Please don't mind me though, all of this laughing is probably the liquor talking . . ." As I calmed down I continued, "But honestly though, you look more like your name would be Alex, or Alvin, or maybe Al . . ." I knew that I was coming across kind of immature but I didn't care. "Yeah, matter of fact me and my girl was just saying that you look like the singer Al B. Sure," I added while smiling a huge Kool-Aid smile.

Sha-Boogie jumped in and said, "I see that you got a lot of jokes. . . . But it's all good. I'll let you get a pass."

"Nah, but come on. Sha-Boogie? Even you gotta admit that a name like that would fit some thugged-out street nigga and you don't fit that description."

Sha-Boogie replied, "Yeah, I know what you're saying but looks can be deceiving. If we had time, I could tell you how I got that name. . . ."

"Oh really?" I asked.

"Really," he replied.

"So, what's your government name? I always ask everybody for their government names when I first meet them."

"My government name is Darius," he replied. "But just call me Sha-Boogie or Sha or Boogie. Please don't call me Darius."

"Oh, that's a cool name though. I gotta remember that in case I ever have kids one day."

We both laughed, then I started to talk. I told Sha-Boogie that I was the owner of the club and that was why it seemed like everyone knew me.

"You own all of this?!"

"Yes and why are you asking like that? You sound shocked or surprised."

"Nah, I'm just impressed," Sha-Boogie replied. "I love anybody that's an entrepreneur. I'm an entrepreneur myself."

"Oh really? So what do you do?" I asked.

Sha-Boogie took a sip from his drink and then he said, "Okay, I'll tell you what I do but before I do let me just be up front with you. I've been coming into this club week after week for about a month now, just hoping that I would see you and get the chance to talk to you. And I finally have that chance. So, I mean, I know that I don't really know you, and I know that there's a good chance that you're involved with somebody already but can I see you one day outside of this whole club atmosphere? . . . You know, like a date? Can I take you out to eat somewhere?"

I had to admit that Sha-Boogie made me feel innocent and young again when he asked me that. See, with the image and reputation that I had, guys didn't have the confidence to approach me and simply ask me what Sha-Boogie had asked me—out on a date.

"You seem real cool, I wouldn't mind going out with you," I replied.

There was brief silence, and then Sha-Boogie smiled.

"See, now, was that hard to do?" I asked.

"Actually, it was a hell of a lot easier than I thought it would be," Sha-Boogie replied. Then he added, "I guess it's true about perception being a low form of knowledge."

"Listen to you! With your deep sayings, 'perception is a low form of knowledge,'" I added as I mocked Sha-Boogie. Sha smiled at me.

"So, now answer my other question," I stated.

"About what I do?"

I nodded my head.

"Well, I run one of the largest black-owned triple-X websites on the Internet."

"Really?" I said with intrigue. "You mean a pornography website?"

"Yeah, black pornography," Sha-Boogie answered.

I know that he had no idea how closely I had been involved in— and to a great extent was still involved in—the sex business.

"That is so interesting!" I replied.

"Are you serious?" Sha-Boogie asked. He sounded kind of surprised by my enthusiasm.

"Yeah, I'm dead-ass serious. That seems like a business that I would love to own. I mean, I'm like this *serial* entrepreneur. I love starting different businesses," I explained as I told him about the hair salons and the hand car washes.

"Yo, word is bond, I have never come across a woman who was intrigued and not turned off by what I do for a living," Sha-Boogie explained.

"Oh, so that's why you figured you would ask me out first before you told me what you do for a living? That was smooth. . . . But I'm as real as they come and I don't trip over things like that. I mean, just look at the way my waitresses are dressed."

"Yeah, I gotta admit that they look hot! And I know that all of the guys who come in here love it!" Sha-Boogie added.

Sha-Boogie and I continued to talk and we also exchanged numbers. I felt like I could have talked to him for the whole night and that was what I wanted to do. Just from the brief conversation that we had had, he didn't know it but he had me so open it was unreal!

I attended to my club duties that night and I rang in 2002 on a real good note. I felt like I was floating on air simply because I had met Sha-Boogie and he helped me to feel young and innocent again. I didn't tell anyone about him until the next afternoon when I spoke to Shauna by phone.

"Girl, I think I met my future baby's daddy!" I said to her.

"What are you talking about?" she asked.

"Remember Al B. Sure, from last night?"

"Yeah," Shauna replied.

"Well—"

Shauna interrupted, "I know the stalker didn't get you that open last night?"

I started laughing as I said, "No, but Shauna, we ended up speaking for a while, and I don't know what it is, but I'm just really feeling him!"

"Well, what is Al B. Sure's name?"

I laughed again as I said, "Now get this Shauna. I know you are gonna fall out when I tell you because I fell out when he told me his name."

I could hear Shauna giggling through the phone in anticipation. "Okay, let me sit up and get ready for this," she stated.

"His name is Sha-Boogie. . . ."

"What?! Sha-Boogie? His pretty ass?!" Shauna said as she began to laugh.

"Yeah, I know. . . . That's the same thing I told him!"

We both laughed over the phone. I explained to Shauna what he did for a living, and that the two of us were going out on a date.

"Wait a minute, does he act in porno movies or does he just own the company?"

I replied, "I don't know, but I think he just owns the website."

"Well, you better find out! The way you talking it sounds like you ready to give him some the next time you see him."

"I'll find out, but it really wouldn't matter to me one way or the other."

Shauna sarcastically replied, "Yeah, you would be the type who would end up marrying a porno star, with your scandalous ass!"

We both kept laughing. When the conversation was over, I headed straight to the shopping mall for a sexy outfit to wear on my date with Sha-Boogie. Yeah, I knew that I was acting way too open and immature but at the same time my soul needed to feel that young giggly and tingly feeling. Sha-Boogie was probably about twenty-six years old and I would be turning twenty-three in a couple of months. There is nothing like being young and fantasizing about a possible love interest, even if it was just a puppy-love interest.

With the life that I had chosen to live, I had sacrificed a whole lot. For example, I had never been to a prom, so I could only envision what it would have been like to be in a prom dress waiting at home for my date to arrive and pick me up in a limo. I would never be able to go back and experience things like that because in a way I had robbed myself of my teenage years. Unfortunately, my living conditions at home had robbed me of a normal preteen experience.

I was starting to think that maybe I needed some normally in my life. I don't know why, but in my mind I just sort of transposed onto Sha-Boogie everything that I thought was normal. Maybe I was going off the deep end way too early and assuming things, but to me, it seemed like I was finally getting the chance to have a normal relationship with a member of the opposite sex.

But would my perception of Sha-Boogie prove to simply be "a low form of knowledge"? Or was that just a bogus theory?

30

SHA-BOOGIE AND I WENT TO a popular New York City restaurant called One Fish Two Fish. I liked the atmosphere at One Fish Two Fish and Sha-Boogie was familiar with the place so that was where we decided to go.

As we sat and talked, I remember thinking how weird it felt to actually be on a real date. In my whole life I had never really had a steady man or anything like that. Yeah, I had been to dinner with guys before but with Sha it was just different. In the past, I knew that after dinner or after a movie I would end up screwing the person. So in essence, in the past, dinners and movies were nothing more than fillers or sort of like the pre-game show that came before sex.

While we ate at One Fish Two Fish, things felt like more than just a pre-game show. And I was determined for the first time in my life to not give Sha any booty until I had given things some time to materialize between the two of us. I hated to think it, but I was starting to mature and look at things from a different perspective.

"So Sha, I just wanna make sure that you know how I roll. I'm a straight shooter and I like dealing with people who are straight shooters. So please, just always be up front and real with me and I'll be real and up front with you."

"That's not a problem, Lady, because I'm not into playing games. Those days are far behind me," Sha replied.

"Now about this pornography thing . . ."

Sha began to smile.

"I just need to ask you . . . Umh . . . Do you actually *get busy* in any of the movies? You do make porno movies, right? . . . I'm mean what exactly is the website about? . . . Just explain to me whatchu do."

I knew that I was fumbling over my words, but I didn't know how to properly phrase my question.

Sha smiled as he ate his food. He began to speak after swallowing.

"Okay, in the past I've actually *gotten busy* in some triple-X movies. But now I'm more into the behind-the-scenes thing."

"You know I'm curious as hell and I wanna see one of your movies, right?"

"Look, I'm not ashamed of nothing, I'll let you see one of my movies. . . . But the thing is it's the producers and really the distributors who make all of the money in the movie business. So, when I was actually in movies, that was before the Internet really took off. It was like in '97 and '98 and I was happy to be making a few hundred dollars per movie just having sex. And even if I wanted to make real money as a producer or a distributor, I didn't really have the money or the connections to get my foot in the door. But when this Internet thing took off I was like I can get paid because I knew that all I had to do was get people to my website. They could download movies that I produced right from my website, so the Internet solved my distribution problem."

"And you already knew porno actresses you could get to perform in your movies, right?" I added.

"Exactly."

"So, you aren't scared about catching no diseases or anything? Or I should say you weren't scared?"

"Nah, see, people always trip about that. But when I was in movies and even now, everybody was constantly getting tested for diseases so we always knew what was up. And when you think about it, how many people today just jump in bed and have unprotected sex with someone that they don't even know? And on top of that, even when people know each other, how many get tests to see if there are any diseases before having sex?"

I remarked, "That is so true. I never thought about it, but in a way the porno business could be safer than the regular everyday sex people are having."

Sha replied, "The porno business is much safer as far as contracting diseases are concerned."

I didn't wanna just stay on that topic but I loved making money and I was trying to pick Sha's brain for information.

"Sha, you gotta teach me that whole Internet hustle. Is there real money in it?"

"Whaaat?! Do you know how many horny-ass niggas there are out there?! I get paid lovely! And the thing is, once I produce the movie my work is done. The website runs on its own. People just come to the website, enter their credit-card information, and then in two days that money from their credit card is transferred right into my bank account."

"Word? So you don't really have to manage anything?" I replied.

"Hell no. All I do is check with my webmaster—the technical guy that knows all of the computer stuff—and he makes sure that my site is up and running with no problems."

"See, that's what I'm talking about! For me, it's like the past five years or so of my life has been one big party. And I never thought I would get tired or burnt out from owning my club, but really it's just the same old thing. I used to get all open when I met stars and rappers but that's nothing to me now. I just kind of wanna slow down and chill now. But I also gotta make sure that my money is right. That means I have to manage everything, because I don't trust nobody. I mean I ain't trying to bring in somebody to manage my joint and have them destroy what I built!"

"I feel you," Sha replied.

Then, surprisingly, Sha explained that he had been involved in distributing kilos of cocaine, a couple of years back. He said he had given that up.

"You know I don't believe that, right?" I said.

"Why not?"

"Sha, I've been on the street since I was like fourteen years old. I know the streets and I can just sniff out niggas who really lived that whole gangsta thing. . . . And no disrespect but I can look at you and tell that you wasn't that type."

Sha smiled as he sipped his drink. "Yo, I'm not trying to impress you by telling you that. I mean, after you told me who you were, I was able to put two and two together. I know who you run with in terms of the Cream Team. But on the real, you can check my stats. Check with street niggas about me and see what they say about my stats."

"So word is bond? You used to move keys?"

"Yeah, when the whole drug thing died down in New York it was still popping in areas like Baltimore. I used to transport drugs into that area."

"So, what happened with that?"

"Nah, I just realized that I didn't have to be risking jail time and all of that or getting snaked by one of my boys, especially since I knew I could make money with the porno hustle. So, I just dropped everything and left all of that drug money on the table and focused on the porno money. You feel me?"

As I chewed on my food, I didn't know what to believe. If in fact Sha was making money from his Internet business, then he really had no reason to lie about the drug thing other than to try to impress me. But he did have a twenty-five thousand dollar watch. He also had a nice house and a nice car, so maybe he was being straight up with me. After all, if I was a guy trying to impress a woman, the last thing I would say is that I was in the porno business and that I had personally been in porno movies!

Sha and I continued to talk and I wanted to tell him about my days as a streetwalking prostitute. And I wanted to tell him all about the Cream Team, but I knew that it was too early for that. The last thing I wanted to do was scare him off, but at the same time I felt that he, if anybody, would definitely understand where I had come from.

"Lady, I could teach you the Internet game. But really, if you went into that game you wouldn't even have to get into the whole pornography side of the Internet and you could still make a whole lot of money," Sha explained.

"How do you figure that?"

"Because you have a club where thousands of people come every week, and you also have a name and a following that people have heard about and wanna be a part of."

"So what exactly are you saying?" I asked.

"What I'm saying is that you need to leverage what you already have by simply taking it to the Internet."

"Okay, but how do I do that?" I asked.

"You ever heard of a webcam?" Sha asked.

"Yeah, I think so."

"Well, basically what you could do is design a website that promotes your club and tells what events will be going on at the club. Of course you could have pictures of your sexy half-naked waitresses on the website. But what you would do is have an area on the website where it would be like a 'member's only' area. And you could charge members like ten dollars or so to have a one-time access code which would allow them to see inside of the club and hear the music and all of that. So even if people were in Los Angeles, or Miami, or Chicago, or wherever, they could feel like they were right there at your club partying with you."

Sha had completely blown me away with that idea. It sounded good as hell, but I just hated doing anything that I did not completely understand. For example, selling sex is something that I understood, the drug game is something that I understood, washing cars is something that I understood, a hair salon is something that I understood, and promoting a club is something that I understood, but the Internet was foreign to me. To me, the Internet was something I would see on the *Jetsons.*

"But how would people in those areas be able to actually party with me?" I asked. "Sha, I don't know this whole computer thing so you gotta break it down for a sista."

"Okay, well, first of all it wouldn't be limited to people in just those areas that I mentioned. Anyone in the world with access to the Internet would be able to access your website, pay the money, log in to the member's area, and see and hear what is going on in your club here in New York City. What you would do is install webcams in different places inside the club and those webcams would transmit over the Internet exactly what's going on at your club."

"In real time?" I asked.

"Yes," Sha replied.

"So, a webcam is like a video camera?"

"Exactly!" Sha answered.

Now it was starting to get clearer to me.

"Lady, think about how many people go to your club and then the next day get on the phone and talk to someone who wasn't there. All you gotta do is get those people to advertise your website for you by word of mouth. And I could show you how to advertise on the Internet itself, it's so easy. Like if you put pictures of your waitresses on my website and hundreds of other websites, when people see those pictures they will get interested. They'll want to know more about who the girls are. If they click on the picture of the waitresses, it will take them right to your website."

"Okay, you're losing me. I don't think I need to understand all of that just yet. But I do understand what you're saying about the whole webcam thing. And I'll think about that and see it's something that I should get into. I mean, it sounds like it would make perfect sense, but I just gotta think about it."

"Yeah, I mean I'm just putting that out there," Sha replied.

"So how much would something like that cost?" I asked.

"You definitely could get that done for like under ten thousand."

That's it? I thought to myself. "But see, I just wouldn't want people having all kinds of access to everything that goes on inside the club. All kinds of things go on in my club, some girl could go down on some guy right on the dance floor and I wouldn't want that just out there on the Internet."

It was really the images of drug dealing and prostitution that I didn't want transmitted across the Internet.

"Well, see, the thing is you would control where the webcams are located and you can turn them on and off whenever you want to. So it's not like people will be able to see every inch of the club nor will they be able to see so clearly to the point where they'll be able to tell what kind of earrings someone is wearing, you know what I mean?"

"Okay, I got you," I replied.

Sha had me open with that whole Internet idea. And in general he had me open the entire night. After dinner we went back to my condo. Sha was cool with us just chilling on the couch and watching a tape of *Def Comedy Jam*. I almost felt guilty for not offering him the booty. I also found it weird that other than kissing me he didn't try to move in for the panties. But as weird as it felt to not have sex with Sha, it also felt liberating.

As days went by, Sha and I were constantly on the phone and constantly in each other's face. He was all that I thought about and all that I focused my attention on. For the first time in my life something other than making money seriously interested and captivated me. And that was Sha-Boogie. I didn't know what real love was, but for the first time in my life I was beginning to feel like maybe I'd find out.

31

IN FEBRUARY OF 2002 I went to visit Cream. It was more than likely gonna be my last visit to see him. Neither of us could believe that five years had come and gone so fast. But it had, and ironically he was scheduled to be released on April 15, the day that income taxes are due. Officially it had been his evasion of income taxes that had landed him in jail.

The whole team had been planning a lavish coming home party for Cream and it was scheduled for the first weekend after his release. We knew that his party was gonna be packed and off the hook. But we also knew that undercover police and federal agents would more than likely be among those in attendance.

Cream had been prosecuted for tax evasion simply because that was the one charge that they knew would stick. However, even though Cream had been out of sight, we knew he had still been on the minds of those in law enforcement. Think about it like this. If there was a school bully who got shipped off to another state, it would cause everybody in the school to breathe a sigh of relief. But if word got out that the same bully was moving back to the area and would be attending the same school, it would cause everyone to be on guard. Law enforcement looked at Cream as a menace to society and as someone who could single-handedly drive up the crime rate in any given city. They were going to watch his every move, and hopefully catch him in the act this time.

So, during my last visit to see Cream, the two of us spoke in detail about the future of the team and about our individual futures. When I spoke, I found myself constantly referring to Sha-Boogie. It was the first time Cream had ever heard me mention Sha-Boogie's name, and his radar went up right away.

"So, you're telling me that you just met this cat on New Year's Eve?" Cream asked.

"Yes," I replied.

"No, what I mean is, you just met him this past New Year's Eve, like forty-five days ago?"

"Yes, Cream, it was this New Year's Eve that just passed." I responded to Cream's sarcasm with a little disgust in my voice.

"So, why is it that everything I mention, you come back with something either referring to *this* Sha-Boogie or something that *this* Sha-Boogie said or suggested?"

Cream may have been a bit jealous, but I couldn't understand why. It wasn't like Cream was my *man* or anything. I couldn't deal with his sarcasm.

"Cream, why you gotta sound like that?"

"Like what?!"

"You know what I mean, you ain't gotta say things like *this Sha-Boogie.*"

"Lady, all I'm saying is that you don't even really know the nigga yet. So I don't understand why his name keeps coming up!"

"Cream, his name keeps coming up because I'm feeling him! It's like I've just been thinking . . . thinking about slowing down a bit and . . . and to me Sha is somebody that I could see myself just chilling with. You know?"

"Nah, I don't know! But what I do know is that here I am getting ready to come home and it's like you're raining on my parade! Talking about you're ready to just slow down, all because of some punk-ass nigga you don't even know!"

"Cream, why you hating?!"

"Hating?! Ain't nobody hating! I'm just being real!"

I paused because I didn't wanna lose it. I chilled for a second to see if I could tell where Cream was coming from.

"Okay, Cream, what I'm saying is this. It's not like I'm trying to let Sha get all close to the team or anything. But I don't see what's wrong if I want Sha to get close to me."

Cream shook his head and then replied, "See, Lady, that's the problem. If you let Sha get close to you, then he is close to the team because you're a major player on the team. Don't you get it?!"

It was dealings and discussions like this one that I had grown tired of. I was tired of living every second of my life looking over my shoulder and wondering if I was making the right moves. I just wanted to live my life and not have it be like a got damn game of chess.

"Nah, I don't get it, Cream! Really I don't."

"Lady, this is what I'm saying. I'm gonna have all kinds of heat surrounding me when I go home. All I'm asking you is to just let me come home and let us sort things out together before you let this nigga get you all open."

In my mind I felt like asking Cream who the hell he thought he was dealing with. I wasn't some naïve fifteen-year-old who he could manipulate anymore. I had had enough of the hustle and enough of the games!

"Cream, I hear what you're saying but—"

Cream cut me off and added, "Lady, I'm gonna drop it but I've always said, before you let anybody get close to you, you gotta test them first. Now in the past I was referring to the whole gangsta thing and the gangsta lifestyle. But it applies across the board in any walk of life, even if you're just thinking about being with someone. You need to test that person first and see what they're really about."

I shook my head. I decided to just talk about business.

"So, are you at least with the whole Internet idea?" I asked.

"Honestly, it sounds good and all, but I ain't with that."

"Why not?" I asked.

"Because I'm not trying to give the police a window into where I'll be chilling at!"

See, there it was again. It was like Cream's every thought was suspicious. His mind must have run twenty-four/seven just thinking about a big conspiracy theory designed to take him down.

I laughed a little, but I knew how to counter Cream's concerns. "So you're worried that the police would find out about the whole Internet thing and then spy on us over the Internet?"

"Exactly! Especially if it's gonna work the way you explained it to me."

I couldn't help but giggle at Cream's paranoia.

"Well, let's say that were the case. Then to me it seems like the Internet thing is the perfect thing to do. Because we would control the cameras and we would control what people would have access to seeing. It would send a message to law enforcement that says we ain't trying to hide nothing, and we can prove it because we are willing to give the whole world access to one of our main spots twenty-four hours a day."

Cream was thinking about what I had said. And he did agree that it made some kind of sense when he looked at it from my point of view. But I knew it made sense, and anyone with a logical mind would have known it was a good idea—anyone except for Cream, who had all kinds of time on his hands, literally, to sit and think about conspiracy-theory crap.

Cream tried to lighten the mood by asking, "So, how was it?"

"How was what?" I responded.

"The sex!" Cream replied with a smile.

"With Sha?"

"Yes. . . . With the way you talking about the nigga, his pretty ass must have turned you out."

We both started laughing and then I jokingly said, "Now that's where you're wrong. Lady has matured over the past five years and she doesn't give it up that easily! I'm making the nigga wait on this," I said as I pointed to my crotch area.

"Really? So you didn't give him none yet?"

"No, honestly I didn't."

"Okay," Cream said as he nodded his head. "There must be something there then."

"Cream, there is something there, trust me. . . . But seriously though,

I just wanna take my money and chill out somewhere because the whole game is getting old to me. It's the same old thing and it's time for me to just move on with life. I was thinking about transferring the club into your name. You could run it just so I could move on and do me."

"So you could do you?" Cream asked.

"Yeah."

"Where is all of this coming from, Lady? It's not just Sha-Boogie. . . . Something else is going on."

Cream was right, it wasn't just about Sha-Boogie. But actually, I didn't know exactly where all of my talk of slowing down was coming from. I just knew that I wanted a change. I seriously was gonna work out something with Cream where he would take over the club and pay me for it in installments somehow, or maybe I would just concentrate on my hair salons and on the Internet hustle that I was gonna orchestrate with Sha. . . . I didn't exactly know what route I was gonna take but it was time for a change.

32

CREAM HAD COMPLETED HIS BID and he had come home. I had been stacking paper for him so he came home to a whole lot of something. The first thing he did was purchase a Hummer SUV. He also purchased a fifty-thousand-dollar diamond-encrusted watch from Jacob the Jeweler along with an iced-out platinum chain, and thousands of dollars of new clothes. Cream wanted to make a statement to everyone on the street, especially to the law enforcement that had wiped him out and took everything from him. He wanted to show that he was the man and that he could never fall off.

Cream also purchased a two-bedroom condo in a nice high-rise building in Jamaica Estates. It wasn't bad for a person who had just come home from the joint after doing a five-year stretch. But Cream had to be careful because all of the lavish in-their-face spending was only gonna land him right back in jail for the exact same crime.

While I wanted to slow down, Cream was the total opposite. I guess he had a lot of pent-up energy that he wanted to unleash on the world. He wanted to make sure that his notorious reputation would once again be elevated to the highest level possible in everyone's minds.

Cream's welcome-home bash was flat-out ridiculous. Although I was in the mode of wanting to slow down, Cream's welcome-home party reminded me of why I had chosen to live this lifestyle. His party had every element of glamour, street life, celebrity, intrigue, sex, and any other appropriate adjective that you can name.

As I danced with Sha-Boogie I screamed into his ear, "I can't believe that the whole world has the ability to watch Cream's party over the Internet right now! That is sick!"

Sha-Boogie replied, "But what is even sicker is that in about a year from now you will be making more money over the Internet than you'll be making from ticket sales and bar sales combined!"

I loved the sound of that. Sha-Boggie had walked me through the process of getting my club onto the Internet. It had been a straightforward and smooth process that only took a couple of weeks. We decided to launch the website with Cream's welcome-home celebration.

During and after the party it was like you could just cut the tension with a knife whenever Cream was around Sha-Boogie. No words had to be spoken but you could just feel that there was no love between Cream and Sha, and really the lack of love was from Cream's side. Sha was cool about it though. And although he and Cream didn't hit it off, Sha did somewhat hit it off with Spinach and some of the other Cream Team members he was becoming somewhat familiar with.

Truthfully, I didn't care who Sha hit it off with. All I knew is that the bond between us had tightened and it was continuing to get tighter. I finally did open up and allow him to dip into my *honey jar.* When we finally did have sex, I felt like it was the first time in my life that I had ever made love to anyone and vice versa. Sex with Sha was off the hook! Even though he was this pretty-face, good-hair dude, he knew how to put it down in the bedroom. The sex was so good that I couldn't stop talking about it to Shauna. I was constantly telling her how sex with Sha reminded me of taking a hot knife and slicing it through a stick of butter, with me of course being the stick of butter. Shauna was so happy for me and she always joked that it was time for her to also get some *"butter love"* in her life.

As time went on all I wanted to do was enjoy and experience the butter love that Sha and I shared. But with Cream out on the streets it was like negative things began to constantly happen. Cream was constantly calling meetings about something or complaining about someone.

Right around the time 50 Cent's hit song "Wanksta" was at its peak, probably around July of 2002, Cream called one of his urgent meetings. He wanted Spinach and me to meet him at the bowling alley at Chelsea Piers in Manhattan. Chelsea Piers wasn't too far from the club but Cream insisted that we meet at the bowling alley.

Spinach and I drove to the bowling alley together and when we got there Cream was already there, waiting for us. He wasted no time getting started. He began by asking us if we remembered Detective Lombardi. I definitely remembered who he was. After all, I had suggested that we kill him back in the days. But I was surprised that Spinach knew who he was. I had always thought that only Cream and I knew who Lombardi was, but I guess over the years Cream had filled Spinach in. Otherwise, Cream himself had gotten sloppy and let his loose lips spread things that he shouldn't have been spreading.

"Yeah, I remember him," I stated.

"Me too," Spinach added.

"I just gotta say that I always knew that he was real with me and was never out to snake me. Not too long after I hit the bricks, Lombardi got word to me to contact him. He told me that he had put in his twenty years on the police force and that he would be retiring in a couple of weeks."

Spinach and I looked at Cream as if to say, "And?"

Cream went on, "He said that he couldn't elaborate and that he definitely didn't wanna risk anything at this point in his life and his career, but he asked me to read between the lines. Then he said, 'The eagle has eyes and ears in your organization and is about to swoop down on everybody.'"

My heart skipped a beat and the three of us looked at each other.

Cream went on, "I just did five years and I'm not trying to go back to prison! And from what I can decipher, Lombardi is basically saying that there is a rat on our team!"

Spinach and I looked at each other.

"Y'all niggas been out here on the street, so y'all know better than I do what the hell is going on and what the hell has gone on. And all

I'm saying is this. I don't care if we gotta murder one hundred people, but if y'all even think that somebody might be a snitch, I want y'all to put their name on a list and one by one the three of us is gonna take out everybody on the list that y'all come up with."

There was silence amongst the three of us. In my silence I was thinking how I had turned myself into a millionaire by the age of twenty-three. Spinach was making a whole lot of money and Cream had cake. In my mind I was like, *I know we are not hustlin' backward.* Cream wanted to continue that "rule with an iron fist" mentality, and it was time to leave all of that nonsense alone.

"Tell me something!" Cream said while raising his voice. "Y'all are all quiet like y'all are the ones talking to the cops or something!"

"Cream, come on now," I arrogantly said.

Spinach began to give names of people he thought had been acting shifty and talking greasy. Cream told him to make sure to add those names to his list.

"Lady, did you tell that nigga Sha-Boogie anything about how we roll?"

"Cream, there ain't no need to bring his name into this."

"Lady! This ain't no joke! Y'all can take this lightly if y'all want to but when Lombardi tells me something, he knows what he's talking about. Lady, back in the days you was telling me that we should kill Lombardi and I knew that he was good people. Just like I was right about not doing that back then, I know that I'm right about him knowing something deep is going on right now!"

"So Cream, if we kill one or two hundred people, it doesn't mean we would definitely have eliminated the rat or the problem," I added.

"Give me some solutions then!" Cream demanded in a sarcastic and angry tone.

"I don't know," I replied.

There was silence for a few minutes.

"Look, we got money, we don't need no headaches of murders and all of that. Let's just take our dough and bounce somewhere out of town and just chill."

"Lady, on the real, you've been talking about 'let's just chill' and about how you're ready to slow down. I find it funny that you wanna slow down and give me the club right around the same time that all of this is going down," Cream stated.

"What!" I replied. "So, what exactly are you trying to say, Cream?" I stood up. I was obviously angry and ready to step to Cream and his paranoid psycho ass.

Spinach jumped in and tried to restore order.

"All of what, Cream? What are you getting at?" I demanded to know.

Spinach again tried to restore peace.

"Lady, you know exactly what I'm talking about! I think that you know there's a rat or you know something more than you've been letting on about!" Cream added with hostility.

"Cream, so you're saying I'm a rat? Do you know how stupid that sounds? I'm the one who ran the show for the past five years so that would mean I must be ratting on myself!"

"Or you could be ratting on us in order to get your ass out of a sling!" Cream continued with his foolishness.

I shook my head and gave Cream the most ice-grille look. I was ready to lose it and just flip on him but I did my best to maintain my composure.

The conversation continued to flow like that until the three of us decided to depart. We left with no real solid plan or course of action. All we knew was that Cream wanted a list of names from Spinach and myself so that we could just start taking out possible rats one by one. Personally I wasn't with that plan. I had put my life on the line for the Cream Team and I had done so much for the Cream Team, but for me there just came a point when I had to draw a line in the sand. I just didn't know how to do that. But I knew that I had to do something because once again, I could sense that it would only be a matter of time before Cream would try to kill me.

I wanted to talk to Sha-Boogie about what was going on, but really I had never been completely honest with him about everything that had transpired in my past. I had told him some things but not everything. I didn't wanna flood him with all of the past situations, but I did want to tell him what Cream was proposing. I sighed as I thought about how tough it had been for me to tell Sha all of the details from my streetwalking prostitution days. Deep down inside I knew that I wasn't gonna be able to spill all of the beans to Sha. But I needed an outlet other than Shauna. I needed someone to talk to who would be able to provide a fresh perspective and yet be able to handle my pile of dirty laundry.

The next couple of days were very hectic and mentally I was a wreck. I was trying to figure out the best thing for me to do but I just couldn't figure it out on my own. I was kind of dodging Cream and letting his calls go to my voice mail. But I knew that avoiding him was helping to raise his suspicions and thereby increasing the chances that Cream would try to kill me.

I tried to relax as best I could. I went to see my mother, and that proved to be so refreshing for me. She had been inviting me to go with her to church again, and she had stepped it up as of late. She told me that MA$E had flown in from Atlanta, Georgia. He was gonna be a guest preacher at her church in Brooklyn, the same church where he had given his life to the Lord. She said she'd love for us to go together to hear what MA$E had to say. I had not been to church with her since that day we saw MA$E give his life to the Lord. I could identify with MA$E and I thought that it would be a good excuse for me to go. I also thought it would be a good time for my mother to meet Sha-Boogie. I was just hoping that he would agree to come with us. After all, he was into the whole pornography thing and that was so opposite of God. Fortunately for me, Sha did agree to come to church with my mother and me, and as he put it, he was only doing it for me. I was just glad that he had agreed to go.

When my mother met him she thought that he was cute and she also thought that he and I made a good couple. She wasn't shy about expressing her thoughts to me and Sha. But mostly she was ecstatic that he had been willing to accompany us to church.

The three of us went to church on a Tuesday night. It was a special service as part of the church's twenty-five-year anniversary celebration. When we arrived I remember feeling really weird, I don't know how to explain it but I was just feeling weird. The church was this huge mega-church that held like five thousand people. So when we pulled up to it I saw this huge line of people and my first thought was that there was some kind of new nightclub nearby that people were going to. The line of people was reminiscent of the lines that I was used to seeing outside my club.

"Tina, these people are not going to a club. They're waiting to get inside to hear MA$E preach," my mother told us.

"All of these people?" Sha and I both questioned.

"Yes, all of these people," my mother nonchalantly replied.

I finally found a spot to park my car. The three of us got out of my Mercedes Benz and that was when it hit me. I was parked in the exact same spot where I had turned my first trick as a streetwalker years ago. It was so eerie, but of course I kept my mouth shut. The three of us proceeded to walk toward the line and waited to be let inside the church.

Once we were inside, the three of us took our seats and waited for the service to begin. It started with some really nice songs which both Sha and I were able to grove to and get into. Then MA$E, who needed no introduction, was introduced to everyone. He came to the pulpit amidst a loud and enthusiastic standing ovation.

In my mind I was like, *Oh my god look at MA$E! He looks so good!* But not in a sexual way, he just looked good in the sense that he had a certain glow about him. I guess he just really looked happy and super successful.

As MA$E began to preach I realized that he was really for real. He had really made a change in his life and he even sounded like a completely different person. Just seeing him and hearing him, flat-out blew me away. Everything that he was speaking about hit home for me like I couldn't believe. Of course he gave his testimony about how he had changed and why he felt the need to change, but he wasn't beating anybody over the head about why they needed to or should do what he had done. He was just simply trying to relay to people why we needed to be in a right relationship with God and how without God we would never be able to police ourselves from all of the sins and temptations that constantly surround us.

Then it came to the point where MA$E made an altar call. He was reaching out to everybody. In particular he was reaching out to all of the young people who were in attendance. Even more particularly I felt like he was personally reaching out to me, even though he never mentioned my name and he had no idea that I was even inside the church. I stood up and saw literally hundreds of people going forward to the altar to give their life to the Lord.

Without saying anything to Sha-Boogie or to my mother I just began to make my way from the row of seats to the aisle. I walked to the front of the church and stood at the altar with many other people. Tears began to stream down my cheeks as I listened and more importantly *believed* what MA$E was saying. He said that right there on that very night God was ready to forgive me and everyone else of all of our sins if we would simply believe that God raised Jesus from the dead and if we were willing to confess Jesus as our Lord and savior. I was more than willing to do that and in fact I did do it that night in front of five thousand people.

I didn't know what to really think, I didn't know exactly what my future was gonna hold. I didn't know what Sha would say or what my mother would say. I didn't know what I was gonna do with my club and all of that stuff. I didn't even really understand fully what I had just been through. But I did know one thing. I knew that when I left that altar and when I left that church building that night, I had begun a relationship with Jesus Christ. I was saved!

It was funny, because in the morning I'd had no idea that I would even be going to church that night. Yet, that night turned out to be one of the best nights of my life, if not the best night of my life. It felt better than any Lady's Night at my club. Truthfully, the night I went to church, gave my life to the Lord, and got saved—that was really Lady's Night. It was my night!

33

THE MORNING AFTER I GOT saved, I woke up and went to my kitchen and made some pancakes. As I sat and ate I realized that I felt like the same person I had been before I had been saved. But one of the ministers at the church had explained to me that I wouldn't feel any different and that no magical spell would take over my body or anything supernatural like that. He also explained to me that no matter how I felt, I needed to be assured of one thing and that was that God had truly forgiven me. He had explained that just because I had given my life to the Lord did not mean that I would be perfect and do everything right and that I need not worry about trying to be perfect. Nor did I need to worry about people trying to define what I needed to be doing in order to prove that I was sincere about my relationship with Jesus.

The minister's words were what I needed to remind myself of as I sat and ate my pancakes. I kept telling myself that I didn't have to put unnecessary pressure on myself to be or act in a way that would give the appearance that I was "religious." All I needed to do was start to do the best I could do with Jesus's help.

When I finished my pancakes and orange juice, I made it back to my bedroom and did something that I had never brought myself to do before. In the solace of my bedroom I got on my knees and I began to pray. I didn't know how to pray, but I just closed my eyes and began to talk to God. I talked to Him about my life and about all that I had been through and about all the wrong I had done. I thanked Him for letting me live to see the age of twenty-three and I thanked Him for my mother and I thanked Him for all kinds of things.

During that prayer I told the Lord that I was scared. I was scared because I didn't know what to do about my image as "Lady." I didn't know what to do with my club or with my relationships with people like Cream, Spinach, and Sha-Boogie. I didn't know how I was gonna stop drinking liquor and stop smoking weed. I was as straight up and honest with the Lord as I knew how. I remember crying and adding in my prayer to God that I didn't know how it was that He could just forgive me based on the fact that I believed in Him and professed and confessed that belief. But I assured Him that I did trust Him. And based on that trust I told Him that I was willing to do whatever it is that He wanted me to do. I wanted to submit and surrender everything in my life and hand it over to God.

I also asked God to lead me to people who could help me and direct me and give me practical answers and practical application to the whole process of "walking with Jesus." And lastly I asked God to help me understand the bible so that if and when I was to open the bible I would be able to understand what I was reading.

When I finished praying I wiped the tears from my eyes. I got up and walked into my living room and picked up the bible my mother had let me borrow the night before. I turned to the back of the bible and looked through the index and I came across names and words that I had heard before or that just stood out to me. I remember reading the name Moses. I had heard about Moses so I decided to turn to the page numbers that were listed next to his name so that I could read about him.

I turned the pages and I started reading about how Moses had killed someone. And when I read that, I had to check the cover of the book to make sure that it was actually the bible that I was reading. After I confirmed that it was the bible I kept on reading and I was blown away by the fact that Moses had killed someone when he was forty years old. The little that I did know about church and God—mostly from TV—I knew that Moses was somebody great. So I put two and two together and I realized that God could even use murderers and consider them great. I knew that I had been a murderer in the past.

I flipped back to the index and I looked for the word prostitute. I flipped to the pages the index listed and I began to read. I read how Jesus had genuinely interacted with a prostitute. And that blew me away. I knew that Jesus was the epitome of holiness and yet he had interacted with someone who was the total opposite. I had been a prostitute and if Jesus loved Mary Magdalene and was concerned enough about her to talk to her then he had to love me and also be concerned about me.

As I continued to read I continued to be blown away. Before I knew it three hours had passed by and I was still reading the bible and enjoying it! I realized that for twenty-three years I did not know about God or know who God was or exactly what He had wanted out of me. I simply never knew how to put the pieces of the "God puzzle" together so that they would form a clear picture of something that I could tangibly understand. I simply had never known, but now I was starting to find out and it felt so good and refreshing.

After praying and reading the bible I called my mother. We spoke for about an hour or so and we had one of the deepest conversations that we had ever had. After we hung up I called Shauna and dropped the bombshell on her. I told her that I had gone to church the night before and had gotten saved. Shauna, of course, thought that I was joking and she kept waiting for me to give her the punch line. As I kept telling her about what I had read in the bible and how I had been praying, Shauna began to realize that I was serious. And as she and I kept talking I started sharing things with her that I had never ever shared before. I explained to her that I knew that God was desiring something different from me.

Shauna gave me a very attentive and supportive ear, although she had in a literal sense become rich by hanging out with me. The question and thought or talk of money never came out of her mouth when I told her that I thought I needed to just walk away from the club and all of the negative stuff. Shauna simply asked me one thing. She said,

"Lady, let me just ask you this, are you committed and serious about God and what you're telling me? Because so many people get on these emotional religious highs and experiences and then before you know it, in a week or two they are right back to living any old way and they forget about God. . . . So, if you're serious then you can count on one thing. I will be there for you and support you in whatever direction it is that you feel you need to go in."

I just loved Shauna's character and spirit. She was exactly the type of person I needed in my life. I assured her that I was serious. I reminded that years prior I had been living on my own on the streets. I had been determined to make it and be a part of the Cream Team. I had successfully accomplished that mission. I went on to say that just like I had been serious about those things at the age of fourteen, I was ten times as serious and ten times as determined to start living for God now at the age of twenty-three.

So Shauna and my mom both had my back, and that made me feel real good. I reached out to Sha-Boogie but I couldn't make contact with him. I found it weird that his cell phone was giving me this message that a person would get when they change their phone number. And I was more shocked and surprised when I called his house and got a message that his number had been disconnected. I had no idea what that was all about and that weighed on my mind a whole lot.

When I reached out to Cream the first thing he wanted to know was if I had my list of people for him. If there was ever a time that I needed God to be with me it was at that moment when I had Cream on the phone. I took a deep breath and told him that I didn't have my list and that I wasn't gonna give him no list. I explained to Cream that I had decided to turn away from the life that I had been living. I had given my life to Jesus.

"What the hell are you talking about, Lady?!" Cream asked.

I calmly replied, "Cream, you heard what I said."

Cream became irate as he began telling me that he didn't have time for no games and for me to be talking like some holy roller when he had the cops and feds breathing down his back.

"Cream, I don't know what to tell you but I cannot and I will not be living like I've been living!"

"Oh come on with that, Lady! You know you gonna be right in the club next week smoking weed and getting drunk and partying like you always do."

I remained quiet. I had nothing else to say and no need to convince Cream of anything. I knew that he was just a man and nothing more than that.

"So, you know that the cops are breathing down my back and you just gonna leave me hanging like that?!" Cream asked. It's funny, he had always told me that only the paranoid survive, and man, was he paranoid!

"Cream, if they are breathing down your back then that means they're breathing down my back as well," I replied.

"Yeah, that's right and that's why I don't understand you!"

"Cream, what is there to understand? I'm telling you, just like when MA$E walked away from rap and nobody took him seriously, I'm walking away from this life of mine. And look at MA$E now, he's still staying true to why he left the rap game."

I could sense Cream's blood boiling right through the phone as he yelled, "Lady, do you think I really care about MA$E and his bitch-ass?! I don't know what all this talk is about, but word is bond, if I didn't know any better I would swear that you were the one ratting me out!"

I calmly replied, "Cream, listen. If you wanna believe that then believe it. But I'm telling you that is not the case. . . . How long have you known me? . . . You know me, Cream. That right there is all you need to know—you know me. And you have to know that when I say I'm serious about something then that means I'm serious about it. So, if you wanna put my name on the list you're drumming up then do whatever it is that you have to do. But all I'm telling you is that I'm done."

Cream did not reply. He simply hung up on me. I stood there and all kinds of thoughts raced through my head. I have to admit that I was scared as heck. I'm human, so I was scared about a lot of things. But I knew that I needed to trust God and turn to him and that is exactly what I did. I turned to God in prayer as I prepared to navigate through all the unknown things that were gonna come my way.

34

IT WAS AUGUST OF 2002. Approximately three weeks had passed since I had become a Christian. For the most part I was managing well and trying my best to stay focused on the things that God wanted me to do.

One good thing about the streets is that it is a training ground that can teach a person how to navigate through life no matter who or where they are. My street experience was serving me in a good way as I began my Christian experience. For example, on the streets you have to rely a lot on your instincts and be able to read people. As a new Christian I was finding that I had to sort of rely on my instincts to some extent also. Only it wasn't exactly my instincts per se, but rather a little voice inside of me. I knew that that little voice was really God talking to me.

At times I would hear weird things from that little voice. I knew that if it sounded too off the wall then it was probably not from God but was more than likely from Satan. For example, if that voice was telling me to smoke weed, then I definitely knew that it was from Satan. Likewise, if that voice was telling me to call some guy for sex then I knew that was from Satan. But if the voice was telling me things like maybe I should pray or maybe I shouldn't go here or there,

I could discern that it was likely from God and I would listen to it. So I learned to use my instincts to read that voice inside of me the same way I used to read different people who would come into my life while I was living the street life. Those two abilities helped me a great deal in the beginning.

But like I said, I'm human, and the one thing that I feared and constantly thought about was Cream killing me in order to silence me. Even though I had no intentions of ever ratting on him, I knew that he was paranoid about being indicted again and that his paranoia would likely be the reason for my execution.

What heightened my fears of execution was that I had not heard from Cream since the day he hung up the phone on me. I had also not heard from Sha-Boogie since the night that he and I went to church. While I longed to speak to and see Sha, I just figured that the whole church thing had scared him off. But at the same time I thought that he at least owed me the respect of calling me and telling me what was up. It was like he had just up and disappeared without a trace. He had changed all of his numbers and the whole nine.

I also have to admit that since I had not heard from Cream, a small part of me wondered if Cream had ordered Sha-Boogie to be killed. *Maybe that was the reason for both Cream and Sha's silence*, I thought to myself.

All I knew was that Shauna was the best anchor that I could possibly have had. Although she herself was not ready to jump into Jesus like I had, she was still willing to be there for me and I respected and appreciated that a whole lot. Surprisingly, for the first time in my life my mother was also a really big anchor for me.

One of the best things that had come out of my decision to follow Christ was that it made my mother and me close for the first time in my life. She and I had some of the best conversations—which I would never have thought possible. I was finally able to lean on her as a daughter should lean on a mother. The conversations that my mother and I had were also very painful and revealing. I told her just about everything I had been through. I didn't tell her about the murder in which I pulled the trigger, but I basically told her about everything else. The hardest part was telling her about my days as a prostitute.

My mother also opened up to me. She revealed so many things to me, things that helped to explain some of the bad decisions she had made in the past. She cried and I cried as we fully reconciled ourselves to one another and opened ourselves to one another.

Then one day in August when I was at my house in Jamaica Estates, my doorbell rang. I went to answer the door and Cream and Spinach were standing there. My heart skipped a beat and I assumed the worst.

"I didn't expect to see y'all," I stated as I smiled and tried to give them both a hug.

"Lady, hurry up and get dressed. We gotta go," Cream stated in sort of a hushed but stern tone.

"Go where?" I asked.

"Lady, I can't explain right now but just trust me. We gotta go," Cream added.

I didn't wanna show my fear but I was scared as hell. No one wants to know the exact day that they are gonna die, but I felt like I knew that my time on this earth was up. Cream and Spinach had come to take me out in the same manner that we had taken out Shamgod.

"Cream, I—"

Cream cut me off. "Lady, look, I understand what you told me about the church thing. Trust me, I do. I'm not tripping over that. But I really need you to get dressed and to come with us right now!"

"Just tell me where we're going so that I can call Shauna to tell her to meet me. She and I were supposed to be hanging out," I said to Cream. The part about Shauna was a lie, but I did want to call Shauna to tell her that I was heading out with Cream and Spinach. This way if I never returned home then at least someone know that I was last with Cream and Spinach.

Spinach remained quiet and Cream spoke. "Okay, call her but just hurry up!"

"Okay, give me two minutes to throw something on," I said.

I quickly went to get dressed. Part of me worried that Cream and Spinach would ambush me and kill me right there in my own house. That was the last thing I would have wanted my sister Mya to come home to.

I threw on a pair of jeans, sneakers, and a T-shirt. I grabbed my cell phone and we were out the door and inside Cream's Hummer. I made sure that I sat alone in the backseat. As soon as we got in the ride I called Shauna.

"Hey, what's up girl?" I said, trying to sound as normal as possible.

"What's up?" Shauna replied.

"Nothing, I was just calling to tell you that we're still going shopping but I will be tied up for a little bit. I'm with Cream and Spinach."

"Huh?" Shauna asked in confusion.

I held the phone away from my ear and I yelled to Cream, "Cream, where are we going again?" I hoped to catch Cream off guard.

He replied that we were going to his man's computer store on Merrick Boulevard in Laurelton.

"Shauna, just meet me in about an hour at this computer store on Merrick Boulevard in Laurelton," I instructed as I spoke into the phone.

"Huh? Girl, what are you talking about?" Shauna asked.

"Okay, so I'll see you soon. . . . I love you too," I said. I knew that Shauna had no idea what I was saying but I had to give her some idea of where I would be in case they needed to look for my body. I also wanted to tell her that I loved her just in case I never spoke to her again.

"You love me? Girl, was you drinking or something?" Shauna asked.

"Okay, I gotta go, I'll speak to you later," I said as I hung up my cell phone. I knew that Shauna must have thought I was a nut.

When I got off the phone I noticed that we did seem to be navigating our way toward Laurelton. Spinach then spoke up and asked, "Lady, when's the last time you spoke to Sha-Boogie?"

"Like three or four weeks ago. Ever since I started going to church I haven't seen him. He just up and disappeared on me and changed all of his numbers and all of that."

Spinach looked at Cream and the two of them just shook their heads. I was glad that I was sitting in the backseat because otherwise I probably would have been shot in the back of the head at that moment.

"What's up, y'all?" I nervously asked.

Cream spoke up. "What's up is that you didn't listen to me and you got involved with that nigga and he was dirty! I told you not to trust that nigga, Lady!"

My heart began racing. I sat at the edge of my seat.

"Dirty? What do you mean by that?" I asked in a real anxious tone.

"Lady, that nigga is a got damn rat bastard! *Pretty-Ricky* . . . a.k.a. Sha-Boogie was nothing but a got damn rat and now all of us is probably gonna get locked up because of his ass!" Cream yelled as Spinach shook his head. I jumped as Cream banged his hand on the steering wheel and looked at me through the rearview mirror.

"You didn't wanna listen to me! I told you to test his ass and you didn't listen!" Cream barked.

I was ready to begin sweating bullets of blood. I was so scared and still in the dark about exactly what was going on. I just couldn't take the pressure and the anxiety so I yelled out with anger, frustration, and fear. "Cream, just tell me what is going on?! Please!"

At that point we had reached Laurelton and we were at the computer store on Merrick Boulevard. "Get out and I'll show you what the hell I'm talking about!" Cream shouted. Then he added, "And what I'm about to show you, don't even question it. Because, unlike you, I did my homework and had Lombardi verify what I'm about to show your dumb ass!"

The three of us got out of the Hummer. We made it into the computer store which was a small, privately owned computer repair shop and Internet café. Apparently Cream and Spinach knew the owner as they greeted each other on a first-name basis.

"Yo, can you bring that stuff back up on the computer that you had on earlier?" Cream asked the guy.

The guy complied.

"Do me a favor and explain to her what you explained to us."

The guy went on to show me the computer screen and it had all kinds of numbers and charts on it.

"Okay, this is a stats log page from an Internet website. Right now I am connected to the Internet and I'm looking at a page that I was able to access with a special technique," the guy said while he winked at me.

I motioned with my hand for the guy to continue on.

"Every website is hosted somewhere. What that means is that the files that produce a website, those files rest and originate on a specific single computer. It's just like the physical headquarters of a business are located inside of some specific office building. . . . You follow me so far?"

"Yes," I replied as my heart continued to race a million beats per minute.

"Well, usually the place that hosts your website, or the company that hosts your website, they can give you these same stats and graphs that we are looking at right now. But there are other ways to get these stats if you know the right people," the guy said as he winked again and smiled.

He continued, "Now these stats are for your specific website for the nightclub. And basically what I was showing Cream and Spinach is that certain computers are *always* logged into your website. Meaning that even when there is nothing going on at your club, somebody is always logged in as a member to your website as if they were watching one of the events or parties there."

My heart sank at that point as I knew what was up.

The guy continued, "See these numbers? Well, each computer that is connected to the Internet has its own unique number just like these numbers that you see on the computer screen. It's similar to each house having a specific phone number. And just like with a phone number, if you know the phone number then you'll be able to trace that phone number to a particular house if you wanted to."

In a dejected whisper I said, "Or like if you have a license plate number on a car then you can trace that license plate number to the owner of the car."

"Exactly!" the guy said. "Now with these two numbers, I had one of my people trace them for me and—"

Cream cut him off and said, "Nah, that's cool. That's enough. I just wanted her to see that."

Cream and Spinach said their good-byes to the guy and then the three of us left together.

We piled back into the Hummer and I was certain that I was

gonna die. I was just hoping that it would be painless, quick, and peaceful.

"Lady, those numbers were traced back to a location in Manhattan and a location in Virginia. And those two places just happen to be the headquarters for the New York Police Department and the FBI headquarters in Virginia!" Cream spoke in a raised tone as we sat idle in the Hummer.

"Cream, there ain't nothing I can say. I—"

"You got damn right there ain't nothing you can say! I had a security guy come by the club and the place was dripping with bugs and all kinds of cameras!" Cream yelled as he interrupted my words.

"You don't know how I need to just hog-tie you to the back of this truck and drag your ass naked through the streets!"

I interrupted Cream. "A'ight Cream! I know that I messed up! That's obvious! So if you're gonna kill me then just kill me and get it over with!"

"Spinach, do you believe the balls of this bitch?!" Cream asked as he pulled out a gun and pointed it at my forehead.

I closed my eyes and inhaled and just waited for the trigger to be pulled.

"Hurry up!" I screamed as I gritted my teeth and kept my eyes closed.

Then the next thing I felt was a blow to my head but I could tell that I had not been shot. Cream had only hit me in the head with the butt of the gun. But in no time he switched into a rage and climbed over the front seats and was in the backseat of the roomy Hummer beating the hell out of me with his fists and feet. He also pistol-whipped the crap out of me.

"Cream, let's just bounce!" Spinach urged. "It's not worth killing her!"

Cream unlocked the passenger door, kicked me, and sort of pushed me with his foot at the same time. His push caused me to fall out of the car and I spilled out onto the concrete of Merrick Boulevard. Then I heard the sound of the Hummer's tires as Cream and Spinach screeched off.

I barely avoided getting hit by two cars that were driving by as I crawled on all fours. I made it to the sidewalk where I sat there bruised, bloody, and with a tremendously sharp pain cutting through my head. I tried to stand up but I quickly stumbled back to the ground. As I began to get my senses back people began coming over to me. This one Jamaican girl helped me to my feet and she walked me into a nearby beauty parlor.

Thankfully, the beauty parlor was not too crowded. But the people all seemed concerned. They came to my aid and asked if I wanted them to call the police. I declined. They tried to clean some of my open wounds—the result of the butt of the gun being slammed up against my head.

My first call was to Shauna and when I reached her on her cell phone I found out that she was right down the block. She had deciphered my phone conversation from earlier and had sort of come to my rescue. I told Shauna exactly where I was and what had happened. Before I knew it, she had come hastily stumbling into the beauty parlor with her designer handbag and car keys in her right hand.

"Oh my god, look at your face!" Shauna remarked.

I hadn't looked into any of the numerous mirrors that were located throughout the beauty parlor and truthfully I didn't wanna see what had become of my face. If my face felt the way it looked, then I knew it would not a pretty sight.

"Why did he do that to you?" Shauna asked.

"I'll tell you in a minute," I stated as I grimaced and winced in pain.

Shauna and I both thanked the ladies in the beauty parlor for their aid, concern, and hospitality and then we left.

We drove in Shauna's car and headed back to her place. I was simply too scared to go back to my house. I phoned Mya on her cell phone and told her not to go back to the house. I ordered her to spend the night with our mother and promised to explain why at a later time. As we drove, I explained everything to Shauna. She tried her best to put me at ease as she told me that if Cream and Spinach had wanted to kill me then they would have done it already. She also told me that if the cops and feds had had the club wired and bugged that they too would have already had me in custody.

Shauna's words came at the right time and they helped to relax me a great deal. In the worst way I just wanted to get to Shauna's place and take some Tylenol, clean myself up, assess the damage to my face, and sort everything out. I needed to figure out what the hell to do.

35

I WOUND UP SPENDING THE night at Shauna's house. I said my prayers and tried my best to fall asleep in Shauna's bed, but I had a pounding headache that just would not quit. I think it was like two or three o'clock in the morning when I actually managed to fall asleep.

All night long I tossed and turned. At around four thirty in the morning I heard this loud noise. I didn't know what the hell it was. But it had been so loud that it had folly woken me up.

"Shauna . . . Shauna! Wake up!" I said as I started to shake Shauna's body. The loud noise had gotten louder. Shauna was in a daze.

"What's wrong?" she asked.

"I heard this loud noise. . . . It sounded like someone was trying to break into your house," I whispered in a nervous tone. I noticed that the clock radio said 4:30 in the morning.

As Shauna and I sat up in her bed, I'll never forget the sound I heard next.

"FBI! Get on the ground! Put your hands out and get on the ground! I wanna see your hands!" the FBI agents yelled as they ripped Shauna and me out of the bed and slammed us onto the floor.

The FBI was in the middle of a predawn raid. They were the ones who had broken into Shauna's house. With flashlights blinding me, I found myself sprawled out on Shauna's bedroom floor with just my bra and panties on. My hands were stretched out in front of me but then they were quickly repositioned above my head and an FBI agent had his knee on my back. Shauna was in a similar position on the other side of the room.

"What are y'all doing in my house?!" Shauna screamed and demanded to know.

"Are there any weapons in here?!" one of the agents asked in a violent tone.

"No, we ain't got any weapons! And y'all still ain't tell me what y'all are doing in my crib!" Shauna yelled.

The agents at that point had our hands cuffed behind our backs. They helped us to our feet. The lights were now on in the bedroom and my half-naked body was fully exposed. Thankfully, Shauna had some decent silk short pajamas on and they did a good job of covering up her body.

I knew that my time was up and that my card had finally been pulled after years of doing dirt. This was how my career as a Cream Team member was coming to a definitive halt. I kept silent and Shauna continued to ramble as one of the agents began to read us our rights.

"You arresting us for what?!" Shauna asked as the FBI agent ignored her and continued to read us our rights.

Shauna looked at me and asked, "Can you believe this?!"

Two agents took us into the living room as others continued to thoroughly search Shauna's crib.

"Can I at least put on a robe or something?" I asked.

The agents looked at me and I know those white boys were loving looking at my half-naked body. Fortunately one of the agents got the attention of a female agent who came and escorted me back to Shauna's bedroom where she assisted me in covering up my body.

"My jeans are right over there, can you help me put those on?"

The agent reluctantly stated that she could not take the handcuffs off but that she would help me.

"Okay, whateva. I just don't wanna be walking around with my panties on," I explained.

Thankfully the jeans I had were not too tight and I was able to squirm my way into them with the assistance of the female FBI agent. She also helped me put on my short-sleeved T-shirt. Then she escorted me back to Shauna's living room. I looked like I had no arms since they were behind my back and covered underneath my shirt.

Before long, Shauna and I were escorted to FBI cars and whisked away to Manhattan with about fifteen other unmarked FBI vehicles following behind us. I was surprised that Shauna had been placed in the car with me because I was sure that they had only come for me. So, as we rode in the car I tried to calm Shauna and reassure her that everything would be okay.

"Shauna, don't worry about nothing. I'm calling my lawyer, Mr. Kellman, as soon as I get a chance and he'll take care of us."

Shauna was angry as hell and responded, "All I know is that they better have had a warrant to just come up in my crib the way they did!"

The sun was starting to rise and the traffic was beginning to build on the street, but we reached our downtown Manhattan destination rather quickly. Shauna and I were taken to different rooms and they attempted to interrogate us separately. They had finally told me why I had been arrested and they asked me numerous questions but I refused to answer anything. I was no dummy and I knew that I needed my lawyer to speak for me.

The first chance I got I called Mr. Kellman. He had helped me throughout the years with all of my business dealings. He had never once questioned whether I was into anything illegal, but I was sure that he must have had an idea that some of my money was being derived from illegal means. When I got him on the phone he told me not to worry about a thing and that he would be there by my side as soon as he could. He also said that he was gonna try to contact who he thought was the best criminal lawyer in the city and have him meet me as well.

As I sat detained for a few hours many thoughts ran through my head. I wondered what my mother and sister would think when they found out that I had been arrested. I wondered how the FBI had known that I was at Shauna's crib. Would I actually do jail time and if so, how much time would I get? I decided to just sit with my eyes closed. As I sat I began to pray, but I kept getting distracted by random thoughts.

I thought about the first time I'd spoken to Cream. I thought about the first time he took me to Club New York. I thought about the time he had given me a gun to use for my protection. I thought about the fight I had had with Mercedes. I thought about the numerous tricks I had turned. I thought about the Spanish guy's dick that had been chopped off. I thought about the time I cleaned up blood after witnessing Cream, Shamgod, and Spinach commit murder. I thought about the murder in which I pulled the trigger. I thought about the girls whose lives I helped ruin by keeping them enslaved in prostitution. I thought about the E pills and the weed that was illegally sold at my club. I thought about how Cream had beaten me for calling myself the First Lady. I thought about how I thought I loved Sha-Boogie and how he had been a refreshing spot in my life—or so I'd thought. I thought about everything that I had ever been through. And while I thought about all of those things I came to one resounding conclusion. Although I had become a millionaire at such a young age, the money I had made was not worth the price. I would have given anything to turn back the hands of time. But unfortunately I couldn't undo the past and I had to be held accountable for all of the wrong that I had done.

My attorney showed up at about 11 A.M. He was accompanied by a high-profile criminal lawyer named was Marvin Thornburg. The three of us sat in a room for a couple of hours. We spoke at length.

"Did you guys get stuck in traffic?" I asked.

"No, nothing like that. Sorry it took us so long but we were speaking to one of the assistant U.S. attorneys. We're trying to sort everything out and get a handle on what's going on," Marvin Thornburg explained.

"So, what am I looking at?" I eagerly asked. "Be completely honest with me and don't hold any punches," I instructed.

"Well, first off, Tina, let me explain something. I'm a straight shooter and I never hold any punches. I tell you how it is so that you won't have any surprises," Marvin responded.

"Now, what is going on is this. There is something called the

RICO law which stands for Racketeer Influenced and Corrupt Organization. Basically RICO is an acronym—"

I nodded my head to show that I understood. Then my criminal lawyer went on.

"The RICO law gives prosecutors wide-ranging and sweeping authority. One of the favorite uses of the RICO law is its ability to go after and take down what they call organized crime syndicates such as the Mafia and things of that nature. The law defines racketeering activity as any act or threat involving murder, kidnapping, gambling, arson, bribery, extortion, dealing in obscene matter, or dealing in a controlled substance or listed chemical. . . . You follow?" I was soaking up everything like a sponge.

"Yeah, I follow you."

"Now, the indictment is a multiple-count indictment. It charges that you are a member of the Cream Team and that the Cream Team has engaged in murder, kidnapping, narcotics distribution, and prostitution. It's also stating that your street name is Lady and that you are right at the top of the organization."

I interrupted, "Well, am I the only one being charged?!"

"Oh no!" Marvin replied. "See, let me explain how the FBI works. They don't go after just one fish. They try to go after the whole school of fish that swim together. This way, they hope to wipe out the entire organization. And in this case they did not just go after you but they rounded up about fifteen people. But the thing with the RICO law is that you're looking at anywhere from twenty years to life behind bars."

My heart sank at those words but I still had enough in me to ask another question. "So, am I correct in assuming that someone like myself—who they consider to be at the top of the organization—would be looking at more time than those at the bottom of the organization?"

Marvin replied, "Well, in general terms, yes. But not always, because a guy at the bottom of the organization could be responsible for thirty murders, you understand?"

I nodded to indicate that I did. Then I asked them to find out why Shauna had been arrested and to also make sure that she was released. Unfortunately, to my surprise, I was told some awful news by the attorneys.

"Well Tina, things don't work that easily. Now while we will represent Shauna, she's not going home anytime soon. She's also being charged under this indictment."

"What?!" I yelled in total shock and disbelief.

"Okay Tina, listen. We will get to Shauna, but let us work this one step at a time."

I shut up and listened. I felt absolutely horrible because Shauna had always been a straight arrow. I had been a bad influence in her life and now she was paying the price for having stuck by me through everything.

The lawyers went on to explain that the RICO law had wide-sweeping authority. As we spoke, all of my assets were either frozen or being frozen and basically in the hands of the government. With the RICO law, the authorities didn't even need a conviction in order to freeze someone's assets. All of my bank accounts, both personal and corporate, were frozen. The club, my cars, my house, my condo—nothing was under my control. And not only for me but for Shauna and for everyone else who was being charged.

I also found out that Cream, Spinach, and a whole host of other Cream Team members had been picked up during the predawn raid. My lawyer went on to give me some options. He explained the massive amount of evidence that was stacked up against me. The wiretap evidence, the video surveillance, and a host of other evidence that went back for years and included everything up until the present. He also explained that there were a number of witnesses prepared to testify against the Cream Team.

I jumped in and asked, "Marvin, I don't know for sure, but I think they may have told you about an undercover cop who goes by the name Sha-Boogie. But even if they didn't tell you about him, I'm sure he was the one who helped get a lot of the evidence and videotapes and all of that. But my thing is this, isn't there a line that the police can't cross while they are investigating? I mean, I went as far as having sex with the guy! There has to be something illegal about that or some kind of conflict of interest," I said in a slightly bitter manner.

Marvin explained that he had been told by the U.S. attorney that Sha-Boogie was not an undercover cop. He was simply a criminal informant who was working with the NYPD-FBI Organized Crime Joint Task Force. Sha-Boogie had agreed to help infiltrate and take down the Cream Team in order to get a sweetheart deal for crimes that he had been involved in. Now Sha-Boogie was in the witness protection program.

"You see, you're right about what you're getting at. Informants, cops, and undercovers cannot do anything illegal while they're investigating. But in this case, the informant, Sha-Boogie, didn't do anything illegal. He simply had consensual sex with you," my attorney stated.

I sank into my seat. I finally understood why Sha-Boogie had seemed to just disappear off the face of the earth. In my head, I knew that regardless of the investigation that Sha had been helping to conduct, he and I had made some kind of emotional connection. Maybe I was crazy and just wanted to believe what I wanted to believe, but I knew in my heart that Sha and I had shared some kind of chemistry. But that was neither here nor there—he would probably soon be on the witness stand testifying against me.

I sat back up in my seat. I explained to Marvin that I was guilty of a whole lot. I wasn't gonna try to hold no punches and I just wanted to tell the truth.

Marvin cautioned me, "Tina, I understand where you're coming from, and it's noble and the right thing to do. But see, right now, while my job is to have you tell the truth, the bigger scope of my job is to get the government to prove their case against you. They have to prove to the jury beyond a shadow of a doubt that you should be held accountable. The jury has to decide to what extent you should be held accountable for the charges that you face."

I understood where Marvin was coming from, but as a Christian I knew that I just had to do the right thing. And I also knew that some lawyers would do anything and say anything in order to spring their client.

Then Marvin surprised me. I knew that he was Jewish simply based on his name but he began to speak to me and tell me about Christianity. He explained that although people do all kinds of wrong and they should not be able to get off, in God's eyes they would be able to get off as long as they had Jesus representing them. Jesus would be able to present a winnable defense to God that would definitely spring his clients. Marvin went on to say that while he was in no way equating himself to Jesus, that he would be playing a similar role as Jesus in trying to get me off.

As Marvin spoke, one of the assistant U.S. attorneys came into the room and asked my lawyers if she could speak with them. The lawyers excused themselves for about ten minutes and then all three of them came back to speak to me.

The assistant U.S. attorney spoke first. She basically told me the same things about the RICO law that my lawyer had explained to me. She went on to tell me how I could possibly be facing life in prison if I was convicted of the charges. After she was done talking she asked me if I would listen to a tape recording. I agreed and she whipped out her tape recorder and pressed play.

With all four of us closely listening to the tape, she asked me, "Do you recognize those voices on the tape?"

"Yeah," I replied as I listened somewhat in disgust.

On the tape, Cream was talking to Spinach about how stupid I was, how I never listened to him, and how flamboyant I was. He spoke at length about how I always start one business after another like some big-time business person. He mocked me on the tape and told Spinach that I must have thought I was Oprah Winfrey or something. Then he said something to the affect of: with all of us being street niggas and all, what the hell did street niggas know about the Internet? The fact that I had even suggested the whole Internet thing was proof of my stupidity. He rambled on and on about how he knew he should have killed me a long time ago and how he just had to go through with it and finish me off. Throughout the tape Spinach would laugh here and there but Spinach stayed true and not once did he bad-mouth me.

I kind of sat there, stunned. I was the one who had religiously visited Cream when he was in the joint. I was the one who had stashed away so much money for him while he was in the joint. I was the one who had sold my body for him. I was the one who had helped to sky-rocket his prostitution business. And I just found it so hypocritical that he was bad-mouthing me about the different businesses I had started and yet he never had a problem spending the money when I would deliver it to him. As for killing me—well, his words on the tape simply confirmed what I had already sensed he had been plotting for a long time.

When the tape stopped, the assistant U.S. attorney spoke and said, "Tina, you heard for yourself how Cream was talking about you. You should clearly be able to see that Cream could care less about you and your well-being. Now, what I'm prepared to do is grant you and Shauna full immunity from all of these charges if you agree to testify against Cream and the rest of the Cream Team members and associates."

I closed my eyes and blew air out of my lungs. And as I closed my eyes I saw an image of Cream beating me in the back of his Hummer. I also saw the time that he had beaten me in his house and then pulled down his pants and chastised me and said that without him I would have been nothing more than a two-dollar hoe. I continued to just sit there with my eyes closed and I blew more air out of my lungs.

I knew that at that moment I was holding all of the cards. And all I had to do was play those cards. In doing so I would be able to spring myself and get off scot-free from a lifetime of corrupt actions.

The assistant U.S. attorney then reminded me that I was gonna be tried for Shamgod's murder. She ran down all of the other charges. She was trying to reinforce what I was up against in order to suggest that testifying against Cream and everyone else was a no-brainer.

Honestly, as I sat there, the only thing that was making me lean toward turning against the Cream Team was the fact that I could help spring Shauna. Personally, I was willing to do whatever time in the joint that I was facing, but I would not have been able to live with my-self if Shauna had been sent to prison.

"Can you just give me some time alone with my lawyers?" I asked.

"Sure, no problem," the lady replied as she prepared to leave the room.

With her gone, Marvin spoke and said, "Tina, it's a sweetheart deal."

"I know," I replied. But I knew that no matter how bad Cream had spoken about me, I couldn't let any resentment or bitterness cloud my thinking. I knew that I couldn't turn into a rat. It just wasn't right. No one on the Cream Team had ever forced me to do anything and I couldn't now turn the tables on everybody.

"Marvin, I just can't do it. I'm gonna have to roll the dice and go to trial," I replied.

"Tina, just think about what you're doing. You're risking jail time for yourself and for Shauna. And not only that, if you don't go through with this deal, you can bet that the same assistant U.S. attorney will be talking to Cream in a minute and trying to get him to turn against you. The government is willing to sacrifice one if it can guarantee that they'll get the majority," Marvin explained.

"Marvin, look, my mother knows of a spot where I stashed a whole lot of cash. I did that so if I died she and my sister would be okay. I know that the government doesn't know about that money. I want you to take your fees out of that money and use it to represent both me and Shauna and do the best job you can. I just can't go through with testifying against Cream and the team. I know I'm rolling the dice but I gotta do what I gotta do. . . . Find another way to help me. Please."

Marvin took off his glasses and rubbed his eyes. He simply replied, "Okay."

For myself, I had to believe that the government had a weak case against me in particular. Even with all of their wiretaps, videotapes, bugs, and witnesses, why were they offering me such a sweet deal so soon? They were offering it because they didn't have a rock-solid case.

I would be lying if I said that I wasn't nervous. Maybe I was cutting my own throat by going to trial. I was placing all of my chips on the table and letting everything ride, all the while knowing that Cream— who was the devil incarnate—would have killed me at any time and not lost sleep over it. He could have been planning to turn the tables and take me down in order to free himself. He had no kind of honor and yet I was still honoring him to a big extent.

Was I stupid?

True street niggas would say no, I wasn't stupid. Everyone else would have said that I was stupid as hell for not taking the government's deal. Time would tell if I had played my cards right.

36

BETWEEN SHAUNA AND MYSELF, OUR combined bail was beyond the seven-figure mark. With all of my assets frozen, I had no way to personally make bail. I did have $250,000 in cash stashed away for my mother and my sister but I had to use that to pay my lawyers and different experts and consultants that my lawyers were planning to hire to help bolster our defense.

Fortunately for me, I had given my lawyer the name of a prominent record industry bigwig who I knew really well. The bigwig, who shall remain nameless, was willing to put up the bail for Shauna and myself. So, after only two weeks behind bars Shauna and I were once again free women. Or at least we were free until our trial came to an end. The prosecution was moving fast and trying to bring our case to trial within like seven months.

It was weird, because for so long I had purposely lived independently of my mother. But now that this whole indictment and arrest had sprang up, everything had been taken from me and I was in a humbled position. Just like *that* the finances in my life had done a complete one-eighty-degree turn. In that humbled position I found myself living with my sister at my mother's place. But my mother was not living with and being supported by some man. She had really changed up her act and was living a completely different life now that she was a Christian.

My relationship with Shauna was somewhat strained. I mean, she was grateful that I was willing to pay for her defense and that I had helped to get her bail taken care of, but she just couldn't understand why I had not taken the government's deal. She purposely began to distance herself from me and I can't say that I blamed her. Really, the only time she and I spoke was when we would meet with our lawyers together. We'd go over our defense strategy and take part in mock cross-examination sessions. I was praying every day to God that no matter the outcome of the trial, that He restore my relationship with Shauna to the way it had been before we had been arrested.

What was also tough for me was that I felt like I had really let my sister and my mother down. They didn't beat me up and they didn't look at me like I was the scum of the earth, but I know that there was some deep-rooted disappointment inside of both of them. So, I guess it was their disappointment in me that ate at me to no end.

Without a doubt, the things that helped me the most while I waited for my trial to begin were my prayers, reading my bible regularly, and becoming a member of the church in Brooklyn where I had given my life to the Lord. I found myself at the church building on a regular basis. There was a Christian bookstore inside the church, along with a restaurant, a gymnasium, and so many other things that helped to fill up my time in wholesome ways.

But the best thing about spending a lot of time there was that I began to meet with the pastor of the church. He and I would speak at length. I explained to him all that I had been through and how I had come to the Lord and then been arrested and was now out on bail. The pastor was filled with so much wisdom. I know that sort of sounds like religious rhetoric but it was the truth. He had a way of taking the most complex things about God and the bible and breaking them down for me so I could immediately start applying them to my life. I loved talking with my pastor and I knew that God had specifically worked it out so that I could get counsel from him and from no one else.

One of the things that I spoke to my pastor about was my inability to accept the idea that God loves me. My pastor eased my fears as he said, "Tina, you have to understand that God's love is unconditional. He loves everybody exactly the same and he doesn't show any favoritism toward any one person. But while his love is unconditional, you have to also understand that *his promises are conditional*. His promises are conditional and based on our obedience to his word. And now that you have decided to change your old way of living, you must make sure that your lifestyle proves that you have truly moved from a life of sin. Now, I'm not saying that you will never make mistakes because you will, but you just have to always be willing to truly repent after you make those mistakes."

I nodded my head in agreement and continued to listen as my pastor spoke to me. "See, Tina, the thing with many people and with things in general is that change is always way too temporary. But you must remember that change isn't an event. It is a process. Long-lasting change is the type of change that you should want to make and that begins with raising the bar in your own life. You will not change what you are willing to tolerate. And more than likely, Tina, you only did what you did in the past and lived the way you lived simply because you only thought to the level of what you had been exposed to."

"That is so true," I said while my pastor nodded in agreement.

I went on, "In the past I had never been exposed to the things of God. I had only been exposed to the streets and to the different hustles on the street. That was all that was real to me and all that I thought about. But as soon as I began to hear about God, I began to think about Him."

My pastor went on to explain that everything in life starts in seed form and then it grows. He told me that the night I had seen MA$E give his life to the Lord, God had planted a seed inside of me.

"It was no accident that you saw that. It was God planting a seed inside of you. And then a few years later God started watering that seed and when you came to church again and gave your life to God, the seed began to sprout. And what you do from here forward will show what type of fruit you will bear," he explained.

I laughed. I told him to just keep speaking because I needed to hear all that he was telling me. "Speak, please just keep speaking, speak . . . I never heard anyone talk like this before," I said as I smiled and moved to the edge of my chair.

My pastor smiled and said, "Everybody's life is determined by choices. And we become servants to the choices we make. But our character is what determines our destiny. Choices are not made in a moment of time, they are rooted in your character."

"That is so deep!" I replied. "So, basically I need to start working on things like my character and my integrity because those are the things that will help me to make better choices in my life?"

"Exactly," my pastor said as he smiled.

"So, what exactly is gonna happen to me as I go forward? I mean, what if I get sentenced to prison?"

"If that happens, it will be a consequence of your past sins and past actions. It is possible to experience the joys of forgiveness while going through the consequences of sin. But sometimes, God's permissiveness will not let you suffer any consequences of your actions. He'll still hate the sins and hate the actions but He'll love you all the way through the process. One other thing that you have to keep in mind is that for everything that happens in the natural realm that we live in, there is a spiritual counterpart or a spiritual parallel. We need to see those parallels so that we can learn from them."

"I don't understand what you mean," I said.

"Okay, what I mean is this. You will go to trial and we don't know what the outcome will be. But personally, I suspect that you will get off and not face any jail time."

"Really? Why do you say that?" I asked.

"I say that because I think God will be using something in real life in order to show you something spiritually. If that happens, He could be showing you that even when everything seems hopeless and when it looks like there can be no chance of forgiveness, a lawyer can step in and convince a jury to let you off. In the same way, one day you will stand before God and you will have to give an account for *all* that you did. While it would seem that all of the wrong you did should be a just cause for a sentence to hell, Jesus will step in and speak for you and allow you to make it to heaven simply because you put your trust in Him."

"Oh, okay . . . I got you," I replied. "But pastor, let's say that I do get off. Then how do I live? I mean, would I not be able to go to a club or do what I like to do? Christianity always seemed so *religious* to me; people always seem to be telling you what you *can't* do. I don't think that I really know how to practically live my life, especially after the way I grew up."

"Tina, this is the thing. Number one, never let anyone but God define who you are. Because when you let a man define you, then you empower that person to judge you. The second thing that you need to understand is that it's not about religion, it's about a relationship with Jesus Christ, plain and simple. Many pastors mean well, but they focus too much on religious rules and regulations and forget that it is all about a relationship with Jesus Christ. The third thing you need to know is that everyone has a purpose and a gift. You have to find out what your purpose in life is and what your gifts are. Then use those gifts to fulfill your purpose in life. In doing so, your focus needs to be on having a positive impact on society. I don't care if you get locked up or if you are free, you still need to find out what your purpose in life is. From what you've told me about your past, it seems to me like you are an incredibly gifted business person. Only you used your gifts in the wrong way."

I nodded.

He went on, "I understand what you are trying to say about how Christians are always telling you what you shouldn't be doing. But understand this, it's not about what music you listen to or who you associate with or any of that stuff. It's not about rules and regulations. While you don't want to have a steady diet of negative influences, you need to always think about this word: *Conversion.*"

"What do you mean?"

"Let's say you get off. You're probably thinking, 'Well, I can't be a club promoter anymore because that is evil. And I can't be a part of the Cream Team anymore because that is evil.' But what I'm telling you to do is simply convert it. Convert what you were doing. If your business was doing bad or doing wrong, then you need to convert that business in the same way you yourself were converted."

"Huh? So you're saying that I could still be a club promoter and all of that stuff?"

"This is what I'm saying. Apparently you have talents that let you succeed in what you do. And you also have a lot of influence over people. The conversion that I am talking about is this. Can you imagine, Tina—or as you were called, Lady—can you imagine society finding out that Lady is still promoting her club but she is promoting it so that people can have a place to come and have a good time where they won't have to worry about drugs and shootings and things like that? What if you started a club for Christians and the focus was playing all-Christian rap music? Do you know what kind of impact that would have? And the whole thing about the Cream Team—I know what you told me the letters stand for but even that can be converted."

"How?" I asked.

"Instead of people knowing that Cream stands for Cash Reigns Everywhere Around Me, why don't you convert that and change it to Christ Reigns Everywhere Around Me? If you do that, then in or out of prison you can still be a part of the Cream Team. But the focus of the new Cream Team would radically change. . . . Do you follow what I'm saying?"

"Yes! I follow completely. I am so glad you're telling me all of this. It's like it gives me so much to look forward to and it is the exact practical application that I was missing."

My pastor said he had a meeting in a few minutes so he would have to leave shortly. But before he left he gave me one last jewel of information.

"Lady, this is what I want to leave you with. I already told you about how change is a process and not an event. But remember that change is a constant thing in life. You recognized that you needed to make a change in your life and you did that by coming to the Lord. But understand that you will continually be faced with changes that you'll have to make and I hope you remember all of what I have told you. But if you don't remember anything else, please remember this: *When change is necessary, to not change is destructive.*"

I thought for a moment about what he had said. Then I added, "You are so right. It's just like if a person is using drugs or having unprotected sex or always driving drunk, if they don't change their behavior somewhere along the line, then eventually destructive things will happen to them, like addiction, diseases, and even death. And the same principles can be applied to any situation in life where change needs to take place, right?"

"You learn real fast, Lady," my pastor stated as he stood up and prepared to depart.

After we finished talking, I hugged my pastor and thanked him for his time. I felt so refreshed because win or lose in my trial I was beginning to understand life and how I fit into the whole grand scheme of things around me.

IN FEBRUARY OF 2003, THE trial had finally gotten underway. At the age of twenty-four, I was on trial and facing years behind bars. Cream, Spinach, Shauna, and I were all codefendants. The other Cream Team members were being tried separately at different times. Shauna and I shared the same attorneys. And Cream and Spinach, who had not been able to make bail, they too shared a common attorney.

Our defense table was crowded and reminded me a lot of the O.J. Simpson trial. During different breaks and recesses, Cream and I would talk. He told me that he knew I had been offered immunity. He said he had nothing but respect for me for not going that route which would have been sure doom for him. I knew that the government really wanted him, because he told me that they had never even offered him or Spinach a plea deal.

He explained that he was sorry about what he had said and what had been recorded on tape. He told me that all the negative things that he had ever said about me was just foolish talk, just him rambling off at the mouth. He swore he never meant any of it. With words, I told Cream that I understood and that I accepted his apology. But on the inside, I knew that it was hard for a zebra to lose its stripes. Plus, I had learned from the bible that what comes out of a man's mouth is often a reflection of what's in his heart. It's just like when someone gets drunk and loses his inhibitions and starts talking all kinds of craziness. Behind that craziness is what he has been holding inside and was afraid to say all along. Once he gets drunk the words he was afraid to say start spilling out of his mouth. So, in other words I knew that in Cream's heart he really believed and meant everything that he had said about me on the tapes.

But Cream had to respect my gangsta of deciding to go to trial. He asked me to be honest with him and to tell him why I didn't rat on him. I said to him, "Cream, you know what? I realize now that with the life that people live on the streets they usually only have two alternatives. They can turn into a rat or they can turn to God. And the only reason that I decided to go to trial is because I decided to turn to God."

The trial lasted about three weeks. During those three weeks the courtroom was packed each and every day. At the trial I got a chance to see firsthand just how the Cream Team had disrupted so many lives. There were people like Shamgod's family members in attendance. There were relatives of the guys that Cream, Spinach, and Shamgod had murdered. Mercedes's mother was in attendance as were the mothers of other ex-prostitutes.

There were also a ton of witnesses that testified against us, but none were more damaging than Sha-Boogie's testimony. And what was ill about Sha-Boogie—and it helped me confirm that he had developed some real feelings for me—was that he lied his butt off when he was on the witness stand. He put words in my mouth and said things about Cream and the team that he claimed I told him firsthand, but he knew in his heart that they were lies. And yet there were things that I'd told him about myself that would have sent me to jail for life but he never mentioned those things. So in a way I think he was kind of protecting me and trying to save face in the only way that he really could. He never looked at any of us in the eyes, not once during his entire time on the witness stand. But what could I say about the man? He played the rat game like so many others have done over the years and he definitely got the best of me. There really wasn't much else to say about him. My heart had blinded me and got the best of me and I was the loser. It's that simple.

Some of the girls who were former teenage prostitutes also testified in a very damaging manner. They recanted horrors of being coaxed and then manipulated, brainwashed, and controlled into a life of sex slavery.

The prosecution presented a ton of visual evidence in the form of crime-scene photos. They turned my stomach. They showed Shamgod's decomposing body. They showed the charred remains of Pete, Dame, Ci-Lo, and Stretch, all members of Shamgod's crew who had been torched by Cream after they had been shot, clubbed in the head, and killed with baseball bats. Ironically, it was at the trial that I finally found out what happened to the bodies of those guys.

The prosecution also detailed with huge pie charts and bar graphs the large amounts of money that the Cream Team raked in over the years. They showed videotape of drug sales that went on inside my club. They showed illegal sex acts that went on inside the club. And they played recorded cell phone conversations between Cream and me, Cream and Spinach, as well as conversations between the three of us as we plotted and planned schemes.

My attorney was an absolute genius. Since I did not take the sweetheart plea deal, he decided to play the psychological card. In building a psychological defense he brought in expert witnesses in the form of social workers and forensic psychologists. Marvin and my entire defense team built up an extraordinary and compelling case that basically displayed how the events of my upbringing had affected me.

I loved the defense strategy, but it opened up some old wounds and exposed so many embarrassing details about my family and my upbringing. I had to recount the numerous times that I had been molested and the time that I had been raped. I also had to talk about how I had been exposed to pornography from as early as I could remember and how I had witnessed my mother being physically abused and beaten by different men. I had to talk about how, as a child, I moved around countless times. I also testified how I had literally lived on the street and slept in the subway in order to avoid the pain and misery of the environment that my mother and sister were in. The fact that I'd never met my biological father also came up, as did the fact that I had been a prostitute under the rule and control of Cream.

My lawyer hoped that if they selected the right jury, and if they played the sympathy angle and didn't try to deny or cover up what I had done, that the jury would look at me in a totally different light and possibly excuse what I had done. Sort of like if a two-year-old baby shoots someone, everyone would look at that as an accident because mentally, emotionally, and psychologically they know that a two-year-old could not possibly understand the concept of murder. Or a better example would be if a battered wife were to kill her husband while he slept in his bed. A lawyer could argue and show that the past beatings, manipulation, and threats by her husband had damaged and traumatized her in such a serious way to the point where it drove her over the edge.

In the same way, my defense wanted to show that my past had affected and traumatized me to the point where it caused me to have serious issues emotionally, mentally, and psychologically. I had detachment issues and anger issues which enabled me to do what I did without fully understanding the impact or consequences of what I was doing.

My lawyer always spoke straight with me. He told me that there was a very good chance that I was gonna do some time. He told me he was trying to set the jury up sympathetically so they'd only charge me with the lesser crimes which carried less jail time.

That was the strategy and it definitely seemed effective. The prosecution did a damn good job of drilling me and trying to break through my defenses. But I was more than happy and satisfied with the job of my defense team.

Shauna was probably the easiest to defend simply because she really had never been involved in any of the illegal dirt. Nor was she on tape saying anything incriminating. There were numerous credible witnesses to back up her story and defense that she just happened to be a real good childhood friend of mine who had come to work for me and had only helped me manage the *legal* doings of the club.

Cream and Spinach didn't have a very good attorney and things did not look good for them. The jury had no reason to sympathize with them. And to make matters worse, in 2001 or in 2002—some time before the indictments had been handed down—a bill had been passed which eliminated the five-year statute of limitations on the crime of kidnapping. So that meant that the prosecution was able to go back years and lay out how Cream and Spinach had systematically lured and essentially kidnapped young girls from other states, brought them to New York, enslaved them, and had them work as prostitutes.

All four defendants and both of the defense teams tried to remain as upbeat and as supportive as possible of each other throughout the entire trial. Finally the trial was over and the case was in the hands of the jury. The jury deliberated for three whole days. And man, I thought sitting through the actual trial was the most horrifying and nerve-racking experience that I had ever been through. But during the three days in which the jury deliberated, I can honestly say that I have never been so scared in my life. I trusted in the Lord but I still was very nervous about my future. I was even more nervous about Shauna's future.

The verdict came in on March 12, 2003. Everyone was notified and given time to get to the courtroom—everyone meaning family, friends, lawyers, prosecutors, and defendants.

As the courtroom filled up with people my heart started to race nonstop and my mouth was unbelievably dry. When everyone was ready and in position, the judge spoke the words that we have all heard on TV. He asked the jury foreman if they had reached a verdict and the foreman said yes.

Things were so blurry to me from that point on. But I remember standing up alongside Shauna and my lawyers as the official verdict was about to be read aloud. Cream, Spinach, and his lawyers also stood up beside us.

Shauna was the first defendant to hear her verdict. As the jury foreman spoke, I kept my head down and my eyes closed and I prayed as hard as I could. I don't know exactly what Shauna was doing but I could sort of feel her hand trembling as I held on to it and squeezed it. Both of our palms were hot and as wet as a river.

Then for each count that was read against Shauna, the words, "Not guilty," flowed out of the jury foreman's mouth. I blew out air from my lungs and I hugged Shauna as she started to cry. Her family and friends shouted for joy as they sat in the packed courtroom.

The only thing Shauna said to me as we embraced was, "Thank God, thank God, thank God!"

Shauna thanked our lawyer, Marvin, and then the judge restored order to the courtroom. The verdicts for Tina Montgomery were about to be read aloud.

Shauna now gripped my hand, and I thought that I was gonna explode with anxiety and fear. I also thought that the entire courtroom could hear my heart pounding. Then the jury foreman began to read, and I kept hearing the words "Not guilty." But my eyes were closed and I wasn't sure if my mind was playing tricks on me. So I opened my eyes and I waited to hear the word "Guilty." But fortunately I never heard those words, and really for a brief second I was just numb. I didn't remember hearing anything for a few seconds. Then I felt the triple embrace of Marvin, Mr. Kellman, and Shauna. I realized that against all odds I had beat every charge that I was up against!

I buried my face in my hands and I wanted to drop to my knees and cry for joy. But instead I very softly thanked the Lord as I took my hands from my face and looked toward the ceiling. I looked over to the jury and I repeatedly mouthed the words "thank you" to them. I embraced Marvin and gave him a kiss on the cheek. I whispered my thanks into his ear, telling him that he was the best lawyer in the world.

The courtroom went wild when they heard my verdict. There were people who cheered for me but most jeered me and the jury's decision. Even though I had never been implicated as the shooter, I remember Shamgod's mother violently yelling that I was a murderer and that she couldn't believe that they had let me get away with murder. Then she actually collapsed and passed out from her overwhelming grief.

Her words stung deep into my soul as I knew that she was right. And I honestly and genuinely felt for her though I could only imagine her pain. But I had gone through the legal process and although it wasn't fair to her or the rest of her family, it was the reality.

The court officers helped to restore order. Everyone prepared to hear the verdicts for Spinach and Cream respectively. I was no longer nervous. I was very relieved but I didn't want to express my emotions out of respect for everyone in the courtroom. So I stood poker-faced and listened as Spinach and Cream were both found guilty on every charge.

Finally, some of the families whose lives the Cream Team had helped to ruin had received some form of justice and vindication. The courtroom erupted in loud shouts of joy.

Cream and Spinach both looked dejected, as did their lawyer. It had to be a huge letdown to them after having watched Shauna and me both get off. I'll never forget the look that Cream gave me. He looked at me as if to say he hated every fiber in my body. You could just feel the hate oozing out of Cream's ice-grille as he was handcuffed and led away by the court officers. And the worst part was that all of his hate was directed at me. Spinach, on the other hand, leaned over and said that he loved us. He hugged and kissed both me and Shauna before he was handcuffed and led off.

There was more legal talk by the judge and some directions were given to everyone. And then I just simply could not believe that I was able to walk out of the courtroom scot-free with my mother, my attorneys, and Shauna. The press was everywhere. They swarmed around me and asked me all kinds of questions and snapped pictures. No one in my camp made any comments. We just wanted to get out of the courthouse and on with our lives.

Shauna went with her people, and the lawyers went their separate ways. My mother, Mya, and I ended up jumping into this hot, black Range Rover with tinted windows. My mother got into the front passenger seat and Mya and I got in the back. We quickly drove off to avoid the media circus. The driver looked very handsome, sort of like a Billy Dee Williams, and he was well dressed. I quietly wondered if he was the new man in my mother's life. If it was, he looked as though he had it going on.

When we reached a traffic light the driver turned around and handed me a big box that was gift-wrapped. "Here. This is from your mother and me," he said.

"Thank you," I said. I opened up the box and to my surprise it was a banging sheared mink jacket. I was shocked because I knew that my mother couldn't afford such a luxury item.

"Ma, I love this mink but I can't accept this," I said.

"Why not? Girl, put it on," my mother instructed.

Mya loved the mink and she marveled at it. As I put it on I asked my mother, "How did you afford this?"

My mother ignored my question and simply said, "Tina, you look so good in that mink!" The driver turned around, looked at me, and agreed.

Then my mother said, "Tina, that jacket is a gift from your father and me to you."

"My father?" I asked with a curious smile.

"Yes. Your father," my mother answered. "Say hello to him . . ."

My heart dropped and my sister and I both looked at each other in disbelief.

"Daddy?" I said with a whole bunch of uncertainty in my voice.

"Yes, baby?" the driver responded.

"Oh my god!" I screamed and I began crying. Mya also was screaming with joy.

"Ma, please don't joke with me like this! Are you serious that this is my father?"

"Tina, I would never joke with you like that," my mother replied.

I could not believe that after twenty-four years I was finally meeting my father. It was so surreal.

Then my father told us that he was taking us to a restaurant. "We got a whole lot to catch up on," he said.

I could not stop crying. I just gazed in disbelief at my father. He looked so strong, successful, and stable, and he just looked like he had it going on. He looked so much better than I had ever imagined.

Then he pressed play on his CD player and 50 Cent's smash hit song "In da Club" came on.

"Y'all like this song?" my father asked.

Mya and I both said yes. Through my tears I said, "That's my jam! Turn it up."

My father blasted 50 Cent's hit song and he began reciting all of the words to the song. He threw his right hand in the air and nodded his head up and down and just jammed to the music. That was one of the best sights and best feelings ever.

As we drove I didn't really reflect on the fact that I had just skated in a major way. But I did know that a lot of things in life weren't fair. Truly, it wasn't fair that I got off scot-free. But like I said, I realized that many things in life were not and are not fair. The most unfair and unjust thing that I knew of was the fact that Jesus had been wrongly sentenced to death although He was an innocent man. But I believe that His death had all been a part of God's plan. And it was His death that truly set me and all others who believe in Him free. Jesus's death, may have seemed like this terrible tragedy, but in actuality it was the best thing that could have ever happened to mankind and it had been part of God's divine plan.

In a similar fashion, God had known me before he created me in my mother's womb and He knew and ordained every day of my life. He knew exactly what I would go through in life. And God also knew that I would beat the charges. Like Jesus's death on the cross had been a part of God's plan to fulfill Jesus's purpose here on earth, my beating the charges had also been a part of God's plan and now it was time for me to live out my true purpose in life.

So, as we drove we continued to jam in the Range Rover and we blasted 50 Cent. But while 50 Cent's voice blared through the speakers, a verse from an old Jay-Z song kept floating through my head. I think the title of the Jay-Z song was "Money, Cash, Hoes," but I knew a verse to the song and it was so appropriate for me and it just kept replaying in my head.

The verse went, "Sex, murder, and mayhem, romance with the streets, I led a life that you could write a book on . . . Man and I tell ya it would be the bestseller."

Epilogue

THE DAY AFTER CREAM AND Spinach were convicted, a New York newspaper ran a picture of Cream in handcuffs looking at Lady with an ice-grille on the front page, the headline appropriately read, "Sour Cream." Cream had never learned to grow better through tough situations, instead he always grew bitter. Cream and Spinach were both sentenced to twenty-five years to life in prison. The majority—but not all—of Lady's assets were returned to her. Lady went on to learn that her father was the most successful African-American real estate developer in New York. But even more importantly, her mother and biological father began romantically seeing each other on a regular basis. For the first time in their lives, Mya and Lady experienced that ideal family situation they had both so desperately desired. Lady was baptized about a week after the trial ended. She went on to start Cream Team Ministries, which stood for Christ Reigns Everywhere Around Me * Together Everyone Achieves More. Through her ministry—which was run through a non-profit organization that she started—she opened up a roller-skating rink and many other businesses, all which gave both Christians and non-Christians a place to go where they could experience genuine and clean fun. Lady was also very instrumental in leading thousands of individuals to Christ. She regularly spoke at prisons and schools, and to young people, at-risk teenagers, and prostitutes about her past, and in doing so she was able to connect with and help many people. Lady and Shauna remained good friends and at the age of twenty-seven Lady met the man of her dreams and they got married. At her wedding her father walked her down the aisle and Shauna was her maid of honor. Lady was determined to have a healthy and happy family and to provide her children with the stable upbringing that she never had. Her family's generational curse ended here.

Acknowledgments

I FIRST HAVE TO THANK my Homey, my Ace, my Lord and Savior Jesus Christ. Thank you, thank you, thank you for staying true to your word. Your favor is resting on me, and I know how blessed I am. Thank you, Lord.

To my wife, Sabine: words cannot express my love for you. I know how much you put up with and how much you give up and sacrifice for us. I am truly blessed to have you in my corner. I told you our harvest season was coming, and it's here! Thanks for standing by my side when things got thick.

To my mother and father: I hope that I've made you both proud. I told y'all when I was in high school that I was gonna do this, and look, I did it! I am your legacy, and my kids, my books, and my company will be my legacy. So when I am long and gone, my spirit and your spirits will live on through my kids, my books, and my company.

To my family and friends, especially my brother, Ronnie, and my sister, Paula, my in-laws, Ryan, and the whole Fourth Crew—Randy, X, Latiefe, Dwight, Reggie, Kwame, J. P., Donnie, Paul: y'all are loyal and believed in me and stood by me. I thank y'all for being true, I love y'all. To the "friends" who doubted me, assassinated my character, and became cold toward me: I love y'all too. Didn't y'all know that my will cannot be broken? But it was all part of God's plan. Y'all can hate me now, but I won't stop now, I can't stop now . . . I'm shining! Huh-ha . . .

To St. Martin's Press, especially my editor, Monique: thanks for believing in me and giving me a shot. Monique, you are a pleasure to work with and I trust your judgment. Thanks for making this book hotter than I originally had it.

To my agent, Scott Miller: thanks for helping me connect the dots. Now let's make a lot of money together!

To all of my fellow authors and industry peeps: I'm riding with y'all, especially the entire Q-Boro Books camp, Erick S. Gray, Anna J., Mo Shines, Kiniesha Gayle, Vonetta Pierce, DeJon, Gerald Malcom, Anthony Whyte, K'Wan, Treasure E. Blue, Crystal Lacey Winslow, Tracy Brown, K. Elliott, T. N. Baker, Kashamba Williams, Jamise L. Dames, Carl Weber, Nakea Murray, Shon Bacon, Candace Cottrell, Linda Williams, Meite, Sidi, Massamba, Tee C. Royal, the book clubs, the bookstores, and the distributors.

To the readers: I listen to all of your feedback; thanks for supporting me. And if there is anybody that I forgot to mention, please do not take it personal and I apologize in advance.

Lastly, but certainly not least, I gotta shout out Christian Cultural Center in Brooklyn, New York, and Pastor A. R. Bernard. There is so much that I could thank y'all for but I think the main thing is, I thank y'all for teaching me that it's about relationship and not about *religion* and *religious* activity. I truly get it now! The word kills but the spirit gives life . . .